SEALING THE GATE

A CHRISTIAN FANTASY ADVENTURE

THE HOLY WARRIORS' COMMISSION
BOOK ONE

TAMARA MAUDELLE

Cover Design: Etheric Tales and Edits © 2021
Editor: Elizabeth Bentivegna

ISBN Print: 978-1-7372915-0-3
ISBN EBook: 978-1-7372915-1-0

Printed in the United States of America

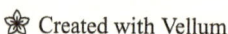 Created with Vellum

ACKNOWLEDGMENTS

To Jodi: You have been my most supportive friend for many years. You've helped me to persevere in my writing and still encourages me in the entire process.

To my friends, Brenda, Wendy, and Marcia: for being my Beta readers. You were constructive and caring and very helpful in assisting me in creating a better novel.

To my amazing mother, Collene, and my sister, Jan: for being my Alpha readers and for your continued support and encouragement.

To my brother, Rick: for letting me bounce ideas off of you and for giving me valued advice regarding military equipment, maneuvers, and procedures.

To my dad who died way too early in his life and in mine. I still remember your laughter and the twinkle in your eyes. You still inspire me and I wish you were here to share in my new adventure in writing. I love you, Dad.

"Put on the whole armor of God, that you may be able to stand against the wiles of the devil. For we are not contending against flesh and blood, but against the principalities, against the powers, against the world rulers of this present darkness, against the spiritual hosts of wickedness in the heavenly places."

"Stand therefore, having girded your loins with truth, and having put on the breastplate of righteousness, and having shod your feet with the equipment of the gospel of peace; above all taking the shield of faith, with which you can quench all the flaming darts of the evil one."

Ephesians 6:11-13, 14-15

CHAPTER 1

I'm falling! The speed of the descent makes my head spin and there's no way I can survive the inevitable impact. The inky blackness consumes me. But wait, I'm also being pulled, so how can this be? The dizzying speed finally slows, and then I'm hovering, over what I'm unsure. A pounding echoes in my head, but I'm unaware if it's my heart or coming from somewhere outside my body. I'm being pulled again, and a sudden electric shock moves through me. After the jolt, everything stops. The banging ceases, but a voice replaces the incessant hammering. Someone's calling my name and my body is being shaken. A hint of light pierces my vision.

"MARA, MARA, PLEASE WAKE UP!"

What's happening? I jolted awake from a dead sleep, then clutched my chest and struggled to breathe. After gulping precious air, I rubbed my hand over my heart as I distinctly remembered an unbearable pain, then the fall. But the discomfort had vanished. I breathed without difficulty and was lying in my bed at home.

1

Someone shook me and I tried to focus on the source of the interruption. I rubbed my eyes and shifted my vision. Standing before me was my mother, staring at me in fear and concern, then in utter surprise.

"Oh, my Lord in heaven, Mara. My dream was true! Are you okay, honey? Please tell me you're alright!" My mom eyed me strangely as I stared back at her worried and shocked face.

"Mom, I don't understand. What's the problem? Was I yelling in my sleep?" I thought I was dead for a moment, so it must have been a nightmare.

I tossed the blankets aside and sat up in bed. *Hmm, so far, so good.* It must be a better day for this painful body of mine. It seemed strange that I hadn't felt my usual nausea and chronic pain when I woke up.

"Mara, wait. There's something I have to tell you. I had a vivid dream this morning and was told, in no uncertain terms, that you'd wake…well, as a new woman. The angel said you'd look different this day, and we should trust in His plans for you. Your constant pain and illness would be a thing of the past too. I didn't know the change would be this drastic. But praise God, He's done a wondrous thing for you!" Mom stared at me with an enormous smile on her lovely face and tears in her eyes.

I climbed out of bed and walked to the large dresser mirror. As I caught my reflection, I shrieked with fear, then stared with unbelieving eyes. *This isn't me!* Feeling lightheaded with shock, I swayed on my feet. Mom rushed to my side, holding me by the arm to keep me steady and upright.

My reflection was of a young woman, not my fifty-five-year-old self. I looked again, turned this way and that, and peered closer. The female who returned my gaze had the same blue eyes, but everything else was different. My hair now hung below my shoulders, returning to the dark auburn color I had when I was much younger, not the pixie blonde highlighted coiffure I wore in my later years. This person was a younger version of me by at least thirty years. I looked at my teeth—perfectly straight and white, and the missing molars were back. But what seemed more strange was that I looked almost ethereal—nothing like the old me. Every feature was shaped perfectly, and my skin positively glowed with youth and vitality—it was clear and vibrant, and there weren't any wrinkles, age spots, or dark circles under my eyes. Then I looked inquisitively down at myself in the pale rose-colored nightgown. My body was now thin and shapely, yet athletic and in excellent shape.

"Mom, is this really me? But how can this be? I don't recognize myself —my eyes look the same color, and I see hints of my previous self, but— I'm so different. I don't understand—why?" I kept running my hands over my face, trying to believe what I saw was real.

She hugged me close and told me to trust the Lord, as instructed in her dream. Curiosity overwhelmed me, and I had to look at my new body. I removed the nightgown and everything in my figure was back where it should be. My breasts had returned to their youthful, high position. *Yee haw!* Even my flabby arms and thighs were now firm and lightly muscled. A Beverly Hills plastic surgeon couldn't do a job this well. Only God could have done something like this. *Was this real, or was I still dreaming?* I donned my gown again and sat on the bed with my mother.

"I'm confused, Mom. Why...how? I look...pretty. But not only that, but I'm young and feel healthy. I just don't get why my looks have changed. There are no memories of anything that transpired during the night except the feeling of falling before I woke up. Why don't I know why God has done this?"

"Honey, all I know is that an angel told me in a dream that you'd be different this morning. Oh, Mara, you're positively stunning. I always thought you were pretty, but now...it's as if God has changed you to reflect His perfection. You must trust in the Lord, my dear. He also said you'd eventually remember and would know the reason for your change. God has chosen who will see you in this new youthful body and who will still view you as your older self. This is all quite interesting, don't you think?"

I hugged my mom again, and we both cried because of this wonderful miracle, and we gloried in God's blessing.

As I gazed at my mother, I thought about what an amazing woman she is. She's sweet, intelligent, funny, and, thankfully, a stay-at-home mom. My mom is compassionate and never met a person she didn't like. She taught me many wonderful things throughout my life, and I'm blessed that God allowed her to stay on this earth for so many years.

Sadie, our Bichon-mix dog, trotted into the room. She whimpered slightly as she pushed against my legs. I glanced down at her; she cocked her head and stared at me, dumbfounded.

"Sweetie, it's me." She jumped up and down as she impatiently waited for a good morning hug. *I won the dog over, thank goodness, but what do I do now, my dear Lord?*

I had a great family growing up in mid-Michigan. I was the younger of two children, with Jonas as my fun-loving brother. We had two wonderful, caring parents, four grandparents, and several distant relatives. But they never understood me and my so-called life. I always felt the nagging guilt for being sick and not having the ambition that my hardworking father tried to instill in me. He said nothing negative—but I swear I saw his disappointment in me from his random glances when I couldn't make it to school again. I still feel shame to this day as a mature adult, even after his sudden death when I was in my late thirties. Of course, he loved me, and I loved him, but I didn't see how he could have been proud of me.

Ever since I can remember, I've had health issues. I was hospitalized several times as a baby with respiratory problems and other maladies. As I grew older, it just continued on the same miserable path of one illness after another, including severe sinus infections twice a year, daily headaches, and chronic exhaustion. On a rare good day, I'd run like wildfire as I took advantage of the blissful pain-free hours. The next day, I'd return to feeling miserable. I could never seem to get enough sleep, either. The exhaustion was debilitating. I missed so many days of school because of sickness that I spent most of my time and effort simply trying to maintain my grades.

My father raised my brother and me as strict Catholics, and for that, I'm thankful, though as a child, I didn't understand. "If you're too sick for Mass, you're also too sick to leave your room," were my father's words. Unfortunately, I spent many Sundays in my bedroom feeling alone and miserable.

As I reached adulthood, the headaches turned into migraines. I still dealt with severe sinus infections and also picked up every flu that reared its ugly head during winter. Thus, it was next to impossible to keep a job for long. My employers would say I was a hard-working and well-liked employee, but they couldn't rely on me to be there every day. I understood, but losing so many jobs affected my confidence and self-worth.

I was perpetually single, didn't date, and had no interest in it. My life was difficult enough, and what man would believe I was too sick to go out or to leave a date early because I was in so much pain? So, I remained single, unattached, and destined to remain childless.

In my early forties, I found a superb job as a software specialist with an understanding boss who was good to me. After working there for several years, I could finally afford to buy a house, and it felt like I had a life until the proverbial crap hit the fan. Eventually, severe illness descended upon me, and I ended up in the emergency room on more than one occasion. I saw several specialists, and although they knew how sick I was, they didn't know the cause. The physicians gave up, and I was on my own; it was up to me to figure this out. Thus, I had to take long-term disability and leave the job and people I'd grown to love.

By this time, I was broke and had lost most of my savings. I could barely care for myself and my little dog, so I sold the house and moved back in with my mother.

The illness remained, but with additional symptoms—nausea, weight loss, nerve and joint pain, insomnia, nervousness, bowel issues, chest pain, vertigo, rashes, shortness of breath—the list goes on.

A couple of years later, I became so sick with some type of virus that I would stop breathing when I tried to sleep. The virus lasted over six weeks (this happened two years before the COVID-19 outbreak). I had high fevers, severe body aches, and hearing loss in my left ear.

After several doctor visits and three antibiotics, I couldn't take it anymore and pleaded with God to either help me or let me die. I'd been a faithful servant of the Lord and didn't understand why I was sick my entire life. The adage—God doesn't give you anything you can't handle—was ridiculous, according to my perspective. Well, I couldn't "handle" it anymore. I cried to Him to give me a sign that He was there, but He remained silent. About a week later, I finally improved, but it was a slow recovery. The chronic pain and numerous other symptoms continued, but I tried to manage each one as it appeared.

After that point, I grew distant from the Lord, wondering, *What was my relationship with Him now? Was I being a hypocrite by continuing my daily prayers and attending Mass when my heart was no longer in it? How did I heal my heart and soul after everything I'd been through?*

CHAPTER 2

*A*fter I moved home, I tried to save money. There wasn't much in my bank account, but there was enough to pay my bills and help Mom with the household expenses. Now that I have a new and vibrant body, I would need to build a new life, which would be difficult. *How would I do this?* That question had no answer. All I could do was trust in the Lord.

For a few days, my mother and I had several discussions about why this could have happened or how I should continue to live as this new person. I was young again, at least in body, and had a new health and vitality I'd never known before. Since the morning of my transformation, a nagging sense of urgency plagued me as if I needed to go somewhere, but to where? I didn't know. Bizarre dreams continually interrupted my sleep as well. They seemed surreal and almost ghostly. There were flashes of bright lights, someone calling my name, and smells and colors so vivid I could still experience them upon waking.

The intense need to run grew overwhelming. I discussed this feeling at length with my mother. We both agreed I should follow my instincts, so I formulated a plan for leaving and what I would require for the journey.

Luckily, the teller at the bank saw me as the old me so that I could cash out my bank accounts, and it was enough to tide me over for a while.

Would I need a new identity? How would other strangers see me—as a young woman or the one on my driver's license? This was a dilemma I had to solve.

Going out on my own could be dangerous and I'd need to protect myself. Luckily, after working a second shift job years ago, I was certified for a concealed gun permit and purchased a 9mm pistol for self-defense. I decided I'd take my weapon with me for protection.

I acquired a sensible and inexpensive wardrobe that fit my new body, paid off a few outstanding bills, and decided I was ready for whatever may come my way. I'd leave Mom with enough money to pay my monthly cell phone bill so we could keep in touch.

I still had my old yet reliable Hyundai, so I had transportation to wherever God was leading me. Hopefully, the good Lord would keep my vehicle running.

It was Monday when I decided it was time to depart. When I had everything in order, I packed up the car and was ready to leave. I knew my mother was frantic at the thought that I'd be alone, but I promised her I'd stay in contact and would be fine.

"Thanks, Mom; I love you!" I gave her and Sadie a big hug and kiss. "What should we do about Jonas?"

"I'll tell him what I can if I can reach him," Mom said. "You know how elusive he can be."

I waved goodbye as I backed out of the driveway. "*I'll miss you, Mom,*" I whispered as I blinked back tears and started my adventure.

I decided to head north, which was just a gut feeling, and kept driving, hoping I'd know when I found my ultimate destination. An hour later, as I traveled down a secluded highway, I thought about everything that had happened to me and what I was about to do.

Panic set in, and I started muttering, "What on earth am I doing? Am I insane?" Turning off the road into a small wooded rest area, I parked the car, got out, and began pacing back and forth. I was still talking to myself and was glad no one was around to hear my ramblings.

"How can I simply leave home and drive to God knows where hoping I'd find myself? What was I thinking?" I stopped pacing and walked over to an old crooked picnic table that needed a good paint job.

I climbed on the table, sat down with a hard "thump," and contemplated my situation.

"God, what is it you want from me? Am I doing Your will, or am I simply delusional in thinking You wish me to drive somewhere specific?" I waited several minutes, hoping He'd answer, but all I could hear were the occasional passing of cars from the highway and birds chirping overhead in the trees.

"Please, God, I need a sign. I'm confused and unsure if I'm doing the correct thing here," I pleaded with the Lord and hung my head in my hands.

Several minutes later, I raised my eyes and gazed at my surroundings. It was beautiful here as the sun's rays shimmered through the trees' canopy, and the summer breeze flitted around me, teasing my hair and cooling my skin with its freshness. I laid down on the table, staring up through the trees, watching the leaves dance in the air as if by magic.

The breeze picked up and something above me changed. I squinted my eyes, trying to get a better view of what was appearing overhead. The trees swayed in a synchronized movement, then parted as if creating an open tunnel from the sky to the picnic table. White doves trailed down through the vortex toward me, one following the other, singing an enchanting, almost hypnotizing tune. I could feel the wind from their flapping wings when they flew around me. Holding out my arm, one landed on me and sat contentedly on its new perch. It peered at me, sang another delightful tune, then rejoined the other doves.

I watched in fascination and heard a mighty voice echo through the trees, "Follow Me, My child, and I will answer your questions." The message repeated two more times, and I waited until the birds disappeared through the top of the tunnel.

After they left, the trees suddenly returned to their natural position. It was as if a rubber band held them apart, then abruptly released, causing several loud clapping sounds as the trunks and limbs banged back together. The sudden movement caused a cascade of leaves to fall from the trees to the ground below. The scent of roses heavily permeated the air. I thought I heard a child's joyful laughter as the breeze danced around me once more. Then it became still and quiet.

Everything had returned to the way it was before. I sat up and looked around me, and the only evidence of what had just happened were the thousands of leaves covering me, the picnic table, and the ground.

Smiling, I brushed the leaves from my body, thanked God for His blessed message, and said I'd do exactly as He'd directed. I climbed back into the car, grinned again with joy, and headed north once more.

After a few hours, I came upon a small town about sixty miles south of Traverse City. I don't know why this was where I stopped, but it felt right, and it was time for a break.

There was a little diner that was nondescript yet inviting. I walked to the entrance and the bell over the door chimed as I entered. A young skinny boy hustled over wearing a coffee-stained apron, and he told me to sit anywhere. I thanked him and parked myself at a booth by the front windows. A matronly server appeared, and I ordered a chocolate milkshake and a BLT with fries.

"I'll get right on that, honey," she said as she rushed back to the kitchen.

As I looked around at the nearly empty diner, I saw an old, fully bearded weathered man of about ninety sitting at the counter perusing a local newspaper. He wore worn-out shoes and faded coveralls over a checkered shirt. The man seemed to sense me as I glanced at him, then he turned around and looked me dead in the eye. For a brief instant, I thought I'd recognized him, but I must have been mistaken. We stared at each other for a moment longer, and he laid the paper on the counter and ambled over to me.

"You know," he mumbled, "I've got just what you're looking for, missy. It's private, free, and off the beaten track, so to speak." He sat down across from me and I waited for him to continue. *This man must be the crazy old coot of the town.*

He reached across the booth and placed his hand over mine. "You're not alone, honey, and I'm here to lend a hand and give you a little guidance, you might say." My eyes widened, and I wondered if he may have a touch of dementia.

The old man continued, "I know you're a bit lost after what has happened, but I assure you everything will come to light, Mara. You'll see.

There's a cabin where you can stay until it's time to move on to the next leg of your journey." He dropped a set of keys into my hand.

"I don't understand. Do you know me?" I asked.

"Kiddo, I guess you can say I know what you're going through and the doubts and fears you're experiencing. Continue to trust in Him"—he pointed a finger to the ceiling—"and you'll be just fine. You'll also need to be careful for the next few weeks and try to stay out of the public eye as much as possible. It'll be safer for you."

"Sure, no problem," I replied with a bit of skepticism. But after what happened at the rest stop, I knew in my heart that God sent this old man to assist me in whatever may be headed my way.

He stood to leave, but I stopped him with a hand on his arm and said, "Wait, I'll need an address and directions to the cabin, please."

He leaned down and whispered, "Have faith; you'll find it. Good luck, Mara." He spun on his heel, returned to his seat at the counter, sat down, and continued perusing his paper.

How did he know my name? The server stood before me as I was about to ask him more questions. She gave me my lunch with a smile and hurried away. I peered over at the old man and he'd disappeared. *Where did he go? He couldn't possibly have left the diner without me seeing or hearing him.*

Looking at the keys still gripped in my fingers, I felt a strange tingle on my upper left arm, then absently rubbed at the minor irritation. *Hmm, I guess I'll go with the flow.* I finished my lunch, paid the cashier, and filled the car with gas at the local station.

I started driving again, hoping I'd know where to go. "Have faith... okay, God, I need your assistance here," I said aloud. That familiar pull returned, and I followed a dirt road heavily lined with fir and poplar trees.

Half an hour later, I drove down a dead-end road to an isolated log cabin. It wasn't anything extravagant, but it was warm, well-kept, and inviting. Surrounding the cabin were several flowering plants, a bed of red roses, and a large dilapidated bird feeder brimming with seed that was alive with cardinals, blue jays, and chickadees.

This is it? It's beautiful. I parked to the right of the cottage in the narrow driveway, grabbed the keys to the cabin, and strolled to the door. I sincerely hoped this was the place God had chosen for me. As I inserted the key in the deadbolt lock, I noticed a beautiful Celtic cross above the door. The lock clicked open, and I stepped inside.

This place was simple yet well decorated, in excellent condition, and with large windows allowing warm daylight to permeate the rooms. It was a log cabin with an overstuffed burgundy sofa with matching armchairs, and a gorgeous, large print throw rug on the floor added a nice, homey touch. The cathedral ceiling was impressive with a tasteful yet rustic chandelier, and sturdy lamps rested comfortably on the corner sofa tables.

The kitchen was compact but adequate; it even had a small island. Upon searching the refrigerator and cabinets, they were well stocked with anything I could possibly need. One small yet comfortable fully furnished bedroom was next to the kitchen. Off the bedroom was a large bathroom with a walk-in shower and a separate claw-foot bathtub.

All this can't possibly be free, can it?

Returning to the great room, I looked out the large French doors off the living space. I unlocked and opened the doors, and there was a huge furnished deck and a wooden path that led down to a glimmering lake. There was a small dock and a sturdy ten-foot johnboat pulled ashore and flipped over. Off to the right, I spotted a short, well-beaten path that led to a small shed surrounded by colorful wildflowers. I inhaled deeply and the scents of pine and the freshwater lake filled the air.

I returned to the car to retrieve my luggage. Several birds flew around me, and one brightly colored cardinal landed on my arm. He looked at me and sang a delightful song, then returned to the bird feeder. Confused, I shook my head and wondered why the birds seemed so unusually tame. I shrugged, grabbed my bags, and returned to the cabin. I hoped this wasn't someone's house. If it was, I'd better prepare to skedaddle if the owners returned.

I settled into this beautiful, peaceful place and hoped I could piece together what had happened to me and what God had planned for my future. As I gazed out the window, I realized it was late afternoon, and I decided to fix a simple dinner and try to relax.

Not having to take all the medications I'd grown accustomed to was wonderful. It was like I was a free woman and was no longer chained to pain and prescriptions. *Ahh, so this is what it's like to be healthy? Who knew?*

After dinner, I sat in one of the comfy armchairs and turned on the lamp since dusk was falling. I thought about the disjointed dreams I'd been having and tried to make sense of them. Well, maybe later. It was time for a nap, and I fell asleep and started to dream.

THERE ARE SO many amazing colors—hues I couldn't have ever imagined. Not on this earth, anyway. There's such a joyful noise too. The sounds of euphoric music and prayerful singing are soothing and filled with love, making you blissful upon hearing them. The smells I'm inhaling are fragrant and sweet. So many ambrosial scents permeate the air, and they're intensely pleasing and calming. I feel no fear, no pain, no uncertainty. I know this is where I'm supposed to be. But where am I? I look down and see no body, simply more colors, lights, and whispers of what I'd describe as clouds that appear to have intelligence and being. I've been here before, and I know this must be a memory, and I'm being pulled toward a magical place. Something here is so incredible and full of love, I can't wait to get near it. Everything is getting brighter, warmer, and more intense. It's astounding.

"Mara," a deep, mesmerizing voice calls out to me. "Welcome home."

I JOLTED AWAKE. *Darn!*

"O, my dear Lord!" I exclaimed in shock. My body died that fateful night—I remember now. That evening, I awoke to an intense pain in my chest that radiated up my neck, down my left arm, and into my back. I couldn't say anything or even move. The pain was so excruciating that my body froze in agony. First, there was darkness, then I ended up in this celestial plane, and the pain vanished. *Was it actually Heaven?* More had happened, but I couldn't grasp it from my memory yet.

I called my mom and approached the subject gently about my death, and she didn't sound surprised. She said she figured something like that must have happened but was thankful to God for delivering her loving daughter from her painful life. I told her about the homey cabin and that I was doing well.

She replied, "I wish your father was here to witness this miracle. But that's probably a stupid thing to say. I'm sure he's in Heaven and aware of what God has done for you. I love you, my sweet baby, and stay in touch."

"I love you too, Mom." I hung up, but immediately thought about Dad. I really missed him.

My father had the best sense of humor, which I remember most about him. He never cared about clothes or how he looked in them. He liked plaids with stripes or prints with paisleys and wore them all together as long as he was comfortable, and it was a running joke between my parents.

I still recall when my mom insisted he purchase new shoes. He finally gave in, and my mom bought him a pair of loafers. He grumbled about the cost but was proud to have them.

There was one problem, however; one shoe had a particular squeak when he put his weight on it. He didn't care and wore them, anyway. My mom finally insisted they take the shoe to a cobbler. But they could find nothing that would cause the incessant noise. It didn't bother my dad; he wore them proudly to church.

Jonas and I were young teenagers at the time, and I remember being embarrassed by that sound when Dad went to Communion. You couldn't hear it on his way up to the altar because of the slow crawl of parishioners, but on the way back, everyone walked faster, and I could hear the *squeak, squeak* as he returned to the pew. Relief flowed through me when the organ would start playing the Communion meditation hymn that covered the shoe's noise.

I finally got the courage and asked my dad why he didn't get rid of them. He'd replied, "Why? They're a perfectly good pair of shoes. Just because there's a small imperfection doesn't mean they aren't worthy of being worn." At the time, I didn't quite understand what he meant by his remark, but I figured there must be some lesson to be learned. *Thanks, Dad.*

His love for God and the church never wavered. I remember staring at him as a child when the church hymns played. Glory filled his face when he sang along. I always hoped that someday I'd have such devotion and delight in loving and serving God. Heaven must have cried for joy when my dad returned home to the Lord.

I decided to turn in for the night. After locking up the cabin and clicking off the lights, I opted to take a hot soak in the tub. It's what I needed in the hope of a good night's rest. I filled the tub, removed my clothes, and entered the bath. As I submerged my upper body into the water, a burning sensation on my upper left bicep made me gasp. Pulling my arm around to get a look, I could only see a faint red discoloration the size of an orange. Hmmm, how did I do that?

Finishing my bath, I decided not to fret over the strange mark. There was enough to deal with for now, but why was there a sense of impending doom as if my life was in peril? A slight shiver went through my body, and even though I tried to deny it, something dangerous was headed my way.

CHAPTER 3

*T*he next morning, I was ready to explore what this day had to offer. It was amazing waking up refreshed, full of energy, and feeling no pain. This continued good health and vigor still surprised me, and I relished every day as if it was a new beginning. It was also astounding how my mind and memory were now acute. I thanked God every day for these beautiful gifts of a healthy mind and body, which I'd never known in my previous life.

I dressed, cleaned up, and headed for the kitchen. I ate a light breakfast, grabbed a book, and strolled to the deck. The morning dawned bright and clear and I loved the early summer weather. It must have rained the night before as droplets of water hung off the leaves of the poplars and glistened in the morning sun. The air smelled like spring rain mixed with fresh grass and roses.

Perfect. I sat in a lounge chair protected from the rain by the house's eaves. After saying my daily prayers to the Lord, I simply enjoyed the view. Staring at the lake, I became entranced, almost hypnotized. I was on my way to remembering the rest of my experience from the night I had died.

I'M BACK in this wonderful place. But now I'm moving through space with beautiful scenery passing below me. There are lakes of vivid blue that sparkle like brightly colored gems and fields of flowers in every color, shape, size, and scent. Grassy meadows of the brightest emerald green dazzle my eyes with their vibrancy. All of these fantastic things appear to glow with love and move in synchronization with music that is so enchanting it brings tears to my eyes. Everything in this splendid place emits love, joy, and glory to God.

I float down to the most magnificent garden. How can anything be this glorious? A small bench appears before me and is made of gold and luminous gems. As I continue to look around, I see many animals. Most I recognize, some not. They all live together in peace, wanting nothing. There's neither predator nor prey here. All are one with the heavenly Father.

I catch sight of something moving in my direction. The shape seems blurry but appears sharper as it moves closer. I know it's a man because I can see a glimpse of his dark beard. His countenance is pure beauty and perfection. He's wearing a white robe with a hood that covers most of His head, and His entire being glows with a stunning aura. I feel fear and apprehension.

"Don't be afraid." This voice comes to me in my head. I'm sitting on the bench, but since I see no physical body, I don't understand how this can be. The man sits beside me, but I only see His profile. The sleeves of His robe are long, so they cover His hands.

"This is one of my favorite places," He says. "The animals are an amazing gift to man by My Father. When they're on earth, all they want is love and respect from humans. Some people can't even give this to an animal, let alone to the Father. So why do they find this small task so difficult? Ahh, that's been the question given to humans for many of your years, yes?"

He turns to look at me and I fall to the ground. "O child, this is not necessary. I love you and I know you love Me. You're a faithful child, and yes, I know you've faltered on more than one occasion, but that's part of the human condition. Our Father made us all who we are. Doubts, frailties, and imperfections, are we."

His eyes are the most incredible color of green and blue. They emit an intense look of love and compassion that reaches into my very soul. As I rise from the ground, He touches my upper arm. Even with no physical body, I can feel the pressure of His hand.

Looking down, I witness the holes through His palms. I cry out in despair and kiss His injury. "I'm so sorry for what You suffered because of us. We continue to sin and hurt each other and simply never learn. You endured agony because of us, but how do we repay You? With unbelief and more sin. Are we really worth it?" I ask in despair.

"The answer to that question is a resounding yes! Our Father is all love and forgiveness. He created man in His image, loves His beautiful children, and has only ever wanted the best for them, like any loving father. You know that's why He gave them His only Son. For everlasting life. The eternal love of our Father is why you're in this place."

"I don't understand," I say to Him.

"The earth is in terrible despair, and evil has been flourishing. So many men have succumbed to the promises of this evil that our Father's chastisement of his children is on the horizon. Millions of lives will perish from this cleansing. That's how dire man's sin has become. This is where you come in, my child."

Gasping at this astounding information, it takes me a moment to answer. I finally respond, "I'm sorry, my Lord, but what can I do? I'm no saint but a sinner, and I've failed Him on many occasions that I'm terribly ashamed."

He pats my hand and replies, "You may think you've failed but are wrong. You've always had love in your heart, which gave you endless compassion for others and every living thing. You felt great remorse for your sins and forgave others who transgressed against you. Although, sometimes, it took a while," He chuckles. It's a deep, soft, throaty laugh.

He continues, "I know everything about you. There's nothing I don't see. Yes, you doubted my Father loved you at times because of your suffering. You were angry with Him on more than one instance and turned away from Him, but you always returned. You consistently believed in Him. Of course, you don't understand why you had to be sick all your life, but that was your cross to bear. I'm sorry for the pun, my dear, but I still have my sense of humor!" He laughs again. I smile with happiness at hearing Him chuckle and joke.

Jesus continues, "This suffering was to prepare you for your next journey and what comes after. I know it's still hard to understand, but you will. You'll know everything once you return to eternal Heaven and be with the Father. You must continue to trust that He knows what He's doing."

Jesus scans the beauty of our surroundings, then turns to me again, saying, "We have a task for you. You and many others My Father has chosen are to correct in the world what has gone so horribly wrong. The evil that has descended on His children must be sent back to Hell, and for the Chosen—this is the massive undertaking that awaits you."

"But how can we cast out evil? We're mere humans. Isn't this something only He can do?"

"Simply put, it must be the children of God who must repair what the children of God have perpetuated. Murder, corruption, apathy, greed, adultery, idolatry, all sin, but most of all, the rejection and blasphemy of My Father. This has allowed Satan and his army to flourish and gain a tremendous grip on the Earth and on My Father's straying sheep. If you accept this task, you'll return to your body and live again to fight this holy war.

"Mara, you're greatly needed among the Chosen. You can stay here or return to fight. You do have a choice. There are no repercussions if you want to remain here and complete the journey to the Father. But, if you return to Earth and take on His holy commission, then when it's time for you to return here, you'll be in one of the highest mansions of Heaven so near to the Father. That's a glorious reward, indeed."

"If I go back, I'll be in a middle-aged, sickly body. How can I possibly do this tremendous task with such poor health?"

"That's not a problem. When you return, your body will have regained its youth, and you'll be in optimum health. You'll need the body of a warrior to fight the battles before you. Once back on Earth, you'll develop the skills to fight evil. And remember, you'll not be alone. Many others will fight alongside you, and God will also give you someone to guide you if the need arises. But you and two others are my Father's favored, as He will

give you more gifts than the other Chosen. My Father will also make the three of you in His image of human perfection." I looked at Him with puzzlement at His last statement, but He simply smiled.

"Your additional skills will be a great asset in the coming battles. Many demons will continue to flourish, tempt, and corrupt many of His children, and it'll be a continuing war for all of His Chosen. This is a major undertaking for all of you; at times, it may seem unending."

Jesus looks intently into my eyes with love and compassion and continues, "You know what you want to do." Then He smiles, and His eyes light up again. "I thought so. My sweet child, you are My little warrior," and He kisses me on the forehead.

He rises to his feet and strokes a large snow leopard standing at His side. "These creatures still amaze me. Do you know My Father is still creating them? The one He's working on now is, well, unusual. It's a cross between an alligator and an anteater," He laughs again. "One last thing— you won't remember your body dying or this conversation with me for a little while after you return to your body. But you will remember. We love you, My child, and We're always with you." He slowly walks away with the leopard padding along beside Him until they both disappear from view.

RETURNING TO CONSCIOUSNESS, I was still sitting in the deck chair at the little cottage. A sizable amount of time must have passed as the sun was now high in the sky, and my stomach rumbled.

God really expected me to do this unbelievable task? How on earth could I possibly do what he'd asked of me?

Continuing to sit in the chair, I contemplated the memories that flooded my mind and digested all this unbelievable information. I was overwhelmed by terror, so I prayed to God to ease my fear and apprehension. Sitting quietly to clear my mind, I waited and hoped for His answer. A warm, gentle breeze picked up and danced around me, then through me.

"Remember, I chose you specifically, Mara. Trust in Me, child." This majestic whisper was carried through the wind and down into my soul.

Taking a deep and calming breath, my fears were replaced with peace and joy. I thanked the Lord for his gracious reply and praised His holy name.

But now what? I guess I'd have to wait, and God would show me the next steps that would be the continuation of my journey.

Contacting my mother, I relayed what I'd remembered about that fateful night. She had mixed emotions about the entire incident, but she didn't doubt my recollection. Taking it in stride, she told me to keep in close contact and be careful.

I asked her if she'd spoken with Jonas. She said she had tried to explain to him how my physical appearance had changed and that I'd decided to take off and 'find myself.' She also relayed that Jonas had been silent for a while, not saying much else, then he finally asked where I was.

"Well," Mom replied, "I couldn't tell him because I didn't know myself. You said there wasn't an address, but you gave me the nearest town." She then stated Jonas seemed worried but hurriedly said his good-byes and assured her he'd call back when he could.

I decided to explore the wooded area which was adjacent to the house. There were clear footpaths, and the denseness of the pines kept the forest floor clean of intrusive brush and weeds. I picked up a skinny dead tree branch that would work well as a walking stick and started down the path.

Entering deeper into the woods, the trails were clearly marked, and I startled a blue jay rummaging through the forest floor. I watched him fly high onto one of the enormous pines while he squawked and complained about the rude interruption of his morning forage.

"Sorry about that, fella," I apologized. Moving on once more, I then stopped dead in my tracks. The biggest wolf I'd ever seen was a few feet ahead of me on the path. His coat was white and he had bright green eyes. I surmised he was a timber wolf. He weighed almost two hundred pounds, and I estimated his height to be three feet at the shoulder.

I stood there unmoving, waiting to see if he was only passing through or if I was his next meal. I decided I'd better drop the skinny walking stick; it wouldn't help me against the beast anyway, and he may see it as threatening. It seemed we stared at each other forever, but; it was probably a few minutes. He finally made a small move but only raised his nose and sniffed the air. Then he took one, two, three tentative steps toward me. I had to do something, say something.

"Uh, hello there, my friend. Fine morning, isn't it?" I muttered, my voice shaking. He stopped, cocked his head back and forth, then sat back on his haunches.

Darn, what do I do now? Should I back away or not move until he finally does? I decided to wait. After a few seconds, he stood up, advanced a few more steps toward me, sat down again, then whined and huffed. He tilted his head again, not taking his eyes off me, then laid down and rolled over onto his back. *What?* I took a few paces toward him, and he stuck his tongue out and pumped his front paws up and down.

"What's this, handsome? You want a belly rub?" He whined again, and I tried touching him. I moved forward, slowly knelt, and gingerly moved my hand, palm down, toward his nose. He sniffed it, then gave me a lick. I rubbed his belly and he made cute sounds of satisfaction.

"Feels good, huh? You gave me quite a scare, my friend. Do you belong to someone? I don't see a collar and you appear to be well-fed." We spent a few more minutes together, but he jumped back up, licked me on the cheek, bounded down the path, and disappeared.

AFTER REMEMBERING my trip to Heaven, there were three uneventful, beautiful, and restful days at the cabin. I spent a lot of time talking to God and continued to thank Him for all the beauty and blessings He'd given me. In the afternoons, I also took the boat out on the lake a few times, slowly rowing around on the water and taking in the calmness and peace. I saw loons, Canadian geese, and an occasional fish jumping. On these boat trips, I realized this was a private lake because there weren't any other cabins along the other shores surrounding the water. That was fine by me since I liked the solitude.

I also enjoyed my daily walks through the woods surrounding the cabin. The wolf always showed up and accompanied me on my stroll. We spent more time together; I threw many sticks for him to retrieve and even saved some of my grilled hamburgers for him as a treat. I decided to call him "Spirit." The name sounded appropriate, and he seemed to like it.

Spirit was a "no-show" on Saturday, and it worried me. I called him many times on my walk, but he didn't appear. It felt like I'd lost my best friend, and I hoped nothing bad happened to him. The feeling of doom crossed my mind again, as well as that fearful shiver. *What was wrong with me?*

CHAPTER 4

Today was Sunday and I was eager to attend Mass. When I first arrived in the area, I viewed a small Catholic Church outside of town.

Upon arriving at the church, there were quite a few cars in the parking lot. Several people talked animatedly to each other on the way to the entrance, and many people greeted me with friendly smiles. As I walked into the quaint brick building, parishioners were kind and welcomed me to Mass.

One sweet older woman and her husband asked if I was alone, and I nodded I was. "You can sit with us, dear, if you don't mind sitting near the front. Most young people hide in the back, hoping no one will notice them. I just don't know why." I smiled, told her I didn't mind, and followed her to a pew near the altar.

It was a lovely church with beautiful Mother Mary and St. Joseph statues, and the enormous crucifix on the altar was ornate yet tastefully done. The face of Jesus on the cross didn't resemble the Jesus I met in heaven, but it was still lovely and serene. There was a beautiful stained glass window on the altar's ceiling. It depicted angels and doves in the glass in a myriad of vibrant colors.

Mass started, and we stood and sang the opening hymn while waiting for the priest, reader, and servers to approach the altar. The Mass was enjoyable and I felt at peace.

As we knelt for the consecration of the body and blood of Christ, I intently watched the priest, and he appeared almost blissful during this part of the Mass. As he raised the host to the heavens, I saw two angels dressed in shimmering white gowns with wings outstretched descending from the stained-glass window. I blinked, rubbed my eyes, and looked again, but they were still there and now hovered on either side of the priest. Their expressions were so joyful that it was hard to peer directly at their faces. I saw shimmering lights dancing around their celestial bodies as they continued to gaze lovingly at the body and blood of Christ on the altar.

The priest continued the blessings, and the angels still hovered, floating on gossamer wings. I couldn't contain myself, and tears streamed down my face. The pleasant woman beside me whispered in my ear and asked if I was alright. I merely smiled at her and nodded, then returned my attention to the altar as the priest finished the consecration. He lifted his head and looked directly at me. His face turned ashen, and he faltered on his prayers but caught himself and concluded the rite. The angels ascended to the ceiling and disappeared through the colorful skylight.

Although shocked at what I'd seen, I finished the Mass and mumbled all the correct responses. When the service was over, I sat down and told the delightful couple I'd like to stay awhile. They said attending Mass with me had been a pleasure and hoped I'd be alright. I smiled again, said I was fine but needed time for prayer, and thanked them both for their kindness.

The parishioners exited the church in a typical rush to resume their day, but I stayed, contemplating the miracle I'd witnessed. I heard quick footsteps from behind me, and the priest who said the Mass appeared next to me.

"I'm so glad I caught you. I was afraid you'd already left. Mrs. McDermott can talk like there's no tomorrow, bless her soul, and I couldn't get away," he said.

I turned to look at him and smiled. He was an older man of about sixty-five with a full head of well-groomed gray hair, bushy eyebrows, bright blue eyes, and an engaging smile.

"I'm sorry for rambling on. I'm Father Martin, and it's such a pleasure to meet you." He smiled kindly, and we shook hands.

"I'm pleased to meet you too, Father. My name is Mara Patrick." I still felt emotional and thought I'd cry again.

"I just wanted—" He started to say something, but the door banged behind us and we heard a whisper of voices. Two of the church staff were talking to each other while straightening up the missals in the pews. "Would you follow me to the sacristy, please? I want to speak with you in private." I nodded and followed his lead; he offered me a chair and I sat across from him.

"I was surprised to see you here today. You shouldn't have come, but I'm so glad you did because you apparently saw something amazing," he continued.

"Father, I don't understand. You were surprised to see me today? I don't believe we've ever met, and why shouldn't I have come? And yes, I did. I thought I saw something wonderful during the consecration."

"I'm sorry, Mara." He shuffled in his seat with embarrassment. "Here I am, rambling on like an old coot, explaining nothing. I had a vivid dream last night, and you were in it. But in this dream, I was given a clear heavenly message that if I saw you, I should tell you to be careful as you may be in danger, at least while you're staying around here. The voice in my dream was adamant about this, and it hounded me until I agreed to warn you."

He clasped my hand between both of his and said, "Will you be careful as the messenger requested?"

"I will, Father, and thank you for caring. I'll do as you ask." What could I say? I'd seen many strange things lately, so anything could be possible. I'd heed his warning.

"Good. Now that we've settled this issue, please tell me what you witnessed."

I related everything I'd seen and tears ran down my face again; he also wept joyfully.

"That's the most tremendous thing. You're so blessed to have seen such an astounding gift from God. I've always felt the most reverent during the consecration of the Eucharist as if I could always feel the Lord coming down from Heaven, and what you saw proved it. Thank you, dear child." He squeezed my hand, offering comfort, and said, "Now, you'd better go. I'll pray that you stay safe under God's loving protection."

As I left the church, I was blessed indeed to witness such a miracle. This was something I'd never forget. *Thank you, Lord!*

THE FOLLOWING DAY, I woke up and felt something wet on the sheets. I jumped out of bed and threw back the light blue blanket and the top sheet. My eyes were drawn to a small bloodstain on the bottom fitted sheet.

"Oh no, this can't be!" I ran to the bathroom, and sure enough, I was menstruating. "Oh, come on! I thought I was done with this. Is this a joke, God? No!"

I had a radical hysterectomy in my mid-forties because of advanced endometriosis. Periods were a thing of the past and I was glad to be rid of them. Rummaging through the bathroom cabinets, I surprisingly found a few tampons. "Eureka!" I bellowed. After cleaning myself up, I changed clothes and stripped the sheets off the bed. I carried them to the bathroom sink and washed out the blood.

"Of all the crappy…."—I muttered, complained, and cussed under my breath while scrubbing diligently at the bedding. Taking them to the efficiency washer and dryer tucked away behind pocket doors in the kitchen, I shoved the sheets into the machine. I was in a snit. "Great…just great!"

Now I needed to take a trip to town. I required some supplies I thought I wouldn't need anymore. Maybe a drive would help diffuse my temper. After eating a small breakfast, I grabbed my purse and returned to town.

It felt good to be with other humans again and be around a town's bustling activity. Although it was small, it still had everything people would need: a grocery store, pharmacy, post office, gas station, tavern, a couple of boutiques, souvenir shops, bakery, two fast-food restaurants, plus the diner where I'd met the old man.

I stopped at the gas station to top off the tank, then drove into the grocery store parking lot and entered the market. I picked up what I needed and packed it into the trunk.

A prickling sensation made the hairs at the back of my neck stand up;

something was dangerously wrong. The trunk was still open, so I popped my head over the lid and looked around inconspicuously. My gaze was drawn to a strange man about a block away in front of the post office. He seemed out of place, not by how he looked but by the way he carried himself. He ignored everyone around him, almost as if he felt they didn't exist. His expression had a blank look, and he was pale but well-muscled and wore dark clothes that seemed too warm for the current summer weather.

When I tried to get a better look at his face, it seemed to blur, and my stomach turned. But the feeling passed quickly. Looking back at him again, I knew I didn't like him. I wasn't usually one to make snap judgments, but something about this guy was wrong.

He turned in my direction, so I ducked down behind the trunk lid. After waiting a few minutes, I peeked again, and the man was heading away from me. I planned to spend more time in town, but this person spooked me. Closing the trunk, I hurried into the driver's seat and drove toward the cabin.

It was a relief to be back at my temporary and cozy home. I pulled a couple of bags from the trunk and walked toward the front door. The bird feeder was busy as usual. *That's odd. How come it was always full? It's never been empty, not once since I'd been here.* I never found a bag of birdseed anywhere in the cabin or the shed—another conundrum.

After unloading the remaining groceries from the car, I put them away. Moving my laundry from the washer to the dryer, I put clean sheets on the bed and tidied up the cabin. I hoped to take a stroll in the woods to see if Spirit had returned, and I also wanted to take the boat out for some exercise. Rowing about the lake helped me think. I also enjoyed the sun dancing off the water and the gentle waves lapping against the metal sides of the boat, which made the *whap, whap, whap* sound.

Deciding to have lunch, I topped it off with a slice of dark chocolate double-layered cake. Everything tasted fantastic, and I savored the sweet flavor of the rich, creamy icing as it slid down my throat.

I started on my stroll in the woods. Seeing the typical birds, chipmunks, squirrels, and rabbits, I was awed when I caught sight of a doe and two fawns a short distance away. Stopping in my tracks, I watched their beauty as they foraged for their food.

The doe must have caught my scent because her head came up and she stared at me. I figured the doe and her fawns would've instinctively run at the sight of me, but she wasn't concerned. Instead, she sniffed the air and began eating again. I walked closer, and she ignored me. This behavior was *not* the typical response of a wild deer. Even when I came within two feet of her and her babies, she still didn't react in fear.

"Hi, momma, congratulations on your twins," I whispered. She raised her head again and blinked at me; the fawns did the same. They slowly walked over to me, and astonishingly, she let me pet her and her precious babies. *Why on earth would she allow me to do this?*

Suddenly startled, she turned her head to the left, stomped her front foot, snorted, and ran off in the opposite direction with her fawns on her heels. I looked to see what had spooked them, and there stood Spirit.

"Spirit, I'm thrilled to see you, baby. Where have you been? Are you alright?" I asked as he trotted over to me. He made a quiet, woofing sound, stuck his nose in my hand, and snuggled beside me. Nothing seemed amiss, and he was his usual sweet self. I hugged him and asked if he'd finish the walk with me. He acted as if he understood my question, and we continued our stroll together.

As we neared the cabin, Spirit did his usual 'time to go' look. He pushed on me twice, licked my hand, and turned to leave. "I hope you won't disappear again." My new best friend bumped my leg once more and trotted down the path away from the cabin. "Goodbye, Spirit."

I returned to the cottage, grabbed a bottle of iced tea, went down to the shore, turned the boat over, and pushed it into the water. Climbing in, I grabbed the oars and started rowing. It was another beautiful day to be out enjoying the peace. Today, I rowed farther across the lake. It was excellent exercise, but I needed a break before I completed the return trip to the cabin. Pulling in the oars, I dropped the anchor and pulled out my cold, refreshing iced tea. *Perfect.*

I heard a splash behind me and turned to find two crimson-eyed loons swimming a short distance away. They must have been a bonded pair because each loon had one black feathered little chick on its back.

"Beautiful, aren't they?" A distinct, deep, familiar voice said.

I spun my upper body around so fast the boat rocked violently in the water. The old man from the diner now sat across from me. Each of us grabbed on with both hands to the sides of the boat, waiting for the wild rocking motion to settle.

"Careful, little girl, you almost dumped us in the drink," he snickered with glee, still hanging on with a tight grip.

"You scared me to death! How could you possibly be here, in my boat, in the middle of the lake?" I shrieked.

"I'm sorry I scared you, Mara: that wasn't my intention. I sincerely apologize," he said apologetically. "Will you forgive me?" he asked with a puppy dog expression in his faded hazel eyes.

"Of course, how can I not?"

"Thank you, dear. Your stay here will soon end, and you must be ready to leave the cabin at a moment's notice. You've had the time you needed to heal, reflect, and remember, but the next leg of your journey has been set into motion. It would be best if you were also on your guard because soon, danger may befall you. I don't mean to frighten you, but my goal is your safety and well-being and to warn you of any possible perils." He gazed at me compassionately, and I noted a hint of worry.

"Do I have to leave tonight?"

"No, but it may be tomorrow or the next—you'll know when it's time. These next few days must be played out according to His will." He pointed to the heavens and smiled.

He continued, saying, "You'll be fine. You know you can trust me, Mara. Now, I must take my leave." At that same instant, I heard a large splash behind me. Whipping around to look, I saw the loons making their ascent to their long runway takeoff. They gracefully took to the skies once more. When I turned back around, the old man had disappeared.

"Darn! I hate how he does that!" I muttered.

The sun was getting lower in the sky and I needed to return to the cabin. After pulling in the anchor, I headed back. Feeling nervous, I cautiously walked up the path to the cabin. As the old man had advised, I scanned my surroundings, trying to be vigilant. Immediately locking the door behind me, I went around the cabin, ensuring the windows and front door were secured.

I took the old man's advice and packed everything I could except the essential items. By the time I finished, it was dinnertime. I barely tasted the meal but ate it anyway, cleaned the few dishes I'd used, then went into the bedroom where I'd hidden the pistol. Pulling my SIG Sauer P365 from its hiding place, I took the weapon apart and checked that everything was in good working order. After reassembling it, I loaded the magazine, chambering in one bullet, and clicked the safety on. Grabbing the two extra loaded magazines, I put them back into the bag. I placed the gun on my bedside table within easy reach in case I needed it during the night.

Returning to the great room, I sat on the sofa and picked up the Clive Cussler book I'd been reading. Still feeling distracted, I hoped I could focus on the novel. It started to rain outside, but I found the gentle pitter-patter sound on the windows soothing. Centering myself, I became engrossed in one of the action scenes when I heard scratching at the French doors. Unfortunately, it wasn't easy to see outside because of the filmy sheers that covered the doors.

I ran silently to the bedroom and grabbed the pistol. Flipping off the safety, I kept the gun pointed toward the floor with my finger off the trigger and crept back into the room. To stay safe, I hid behind the kitchen island, which obstructed the intruder's view of my location. The lights weren't on yet in this part of the cabin, but there was enough illumination for me to get around. I waited while my heart raced.

Stay calm, I told myself. *Scratch, scratch.* What *is* that? I heard a loud whine, then a bark.

"Spirit, is that you?" My voice sounded hollow to my ears. He barked again—I'd know his bellow anywhere. Still keeping my hand on the gun, I rose, loosened my death grip, and approached the doors. It was Spirit. I could see his white head as he paced back and forth across the deck. Unlocking the door, he bounded in. He didn't appear too wet, but I grabbed a towel from the kitchen and wiped him down. He licked my face and made happy chuffing noises.

"What are you doing here, my friend? Don't get me wrong; I'm ecstatic you showed up." He licked me again. "Stop! Yes, I love you too. Are you hungry? Today, I picked up a bag of their best dog food at the store. I spared no expense." He huffed and wagged his tail in reply. "You got it. Your dinner's coming up." I grabbed two large bowls from the cupboard and filled one with dog food and the other with water. "There you go, my good friend. *Bon appétit!*"

When Spirit finished his food, I cleaned the dish and set it aside for his meal in the morning. I turned out the light, and exhaustion set in, and I strolled to the bedroom, keeping my trusty gun at my waistband. Spirit watched me intently and refused to leave my side.

We both went into the bathroom and I decided on a hot shower. I removed my clothes, and Spirit kept his gaze trained on me. "Hey, bub, this is embarrassing." I giggled, but he yawned, laid on the floor, and closed his eyes. "Thank you. You're a gentleman." I had to laugh because this giant wolf lounging on the bathroom rug left very little room for me to maneuver.

After my shower, I walked to the bed with Spirit following. I placed the gun on the bedside table and sat on the edge of the mattress. Spirit looked back at me and whined.

"Okay, come on up, but don't be a bed hog." He jumped up, and the mattress rocked under his weight as he stretched out beside me.

"Hey, you don't snore, do you?" He lifted his head, gave another huff, smiled, and licked my cheek again. "Eck, I won't have any skin left at this rate, bub. By the way, how did you know I could use some company tonight? Did the old man send you? Yeah, I know you wouldn't tell me even if you could. Goodnight, my dear friend." I kissed him on his nose, turned out the light, and said my prayers.

As tired as I was, sleep eluded me, and I stared at the shadows dancing across the ceiling. A twinge of fear still lingered. The image of that dark stranger I spotted in town flashed through my mind. But along with this frightening man's face, I witnessed myself fighting him with a large sword.

Huh? It was plain creepy, but I knew it was important. *But what does it all mean?*

CHAPTER 5

*L*oud snoring came from under my chin when I woke up the following morning. I lifted my hand and felt long, thick fur, then a cold, wet nose. Spirit had nestled against me during the night and laid his head over my neck. His snuggling comforted me, and it made me love him even more.

I did remember, though, dreaming about a tall man with bright green eyes, and we ran and frolicked on a beautiful tropical beach. We laughed joyously as we tumbled onto the warm sand and held each other's hands. He turned his head and looked at me with an intense love that I felt down to my toes. The handsome man was about to say something when Spirit roused me with his loud snort. I wish I could remember exactly what the man looked like. Most of his face had been a blur, but I can recall his eyes vividly. *Oh well, c'est la vie.*

"Speerif, I haf to get uph." I could barely move my chin to form the words. I heard another sharp snort, then felt him lift his head. He licked my face, then rolled over onto his back. "You're a goof, baby." He pumped his paws in happiness and I rubbed his furry, warm belly.

After breakfast and tidying the cabin again, I looked at him and asked, "Okay, what should we do now?" I still had issues with Spirit clinging to my side. He wasn't afraid and looking for comfort—he appeared to be protecting and guarding me. But from what, I wasn't sure.

After my daily prayers, I read while waiting on the laundry. My wolf companion didn't seem to mind. He laid on the floor with his head on my feet while I lounged on the sofa. Spirit was obviously on edge because every ten minutes, he got up and strolled from door to door, sniffing and listening, then returned to sit at my side. This reminded me I hadn't placed the gun under my belt this morning. I walked back to the bedroom, retrieved the weapon and the two extra-loaded magazines, and tucked them into the gun holster.

I finished my book and we still had time to do something before lunch. The sheets were clean and put away, so the cabin was now ready for the next inhabitant.

My wolf and I needed some fresh air. "Come on, my friend. Let's go down to the dock for a bit." He jumped up and was excited about our brief excursion. The summer morning rain had inspired the birds to sing with abounding joy. We both strolled to the end of the dock, and I sat down with Spirit clinging to my side.

I gazed into the water and saw a school of minnows swimming as if in a choreographed dance. "Sorry, fishies, I didn't bring any bread to feed you." Spirit stood and peered into the water to see who I was talking to. He jumped up and down on his front feet so the dock would vibrate and the fish would bounce away in unison, then return. "You can see them, can't you? You're one amazing wolf." I gave him another hug. I used my phone to take a few selfies of Spirit and me so I'd have photos of my new best friend.

We enjoyed the peacefulness of the lake. I also prayed God would continue to help me with everything that may lie ahead. Prayers were said for Spirit too, that he'd always be safe, happy, and healthy. I grabbed his big, beautiful, furry face and said, "Spirit, I don't know if you're aware of this, but you've brought such joy into my life. We haven't known each other long, but our bond is strong, and I'll never forget you. I love you so much; you know that?"

His beautiful green eyes stared into mine as if to say, "I love you too." He still didn't move, but I felt him huff and he pushed closer against me.

After I pulled away, he licked my face again. I laughed, he whined, and we returned to the cabin for lunch.

After a quick meal, I puttered around the cabin. The nervousness still plagued me and I didn't know what to do with myself. I left my purse and luggage in the bedroom because I may still have a day or two here. After I snapped several more photos with my phone, I realized I'd miss this place.

I wanted to take Spirit for another walk. He was still edgy, and I assumed he was getting it from me. Even though he was hesitant, he finally accompanied me. Locking the door behind us, we walked down the path to the woods. I tossed a stick for Spirit and he retrieved it and brought it back to me.

We hiked farther into the woods and I threw another one, but he wasn't interested. He moved closer to me, then directly in front of me, blocking my way. Spirit stared ahead and sniffed. A faint, unpleasant odor filled the air, and it smelled like rotting garbage steeped in vinegar, with a burnt note like charcoal. It wasn't something I'd ever smelled before, but I would never forget it.

Then the hackles rose on the wolf's back and he growled. "Spirit?" He continued growling and kept his body close to me to stop me from advancing. A rustling sound was about twenty feet ahead, but I couldn't see anything amiss.

I pulled my SIG from the holster, thumbed off the safety, and kept the gun pointed toward the ground to my right. Although scared, I kept my wits about me and waited. Grunting noises came from my right and my left, then directly ahead. Spirit wasn't sure where he should stand to defend me, so he stayed still, but his growling grew louder and more vicious.

I could now see dark figures, and they were coming closer but not saying a word. As they approached, their faces came into focus. I recognized the intruder to my left as the strange man I'd seen in town the day before. They weren't friendly, as each man carried a lethal-looking knife.

"Stay away! I'm armed and I'll shoot to defend myself," I warned.

They continued advancing, and the one to my left started charging toward me, so I fired two shots in succession. The man I'd shot square in the chest kept approaching my position. The two seeping bullet wounds appeared to have had no effect, and he moved closer. I fired two more shots at him, but it still didn't slow him down.

Now he was only a few feet in front of me. Spirit turned into action and leaped onto this attacker. They both went down, but the other two had also advanced on me while making low grunting noises. I saw anger, hate, and determination on their faces. I fired two bullets at the one on my right, aiming for his forehead. Unfortunately, only one shot hit my intended target. One of my rounds only grazed his temple, but it knocked him to his knees, and he shook his head as if to clear it. The second bullet hit a poplar to his right, sending a sliver of wood flying several feet.

Just then, a fourth figure appeared to my left. *Not another one. I can't do this, Lord.* As I turned my aim back to the man on the left, I realized he wore military garb. This person didn't act like the other men who were attacking me. He seemed more human and looked familiar as if I'd known him many years ago. This individual barreled toward the middle attacker, firing a sizeable semi-automatic rifle. This intruder went down, but the man in fatigues kept moving toward the man he shot.

I trained my eyes on all four men, wondering what to do next. Spirit killed the first man by ripping out his throat and was descending on the assailant to the right, who I'd grazed in the temple. The military man ran up and knelt on his quarry's chest, pulled out a huge knife, and sliced the man's throat from ear to ear. Three other men wearing military camouflage ran toward the scene from all directions. One of these males went to the attacker I'd shot in the temple. He said something to Spirit, which made the wolf sit back and heel. The man then quickly dispensed with the assailant by shooting him in the head using a large handgun.

Now that my 'enemies' were eliminated, I fell to my knees, still holding my weapon in a fierce grip. I couldn't move or talk and had to force myself to simply breathe.

My first rescuer walked to my side, saying, "It's okay, sis; you're safe now." He crouched beside me and gently unclenched my hand from the gun.

One soldier approached each of the dead assassins, making sure they were truly deceased. He spoke on a handheld radio, but I couldn't understand what he said. I was still trying to pull myself together.

One of the other men moved closer to me and waited, but for what? I wasn't sure. He looked like he may be in charge, and he said to the man crouching next to me, "Come on, man. Talk to her, Jonas."

Wait a minute, *sis?* This jolted me back to reality, and I stood abruptly and turned to the blond man who had called me "sis."

"Do I know you?" I asked. He was tall, slim but muscular, had bright gray-blue eyes, and had a handsome face with one dimple to the right side of his mouth. I grabbed him by the collar and pulled his face closer to mine.

"Jonas?"

"Yeah, 'fraid so."

"You're young again too?"

"Yeah." He had that silly grin that I remembered so well and he gave me a big hug. This man resembled the Jonas I knew, but God also made him with perfection. I couldn't help myself and simply stared at him in awe, and he also studied me in return.

He backed up a bit, then looked down at my shirt. "Uh, sorry about that." My gaze turned to the front of my top, and I saw blood and other unidentifiable substances that had transferred from his shirt to mine.

"You look incredibly different, Jonas, yet the same. I know...that sounds weird," I stuttered.

"So do you, sis. You're stunning, by the way." Jonas leaned in and kissed my cheek.

The man I thought was in charge moved closer and stared at me quizzically. Returning his gaze, I felt an electric jolt of awareness, chemistry, and a sense that I'd known him forever. I tried to look away, but I was drawn to him and didn't want to break the connection.

He was tall, about six foot four, athletic, and well-built. His thick black wavy hair fought to escape the confines of his military cap. He had intense green eyes—wait, those eyes—they were the same ones from this morning's dream. I remember them clearly and this was the same man—*it had to be.* It was impossible to look away, and I studied him and noted a firm mouth, a strong face, and a square chiseled jaw with a cleft in his chin. Even in the state I was in, I could appreciate this fine-looking male. His face wasn't pretty, but his rugged, masculine look oozed sex appeal.

Was meeting this man an omen, or was it simply a flight of fancy on my part?

He'd been looking me over too, with a perplexed look as if trying to place where he'd seen me before. I could imagine what a sight I must be. He shook his head as if to clear it, then moved his gun to his left hand, lifted his right to me, and said, "It's a pleasure to meet you, Mara." His voice had a deep, smooth timbre, and I could detect a hint of an Irish lilt. I shook his hand and felt that instant awareness again but passed it off as a reaction to the stress of almost being killed.

"Thank you. And you are?"

"Sorry about that; where are my manners? My name is Finn, Finn McKenna. Welcome to the group. I'll introduce everyone else once we get on the chopper."

He gave me a nod and a big smile and said to the other men, "We need to get moving, ladies," he chuckled, and the other men shook their heads.

"The clean-up crew is ten minutes out, Finn," said a wiry red-headed young man with freckles and blue eyes.

"Thanks, Chuck. Let's bug out!" Finn answered.

"Wait! Is anyone going to explain these creatures to me? What's happening here, and where are we going in the chopper? Who are you, and how did you know I was in trouble? And...wait, where's Spirit? Has anyone seen him?" I looked around frantically, but he was nowhere in sight.

Finn returned to me and said, "I'll explain everything later. But first, we have to get out of here. The odds are that more of these 'things' are on their way, so time is of the essence. Now, this Spirit, you mean that huge white dog?"

"Wolf," I corrected.

"Well, I can assure you he's fine. I saw him walking out of here and he had no apparent injuries." He continued, "One of my team is retrieving your things from the cottage, and we'll transport your vehicle to our next location."

He moved closer to me, stooped down to my five-foot-five stature, looked directly into my eyes, and said, "Trust me, Mara, this is the next leg of your journey." He retreated a step and added, "By the way, you did an outstanding job today for a newbie. But you need a lot more target prac-tice." He winked, turned on his heel, and followed the other two men.

Jonas stayed by my side and said, "Come on, pipsqueak, we have to go."

I took one last look around, hoping to glimpse Spirit. *Until we meet again, my friend.*

But where the heck were we going, and who were these military men? And what were those things, and why did they want me dead?

CHAPTER 6

I followed the three men in the lead while Jonas stayed in the rear directly behind me. They were still on high alert, so as I walked, I removed the half-empty magazine from my gun and slid in a full one. Jonas whispered behind me, "It's about time you did that." I smiled softly to myself, raised my hand behind me, gave him my middle finger, then heard his familiar chuckle.

We must have walked at least forty-five minutes. I could now see a bright clearing about twenty-five feet ahead. Finn, who was in the lead, raised his hand and made a circling motion with his index finger. Everyone stopped and formed a circle facing outward. Finn gave another signal to his men and continued to the clearing with his weapon still drawn. He disappeared, and I waited with bated breath for him to reappear.

I whispered to Jonas, "What are we doing?"

"We're waiting for him to return to tell us it's safe to proceed to the chopper. This formation is necessary in case the enemy tries to attack. Trust me, you'll learn all this soon," he whispered back.

After several minutes, Finn returned and said, "We're clear. Let's move."

As we trekked into the clearing, a large helicopter was waiting for us to arrive. The rotors were spinning at a low rate, and I could barely hear the rotation. It was all black and had a matte texture. The heavily tinted windows didn't completely block the interior because I could see a faint outline of the pilot in the front seat.

Finn approached me, took my arm, and said, "We've got to go." He guided me to the chopper, and everyone hunched their bodies as we neared the helicopter. Finn settled into the copilot's seat as we piled in.

I connected my seatbelt, then Chuck, who stood next to me, handed me a headset to wear. Returning a weary smile, I mouthed 'thanks.' Jonas had the other window seat. Another team member sat between Jonas and Chuck, but there wasn't time yet for introductions.

Finn looked back, checking that we were secure in our seats; he then gave the pilot a thumbs up. I felt more vibrations as the pilot brought the rotors up to speed for take-off. We rose into the sky and were on our way somewhere, and I had no clue where.

It was quiet in the headset for a few minutes, then Finn asked, "Mara, are you okay back there?"

"Yes, actually. This is thrilling. I've never been in a helicopter before. Are they always this luxurious, smooth riding, and quiet?"

I heard his soft chuckle. "Uh, no. This is an Airbus H130. An excellent chopper, but we had several, what you could call 'enhancements' done." I heard a few chuckles from the men beside me.

"What enhancements?" I asked.

"For starters, we've installed an upgraded 'stealth mode' capability, mounted and concealed armaments, and satellite blocking equipment, just to name a few. But we have several more of these babies, and they're all equipped a little differently, depending on the needs of a mission. We also have one Chinook CH-47 if the need arises. But my favorite is the S97 Raider."

The other men mumbled in agreement. Finn continued, "It's the latest and greatest for military use. That baby really moves and can do just about any maneuver required by the pilot. We were lucky to acquire this bad boy."

"I'm in love!" Chuck crooned, mimicking the voice of a little girl.

"Ahh, knock it off, Chuck! Hey, do you need the air sick bag yet?" I heard the men snorting with laughter. This comment came from a team member I hadn't officially met. Chuck made a rude yet comical face at him and laughed as well. "Sorry, miss, they haven't introduced us. I'm Jasper Wheaton. A pleasure to meet you." He thrust his hand around Chuck's thin frame and over to me.

Jasper continued, "We call him Chuck because when he first joined the group, he'd puke on every helicopter training mission we took for about four months. So, we nicknamed him 'Chuck' as in, upchuck. His actual name is Norman Simmons, and he's still in training. Once he completes it, he'll join one of our other mission teams—we refer to this group as the Alpha team."

After shaking his hand, I said, "The pleasure's all mine, Jasper."

I instantly liked Jasper too. This soldier was another large man of about six feet in height and built like a truck. He was African-American with short-cropped hair and eyes that were a beautiful tawny gold. His smile was infectious, warm, and sincere. He had a strong, soothing voice and a definite Southern accent.

"Before you ask," Jasper continued, "I'm from Georgia. And," he glared at the two men on either side of him, "I'm *not* the one with the accent." More laughter echoed through my headphones.

"Since we're making introductions," said Finn, "Basheer Nazari is the gentleman sitting next to me. He's from Lebanon and one of the best pilots I've ever had the pleasure to fly with."

"My pleasure to meet you, Mara. Welcome to our humble yet totally 'off our stoner' group." He had the accent of someone from the Middle East. His voice was low and melodic and pleasing to the ear.

"That's 'rocker,' Basheer," corrected Jonas.

I couldn't help myself and giggled. "You're quite a group, and I'm pleased and thankful to meet you all, except my brother, of course." I hooted and reached over the two men between us, squeezing Jonas's hand. "I also want to say thank you for saving my life back there. But 'thank you' seems inadequate. Anyway, you men are amazing, and I'll say thank you again."

All the men mumbled, "Aw shucks," "No problem," and "You're welcome" at the same time.

I continued, "Is anyone going to tell me what's going on and who, or what, were those creatures back there?"

"You're still in shock," Finn said. "Give yourself a chance to relax and recuperate. I'll explain everything when we return to base. First, you'll need to settle in, get a meal, and get a good night's rest. Don't worry; I won't leave you in the dark. Always remember, you're one of us and we always stick together."

"*Dei Bellator!* Warrior for God!" they answered in unison.

Everyone stopped talking and was immersed in their thoughts. I relaxed and contemplated what had happened and who these men may be. Were they part of some clandestine military operation? I guess I'd have to wait, as Finn had said.

As I glanced at Jonas, we smiled at each other, and I remembered our lives together when we were young. We used to have a great relationship, engaging in fun and good-natured teasing. He was always more animated when we were together, and we loved being in each other's company.

Jonas was highly intelligent but never boasted about it. He was generally a loner but had a few good friends throughout the years and still does, though not many. I believed he liked it that way.

My dad and Jonas never had a good relationship. They rarely saw eye-to-eye, and I think it was because they were both stubborn.

Upon graduating high school, Jonas enlisted in the Army. His decision shocked my father, and Dad went through many emotions, but the anger won. They argued back and forth until my brother stormed out of the house. I saw tears in my father's eyes when the door slammed behind Jonas. My dad must have known that his son's choice could be dangerous. Jonas could end up in some God-forsaken place or fighting for his life.

Jonas trained hard to become an Army Ranger. He spent several years in the military and we saw very little of him. He never talked about his job or where it took him, as every one of his missions was top secret.

On the rare occasion Jonas visited, he wasn't the person I'd known as a child. Instead, he was nervous, wary, angry, and sullen. My family concluded it was PTSD, and even though we tried to persuade him to get counseling, he denied anything was amiss. When he left, months would pass before we heard from him again. We worried, not knowing if he was dead or alive. Even when my father passed away, Jonas was notified but didn't attend the funeral.

My mom and I finally heard from Jonas a couple of years later, and he said he was retiring. Jonas had had enough of that lifestyle and needed to move on. He said he'd found a large wooded lot in the Upper Peninsula and was building himself a house. We weren't pleased about how far away it was, but we understood. Jonas enjoyed being left alone, and we respected his wishes. This was the life he'd chosen, and apparently, he needed to live in seclusion.

But about six months ago, something changed. We discovered Jonas had sold his house and had moved on again. We tried his cell phone, but it was no longer a valid number. He finally called a month later and told us he was building another house, but it would be off the grid. I asked him for his phone number or address, but Jonas said he'd always contact *us*. It was a brief, matter-of-fact conversation, and he abruptly disconnected the call. His voice even sounded different: more confident and energetic. When he finally phoned again after another month, he gave us a number, but we were told only to use it in case of an emergency. This must have been when Jonas had died and returned to do the Lord's work.

The droning of the helicopter engine and rotors eventually lulled me to sleep because the next thing I knew, I felt a touch on my left leg and opened my eyes. I didn't know how long I'd been asleep.

Chuck drew my attention and pointed out my window. "We're at our destination and are going to land," he said.

I gazed out the window and only saw a large, dense forest of trees and areas of thick vegetation. We were descending, but from where I was sitting, there was no visible landing pad or clearing for Basheer to set down the helicopter. I glanced at Chuck with a puzzled look on my face.

"Just wait," he murmured with a grin. "This is my favorite part."

Within a few seconds, a large area of dense vegetation stirred. I inched closer to the window and almost banged my forehead against it. It *was* moving. It slid to the right of my vantage point. The chopper had stopped its forward motion and was in the middle of a hover, simply waiting. The area that had moved uncovered a deep, enormous underground cement landing pad. We slowly lowered into this cavernous space to an "X," designating the landing target, and gently touched down. *Now that was a sight to behold.* The chopper's rotors slowed, and the team unbuckled their seatbelts and removed their headsets.

Finn had already left the chopper and was opening my door. "We're here, Mara. Welcome to your new home in the beautiful state of Idaho," Finn announced.

I jumped down and looked around. This hangar was massive and well-equipped. I noted several other choppers like the one we exited. There was a huge one which must have been the Chinook, and then I saw the Raider. It looked like a giant, black, dangerous dragonfly.

Finn saw the look on my face and remarked, "I told you. It's one cool-looking machine." He smiled at me and winked again. He had to stop doing that because it made my knees weak.

There was a lot of added security here too. Many well-armed guards were posted around the hangar as well as high-tech security cameras.

"Come on, we need to get you to your quarters. Someone will deliver your luggage to your new place directly," Finn said as he led me across the massive hangar to a bank of elevators.

I looked back, and the rest of the team stood by the chopper, talking and laughing with each other. I waved to them, and they saluted back. "What about the other guys?"

"Don't worry, you'll see them later."

We entered the elevator, and Finn pulled a card from his front shirt pocket, then slipped it in front of a laser reader on the panel. Finn pressed a button that was marked 'Housing.' There were two other floors with the same title. Eight floors were listed on the console panel, and the elevator had doors on both sides, like in hospitals. The doors closed with a soft whoosh and we descended.

When the elevator stopped, the sign above the door I was facing read 'SL3-1'. Finn grasped my arm and turned me around to the other set. The sign above it read 'SL3-2'. Finn pressed a button, and the exit opened to a brightly lit area and three long hallways.

"The other elevator door leads to the 3-1 apartments," he said. A letter designated each hallway. The entries to the hallways had signs that listed all the apartment numbers.

"Mara, you'll need to always keep one of these security cards on you. The small one is generally easier to carry. You can attach it to a key chain, wristband, or anything else that may work for you." The cards looked like his but had a unique set of numbers. "Don't worry; you don't have to remember those digits." He smiled and squeezed my arm. "However, you'll need to memorize your floor and room number. You're on floor Sub Level 3-2, hallway B, room number four. Your security card will be your room key as well. Got it?"

"Yes."

He guided me down the "B" hallway to room four. He took my smaller security card, tapped it on the room laser reader, and returned it to me. I heard a click and the door opened.

My new home was delightful. It was a cozy, one-bedroom apartment. Though small, it was thoughtfully laid out, and every space was used efficiently. The apartment was sparsely decorated and painted in neutral colors of beige and white. The main living area included a comfortable sofa, a matching recliner, and a lamp table. Across from the couch was an entertainment center with a large television. Beyond the living space was an adequately sized designated office area that was fully equipped. Off to the right was the bedroom. There was a full-size bed with a beautiful patterned quilt, a bedside table with a lamp, a dresser, and a large clothes closet.

"Sheets and pillowcases are in the closet," Finn said.

To the right of the bedroom was a bathroom that included a stackable washer and dryer.

The kitchen was on the right side of the entrance to the apartment. It was tiled in a color that matched the beige living room carpet and contained everything I might need. The cabinets and drawers were fully stocked, and they supplied the fridge with the primary food groups.

"My goodness, Finn, this is excellent. This place has everything anyone could possibly need. It's lovely and homey."

"I think so, too," he agreed. "When it comes to your preferences of food and supplies, you can use the phone or TV to order what you require, and it'll be delivered. There's also a large grocery store on another level if you prefer to do your own shopping."

He continued, "We don't do any significant decorating because we like to leave it to the individual to select the things that fit their personal taste. There's a shop in the Plaza where you can find paintings, trinkets, knick-knacks, etcetera, that you may like. The base supplies a generous allowance for apartment decorating. When you visit the store, they'll provide you with all the necessary information on the allowance.

"We've added safe light therapy to every apartment. You can see them along the top of every wall in each room. The timing of the lights follows the daylight in this time zone. At dawn, they gradually come on, then stay bright throughout the day. When dusk approaches, they dim, then turn off until the next morning, of course. You can adjust or turn any of them off using the wall panel in the kitchen. We've found that living underground can become depressing, and these lights are quite therapeutic," Finn said.

I noted these lights gave the rooms a warm glow as if the sun was cascading through light-filtering shades. "This is wonderful, Finn. I love this place!"

"Since there are no windows, there aren't any picturesque views," he remarked with a light frown.

"Yeah, there's that." I wrinkled my nose. "But what can one do? I'll have to speak to the concierge about it."

He laughed and said, "I think you're one of a kind, Mara. I believe we'll get along perfectly."

Just then, there was a knock on the door. A young man stood in the hallway with my luggage. Finn had him bring it in and said, "I'll be leaving now so you can settle in. Someone will bring dinner for you to your room tonight. Try to get some sleep, will you?"

He moved towards the door but turned back, saying, "Oh, I'll be back to pick you up in the morning around nine. We can have breakfast together to discuss a few things. Will that work for you?"

"Sure, that'll be fine. Can I use my cell phone down here?" I began looking for it in my purse, but it wasn't there.

"Sorry, Mara, but we had to destroy your phone. The signal from your cell was how we, and those assassins, found you. Don't worry; we'll provide you with a new phone tomorrow, so you can still contact your mother. 'Night, Mara. Sweet dreams, love."

"Goodnight." After softly closing the door, I turned around and leaned against it. Why was I drawn to his man? He was good-looking, yes, but there was something else about him. In some strange way, we were connected on a spiritual level. There was another flash in my mind of the two of us wearing military fatigues and trekking through a jungle. *How odd!*

CHAPTER 7

*a*fter Finn departed, I contemplated everything I'd seen, heard, and experienced over the last few weeks as I unpacked my belongings. I changed into comfortable sweats and figured the shirt I'd been wearing was beyond saving. The substance I'd suspected was blood that had transferred from Jonas's shirt to mine hadn't hardened the way blood dries, and it wasn't a dark red either. Instead, it was still slightly damp and looked like black oil. It even had the same smell I detected in the woods when I encountered those strange killers. I threw the shirt in the garbage bin and tightly closed the lid.

My head spun with endless questions, and I found it overwhelming. I wished I could call my mother and discuss everything that had transpired today. Especially the news about Jonas showing up out of the blue and that he was also young again.

As Finn had said, someone delivered a meal to my room. I sat at the desk and uncovered the tray. It amazed me that the meal was delicious. I figured it would be tasteless, like hospital food. This was just a military base after all, right? I was exhausted and figured I couldn't eat, but I consumed every bite.

As I prepared for bed, I looked at myself in the vanity mirror. "You look like death warmed over, Mara." My usually bright blue eyes were dull, and my face had a gray cast of exhaustion.

Something caught my eye. I looked at my left upper arm and the spot was now more pronounced. It was about the size of a small orange and dark red. There was a symbol of some kind, like nothing I'd ever seen before. It almost looked like the shape of a three-leaf clover and raised slightly above the skin. I rubbed it and felt no pain, then I ran my fingers over the mark, following every detail.

"What is this?" I asked myself out loud. *This is just too much to think about tonight.*

I set the alarm clock for seven-thirty, so I wouldn't be late when Finn arrived at nine. After climbing into bed, I said my prayers and immediately fell asleep.

The following day, I dressed in snug black jeans and a red silk blouse. I took extra care with my make-up and hair because I was seeing Finn and wanted to look my best. After debating whether I'd need my trusty pistol today, I decided it was probably moot in a place like this. I put the weapon and extra cartridges into a spare box at the top of the closet. I safely nestled my security key card in my jeans pocket.

Finn arrived at precisely nine. My heart skipped a beat when I heard his soft knock on the door. I was looking forward to seeing him again, plus I wanted answers to all my questions.

"Good morning, Mara. I trust you slept well." His bright green eyes flashed with that good ol' Irish charm.

"Yes, I did. Thank you." I stepped into the hallway and closed the door behind me.

He looked different this morning, more civilized and less dangerous out of his combat fatigues. Since he wasn't wearing his cap, I finally saw his thick head of black hair, which tended to curl. He pushed the long hair on the side of his head behind his ears. The length of it touched the neckline of his sweater, and a small wavy curl hung over his forehead.

Finn must have noticed me looking at his hair because he unconsciously ran his hand through it and uttered, "Yeah, I need a haircut."

"It looks great, Finn. I know many women would kill to have hair like yours," I assured him. He gave me his usual cocky smile, which showed off his perfect white teeth.

"Well, thanks, love, and you look gorgeous this morning." His compliment stressed the stronger Irish accent. There was a nervousness in him today that I hadn't seen yesterday. He was like a young schoolboy on a first date, and I found it sweet and comforting. *So, he's not so tough after all and has a nice, sensitive side.*

Dressed in a navy knit pullover, he'd pushed up the sleeves, which showed his muscular forearms and an expensive watch on his left wrist. The sweater hugged his muscular, broad shoulders like a glove. His pants were lightweight khakis that matched his stylish shoes. With his rugged good looks and classic style, he could've just stepped off the cover of *GQ Magazine*.

His voice turned serious, and he said, "We have a long day ahead of us, Mara, so we'd better get our breakfast. Shall we?" he gestured toward the elevators.

"Definitely." I moved to walk beside him and detected a whiff of soap, mint, and a delightful light spice-scented aftershave.

He led me to the elevators and we made our way to the floor SL-6.

"Finn, I noticed you didn't use your security card."

"We only require them for a person's living quarters and any areas that are ingress to this facility."

The elevator stopped, and we exited into another large hallway. Well-marked signs and arrows indicated "Dining Area" to the right, and on the left, it said "Plaza."

As we walked to our right, it opened into an expansive, bright area with several large restaurants in a variety of cuisines. Many people of every race and ethnicity milled about and seemed in good spirits. A sizeable three-sided sign displayed a list of all the places to eat, including a location map.

"Oh my, this is amazing, Finn! It's huge, and there are so many restaurants."

"You're seeing only a small portion of this facility. Anything particular you'd like for breakfast?"

"I'd love an omelet."

"I have just the place, Mara."

The restaurant he selected was charming. It was how I imagined a small café in Paris might look. The area wasn't overly crowded and the hostess greeted us. Finn whispered something to her, and she said, "No problem, Sir."

She led us to a small private dining area with only one large table. Finn graciously held out my chair and sat down next to me. "We need privacy because we have much to discuss."

A young female server approached our table and gave us each a glass of water and a menu. I noticed no prices on the menu, and most of the food was labeled certified organic. The server waited patiently, took our order, smiled, and left.

"Mara, I know you have a million questions, and I wish I could answer them all this morning, but everything you'll need to know will take time. We also have questions for you as well. However, we'll give you time to adjust to everything you'll learn about us, this facility, the enemy we're fighting, and how we plan to succeed.

"First, I know you're anxiously waiting to hear what those things were and why they tried to kill you yesterday. We call them myrmidons because they're the henchmen or flunkies, if you will, for higher demons from Hell. We've discovered they only have one goal: to kill the Chosen of God or anyone that interferes with this goal. It's our job to find the newly Chosen because, as you know, they're unaware of their skills and the danger they may be in, and are untrained and probably haven't remembered their trip to Heaven yet.

"At this early stage, the myrmidons have a much higher chance of taking out an innocent Chosen One. We've found these myrmidons have little in the way of intelligence and seem to act as if they're programmed for just this purpose. We've also learned that the general public doesn't notice them and is unaware of their presence. You'll learn more about these nasty creatures and how we kill them when you start your training.

"Now, about this facility. It's in the heart of Idaho, on and below several hundred acres, and everything anyone could need is available here. You saw part of the living quarters; we can house up to three thousand people comfortably. You also saw the hangar, and we also have a large motor pool. Our central security station is also on that level, as well as the armory and military supply, satellite and radar stations, and of course, air traffic control. That section's only other ingress and egress is hidden on the side of a mountain that leads to the motor pool. The Plaza contains grocery stores, clothing shops, pharmacies, hair salons, and specialty shops. At the other end of this restaurant section, there are several places for entertainment, including a bowling alley, a cinema, an arts and crafts center, an arcade, etcetera.

"We included the Worship Center, which is on this level too. There are places of worship for every religion as well as priests, ministers, pastors, rabbis, imams, and the like. Since I know you're Catholic, we'll give you the times for the Masses so you may attend on Holy Days and Sundays if you wish."

The server brought our food and drinks. We thanked her, and she left us alone to eat our meal.

He continued, "On level two, there's the infirmary with highly qualified and skilled physicians, nurses, and specialists in every field of medicine. This includes highly equipped surgical suites and laboratories. There are also science and research labs in that area. We have dentists on staff, including everything they require to conduct their business." At his comment, he made a squeamish face. I guessed he wasn't too fond of going to a dentist, and it made me smile.

"We have an extensive training center with several classrooms on level seven. We train our people on military tactics and strategy, hand-to-hand combat, martial arts, weaponry, recon, surveillance, and anything else our people need to accomplish our goals. In addition, there's an Olympic-sized swimming pool, an extensive gym, hot tubs, and a couple of masseuses.

"There's another area in the bottom at level eight of this base, which contains everything needed to run this place. It includes laundry, IT, power grids, generators, sewage treatment, water pump and filtration stations, furnaces, oxygen supply with scrubbers, and a recycling center. We're completely self-contained. We also have south elevators that will take our people to the other end of every floor, which allows quick access to these areas. Of course, we also have several freight elevators."

I interrupted because I couldn't contain my excitement, "My gosh, you have an entire city down here. It must cost a fortune, so how is it funded?

53

Is this a top-secret facility run by the government? How can the bottom floor possibly run this entire base? Sorry for all the questions, but this is so mind-boggling!"

He smiled that charming, melt-your-knees grin and said, "Oh, yes. Private benefactors keep this place well-funded. And it's top secret but has nothing to do with any government. Only those that the man upstairs has specifically selected know about this place. Our enormous staff keeps this facility running like a well-oiled machine.

"We also have a full-service staff, custodians, guards, maids, restaurant staff, delivery personnel, and watchers. The watchers are our eyes and ears from all over the world. We call all these people Auxiliaries; we have probably over fifty thousand. The Chosen handpicked this group to assist us in our lives. Some of our Chosen devised this base's mechanics, architecture, security, and infrastructure, and their gifts from God allowed them to figure out the logistics."

"Do these Auxiliaries who work here reside on the base too?" I asked.

"Aye, many do. To keep this base secure and confidential, we try to minimize our exposure to the locals in the area. We ask that everyone only shop or do business within this facility. That's why this place is self-contained and has everything anyone would require.

"There's an abandoned military airbase on the outskirts of this property. We renovated it and have a small staff to make it look like a viable operating facility. We also use the hangar and runway on the old airbase for our planes. On the rare occasion a delivery, personnel, or one of our aircraft is seen by Joe Public, they merely surmise it's from the old airbase."

"How long have you been part of this group and base, Finn?"

"About six years since the inception of this place."

"Are you the leader of this facility, then?"

"I wouldn't say I'm the boss, but I'm one of the three people who run this place, and we're also Chosen Ones. There's an advisory board composed of five members that assist us in the many decisions that must be made. They're not Chosen but Auxiliaries. There's one with much more authority than the three of us and the board. But we can discuss her later."

"Is this the only facility?"

"No, but it's the largest. We have four others that are placed in strategic locations around the world. The Chosen are needed everywhere. Mara, can you tell me how this all started for you?"

I furrowed my brow and was hesitant to reveal my story.

"Look," he stated. "I'll start. My true age is sixty-seven years old. I too, was chosen by God to return, join the others and be part of this war. I believe this body of mine is approximately thirty-one years of age." He looked at me and wiggled his eyebrows up and down, just being silly to make me feel at ease. And it worked.

I sighed with relief and started my story. "A few weeks ago, I died in my sleep, went to Heaven, and was allowed to stay or return to the living and fight evil. I chose the latter, woke up the next morning, and was no longer a fifty-five-year-old woman, but I'd returned to somewhere in my late twenties. It was weird then, but strange things keep happening." I didn't want to tell him yet that I'd spoken with Jesus or provide any details of that conversation. "I feel, though, that you already know this about me."

Finn studied me for a moment, then returned to his matter-of-fact tone. "I know some of it. You're a Chosen One like me, but that's about it. Our first job is to locate, protect, and bring in all Chosen Ones to this facility, and then we test, educate, and train them. The ultimate goal is to keep them safe and provide enough education and training to survive the battles they must engage in. We tracked you with the help of your brother. Your mum told Jonas about your change in age and appearance, so he helped us find you. We're relieved we arrived on time. It was because of God's heavenly aid that we did."

He glanced at his beautiful black and silver watch and frowned. "Mara, we'll have to continue this at a later time. I have an important meeting I must attend."

"No problem," I said casually, wanting to spend more time with him. I connected with Finn on a level I didn't recognize. It was a pull that was slowly growing stronger every time we met. I didn't know how I felt about it or what it meant.

We stood and walked out of the café, but I put my hand on his arm and said, "Finn, we didn't pay for our meal and tip the server. I want to take care of it if you don't mind."

"It's very kind of you to offer, but I forgot to mention there's no cost for anything in this facility except for the Plaza. Everything else is fully covered. Also, you'll receive a regular salary. An advisor will provide this financial information in a couple of days." I was confused again, but I let it go for now.

Finn escorted me up the elevator to the door of my room. I turned, thanked him for the breakfast and information, and hoped we could get together again sometime soon. When my eyes lit on his face, he gazed intently at me, and there was that undeniable connection again. By the intense look in his eyes, he felt it too.

After a few moments, he shook his head as if to clear it, gave me another charming smile, and said, "It was my pleasure, love. We'll get together soon—I'll make sure of it. On another note, Jonas will pick you up early this afternoon for a guided tour. I believe it'll be the perfect time for the two of you to catch up."

"Thank you. I'd love to spend time with my brother."

"My pleasure, *mo áthas*," he whispered, then kissed the back of my hand and departed down the hall to the elevator.

I stood quietly for several moments, smiling. "My joy," he'd said. My eyes opened wide. *How did I know that? I don't speak Gaelic—or do I? Things get weirder all the time.*

CHAPTER 8

A pleased smile remained on Finn's face as he walked into the meeting room, and a booming voice greeted him.

"You're late, my friend. Catching up on your beauty sleep, pretty boy?"

Finn laughed and said, "Very funny, Kincaid. I was on a date with an exquisite, witty woman."

Edison Kincaid was a burly man in his thirties with dirty blonde hair, a neatly trimmed goatee, and a rapier wit. He was second in command of the base, behind Finn. Edison was Australian to the core, and he was also well-liked by everyone.

"You paddies have all the luck," Edison joked.

"Come on, gentlemen, let's get this meeting started. I have tickets to a mud wrestling match this afternoon," interjected Helen as she winked at the two men.

"Will do, Helen. We wouldn't want you to be late for the match," Finn said, and they all laughed.

Helen Bouchard was a tall, graceful, classic beauty of about thirty-three. She was Canadian by birth and had been a widow for the last five years. Two myrmidons who'd been after her had inadvertently murdered her husband. She still blamed herself for what happened but never talked about it to anyone, not even her closest friends sitting at this table. She was the third Chosen One in charge of the base, but her expertise included facility operations and personnel.

All three sat along the same side of the conference table. Across from them on the wall was a large monitor. Finn was about to push a button on the console before him but paused as he looked at his colleagues with a concerned expression. "Are we ready? Remember to be as vague as possible, aye?" Finn asked.

They both nodded in agreement and Finn pressed the button. Five people of varying ages, races, religions, and occupations appeared on the screen. Each person was on a separate video, which displayed their name and country.

"Welcome, everyone," Finn said as he greeted the people on the live feed. They responded in kind.

Finn continued, "This meeting will remain informal and confidential. I know you're anxiously awaiting any updates we may have, so we'll provide what we know. God advised us that the Chosen selection is close to completion. We now have two thousand nine hundred and ninety-two. Some were just brought into safety within the last couple of days. As you know, evaluating and training these new people will take a few weeks, and it will begin tomorrow. After completing their assessment and training, we'll wait for additional instructions."

"Do you know if any of them may be the ones we've been waiting for?" A man on the screen asked in a heavy Italian accent.

"I'm sorry, Cardinal Marchesi. At this point, we still don't know their identities. All of our Chosen have been honest and forthcoming, so I truly believe the three are unaware of their designation. I'm sure it'll come to light by the Lord when He's ready."

"So, you can't tell us anything?" A dark-haired woman named Isabella Rojas from Venezuela said curtly.

"I'm sorry, Isabella. I wish I had more for you," answered Finn.

A man in a turban spoke up. "We must trust Allah to tell us who His favorite three are when the time is right."

"I agree, Imam. Unfortunately, there isn't much we can do but continue the course." This comment came from a Rabbi with a strong accent who wore his kippah.

"We'll stay vigilant and wait for more instructions. Does anyone have anything they wish to discuss?" Finn asked the group, who shook their heads.

"We'll notify you of any further developments. Thank you, and may God be with us."

Everyone on the screen bid farewell and the video went black.

"I feel like a bloody idiot having to lie to them," Edison retorted.

"I know, my friend, but we don't know yet which one has betrayed us. Whoever it is, has already killed four of the Chosen. Besides us, those five people were the only ones who knew where those four Chosen would be and when. Our prophet was adamant yesterday that one of the five committed this horrific atrocity. It's a blessing that none of them know where our bases are located," Finn said.

Helen added, "If our prophet can't pinpoint who it is, how can we figure it out?"

Finn replied, "We'll evaluate this last new group soon. I strongly feel that at least one of them will help us. Any of these new Chosen could be the favored. Let's hope their tests will give us the answers. In the meantime, our people at each facility must remain on base. We don't want any more of the Chosen spotted by any of Lucifer's myrmidons until we catch our betrayer. Until we resolve this issue, we'll continue to be vague in our weekly meetings."

"You were correct not to tell them we now have all of God's Chosen accounted for. It's good to keep them guessing for now," Edison said.

"I'm surprised they aren't more upset by the cursory information we've given them the last few meetings. Isabella was right to be peeved. Anyway, good meeting, my friends. And we pray to our Lord that we discover the identity of our betrayer," Helen replied.

"Amen," agreed Finn.

I RECEIVED a call from Jonas after Finn left, and he said he'd pick me up at two this afternoon. He also told me to turn on the television and review the menu. This was a strange request, but I agreed to take a look.

For the time being, there was time to kill. As I perused the room, I spotted a black book on the desk. It was a phone directory for every area on the base. Looking up the numbers of the hair salons in the Plaza section, I found one that had an opening, and they could take me within fifteen minutes.

Two hours later, I said, "Perfect, it's exactly what I wanted. You're a genuine artist, Amanda." I praised the stylist and looked at myself in the mirror again. My long, dark auburn hair was now highlighted with varying shades of gold and red, which complimented my natural coloring. The stylist gave it a slight trim, allowing my natural curls to flourish. This definitely fits the new me. It reflected a spunky, young, "don't mess with me" vibe.

After returning to my place, I ate a chocolate bar, turned on the television as Jonas had instructed, and found a guide on the screen. The first selection was channel one, "Your Schedule," then channel two, "Facility Directory," and finally, channel three, "On-Line Store." The rest of the listings were regular television stations.

I selected channel one. My name was at the top, followed by a list of each day of the current week. I selected today's date, and it said "Open Day." I tried tomorrow, which was Thursday, and it gave a list of times, locations, room numbers, and descriptions for every appointment scheduled for me. At the bottom right, I selected the "Print" button, and my schedule was printed from the peripheral device on the desk. Jonas would be here any moment, so I'd review it later. I folded it and tucked it into my pants pocket.

Jonas arrived, and I opened the door with excitement. "Wow, sis, I love the new look. You're positively spicy!"

"Thanks. I think so too." I giggled as I closed the door behind me.

Jonas was a perfect guide. He led me around the base while giving detailed information about each area. I didn't know how I'd remember it all.

After showing Jonas my schedule, he said, "They gave me the same one on my first day." He told me not to worry about the medical exam—it was just basic stuff—and he teased, "But, they'll take your blood." He mimicked the accent of a television vampire.

I laughed and commented, "I've missed you, Jonas. To see you back to your old self is such a blessing."

"I *am* happy, Mara. To get this second chance…I want to do it right this time, you know?"

"I do." As I hugged him, my stomach growled. "Oops, sorry about that. I only had a candy bar for lunch."

He laughed. "I'm hungry too. Let's find something to eat. Shall we get pizza?" We both had always loved pizza pies.

"Definitely, yes!" I concurred as I tucked my arm into his.

"Brilliant minds think alike."

He escorted me to an Italian restaurant; according to Jonas, it had the best pizza he'd ever eaten. The hostess found a quiet table near the back that would allow us more privacy.

"Now we can talk about our old and new lives," he said.

"Yes, please. Jonas, what happened to you, especially after you moved to the U.P.? We missed you terribly, but you didn't want anything to do with your family anymore."

"I'm sorry, Mara. My withdrawal had nothing to do with our family. I couldn't get over what I experienced while in the military. So many horrible things happened while I was deployed, and the stress of it all consumed me. There were therapists, counselors—many doctors, but nothing helped. I merely wanted to be alone in my misery. It became worse when Dad died because more guilt set in."

"I assumed you'd have come to his funeral, Jonas. I know you two had your differences, but I also know you loved each other."

"But I was at his funeral, Mara. I stayed out of sight in the back because I couldn't face anyone. When I saw you and Mom crying, I was about to come forward to be with you, but the fear took over again. I hated myself for that." Tears pooled in his eyes, and he turned away in embarrassment.

I gave him a few moments, then said, "I'm glad you were there. Mom would be happy that you showed up too. You were always hard on yourself —you'd been through horrors that most of us could never understand."

He clasped my hand and said, "Thanks. During those few months, I had trouble breathing; I always felt winded. Finally, I went to the V.A. and saw one of their doctors. He sent me for several tests, and they discovered I had stage four lung cancer."

"Oh, Jonas! Why didn't you tell us? You should have been with your family through all of this."

"I couldn't, Mara. The feeling of defeat overwhelmed me and I was glad I was dying. A buddy of mine provided me with some strong drugs, but the pain became so bad I went to the streets to buy Fentanyl. One night, I knew I was near the end. The pain was unbearable, and I could barely suck in any air, so I swallowed several of the Fentanyl. I didn't do it to kill myself; I just wanted the pain to disappear. I died that night, Mara." By this time, tears spilled down my face.

"Oh, Mara, I didn't tell you to make you cry. Yes, I died but I went to heaven and spoke to Jesus. I mean, Jesus Christ, our Lord and Savior. He gave me the choice to stay or return to do this." He raised his hands, indicating the entire facility. "I returned to earth as healthy as a horse and young again. But, best of all, it was all gone: the flashbacks, fear, and PTSD. I couldn't return home because I figured you and Mom wouldn't recognize me and would shoot me where I stood." We both laughed at his comment. "So, I decided to stay at my 'off the grid' home for a while and figure things out. Anyway, enough of my story—now I want to hear yours."

I told him about my encounter with death, my trip to and from heaven, and that I also saw Jesus. Plus, I described my experiences regarding the unusual cabin, the old man, and Spirit.

He listened intently and raised his eyebrows near the end of my story. "You saw an old man, too?" he asked incredulously.

"What? We both saw him? What did your old man look like?" Our descriptions were similar but not exact. "I wonder if all the Chosen see the same old man?"

"I don't know."

We ate our delicious pizza in comfortable silence and contemplated what each other had experienced.

"I'm so full and can't eat another bite. You're correct, Jonas; this is the best pizza I've ever eaten."

He gave me a thumbs up, his mouth full of pizza.

Once we finished our meal and the server cleared our table, I asked Jonas if he ever had any weird experiences with animals.

"Yeah. After I returned, I encountered a large cougar hanging around my home. It took a few days, but he kept coming closer, and I talked to him. The next day he approached me, bounded up the porch steps, and sat beside my chair. He even put his front paw on top of my foot and purred. We became best of friends. I named him Phantom because he'd have a way of disappearing as quickly as he came. We were close and became good friends like you and Spirit."

We sat there for a few minutes, thinking about everything we'd experienced, and then I asked, "Jonas, do you have some kind of mark or tattoo on one of your upper arms?"

"I do. It's on my upper left arm, and I don't know what it is."

"Me too. It's the same location and I can't make it out either."

He looked around the restaurant and said, "I guess we better leave— they have customers waiting for tables. Besides, I have to meet a beautiful young lady at the bar for drinks shortly."

"Jonas, you dirty dog. Already found a girl to your liking, huh?" I teased.

He grinned as we left the restaurant, turned to me, and said, "Mara, I almost forgot—Finn asked me to give you your new cell phone. It's encrypted and secure." The phone looked like the old flip-style type but was jet black, slim, and modern-looking. Jonas told me it was set up just for me, and only I could use it: they matched it to my DNA. I raised my brows with an incredulous look on my face.

"I know. This place has the best and latest technology. It's pretty cool, eh?"

"I would say so. Am I allowed to call off base? I want to phone Mom."

"Yes. You can call off base, and Mom would love to hear from you. I just spoke to her this morning. But Mara, don't say too much, other than we're fine and are staying together at my cabin. We need to keep information at a minimum with her right now. We know little at this point. Okay?"

"You're right, Jonas, I agree. Of course, I wouldn't know how to explain all of this anyway," I admitted, laughing a little.

"Would you like me to escort you back to your place?"

"No, but thanks. I'll be fine. You go woo that gorgeous woman." He hugged me and walked off to meet his date.

I returned to my place and prepared for bed earlier than usual. My first appointment tomorrow was scheduled for seven thirty.

Freshly showered, I plopped on the sofa and turned on the television. My fingers selected the directory channel. It was a complete list of everyone on the base, including their apartments and phone numbers. Just out of curiosity, I looked up Finn's and Jonas's apartment and cell numbers. They were on the same floor and hall as mine, only a few doors down.

I decided to watch an old John Wayne western movie that had always been one of my favorites, but after a half hour, I kept getting distracted. It was like something was poking me in the back of my mind. It wasn't a good feeling, but maybe I was tired. I went to bed, said my evening prayers, and fell asleep.

Standing before me is a tall thirty-year-old woman with long black, shiny hair and dark brown eyes. She isn't what I'd call pretty, but more regal, and she has a distinctive face. She's wearing a dark brown suit with matching shoes, and I can see a pin on her jacket lapel that has an image of a fox painted on it. Looking at me, she stares as if she will ask for help. The woman glances around and walks away from me. She makes her way through a large crowd inside a park with a statue of a giant horse surrounded by bright red shrub roses. The woman looks around, then starts to run from something. I watch the statue come to life, but the horse turns into a dragon. Its eyes are ruby red, and instead of fire spewing from its mouth, it's a slimy black ooze. It jumps over the fountain, chases the woman, and catches her in its powerful jaws. The lady turns to look at me in sheer horror, but then her face changes, and she's now gazing at me with an evil sneer and appears to be gloating at her predicament.

A voice inside my head says, "Her time is running out." I look at the woman once more, and the dragon swallows her whole. I hear the message again, "Her time is running out."

~

I IMMEDIATELY SAT UP, breathing fast, and the voice still echoed in my head from the dream. Getting out of bed, I strolled into the living room and turned on the television. After lowering the volume, I returned to my room, leaving the door ajar, and climbed back into bed, hoping I wouldn't have that nightmare again. I found the distant droning voices and soft lights from the TV comforting. Staring at the ceiling, I reviewed what I'd seen in the dream. This woman was unknown to me, but it seemed so real.

Was the voice referring to her or me? Whose time was running out?

CHAPTER 9

he alarm clock's beep woke me the next morning at six. The television was still on from the previous night. I turned up the volume and the news was broadcasting, which I rarely watched anymore. The chaos in this country had never been worse. COVID-19, or the so-called "outbreak" a few years ago, seemed to be the catalyst for it all. The news media's bias fueled the nation's civil unrest, and evil took care of the rest. I quickly changed the channel to order the groceries I needed and requested delivery for this afternoon.

After a quick breakfast, I made sure I had my key card and today's printed itinerary and headed to the elevators. According to the schedule, my first appointment was on the medical floor. I found my way there and followed the signs to the correct room. Jonas had been right—it was a basic physical exam, and they also took my blood. After that was completed, I was free to go to the next scheduled appointment on my list. Luckily, it was on the same floor and down the hall.

I opened the door that said, "Testing and Analysis." After being greeted by a young man who knew me by name, he led me to a room resembling a therapist's office. I sat on a comfortable sofa across from a plush wingback chair.

After a few minutes, the door opened, and a beautiful woman about forty years old stepped in. She had thick brown, shoulder-length hair and bright green eyes behind fashionable reading glasses.

"Good morning, Mara. I'm pleased to meet you. My name is Dr. Brianna Martin. But please call me Brianna. I'll evaluate your brother today too." She held out her hand and gave me a warm, firm handshake, then sat in the chair across from me.

I returned her pleasant greeting, and she said, "I'm sure you're wondering what we're here for today, hmm?" I nodded my head.

"My job is to test and evaluate your present abilities or gifts since your return after death. I'm also here to assist you with the stress and all the emotions that'll come up in our fight against evil. I'm here anytime, day or night if you need me." She paused for a moment, and I saw the sincerity in her eyes.

"All the Chosen have psychic abilities. Some have very little, and there are those with greater ones. For example, one has limited telekinetic powers, and another can manipulate anything mechanical with a simple touch, like unlocking a door. There are Chosen Ones that have off-the-chart IQs after God selected them. How about you? Has anything seemed strange to you, or have you had visions of any kind?"

I fidgeted for a moment, reluctant to respond. What do I tell her? Should I say anything about my experiences after my return from the dead? I'm sure she already knew about the weird maniacs who tried to kill me and wouldn't die.

She sensed my uncertainty and replied, "Mara, many of the Chosen were hesitant to tell anyone at first. It's understandable. You and they have been through a lot and seen things most people wouldn't understand. You can rely on me. Whatever you tell me, I'll believe. We're on this path together and will finish it together."

I believed her and could sense her fear that I may not trust her. *But how could I perceive her feelings?*

"You just read me, didn't you? Most of the Chosen are empaths and you are as well. Now, can you talk to me about your experiences?"

I followed my gut instincts and relayed everything about my life before and after I died. Although, I didn't mention the nightmare from last night since it was only a dream. She listened intently and nodded her head from time to time. When I finished speaking, she seemed surprised and a bit delighted.

"You have a mark on your arm. May I see it?"

I rolled up my sleeve; she peered at it closely and ran her finger over the raised skin. "Hmm," she muttered, clearly puzzled by it.

"Mara, every Chosen One has an imprint on their arm. Each one is unique but still similar in design. Even though it hasn't fully come through yet, yours is entirely different. Do you mind if I take a photo?"

"I guess that'll be fine."

Brianna nodded, then grabbed her phone and took a couple of pictures.

"Mara, I have to be candid. I think yours is unique, although I don't know why. Hopefully, it'll come to light later. Now, let's move on, shall we? Can I try something with you?" I agreed, and she continued. "Please lie back and try to relax as much as possible. Will you do that?" I nodded and did as she requested.

I was comfortable. It helped that I hadn't slept well last night. She told me to close my eyes, clear my mind, and continued to give me instructions. Relaxation set in, but I was still aware of everything around me, so she hadn't hypnotized me.

"Now, open yourself up and let any image fill your mind." I did as she instructed and let my psyche drift.

I SEE STRANGE, unrecognizable images. Something is taking shape, and it's the woman from my dream again. It's like a movie re-run, and everything is the same, then the scene goes black. Now other images are coming into view. I see one giant beast with enormous wings, blazing eyes, and a flickering tongue, then three smaller ones that look similar to the first, engaging in a violent battle. It's brutal, dark, and terrifying.

I PULLED myself out of the images, opened my eyes, and sat straight up.

Dr. Martin saw the terror in my eyes, moved over to sit beside me, and clasped my shaking hands in hers. "Are you okay?"

I blinked several times and focused on her face. "Y—yes," I stammered. "I just need a minute." After several calming breaths, my head cleared, and my heart returned to its normal rhythm.

"Better?" she asked, and I nodded in agreement. She let go of my hands and returned to her chair. "You've now broken through the barrier that has been in place since you returned. These gifts come to the Chosen slowly so as not to shock them. You've just discovered one of yours. Can you describe what you saw, or would you rather wait until our next session?"

I told her about seeing a woman running from a monster, then the next scene of the battle of the beasts.

"You've done well, Mara. I have to warn you, though, now that the barrier is down, you may start having more visions, and not at the most appropriate times. I'll give you some tools to help control the visions and stop them when they're too disturbing."

She talked with me for forty minutes, explaining how the tools worked, and gave me exercises to control and manage them. She said developing the skills to handle the visions would take time.

"We're done for today. I'll schedule another appointment next week, but my number is already on your phone if you need anything. Any questions?" I said I had none, we shook hands, and I left the office.

I pulled out my schedule from my jeans pocket: my next stop was the financial office. Okay, I liked this one because my funds were dwindling. Going to the next floor, I found the financial office's appointment room. A large older man with thinning gray hair and gentle, kind brown eyes greeted me. His name was Frank Maynard, and he was a financial advisor. He had me sit across from him at his desk, pulled out a folder and clicked his tongue.

"Okay, my dear. Let's get started." He handed me a sheet of paper that contained my name and facility I.D. number. It also listed my weekly salary and where and how the funds would be distributed. My eyes widened in shock and disbelief.

"There must be some mistake. These numbers—they can't be right. It's way too much." I muttered as I handed it back to him.

He reread it and said, "No, Mara. These figures are correct. Your job is a highly skilled position and dangerous. It's called hazard pay, my dear." He smiled and continued, "I'll give you some cash today, and the rest will be deposited weekly into a private bank owned by this facility. There are several ATMs on the Plaza floor if you need to withdraw funds. Use your current security card and this pin to access your accounts."

Frank handed me a card with a PIN and a thick envelope that contained a stack of money. "Memorize the digits, then shred the card." He also handed me a bank book and a supply of checks for the checking account. "You now have all the information you need to access your financial data online.

"This is your new birth certificate, social security card, passport, credit card, and driver's license. The address on these items is fake, but it'll pass the sniff test. It's still your birth name, but we've already updated the public and private records to the new identity." He handed me another envelope containing all the documents.

As I was about to speak up, he raised his hand and said, "Don't ask. It's too difficult to explain how this place accomplishes the things they do. What they may miss, the good Lord handles," he joked lightly.

I did my best to fold the items he gave me and stuffed them into my pockets. After this appointment, I'd have to return to my apartment and safely stash them away.

"All the taxes and social security deductions are on top of your pay, so you don't have to worry about that. When tax time rolls around, we'll take care of it for you. Mara, you're now legal and in the black. Do you have any questions for me?"

"I don't know. Can I think about it?"

"Not a problem—call me anytime, day or night, kiddo. It was a pleasure meeting you, Mara." We shook hands. I thanked him with enthusiasm and walked away, still staring at the number on the sheet.

Wow! I never dreamt I'd get rich doing God's work. Except the term "hazard pay" didn't sit well with me, and exactly how *hazardous* would this job become? A shudder went through me, and the image of the evil dragon appeared again in my mind. *What did I get myself into?*

CHAPTER 10

I returned to my place and received a call from Jonas. He asked if I could join him and Jasper for lunch. After agreeing with excitement, I dropped off the paperwork and documents I'd received, grabbed my purse, and went to meet them. I heard a voice calling my name as I arrived at the plaza and restaurant floor. I looked around and spotted Jonas with Jasper, who motioned for me to join them.

I smiled brightly as I walked over and gave each man a big hug. "It's great to see you two today."

"Oh, we've been around. We've just been busier than a one-legged cat in a sandbox," Jasper replied comically in his sweet Southern accent. "You look mighty fine, Mara. Love the hair too." I squeezed his hand in appreciation of his compliment.

"We were able to coordinate our lunch breaks today from work. I'm glad you could join us," Jonas replied. "How about plain ol' American cuisine today? There should be something each of us would like." We agreed and walked to the restaurant Jonas had selected. We placed our meal order, and as I glanced at Jonas, he was obviously eager to tell us something important. He couldn't sit still in his seat.

"Okay, bro, what gives? You look like the cat that ate the canary." I punched him lightly in the arm, and he smiled with the biggest Cheshire grin.

"I met with Brianna today and you'll never guess what happened. I discovered I have an amazing talent. She asked me to lie down on the couch and close my eyes. It took a while, but then I left my body."

"What in tarnation are you talkin' about, man?" Jasper demanded in astonishment.

"I mean, my spirit left my physical body. I could move through objects and even travel to other areas on the base simply by thinking of where I wanted to go. What's so weird too, is that when I looked behind me, there was a semi-transparent umbilical cord that sparked with electricity between my physical body and my spiritual one. It was the only thing in the room with any color—everything else was in white, gray, and black hues. But the cord glowed with different shades of vivid blues and silver that ran back and forth in time with the electrical sparks. It was amazing." Jonas squirmed in his chair with excitement.

Jonas continued, "On my spiritual journey, I visited Poppy, who was meeting with one of her colleagues. I returned to my body and relayed to Brianna everything I'd seen. She told me what I did was called astral projection or spirit walking."

Jasper responded, flabbergasted, "Well, butter my butt and call me a biscuit! Are you sure you weren't dreamin'? I mean, can you confirm you actually visited other areas of the base?"

"Yeah! Brianna called Poppy and verified my account—from what they'd been discussing, the clothes both of them wore, down to the strawberry muffins they were eating. I even described when Poppy dropped a green file folder onto the floor. And that was weird too—the only thing with color was the folder."

"Heavens to Betsy, buddy. I have to say, that's plum awesome!" Jasper said.

"My gosh, Jonas. This *is* stunning! I mean, the ramifications of what you could do with this gift. You better not start spying on me, or I'll kick your butt from here to Sunday." We all laughed, and then I told them of my experience with Brianna.

"Y'all are gifted. I wonder if I can do any weird things," Jasper said, with a thoughtful look on his handsome face.

I remarked in assurance, "I'm sure all the Chosen have some psychic abilities. But I don't think everyone has discovered them yet. I'm sure time will tell." Jasper nodded, and we sat in silence for a few moments.

Jonas spoke up and asked me what appointment I had for the afternoon, so I pulled out my schedule and answered, "Combat Analysis." They both groaned and Jonas rubbed his hand over his face.

"What?" I asked.

"It was embarrassing," Jasper said. "I didn't want to hurt the trainer. I'm a big galoot and was afraid of squashing him. Luckily, I persevered and eventually won the match."

"Don't worry, Mara, we're the Chosen and God instilled it in us," Jonas replied, trying to keep me positive. "Just do what comes naturally, and you'll be fine."

"Thanks, guys, I appreciate it. I guess I'll run to the Plaza and buy a couple of sweat-suits." They wished me luck, said their goodbyes, and left for the elevators.

After purchasing workout clothes, I returned to my room, changed into my new attire, and had just enough time to get to the appointment. Since I was already tired, I was thankful this was my last one for the day.

I found the correct workout room in the "Training and Exercise" wing. It was a large room with several groups of mats placed strategically on the floor for hand-to-hand combat training.

There was a separate observation area along the outside at one end of the room. It had mirrored glass so you could watch yourself train, and the observers on the other side were hidden. As I stared at the glass for a second, I had a strange feeling I knew someone in that room.

A large, well-muscled man in his forties with short military hair and a tough-as-nails face approached me, saying, "You must be, Mara. I'm Jackson Donahue, your combat trainer. It's a pleasure to meet you." He gave a crooked smile that matched his off-kilter nose.

"Are you ex-military, Jackson?"

"Yes, I am, and proud of it. I've trained many fine men and women in my day. Don't be nervous, Mara, you'll do fine. I'm here to see what you know about self-defense and combat maneuvers."

"I don't know anything, Jackson. Sorry."

"Sure, you do; you just don't know it yet. I'm glad you've dressed appropriately. However, please remove your shoes and socks."

I did as he requested and waited for his instructions. He had me stand in the middle of the mat and walked around me. Then he moved in front of me, standing merely a foot away, and looked down into my eyes. This man was a good six inches taller and seventy pounds heavier than me. Looking back at him, I raised my eyebrows. *What on earth did he expect?* I was waiting for him to begin the lesson.

"Mara, what are you going to do? I'm the enemy and want to kill you. Well?" He moved even closer, then grabbed me by the throat with one hand. It didn't hurt, but he had a firm grip. I stood there and did nothing, so he sighed and moved away. He then lunged at me, but I only stepped back.

He moved behind me, but I could feel his presence. Grabbing me, he pinned my arms to my sides but still wasn't hurting me.

My feet were glued to the mat, with Jackson holding me in some type of lock. I gritted my teeth. *What does this man want? I told him I knew nothing about hand-to-hand combat. He's ticking me off.*

Jackson let go, then moved his position to face me again. "What's wrong with you, soldier? Do you like being pushed around? Okay, then, let the games begin." He shoved me hard. I landed with a thump on my butt several feet from him. *That was going to leave a mark.*

BEHIND THE OBSERVATION area sat two men. One groaned and made an awful keening sound.

Finn sat with fisted hands and he grunted in pain. Sitting next to him was Edison Kincaid.

"Come on, Finn, you've watched the first training session for many of the Chosen. So what gives, mate?" He saw Finn's face as he watched the movement on the mat. "Ahh, so this is the little lady that caught your eye. She's stunning, so I understand your infatuation."

Finn didn't reply to Edison's words because he panicked as he watched Mara on the mat. This was no fun at all. Come on, Mara, let the gift take over. Don't ignore it, love.

Finn couldn't take it anymore when he saw Jackson shove Mara to the floor. He got up to charge out of the room and attack Jackson. Edison grabbed Finn by the shirt and yanked him back to his seat, saying, "Get a grip, mate! Finn, look at me!" Edison gave him a bit of a shake to get his attention. Finn finally turned his head to glare at his friend. "You know this has to be done, and you've known Jackson for years. He knows what he's doing and he'd never really hurt Mara. Tell me you understand."

Finn drew in several deep breaths and his muscles relaxed. "I hear you, Edison. I just—I mean—I can't let anything or anyone hurt her."

"Aw, you've got it bad."

The two men continued to observe the scene playing out on the other side of the glass.

Mara got up, but her expression changed to utter calm and concentration. Staying in place, she appeared in control and at ease. She waited, her stance shoulder-wide, and she bided her time until Jackson approached. He charged at her, but she anticipated his move. Running forward, she slid down when she neared him, and used her feet to displace Jackson, knocking him down, and he landed on his stomach. Mara jumped up, straddled him, and reached up to put him in a headlock. He bucked her off, and she flew back a couple of feet and landed upright, ready to attack again.

The trainer ran toward her, but she flew up and hit him high in the chest with her feet. This move knocked him down again, but she kept coming. He rose to his knees, but she grabbed his arm, flipped him backward, and had him locked in place by the position of her body. Jackson looked stunned, as if he had no clue how she'd done this. She could have easily snapped his neck in this position. But she merely released him and stood up. Mara wasn't the least bit winded, and Jackson laid on the mat with a look of shock and even a bit of fear.

"That's my girl!" Finn stood and hooted out loud. Both Finn and Edison gave each other a chest bump and a high-five. "Yes!"

"Finn, have you ever seen a Chosen do anything like that before?" Edison asked incredulously.

"Actually, I have. I saw her brother do something like that last week. She must be the second one of the three. I'd bet my life on it." His brow furrowed deep in thought, and worry filled his eyes.

~

I STOOD on the mat momentarily, contemplating what I'd accomplished. *Was that me?* Jackson was still prone on the ground, wondering whether he should rise. I strolled over to him, offering him a hand to help him to his feet. He hesitated, then accepted.

"Wow, Mara, I don't know what to say except you kicked butt today. I'm so proud of you! I've never seen a move like that in all my years of combat and martial arts training. I'm excited to see what you'll do next, and your brother has the same exceptional abilities too, though he's had a lot of formal military training. Strange, though, you and your brother's reactions were much like Aaron Taylor's. His moves were similar." His expression reflected both thoughtfulness and puzzlement.

"Mara, I want you to consider a couple of things when you're fighting. Always remember, objects in any space where your fight takes place can be used as lethal weapons. The second thing, your petite size *can* be to your advantage. In your continued training, these things will be explained to you." He patted me on the back and continued, "We'll schedule more sessions starting next week, okay?"

I nodded, and he walked toward the benches to grab a towel. He still smiled but was now walking with a definite limp.

CHAPTER 11

I absently rubbed my upper left arm as I left the training room and moved down the hallway to the elevators. *Now, that was an interesting day. Strange, but interesting.*

As I returned to my apartment, shopping bags were on the kitchen counter and table. The store delivered the groceries, and they kindly put the perishables away. I'll take care of everything else after I clean up.

The shower was heavenly. I spent a long time letting the hot water beat on my sore muscles, feeling my tension melt away. Afterward, I went to the foggy mirror and wiped it off to view my reflection. I looked closer because the mark on my left arm was more prominent now. It looked like a three-leaf clover but broader in the center, where a symbol was emerging. There was also a faint outline in the middle of each section, but I wasn't sure what it could be. I shrugged my shoulders and decided to ask Jonas or Finn about it.

I put my purchases away except for the bracelet I'd ordered. The jewelry was a simple design made of white gold. It had a small compartment on the outside like a watch, but it was made so the small security card would fit perfectly, and the cover latched securely. There was a cross engraved on the surface. I found it fashionable yet practical.

My cell phone rang and it was Jonas. "I just got off work and wanted to know how the training went today. Was it as bad as you imagined?"

"At first, it was uncomfortable. But when he made me mad, something changed. I calmed and then kicked his butt." Laughing, I said, "Actually, I only pinned him to the mat. I've no clue how I did it, though, or if I could do it again. Jonas, what happened with you in combat testing?"

"The military extensively trained me, so I figured I'd do well, but Jackson has several black belts in martial arts. He tossed me all over the mat. But, like you, something came over me, and I attacked him. I matched him move for move, then won."

"What are we, Jonas, ninja warriors?" I asked, giggling.

He chuckled too, then said, "I've got to go now. I have another date tonight."

"You have to tell me about her when you get the time. I want to know everything and I love you, butthead."

Jonas snorted. "I love you too, pipsqueak. I'll promise to give you the lowdown on her." Then with a "catch-ya-later," he hung up.

It was close to five o'clock, and I was about to decide what to have for dinner when my phone rang again. I saw it was Finn, and my heart raced as I answered. "Hello, Finn."

"Hi, Mara. Do you have any plans this evening?"

"No, I was trying to decide what to fix for dinner when you rang."

"How about you come to my place? I can order takeout, and you won't have to do a thing. You've got to be exhausted tonight, so we'll keep it simple and relaxed. What do you say?"

"That sounds great. I'd love to come."

"Great, you know where I live?" I replied I did, and he continued, "Dress casually. How does five-thirty sound?"

"Perfect. Should I bring anything?"

"Just you, love." He hung up.

I hurried to the bedroom to decide what to wear. I opted for a silky, dark purple short-sleeve blouse, tight black jeans with a belt, and strappy black sandals. I slipped on silver hoop earrings and headed to the bathroom to apply more makeup and touch up my hair.

I practically skipped to Finn's apartment, knocked, and the gorgeous man appeared in the doorway.

"Mara, you look beautiful, and your hair is stunning." He reached out and gently caressed one curly tress between his fingers. I felt a small thrill of pleasure, even from his innocent touch. "Please come in, love."

"Thank you." I gazed intently at him and said, "You got your hair cut too. It looks great."

"Aye, I figured it was time. I probably could've put it in a man bun." He chuckled.

It was now shorter, in a typical layered cut, making him look even more handsome. He wore a black silk t-shirt with gray jeans and loafers, making him look stylish yet comfortable.

Finn said, "They should deliver our dinner in about forty-five minutes. Can I get you something to drink? A glass of wine, beer, soda, sweet iced tea?"

"A tea would be great, thanks!"

"Coming right up."

This gave me time to look at his apartment. It was beautifully decorated in blue, brown, and tan hues, with splashes of burnt orange in the throw pillows and the paintings.

I spotted several personal items located around the living area. There was a framed photo of a regal yet older woman standing beside a young boy. I picked up the picture as Finn returned to the room with our drinks.

"That was my sweet, beautiful Nana. She raised me from the age of four until she died when I was fifteen. I loved her dearly." He had a melancholy look in his eyes as he spoke of her.

I looked closer at the photo, and it was definitely Finn. He had the same gorgeous bright eyes, thick black hair, and a twinkle in his eye. He looked like he'd been a handful.

"I'm so sorry, Finn."

"It's okay. Everyone has their story. A drunk lorry driver killed my parents, but my Nana took me in, and we loved each other. I don't remember my parents, so I think of Nana more like my mother." He gestured toward the sofa and we sat down.

"We never had much money, and when Nana died, I ended up on the streets. I ran with other homeless kids, and we survived as best we could."

I sat there and listened, not knowing how to respond.

"I'm not proud of that time in my life, Mara. But it's part of what made me who I am today. Back then, I was a thief, bully, blackmailer, swindler—whatever I needed to be to stay alive. Strangely, I was good at it but wasn't proud of who I'd become. I could only think about how Nana would've felt about my current lifestyle. She raised me as a strict Catholic and would've never approved.

"I had one excellent friend by the name of Calum. We'd become as close as brothers. When I turned seventeen, we were involved in a large drug deal with a bigger gang. At the end of the deal, some drugs turned up short, and they thought Calum had taken them. I wasn't there when they cut his throat from ear to ear."

"Oh, my Lord, Finn. How awful!"

"It broke my heart, and the guilt took me to a very dark place, but that made me want to change. I decided I'd had enough of that life, and it was time to get my act together and live a better one. Luckily, I'd saved enough money from my nefarious activities and headed to the States—New York City, to be exact. I arrived with next to nothing and stayed at a shelter. Every day from dawn until dusk, I searched for work. My goal was to learn how to earn a decent living and be respectable. I went from one company to another until I found one that would take me on.

"The real problem was that I had no high school diploma or experience to qualify for a decent job. But one owner and CEO of a large, successful corporation saw something in me. I'll never forget what he told me when we first met: 'I always interview everyone who wants employment here. This is my company and family, and I say who works for me.

"His name was Clinton Hollister. Although a gruff man, he had a heart of gold. He took me under his wing and showed me the ropes. Don't get me wrong, I started at the bottom and worked hard to get ahead. A month later, when Clinton heard I lived at the shelter, he said, 'You'll move into my house and become the man you should've been.' Clinton lived as a confirmed bachelor and brought me into his enormous home; he bought me a wardrobe and anything else I needed. He didn't spoil me, Mara. He ensured I knew the value of everything I worked for and toward.

"I finally obtained my G.E.D. He sent me to college, where I earned my master's degree. I did all this while working long hours. He drove me hard but fair. After I learned everything I could from Clinton, I told him I wanted to start my own business. I assumed he'd be angry, but he said it was about time I left the nest. He knew I was bored and needed something of my own. That man knew me well, Mara. I loved him until he died at ninety-two."

Finn continued, saying, "I saved enough capital and finally started my own business. It was a thriving success and I started a few more. I'd made it to the big time. One thing I knew for sure was that I was superb at making money. But I always made it on the up-and-up, never anything underhanded or illegal. I was an excellent employer and never received any complaints about my leadership; I was fair and rewarded highly for hard work and dedication. But that fear of returning to poverty haunted me. So, I started stowing my fortune in a vast number of places. Some were in Swiss banks, but I didn't trust them either. I found other places to hide it all."

Finn sighed, then finished his story. "By the time I turned sixty-one years old, I was filthy rich but very alone. I spent all that time making money, but ultimately, I had nothing of actual value. Sure, there were plenty of women, but they meant nothing to me. I never fell in love or had children. The loneliness took me into such a deep depression that I decided to take my own life.

"That night, I begged God to help me not to commit suicide and pleaded with him for hours on my knees. As I put the gun to my head, something miraculous happened. An angel appeared before me, giving me a chance to save the world. I thought, *how amazing would that be?* I cried tears of joy to the angel and God for giving me a reason to live and a chance to have a real purpose on this earth. The next morning, I was young again."

He stopped talking and sat quietly, then turned to me with a look of fear and anticipation.

I returned his gaze with tears in my eyes and stroked the side of his face. "Finn, you had a sad yet amazing life. You pulled yourself out of misery and turned yourself into a good, loving, and giving human being. I don't think I'd have had the courage to go through your trials. I'm so proud of you." I reached across and kissed him warmly on the cheek.

"Mara, I didn't tell you all this so you'd feel sorry for me or to make you cry. I told you because I think we have an amazing connection. I'm praying that you feel it as well. If our relationship is going where I hope it is, I want you to know everything about me. Both good and bad."

When he said these heartfelt words, my heart skipped a beat. I stared deeply into his eyes and replied, "It's there because I feel it too—this strange and overwhelming link we have. I feel blessed you confided in me, and I admire the strength it took for you to overcome all these hardships. If God has brought us together, I want to take full advantage."

Finn held my face, leaned in, and gave me the sweetest kiss imaginable. It stunned me at the sudden surge of emotion and awareness when his lips touched mine. Wanting to explore more of what I felt, I grabbed the front of his shirt to prolong the kiss. This was new to me, and I moaned in pleasure. However, we were rudely interrupted by a knock at the door.

Finn swore, pulled away, and got up to answer it. It may have been an inconvenient interruption, but the food smelled delicious.

He turned to me with a sheepish grin on his handsome face and said, "Let's eat!"

After dinner, we returned to the living room sofa, where we made ourselves comfortable, and Finn pulled me close to him.

"Now, to another subject. I want to meet with you and Jonas within the next few days. There are things I think we should discuss. But at the same time, I'll introduce both of you to my two colleagues."

"Not a problem. I'd like to meet them, and I'm sure Jonas would too." I replied and stifled a yawn. "I'm so sorry. I guess I'm more tired than I thought."

"You've had a long and somewhat rough day, so it's not surprising. You gave Jackson quite a workout." He wiggled his eyebrows.

"You rat. You *were* watching me." I gave him a light punch on the upper arm.

"Ouch! I must say, you're one lean, mean fighting machine," he kidded.

"Oh, puulease!" I joked, dragging out the word. "By the way, how did I know you were there, Finn? Don't you think that's odd?"

"Not really. All the Chosen can sense each other, especially within close proximity. It's quite fascinating. But I think we also have some special connection since we can sense each other specifically. This is something I don't understand and have never seen before. Come on, Mara, let me escort you to your place."

"One more thing, Finn: my mark changed after my combat session. It's now more pronounced. Should I be concerned?"

"Do you mind if I take a look? Brianna sent me the photo she took of your tattoo this afternoon. It looked exactly like Jonas's."

I lifted my sleeve and he peered at it with a furrowed brow. "It *is* like your brother's mark. Some symbols are now starting to appear within the triad. I hope you'll let me know if any more changes occur." He appeared all business again but gently squeezed my shoulder and kissed me quickly.

"Then every Chosen One has a mark?" I asked.

"Yes, they do. Every tattoo has a unique design. Each has a circle, and within that circle, a series of lines, arcs, and dots. They remind me of star constellations, and no two are exactly alike—except for you and Jonas. Our religious scholars tell us each mark represents a specific angel of Heaven. The angel on a Chosen One's arm is their protector and guide. This is just an educated guess, but we believe it's correct."

"What is your mark, Finn? Like the star constellations too?"

"This is mine." He lifted his sleeve and it differed from mine and Jonas's. It was ornate and beautiful in design. "My mark is similar to fourteen of the other Chosen who designed and built the five bases. We didn't have to wait for our marks to develop. They appeared instantly upon our return. Very knowledgeable religious scholars analyzed them. They concluded that these symbols represent the Principality Angels. Pretty cool, huh?"

"What's the purpose of Principalities, Finn?"

"All I know is that they aid groups of people and even the church. Some of them lead and others assist other individuals. We assume these angels were, and are, our guides for the task ahead. They taught us how to get everything designed, built, and running and how we should prepare all the Chosen for the upcoming battles."

"This all just boggles the mind, doesn't it?"

"That it does," was all he said.

He took my arm, escorted me down the hall to my apartment, asked for my security card, and opened my door.

"I had a great evening with you tonight, Mara. I hope we can spend a lot more time together."

"I hope so as well, Finn." I hated that our evening was concluding.

"Goodnight, love."

"Goodnight."

I thought he'd give me a passionate kiss, but he took my hand, turned it over, and sweetly kissed my palm. He gave it a gentle squeeze as he looked deeply into my eyes, then turned around and strolled back to his place.

I closed and locked the door behind me with a giddy grin. Then, I called my mother to tell her about Finn.

After enjoying a long conversation with Mom, I disconnected the call and turned on the television. I needed to check my schedule for tomorrow. The weapons training was scheduled for a few hours late morning, then one long classroom seminar in the afternoon. After printing the program, I went to my bedroom.

I prepared for bed, set the alarm clock, and climbed into the inviting sheets. Weariness filled me and the bed felt heavenly. I turned out the light and fell immediately asleep.

That dream about the dark-haired woman and the dragon returned, and it was an exact repeat. Anger filled me at having to watch it again. *Aw, come on. Let's finish this so I can have a decent night's sleep.* It finally ended before it came to fruition, but I couldn't help but wonder why I kept dreaming about this female. My gut told me intense evil was connected to her, but what did all this have to do with me?

CHAPTER 12

I went to my first appointment, ready for anything. The instructions stated we weren't to bring any outside weapons to the class today, so I left my Sig in my room. I found my first class and expected it would be a target practice site, but it was an ordinary classroom.

Some people were already sitting at tables, and others entered the room behind me. Nine Chosen Ones, including me, attended this class. We greeted each other and chatted for a few minutes. But for some reason, I kept staring at a very handsome young man in his late twenties who introduced himself as Aaron Taylor. He was tall, with a thin, athletic physique, and had short, curly brown hair and expressive blue-green eyes. I don't know why; he just seemed familiar, like I should know him. He looked at me the same way as if he was also trying to figure out where he'd seen me before, but I knew I'd never met him before today. Throughout the day's training, we glanced at each other in puzzlement. *Hmm, another puzzle to solve.*

When the instructor entered the room, I recognized him immediately. It was the pilot who flew the chopper for the group who rescued me.

"Please, everyone, take a seat. We have a lot to cover this morning before target practice begins. There's a manual in front of you which we'll follow for the most part, and before you ask, yes, you can take it with you." He smiled and continued, "My name is Basheer Nazari, and I'll be your pilot today. We have clear skies and are currently cruising at thirty thousand feet." Everyone hooted with laughter, and I guessed they also knew him.

"Now, let's get started." Everyone opened their books and the class began. Basheer was entertaining, and his jokes kept everyone in stitches. He reviewed the different weapons the Chosen used at every facility: why they'd been selected, what we used for ammunition for each one, and how they should be held, handled, and stored. Everyone took notes because this information may save our lives.

"We supply every weapon. But this is most important; all ammo must, and I stress, *must* come from this facility's armory. There are no exceptions. Is that understood?" He pointedly looked at each individual in the class to stress his statement.

"Yes, sir!" we replied loudly.

"Good! This emphatic rule will be explained in another class this afternoon."

The lesson continued, and we asked questions, which Basheer patiently answered. Eventually, he said it was time to move on to weapons training at the shooting range. "We'll now take a ten-minute break, then head down the right side of the hallway and follow the signs to the gun range. Once there, you'll receive a range bag with your name on it. It has all the protective gear you'll need for today. So let's get moving."

Each student had their own personal instructor at the range. They showed us everything we needed to know about each weapon: how to assemble, disassemble, release a jam, and load and reload quickly. We were told they'd assign each person their specific weapons, but they'd have to be stored in the armory when not used for practice or missions.

I loved target practice and handling and shooting all the different weapons. The large automatic and semi-automatic rifles were my favorite. After firing a few rounds from each gun, my shots were spot-on.

Basheer approached me when the instruction ended and commented, "You're an excellent shot, Mara. You've done well today and were as good as Finn and Jonas when they started. You'll do well, my dear." I graciously thanked him and shook his hand.

I grabbed my gear since it was time for lunch, and my stomach growled in anger. *Okay, I'll feed you.* As I walked from the room to the hallway, Finn stood casually against the wall with his arms folded.

"Hi, Finn! It's great to see you today. Are you waiting for Basheer?" I asked. His face lit up, and he gave me a wolfish grin.

"No, I'm waiting for you." He gently wrapped one of my curly tresses around his finger that escaped my French braid. "I like the braid, but it's stunning when your hair is down."

"Really? Thanks for the compliment." My face flushed from his flattery, and I grinned happily that he was here to see me.

"Ready for some lunch?"

I gave him an emphatic yes, and my stomach growled again. He chuckled, looked to see if anyone was looking, and kissed me quickly. Finn carried my range bag, and we went to the restaurant floor.

After we were ushered to a table, Finn turned to me with a serious expression. "Mara, I received a text from Basheer after today's training session, and he recommended you take the sniper course. We need well-skilled sharpshooters because we only have a select few at our facility. There's only Jonas, Jasper, Edison, and one other. I've had all the training but haven't had time to keep my skill polished. We need more, so would you be willing to join our sniper team?"

"You invited me here to talk business, not pleasure, Finn?"

"Not initially. But I wanted to get business out of the way first. Well?"

"I guess. But I know what snipers do, and that concerns me. I don't think I could ever take an innocent life, Finn. That's not who I am."

"We don't kill innocents, Mara. It's exactly the opposite. We mostly target the myrmidons and demons, though I have to be honest, God may request we take a human life. Sometimes, we've no choice in the matter. It's His will."

I sat there for a few minutes considering the idea, then said, "I understand. I'll take the training."

"Thanks. You're doing the right thing, I promise."

Finn stated he wanted to know more about me. So I gave him my entire life history, such as it was, and he was an avid listener.

"My life was boring compared to yours, Finn. I did nothing significant in my life and have diddly squat to show for it. I'm hoping this next life will allow me to make a difference. My wish is to fall in love and raise a family—at least, someday."

"Mara, you were, and are, a courageous woman. You also have been through a lot and had the grace to endure and not become bitter. I think you should be proud of your previous life." He took my hand and kissed the back of it.

"Thank you. I needed to hear that from someone other than my mother."

I went on about my history, just some of the little things I'd enjoyed, including all the pets I had growing up: cats, dogs, horses, snakes, lizards, rabbits, and hamsters. "I loved all the animals, but my favorite pet was a black and white Maine Coon cat. My baby was special, and I'd never had a feline like him before or after. He was the most loving, intelligent, and comical pet I'd ever known. My kitty, Bo, lived to the ripe old age of twenty. For that, I thanked God every day, but I still miss him. Oh, my goodness, I've droned on and on about a cat. I'm sorry, Finn."

"On the contrary, I loved it. It tells me a lot about your sweet, loving nature and how much you regard everything you're given. I'd have loved to have a cat like that. However, I did have a dog once, many years ago, when I was on the streets. My pup was a stray, and I called him Fagan. He was a multi-colored mixed-breed mutt with enormous, expressive eyes and a loving, protective nature. He kept me warm on many chilly nights, and we cared for each other. I had him for about three years until I woke up one morning, and he'd died in his sleep. It was sad, but I knew he was old and had a good life with me." Finn's face reflected love, happiness, and remorse as he recounted his story.

"Animals are amazing. I'm glad God created them."

"I agree. Do you have any photos of Bo?" Finn asked.

"Uh, no. Not with me, anyway. I transferred some to my phone a few years ago, and I used that cell to take photos of that fabulous little cottage and my dear Spirit. But that phone's gone."

"I'm so sorry about that, honey," he said sincerely.

I told him it was fine and I still had photos at my mother's house of Bo, and I had the memories of the cottage and Spirit in my mind, and I'd never forget them.

Glancing at my watch, I advised him I had my afternoon class in a half-hour. I'd need to return to my apartment before class to drop off my range bag and change clothes.

"In that case, we should get going. You'll enjoy this upcoming class, and you'll receive a lot of information today. It should answer many of the questions I know you'd like answered."

Finn continued, "Mara, I have a favor to ask of you. Would you mind joining me for dinner again tonight? I've also invited Jonas. There are a few things I'd like to go over with both of you, and Jonas has already agreed. I was thinking my place at around seven?"

"Of course. Not a problem. I'll be there."

"Oh, by the way, I know you're a practicing Catholic. Would you like to attend Mass with me this Sunday? I'd love it if you'd join me."

I wanted to jump up and down at his invitation, but I politely and calmly answered. "That would be wonderful, Finn. Thank you."

"It's a date. I'll call you so we can discuss the details." He kissed me quickly before I entered the elevator and headed to my apartment. Just thinking of Finn made me giggle like a schoolgirl, and I couldn't wait to see him again. I would've danced a jig in the elevator if I didn't think I'd look stupid.

Oh my, Mara, you've got it bad!

CHAPTER 13

This next class was one I'd been anticipating, and Finn had been correct. It *was* fascinating because the instructor was Edison Kincaid. He said he was one of the Directors or "head-honchos" of this place. His Australian accent was music to my ears, and his wit was entertaining. He started by speaking with the nine of us, then made several clean and funny jokes. Edison had everyone in tears by the time he began to lecture.

"Alright, children, listen up. We have much to cover, and I'm sure you'll have questions when I'm finished."

"The Chosen—which consists of every one of you as well as myself—are comprised of many different nationalities, races, faiths, ages, and backgrounds. Not all Chosen have died to be selected by God; some were visited by angels or spirits from the Lord. Every account is different and doesn't make one Chosen any more important than the other. You're all essential. Does anyone know specifically what we've been 'chosen' for? We know the ultimate goal is to slay the evil here on earth. But as to our specific tasks—not all of us know exactly what our parts are in this war. Most *do* know, but others are still learning. The Lord selected some as warriors and some for other important tasks. God tells each Chosen One when the time is right."

"The Lord's selections started about six years ago. We're unsure who was the first, but that doesn't matter. All we know is that we have close to three thousand of you worldwide."

The vast number shocked us, and we intently waited for him to continue.

"Every one of you has a mark on your arm imprinted by God. We're quite certain these tattoos represent the angel God sent to protect and guide each Chosen One. We conclude that God has sent us close to three thousand different angels. Quite amazing, don't you think?" We nodded in agreement.

"Every one of you has unique talents, abilities, and gifts. They don't manifest themselves right away, either. They emerge when needed or when the good Lord decides you're ready. There are three gifts we know we all share. One, we can speak and understand any language spoken on this planet. Two, we know when other Chosen are nearby, and three, we're aware when any of Lucifer's myrmidons or demons are within our proximity. These abilities are crucial in our survival, so remember that, mates.

"We've discovered there are four distinct classes of us. The first is the Principals. God selected them to design, build, and run these facilities and give a home, training, and any additional support. There are fifteen people in this group. These fifteen are composed of three leaders at each facility. At this location, the bloke standing before you is one of them, plus Finn McKenna and Helen Bouchard. Finn and I handle all the military logistics of this place. Helen oversees this location's daily operations and has an extensive staff to assist her.

"The second group is the Warrior class. They're going to be upfront and center in skirmishes and battles. This group must face the devil's myrmidons and return them to damnation.

"The third type is the Foundation. They are vital to our success. Without them, what you see in this place"—he raised his hands indicating the entire facility—"and have experienced while you're here wouldn't be possible without these strong and dedicated people. They're the ones that support, help train and care for all of us.

"The fourth, which is new to us and we're still learning about, is what we call the Gatekeepers. This small last group is a subset of the Warrior class. We're not sure what God selected them for; we know it's something big. We'll advise you if we learn anything more about the Gatekeepers.

"When you arrived here, your doctors, teachers, and trainers compiled your test results, which indicate which group God selected for you.

"This facility is our primary base. We also have four others like it across the world. We did this because we never know where or when we may need to do any of God's tasks. Time is always of the essence when we're dispatched for a mission.

"Many have asked if we have any idea what will happen to all of us when our battle is completed. I can honestly say that your guess is as good as mine. We expect we'll return to the private sector and go back to living our lives, hopefully, better than we did the last time.

"I'm getting to the nitty-gritty, my friends. Now that the Almighty has selected you, we know that you must, and I repeat, you must live a God-loving, God-obeying life. Sinning is a grave mistake. The Man upstairs will not take kindly to it and will let you know swiftly and without mercy.

"For example, a Chosen, who shall remain nameless, became lonely during an extended surveillance mission in Hong Kong. He headed to town, ignoring the voice thundering in his head not to do what he had planned, and found himself a lady of the evening. The man thought to himself, *what could it hurt? It's only one time. God gave man the urge to procreate, right?* The bloke found himself a 'lady,' guided her to a back alley, and started the dirty deed. Out of nowhere, a humongous angel picked him up and tossed him like a ragdoll up to the fourth-floor balcony of the alley apartment building. He broke both legs, one arm, three ribs and cracked his clavicle. After being released from the hospital, the bloke went straight to a priest and begged forgiveness. God forgave him because he's still an influential member of the Chosen. I assure you, he'll never make that mistake again. I see the look on your faces. He's not at this facility, so don't try to ferret him out, mates!" He finished with a hoot of laughter.

"Now, on another phenomenal subject—our special ammunition. When we first encountered these bloody myrmidons, they were next to impossible to kill. The only way at that time was to cut off their heads. Not fun, my friends, and getting that close is a dangerous risk. So, our Heavenly Father came up with a plan for this dilemma. Any weapon will do when killing those creepy creatures, but the ammo—that's the key. There's a group of Greek Orthodox monks in an ancient monastery in Turkey who produce our ammunition and the steel for the blades of our knives. God gave them, and only them, the formula for making these bullets and the steel. Besides removing their heads, this ammo and the special blades are the only things that can kill a myrmidon. We use too many bullets when shooting them, but this's because of our adrenalin and fear. It's still recommended that you make one shot to the head or cut their throats with these special blades if you're close enough.

"After your training is complete and you're between missions, you'll be assigned a job based on your skills or gifts bestowed upon you. It takes a lot to keep this place running, and there are still sections on all the bases being designed, built, or renovated. We need expertise of every kind at our facilities. We never give you a job you don't like. I remember a quote from Mark Twain, 'Find a job you enjoy doing, and you'll never have to work a day in your life.'

"Everything I've reviewed is in a packet by the door, including additional information on the leaders of each facility, advisors, supportive personnel, etcetera. You're to take one with you when you leave. Please take the time to read all the information. Thank you. Are there any questions or comments?"

Several questions were asked, and Edison was polite and concise with his answers. When the seminar concluded, I returned to my room with the information packet.

I sat on the sofa, trying to take it all in. Of course, Finn and Jonas told me some of it already, but the scale of this massive undertaking was only beginning to sink in. *What are we in for? Am I one of the Gatekeepers, and what does that even mean?* I never really thought about what this could entail. *What big thing are we supposed to do?* It all seemed pretty terrifying.

My dear Lord and Savior, I know we need to trust in You, but this whole thing sounds like a real humdinger.

CHAPTER 14

*a*fter my shower, I selected something simple yet elegant for tonight's dinner with Finn and Jonas. I was looking forward to this evening, not only because I'd see Finn but also Jonas. I'd missed his companionship after he left home.

As I neared Finn's apartment, I heard laughter from inside and knocked on the door. Jonas answered.

"Hi, Mara. Come on in. Finn is setting the table, and they'll deliver dinner in a half-hour."

I followed Jonas into the kitchen, and Finn offered me a cold beer, which I eagerly accepted.

"Let's go into the living room and get comfortable," Finn said.

Jonas and I sat on the sofa and Finn stood with his back to the entertainment center.

"I wanted to talk with you in private because there's been a development we need to discuss. As you know, you have distinctive marks on your arms. Unique, I assumed, to just the two of you. However, we recently found a third Chosen who has your matching symbol. His name is Aaron Taylor, and he came in at the same time as you, Mara. Do either of you know him?" He handed us a photo and Jonas stared intently at Aaron's picture.

I shook my head and said, "I met him briefly in class today but don't know him. However, I felt like I should have, and I thought it was strange at the time. Have you met him before, Jonas?"

My brother shook his head in confusion.

Finn hesitated to continue and rubbed his forehead between his fingers as if he had a massive headache.

"Finn, are you okay?" I inquired.

"Yes. I'm fine, Mara." He gave me a quick smile. "As you know, we physically examine anyone new who enters the facilities. Part of that physical is bloodwork. We keep some of it stored in case further testing may be required."

"That nurse took an awful lot of mine, and I thought it odd," Jonas said.

Finn shrugged and continued, "After Brianna brought your distinctive mark to the principals' attention, we asked for additional blood testing. We did the same for Aaron. Some tests aren't back yet, but we know the two of you are related to Aaron."

Jonas and I eyed each other in puzzlement and turned back to Finn.

"All we can tell you is we don't know him," Jonas said firmly.

"Maybe he's a distant relative?" I asked Jonas, and he said he doubted it.

"This is where it gets weird," Finn replied and peered at us with a somber expression. "According to the test results, Aaron is a *very* close relative. Close as in, I mean, he's your brother."

We both gaped at Finn and began talking at once.

Finn held up his hand, and we quieted. "One at a time, please. I know this is shocking, but we have to solve this issue."

"I swear, Finn," Jonas proclaimed, "we don't have another sibling. Could he be a half-brother we never knew about?" Jonas looked between Finn and me as he asked the question.

"No, the DNA doesn't lie. The three of you had the same mother and father. In his interview, Aaron said his age before his return was fifty-nine. Returned age of twenty-nine, so he was born two years before you, Jonas. We confirmed Aaron's story. He grew up in Vancouver, Canada, and we have his school records, social security information, and driver's license, you name it. We just received a copy of his birth certificate, but we're currently having it researched and verified. He was raised by a single mother by the name of Virginia Taylor. We're still digging for information on her, though we've found little. That's all I know at the moment, but I promise I'll let you know if anything new develops."

Finn continued. "We haven't spoken to Aaron about this. And, until I discussed this with the two of you and we've completed the research, we don't plan to either. When we get all the facts, then we'll meet with him. I assume you'll want to speak with your mother about this, but I recommend you hold off until we learn more. Do you both concur?"

We agreed with Finn's request.

"Dinner should be here soon, so let's talk about lighter subjects," Finn said kindly.

Dinner arrived, and Finn did an outstanding job of keeping us distracted and not thinking about this recent development. By the end of the meal, we laughed and had a great time. After departing Finn's place, Jonas said he'd call me tomorrow to discuss how we'd approach our mother on this sensitive subject.

After returning to my place, I couldn't stop thinking there must be some mistake. Mom and Dad would've never kept something like this from us. So there must be some logical explanation. There just *had* to be.

The next day, I looked forward to purchasing a new wardrobe. Having the money to do this was a novel experience for me, and I couldn't wait to start. Of course, I'd still be frugal and not buy anything too expensive or something I certainly wouldn't need, but I smiled as I headed to the Plaza.

As I entered the elevator, my phone rang. It was Jonas. "Hey, poodle face, you want to meet for lunch today?" I rolled my eyes at the funny name he called me, then told him I'd love to. We agreed to meet at our usual pizza place.

I disconnected the call, and it rang again as I put the phone back in my purse. "What did you forget, butthead?" I teased him and added a loud snort.

There was a long pause before I heard a reply. "Mara, it's me, Finn. Sorry that I'm such a butthead," he chuckled in good humor. In my haste to answer the phone, I hadn't looked at the caller I.D.

I giggled with embarrassment and said, "Sorry, Finn. I thought you were Jonas. How are you today?"

"I'm great. I hope you're doing well too."

"Actually, I'm having a fabulous time. I'm going to the Plaza to shop for a new wardrobe, and it's long overdue."

"Good for you; you deserve it. I must have perfect timing today because I hoped you'd like to go to brunch after Mass tomorrow. Oh, I should also let you know that formal events always pop up now and again. How about buying something long and sultry?" His voice deepened and slowed. "It's always a monkey suit for me." He laughed.

"I'd love to have brunch with you tomorrow. Thanks for letting me know about the formal events. I hope I can find a shop that has proper evening wear."

"I have the perfect one for you. I'd recommend "Crème de la Crème." They'll have anything you could want in this line of clothing."

"Thanks, Finn. I'll check them out."

"I'm looking forward to taking you to church tomorrow, even if you called me a butthead."

"Hardy har har," I replied sarcastically but still snickered.

We agreed on the time and place and said our goodbyes.

I scanned the Plaza and spotted the boutique he'd mentioned. The dresses and gowns were expensive, and their beauty made my jaw drop. Finally, I found exactly what I was looking for, paid the cashier, and left the store.

It was another hour by the time I had everything I needed. My purchases were to be delivered to my apartment later this afternoon. This was an added perk of shopping at the Plaza.

I met Jonas at the restaurant, and we reminisced about our childhood, then discussed how to approach Mom about Aaron. When the time came, we'd try to bring it up gently and hoped we wouldn't upset her.

The Plaza staff delivered my purchases that evening. After putting my new clothing away, I placed my newly bought home décor items around the apartment, and they brightened up the place. The only things missing were a large painting and a few framed personal photographs.

After fixing a quick dinner, I prepared for bed and selected another book to read out of an already-stocked bookshelf in one corner of the living room. It was a mystery romance novel, and I figured it would be a light read.

As I finished the fifth chapter, I heard a voice saying, "*Help me! I don't have much longer.*" I shook my head and glanced around the room but saw no one. A little later, I heard it again, but the voice was barely a whisper. Getting up, I walked to the door and peered into the hallway. There was no one outside my apartment. A few men down the end of the hall were joking about which one was tougher and meaner. I rolled my eyes and closed and relocked the door. It must simply be exhaustion that made me hear things that weren't there. After turning on the TV to a low volume, I left my bedroom door open a crack and fell into a deep sleep.

The dream returned. This time, the only change was the woman transformed into a fox, and the dragon ate it. *Come on—stop this stupid dream!* And it did. The remainder of my sleep was deep, restful, and uninterrupted.

The following day, I grabbed a croissant and readied myself for Mass. Finn arrived, and he looked handsome in gray slacks with a matching polo shirt and a black suit jacket. "You look gorgeous, as usual, love," he declared.

"Thank you, Finn. This is one of the dresses I purchased yesterday." It was a short-sleeved summer dress in a light, colorful pastel print. I grabbed my purse and we went to the worship center.

We stepped off the elevator and found the floor packed with people. Seeing so many individuals coming to worship the Lord made me smile. There were chapels for every denomination imaginable, as well as temples and mosques.

Finn steered me to one of the Catholic chapels: three were at this facility. He advised me they based the number of worship centers on the number of people of each religion.

We entered the church and waved at those we knew. I even saw Jonas with a beautiful young woman. She had gorgeous, short, dark hair and a lovely face with delicate features. Finn guided me to a pew about a third of the way back from the altar. Jonas and his girlfriend sat a couple of benches behind us.

The chapel was incredible. Religious statues and candles were everywhere, and the church smelled sweetly of frankincense and myrrh. The Mass started and Finn insisted on staying close to my side. Giving him a giddy smile, I turned my attention back to the service. I hoped to see the angels again but doubted it would happen. To my surprise, during the consecration, the angelic beings descended. My eyes blurred with tears, and Finn gave me a concerned and quizzical look.

He whispered into my ear, "Are you alright?" I nodded yes because I couldn't speak. I grabbed tightly to Finn's hand and told him to look at the altar. As he turned, his face transformed into pure bliss, and tears slipped down his cheeks. I stole a glance at Jonas, and he was also transfixed with joy as he gazed upon the altar.

When it was communion time, Finn looked at me in wonder, and I gave him a knowing smile. For some reason, I knew if I held his hand, this would allow him to see the angels.

After Mass, we spoke with several people we knew and left the chapel. I wanted to talk to Jonas, but he was engrossed in a conversation with his friends.

Finn couldn't contain himself any longer. "This is what you saw before?" I nodded. "That was incredible." His Irish lilt was more pronounced when he became excited or angry. He was like an overjoyed little boy. Finn would have skipped down to the elevators if there'd been enough room. I gave his hand a gentle squeeze and kissed him on the cheek.

"I didn't see them until you took my hand," he said.

"I don't know why unless it's our connection, Finn. Jonas can see them too, and I assume he'd also seen them before."

The place he chose for brunch was an old café style place with round tables and checkered tablecloths with candles on top. They decorated the restaurant with murals of colorful trees, flowers, and assorted birds, which was lovely. We ate our meal and talked for over two hours.

After we left the café, we held hands and strolled around the Plaza, engrossed in watching everyone enjoying their day. We sat at a small fountain and relished being in each other's company. To my delight, we spent the entire afternoon together, had a light dinner of sandwiches and soup, and just as we finished our meal, Finn received a phone call. Unfortunately, what he heard on the other end didn't make him happy. He only said with a grimace, "I'll be right there," and hung up.

"Mara..." he said, obviously not wanting to tell me he needed to leave.

"I heard. You have to go, but I had the most wonderful day with you."

"Me too, sweetheart."

"I can walk myself back to my apartment. You go on ahead and attend to your emergency."

"You're one special woman." He kissed me, gazed into my eyes, and said, "I'll call you later."

I nodded, smiled brightly, and Finn strode to the elevators.

As I watched him walk away, I wondered what was so urgent that he had to leave abruptly. It couldn't be good since concern and worry clouded his expression.

CHAPTER 15

"*W*hat? How can this have happened?" Finn asked Helen and Edison in astonishment, then paced the board room.

"We don't know, Finn," Helen asserted, replying to his justifiable outburst. "We only know that someone abducted one of our newly returned Chosen. For what purpose? That answer is still unclear. We have to pray he's still alive."

"Finn, stop going off like a frog in a sock. We're all upset, but we must calm down and think this through," Edison said sternly.

Finn inhaled a few calming breaths and nodded to Edison in agreement, smiling lightly at Edison's Australian turn of phrase.

"All we know," Edison continued, "is that one of Lucifer's bloody hell-hounds absconded with him. They took Jake Mathison from a wooded area near his home in Mexico right when he was most vulnerable. It was simply bad luck that they found him before we did. There was a witness. An ornithologist was up in a tree taking photos of a rare bird, and he saw the whole thing."

"Did he get any photos of the kidnapping, Edison?" Finn asked.

"The man was too petrified. In his description, an ugly and foul-smelling monster attacked a young man in fatigues and carried him off like a ragdoll. Our man Mathison was taking a whiz, poor bugger."

"But that doesn't make sense. They've never captured anyone, only killed. That's all we've ever known them to do. It's also surprising that the man in the tree noticed the myrmidon. I thought only the Chosen could see them," Helen replied.

"I'm assuming maybe when a myrmidon commits a violent act, he becomes visible to the non-Chosen," Edison said.

Finn thought for a moment while rubbing his chin. "That makes sense, and I think we should look into this theory later. Regarding the abduction, maybe the Devil's game plan has changed. He hasn't had any luck getting information about us or finding our bases. Maybe it's another tactical move on his part. Or, what if it isn't the Devil at all? Could it be our betrayer?"

"It's possible. But we better pray to God we find this young man quickly. Right now, his future looks grim," Helen said.

"What about our prophet?" Finn asked.

"She hasn't been able to get any answers yet, but she's still working on it. To her knowledge, the young man is alive and being held somewhere south of the U.S., but she can't pinpoint his precise location. I think she could find the answer eventually, but time isn't on our side," Edison replied.

Finn concurred while tapping his fingers on the table in frustration. He said, "Let's order plenty of coffee, and we'll dig in and see if any of our other facilities can provide additional information."

Finn, Edison, and Helen spent time on a video conference call with the principals from every base. They discussed all possible reasons for the kidnapping and who may have been involved. They strategized about what steps to take next, including any Chosen Ones who may be able to assist in the search.

It was after two in the morning when they called it a night to get a few hours of sleep. They had problems concentrating and were repeating themselves.

"Let's meet here in the morning around seven," Finn said. After returning to his apartment, he went to bed and crashed, not even bothering to change his clothes or remove his shoes, and was sound asleep when his head hit the pillow.

. . .

I'M DREAMING AGAIN, but if I wake up, it'll go away. I jerked back to consciousness and thanked the Lord the nightmare was over. After flipping on the bedside lamp, I went to the kitchen for a glass of water. The lights were blinding in the kitchen when I turned on the switch and had to take a moment to adjust to the brightness. I filled a glass with water, downed half of it, and walked toward the living room. Then out of nowhere, a painful brilliant glare attacked my vision.

I immediately dropped the glass and covered my eyes with my hands, but the overwhelming brightness persisted. Finally, I screamed in my head for it to go away, then the light changed to something terrifying.

~

THAT WOMAN IS THERE AGAIN from my dreams. It's her, but she's different. Her eyes are vacant of humanity, and only darkness and evil determination remain. She's in a cold and dank room with cement walls and floors. This place is windowless and one bare bulb hangs from the ceiling. Her mouth forms a sneer which makes her once pretty face ugly.

She's looking at something, so I gaze in another direction and see a young man bound to a metal chair by wire. His hair is brown and curly, plastered to his head by his sweat, and his young, innocent face is bruised and bleeding. They've removed most of his clothes, and bloody welts cover his chest and arms. His feet are bare, and his toes are curled from pain. I have an instant connection to him because he's a Chosen One. Even though I scream out loud, I can't hear my cry. The only sounds I hear are from the dank, cold cement room.

The woman interrogates the captured victim, insisting he provides the information she's demanding or the pain will be unbearable. She sneers again and nods to a bulk of a man standing beside their hostage. The huge thug picks up a wicked-looking scalpel and slices off the Chosen One's right ear. The poor man howls a painful scream, then the woman's henchman takes the scalpel and holds it to his other ear. The Chosen One refuses to tell them anything, and by the look on his face, he's steadfast in his resolve. The woman stops the large male and says, "We've wasted our time—this one won't tell us anything. Don't worry; we can find another."

The woman then turns and stares directly into my face and screams in terror. Her eyes are filled with tears and they reflect utter desperation. She then says, "Please, help me! Save me from him. Time is running out, and it'll be too late!" She keeps chanting these words.

Then, the entire dream starts again from the beginning and replays. "Stop! Stop!" I'm yelling out loud. But it won't cease. Finally, in self-preservation, I roll into a ball on the tiled floor begging for it to end. I swear I hear a man's voice calling at me in the distance, but I can't make out his words.

"Help me!" I scream again.

~

FINN WOKE from his dead sleep in terror. "Mara!" he gasped. Something was wrong.

He ran out of the apartment door and bumped into Jonas, who only wore jeans and no shirt or shoes. His hair was tousled from sleep. Jonas muttered, "Mara!"

They both stared at each other for a brief second, then ran down the hall to Mara's apartment. They banged on her door and called her name, but she didn't answer. Several neighbors down the hall opened their doors to investigate who was causing the ruckus. Finn and Jonas ignored them.

Since Finn hadn't removed his clothes from the day, he still had his phone in his pocket. He quickly dialed a number and said, "This is Finn McKenna, Security I.D. number Victor seven, eight, nine, four, alpha. I need an emergency unlock on Apartment SL3-2, B4."

A computerized voice answered Finn's request by saying, "Identification confirmed. Emergency unlock activated for SL3-2, B4." There was a hard click and the door unlocked.

They both ran in and found Mara lying on the kitchen floor in a fetal position. Her hands gripped her head, and she repeatedly screamed, "Stop! Stop!" and "Help me." Finn and Jonas ran over to Mara and tried talking to her, hoping for a response. Finn picked her up and carried her to the sofa, murmuring and trying to make her focus on the present.

"It's not working, Finn. What do we do?" Jonas asked in a pleading voice.

Finn took another tactic: he started yelling at Mara, demanding an answer. He lightly shook her twice, then repeated his command. Finally, she stopped whimpering, relaxed, and focused her eyes.

"That's it, my love. Come back to me," Finn murmured, stroking her hair. "Welcome back." She turned her gaze to Finn, and he kissed her forehead. He still held her in his lap and Jonas sat next to them. Thankful relief replaced the sheer helplessness on their faces.

I COULD FINALLY FOCUS on the present, and the horrible vision had subsided. Gazing at Finn and Jonas, I thanked them repeatedly for coming to my rescue.

"Mara, you scared us to death. Are you okay?" Jonas asked urgently with fear in his eyes.

"It was so awful! I don't understand what just happened. It was like I was living a nightmare. Oh, Finn, why do I keep seeing this woman? Who is she? Why was she torturing the young Chosen man? Why was she, then, begging for me to save her? None of it makes sense."

I couldn't stop the tears, and Finn held me close, tucking my head under his chin. "It's alright, sweetheart. We'll get the answers, I promise."

"We will, Mara, we'll figure this out. We're here for you and will do everything to protect you from whatever or whoever is doing this." Jonas held my hand as his protective brotherly instincts took over.

We sat together for a while, and they gave me time to recover. It was apparent Finn had his suspicions about what had occurred, but he was kind enough not to push it for the time being.

I continued to sit curled up in Finn's lap, held tightly in his arms. However, I knew I had to pull myself together and make sense of these dreams or visions.

There was a frantic knock on the door, and Jonas went over to answer it.

It was Aaron Taylor, and he looked pale, half-asleep, disheveled, and worried. I heard him ask Jonas, "Is everything okay?" Aaron rubbed his head in confusion and looked at Finn and me on the sofa.

Jonas answered, "Yes. Everything's fine, but thanks for asking." They said their goodbyes and Jonas returned to my side with a puzzled look. "That was weird. I wonder why he stopped by. Is his place in this hallway, Finn?"

"I don't believe so. It must simply be a coincidence," Finn answered and turned his attention back to me.

I reluctantly pushed away from Finn and slid down next to him on the sofa. Both men watched me quizzically, maybe wondering if I was a bit daft. "I'm better now. Thank you both for coming to my rescue. How did you know I needed help?"

"For some reason, we both knew you were in deep trouble and ran over here. I bet your neighbors think we're all crazy," Jonas said, and Finn nodded in agreement.

"My phone's been vibrating since we arrived. I think your concerned neighbors have been calling security. I'd better phone their office and let them know all is well. Excuse me for a minute." Finn stood, walked a few feet away, and called security. He then went to the kitchen and dialed another number. Finn started speaking to another individual while glancing in my direction.

"He's talking to someone about me, Jonas. Is he calling the men who'll put me in that white jacket with the long sleeves that tie in the back?" I asked Jonas in a joking voice.

"Nah. He's in love with you and would never let that happen." After his remark, I stared hard at Jonas, but he wouldn't elaborate.

A few minutes later, Finn walked back and stood before us, staring at me in puzzlement. I just realized I was wearing a skimpy silk nightgown and a pair of bikini panties.

"Excuse me while I put on some clothes. I suddenly feel naked."

"Don't change on my account, love." Finn gave me a comical smile that cheered me up immensely. I stuck my tongue out at him, smiled, and walked to the bedroom to change into something more presentable. I was back in the living room a couple of minutes later, and both Jonas and Finn were obviously talking about me because their conversation halted as soon as I entered.

"Okay, now what?" I asked, with my hands on my hips.

"I've called a meeting of this facility's principals, and I need you and Jonas to attend. We must do it now. Can both of you meet me by the elevators in twenty minutes?"

We agreed, and Jonas and Finn went to their rooms to change clothes. I was already dressed, but I washed my face, brushed my hair, and put on some makeup. Since my pallor made me look like a zombie, I added more blush to my cheeks.

Jonas and I met Finn at the elevators, and he asked us to follow him. For some reason, Fin led us through a strange route from inside a locked utility closet to a hidden hallway with another set of elevators.

"Only a select group of people know about these lifts. They lead to a floor not listed in the other main bank of elevators. The floor is SL-9. It's where we hold our private meetings and conferences with our other principals and advisors. You two will have access to these two elevators and floor by dawn today," Finn explained.

We followed Finn into the elevator; the floor was listed as SL-9. I mused to myself, *Interesting…a hidden and private floor. How James Bondesque.*

After exiting the elevator, we headed to the right to Meeting Room A. As we entered, I spotted Edison Kincaid and a woman I hadn't seen before.

"Jonas and Mara Patrick, meet Helen Bouchard. I know you've both already met Edison Kincaid." We greeted each other and Finn gestured we take a seat.

"Mara, I know this won't be easy, but you need to tell us in detail about these nightmares and this powerful vision you experienced tonight. I can't stress enough how important this information may be. Will you do this for us?" Finn asked gently.

"Yes, I can," I whispered. Jonas clasped my hand and squeezed it.

Trying to be as thorough as possible, I provided every detail of the dreams I'd been having, the voice I thought I'd heard the other night in my apartment, and what it had said. I then recounted the details of the latest vision from tonight.

When I finished, I gazed at each of them, awaiting a response. Jonas watched them too. The principals appeared to be in deep contemplation. They looked at one another with knowing expressions, raised their eyebrows, nodded their heads, then turned to stare at me once more.

"Mara, you say this woman had shoulder-length dark hair, dark eyes, and had a pin with a picture of a fox on it, then later the woman turned into a fox?" Helen asked.

"Yes, it's weird, I know."

"The young man you saw being tortured, are you sure he was a Chosen?" Edison inquired.

"Yes, positive."

Finn stood, moved to a file cabinet, opened a drawer, and removed several folders. He pulled photos of seven women with dark shoulder-length hair and brown eyes and laid them on the table. "Do any of these women look familiar?"

I immediately tapped on one of them. "That's her! She's the woman in my visions."

"Our betrayer," whispered Helen.

"What do you think, Finn? Could she be the one?" Edison asked.

"What are you talking about? What's going on? Why am I dreaming this? I only know that in my gut, we have to save this woman, and now we have to save the Chosen One too." My voice had a frantic edge, and I bit my lip in frustration.

Edison pulled out a laptop and typed for a few minutes, keeping his eyes on the computer screen. He'd glance up now and again, then return to his work.

"Mara, you said she was innocent, then evil, but then begged you to save her, right?" Helen asked, pursing her lips in concentration.

"Yes, like she was fighting to get away from someone or something and needed help."

The three looked at each other again, and Jonas finally demanded, "That's enough questions! The three of you know what's happening, so stop being cryptic and tell us what you know!"

"You're right, Jonas, and we're sorry about that. We only want to be sure about what Mara witnessed and how it relates to this woman," Finn said apologetically. "Within the last few months, we discovered a traitor among us. There's someone who's been killing some of our Chosen. There are four dead so far, and another has been abducted. He's a new recruit named Jake Mathison, who was taken early yesterday in Mexico. We've been trying to discover the identity of this betrayer, but we haven't had any success. Until now, that is. Mara, you've been seeing this traitor, and I believe she's fighting a possession by a demon. Her name is Isabella Rojas, and she's one of our five advisors. Her maiden name was Fox, which explains why you kept seeing a fox. It was a clue to her identity."

Finn then continued, "Back in the eighties, when she still lived in the U.S., she fell in love with a Venezuelan government attaché and eventually moved with him to his country. She joined our group only ten months ago. A priest specifically chose her as an advisor. This priest lives in a small town outside of Caracas, and we all respect him and trust his recommendations without hesitation. We were relieved to find her because we had zero assets in South America. Within one month, she'd gained ten additional assets and said she'd get us close to a hundred by the end of the year. This would be the help we'd need to gain a foothold in that continent. She'd said these assets were beyond reproach and would be highly valuable to our cause. They were devoted to God and passed every test we gave them for loyalty to our Lord.

"About four months ago, her husband had a minor infection and needed antibiotics. Medicine is a scarce commodity due to the political unrest they've been dealing with in this country these last few years. They were unable to procure this simple antibiotic, and her husband died. After his death, her despair at his loss due to her country's political injustices caused her to fight against the current government. She then became an activist and started her own group, protesting against the current regime and marching for democracy. Something else must have happened to Isabella to have caused this complete one-eighty."

"Finn," Edison said, "My sources say she hasn't been in Caracas for at least two months and hasn't been seen by our priest or her followers since. We have some information on the ten assets she told us about. Although we've only been able to reach one of them so far, he states she's no longer in contact with him, and her behavior has become erratic and almost manic.

Isabella hadn't given any of her recruits a way to communicate with us, which is standard protocol for new assets. So, they couldn't advise us of her change in behavior and disappearance."

"But she's been on video conferencing for those two months. So where is she broadcasting from?" Helen asked incredulously.

Everyone shook their heads.

"Finn, can you find me maps of, I'd say—South and Central America? I want to try something if you don't mind," I requested.

He gave me a puzzled look and asked Edison to retrieve the maps. I set them in front of me on the table, began concentrating on the photo of Isabella, and thought about where she might be. Focusing on the Central American map, I ran my finger back and forth and let my mind take over. I found nothing. Then I moved on to the South American map and ran my fingers over it. My finger stopped, and I knew this was Isabella's current location.

"She's there. I'm sure of it," I said confidently.

Everyone looked at where I was pointing, and Edison asked, "Are you positive, Mara? This place is in the middle of nowhere and is surrounded by mountains. If you're correct, infiltrating this area will be a real pain in the arse."

Finn said, "Look into it, Edison, and let's see what information we can acquire on this location. We'll also get our techs to research the origin of her last phone contact. Also, please get in touch with our other principals and see if they have any current data on her. In the meantime, we must get a few hours of sleep because we have a long day ahead."

"Finn, she said she was running out of time, which concerns me. However, I'm sure my vision was not of a past or current event but of one to come. In my gut, I feel we may only have, at the most, ten days to find her and the Chosen One," I replied.

"I'll take your gut instinct anytime, Mara. You heard her, my friends; time is of the essence. It's now a little after four in the morning. Let's meet back here at eight-thirty. All agreed? We're all dead on our feet, and we have a lot of work to do within a short time." Everyone nodded.

"Thank you. Now get some rest!"

I wondered if I could ever sleep at my place again. Jonas said he was heading up and asked if I was too. I answered I wanted to talk to Finn first and told him to go on ahead. After seeing the anxious look on his face, I reassured him I was fine and would see him in the morning. He kissed me on the forehead and left the room with the others. Finn was still on his phone, and when he hung up, he put the photos and files away and motioned me to the door.

"Let's get some sleep, kiddo." He took my hand in his and we headed to our apartments. Finn dropped me at my door, but I hesitated to enter. He noted the look of apprehension on my face and said, "You don't want to be alone yet, do you?"

I shook my head and stood there, staring at the door. Finn said, "I tell you what, go into your place, put on something comfortable, and I'll return in a few minutes. Okay?"

After agreeing with him, I went inside, leaving the door ajar. After changing into plush sweats and a soft pair of socks, I padded into the kitchen for something to drink. The broken glass fragments sparkled on the floor along with the spilled water, and I knelt, carefully picking up the shards. Finn returned, wearing a cozy and worn college t-shirt and a pair of sweatpants. He pulled me gently by the arm and said, "Leave it, Mara. I'll have it taken care of tomorrow. We need to get some sleep."

He led me out of the kitchen while turning out the lights. I watched him as he took a moment to shut off the TV, which I'd forgotten was still on. Then he led me back to the bedroom and shut the door. Finn guided me to the bed, pulled back the covers, and tucked me in. Then, strolling to the other side, he pulled back the blanket, took out his phone to set the alarm, and turned out the lights. "Goodnight, Mara. I pray your sleep will be deep and peaceful unless you dream of me." I heard laughter in his voice, and I giggled too.

"Thanks, Finn. I couldn't bear being alone in case it happens again."

"No problem." He reached over, pulled me to him, and pressed my head to his chest. "Now close your eyes and sleep because I'm not leaving you, sweetheart."

After his whisper, I closed my eyes, felt Finn's body's warmth, and heard his steady heartbeat against my ear. I only saw Finn behind my eyelids, looking at me with those clear, green eyes and a heart-melting smile.

Snuggling in closer, the images from the nightmare still flashed through my mind. *Is this my life now—seeing these horrific things and not knowing if I could stop these evil events from happening?* Only God knew the answers to these questions, and I prayed He'd give me the knowledge and strength to do whatever He may ask of me. *God, I'm listening...*

CHAPTER 16

I woke up slowly from a deep sleep, and it took me a moment to orient myself, but I quickly remembered the previous night. The pillow beside me was empty, and I could hear running water from the bathroom. Finn meandered out while drying his hands on a towel.

"Good morning, sleepyhead," Finn said, smiling. He looked fabulous, even with his tousled hair and morning stubble.

"Good morning. What time is it?"

"It's six-fifteen in the morning and I need to get moving. I must return to my place, shower, shave, and change my clothes. There are several phone calls to be made before the eight-thirty meeting with my team. We have a lot of intel to obtain before any plans can be devised for extraction. You catch up on your sleep, sweetheart."

"Finn, I can find their exact location. I know it's in here." I pointed to my head as I jumped out of bed. "It's my job to help you find them, so please don't shut me out of this mission." This was important to me, so I didn't care what I looked like or that I had morning dragon breath.

"Mara, I promise we won't shut you out: I'll keep you informed and bring you in *after* you meet with Brianna. You don't have a handle on these visions yet, and you'll need a crash course on controlling and using them efficiently. I know this is your baby. Now get a few hours of sleep and call Brianna for an appointment with her today. Agreed?"

"Okay. God chose me for this task no matter what it may entail. You need me, and so does Isabella. With my whole being, I know I *have* to be part of the extraction team when the time comes, regardless of whether you think I'll be ready. You won't find her or Mathison if you leave me behind." I gave him a look that meant business.

He walked toward me, pulled me into his arms, and looked deep into my eyes. "I believe you. You're integral to this situation and will be fully briefed on every development. I promise." He kissed me, then returned to his apartment.

I met with Brianna. She provided more tools to help me control or even stop a vision. However, since I hadn't tried them yet, I hoped they would work. I practiced a few simple exercises until they became second nature.

She also had me practice locating different people I knew on the base. Using a facility map, she guided me through focusing and honing in on one person at a time.

"I did it! I found Finn," I squealed after Brianna confirmed Finn's current location.

"Mara, finding someone within the same vicinity differs from locating a person across a long distance. It would be best if you met with me over the next few days for more practice. Okay?"

"Definitely."

As she requested, I had several sessions with Brianna. I also had a grueling schedule of training, which included combat, weapons and target practice, military tactics and maneuvers, and everything else related to skills I'd need for the upcoming mission. In the evenings, I spent time in the gym lifting weights, running on the treadmill, and swimming laps in the pool. I didn't want anyone to think I wasn't up to the job.

Aaron was side-by-side with me through all the training. We started to know each other better, and it brought me closer to him, and I think he also felt a brotherly connection to me. We discovered we had a lot in common and even had the same bizarre sense of humor. The love for my new brother grew, and I was glad God brought us together, although it was difficult not divulging what I knew about his past and that we were siblings.

I continued spending my lunch hours with Brianna, working on my psychic skills. My visions were more easily controlled, and I continued locating people on the base with only my mind. I enjoyed this part of my gift because it was like a game of hide and seek.

Being so busy, I saw little of Finn during these few days, but he called several times and kept me in the loop, as promised. The calls always started business-like, but after we completed the updates, he took the time to ask how I was doing and was sweet and considerate.

Jonas called—to check up on me. He talked a lot about Poppy, and he apparently loved her.

Later that afternoon, Finn called while I was finishing target practice and said he'd like to meet with Jonas and me that evening. There was news regarding Aaron and he wanted to give us an update. He said we could meet at his place, but a custodian was working on a small water leak in his kitchen, so I invited them both to my apartment for pizza.

Finn and Jonas arrived at the same time. Finn had a leather briefcase in one hand and yellow roses and baby's breath in the other. "These are for you, beautiful," he whispered, handing me the flowers.

"Finn, they're lovely. Thank you!" I kissed him, then buried my nose in the roses. "Let's go to the kitchen and eat." We ate our pizza, brownies, and beer, took turns telling ridiculous jokes, and laughed until we cried.

After dinner, we carried our drinks to the living room and sat on the sofa. Finn looked around and said he loved what I'd done to the place but stared at the large bare spot on the opposite wall.

Knowing he'd ask why there was a huge blank space, I said, "Before you ask, I couldn't get the painting I wanted. I know what I'm looking for but haven't found it yet. Not at the Plaza, anyway."

"What would that be, Mara?" Finn asked with curiosity.

"I want a beautiful, sunny, tropical seascape. My version of heaven on earth. A warm, private oasis with the scent of the salty sea. I love the feel of the warm ocean breezes, the sound of the gently breaking waves against the sand, and the wind blowing through the palm trees. That's paradise to me, Finn." I had a happy, dreamy look on my face.

Finn smiled at my description. "It sounds amazing to me. I wish we could be there right now."

"Me too," I said.

"Me three," Jonas agreed.

Finn waited a few moments, and then his face grew serious. "I need to update you both on the status of everything we've found regarding Aaron. It's a long, complicated story that will take time to tell.

"But first, there's some new intel regarding our current situation with Isabella Rojas and her Chosen hostage. It's been tough getting information out of Venezuela. As you know, we don't have a good presence in this country, but we do have one asset. He's been accommodating and has given us the names of three others who Isabella procured before she went to the other side. We have to work with these four down there, besides the priest. But, these assets are well trained, and we know they can be trusted," Finn said.

"I won't lie to you two; this will be a difficult extraction. Using our satellite imaging and Mara's help, we've discovered the location of their hideout is underground. According to one of our new assets, this site has two tunnels leading in and out, and after two days of recon, very few people have come and gone. We've no clue how many are in this bunker. All we know is that guards are protecting the entrances, and our watchers have seen many myrmidons patrolling as far as a mile from the hideout. Their patrols are random with no pattern, so they'll be unknown when we decide to go in. As Mara said, time isn't on our side. We'll notify you once we have a plan and then move out. You'll need to be ready to leave at a moment's notice, and I expect that'll be in a day or two.

"About Aaron...four years before you were born, Jonas, your mother was pregnant with her first child. As far as I know, it was a normal pregnancy, but you'll have to ask your mum to confirm this. When her labor started, she went to the local hospital for delivery. That's where the story gets complicated.

"Unbeknownst to your mum and dad, a young nurse was working in the delivery ward that had lost a two-month-old baby to crib death when she had lived in Wisconsin six months earlier. After the death of her child, she left her husband and removed herself from what little family was left. Her name was Sandra McCallister, and she had transferred to the Michigan hospital shortly thereafter. Why, I don't know. But apparently, she was developing a plan to replace her dead child, and she waited until the perfect opportunity arose. She needed exact timing to pull this off, and it was when your mother came in to deliver her first son.

"In another hospital room a few doors down, a young single mother with no family died during delivery, along with her newborn son. This was what she'd been waiting for. She took the dead child, hid it somewhere, and went to the next delivery—your mum. Sandra was the only one in the room for the delivery, as the doctor was helping a breech baby down the hall, so she had ample opportunity to make the switch. When your mum finally delivered her son, Sandra claimed he wasn't breathing. Sandra told her that her baby wasn't doing well and she had to take the child down the hall. She then switched the babies, and a few minutes later, she brought the other woman's dead boy to your mum and told her he had died. You remember that back in those days, the family wasn't allowed in the delivery ward. There wasn't any security either, so there were no other witnesses.

"I'm sure it devastated your mum, and Sandra had your mum hold the dead little boy to say goodbye. It's tragic and hard to believe someone would do something this horrendous, but Sandra did. She desperately wanted her son back; in her mind, this was how she could accomplish her goal. So, your mum's baby survived, but this grieving, demented woman kidnapped him. Sandra quit her job that same day, moved to Vancouver, created a new identity, and claimed the child as her own. Her new name was Virginia Taylor, and she named her son Aaron. She even bought herself and her new baby fake birth certificates. I have copies if you'd like to see them."

"How do you know all this, Finn?" I asked.

"We were lucky: Virginia kept a diary. Before her death, she left a letter and the journal for her one and only friend she had while in Vancouver. She told her friend not to open it until after her death. It was all explained in the diary, and she even listed your parents' names.

"Now, about Aaron. He didn't have a good childhood with his so-called mother. We think the guilt of what she'd done drove her to alcohol and street drugs. By the time Aaron entered grade school, Virginia had become a full-blown addict. She left him to his own devices, and he raised himself.

"Aaron had two things going for him, though: he loved school, and the man who lived across the street took a fatherly interest in him. This gave him a reason not to be home with his drug-addicted mother. He was an exceptional student, and the neighbor, a retired mechanical engineering professor, taught him everything he knew about the trade. Aaron ate it up and excelled in anything mechanical. After Aaron graduated from high school, the retired professor got the boy a scholarship at an Ivy League college. He acquired two Ph. Ds, one in electrical engineering and the other in mechanical engineering. It's all a long story, but it explains how Aaron is your brother."

Jonas and I sat in stunned silence and had no clue how to respond. After a few minutes, I replied with tears in my eyes, "Poor Mom."

Then Jonas added, "Poor Aaron. Finn, this is awful! How do we tell Mom? Geez, how do we tell Aaron?"

"I don't know," Finn replied. "I think the three of us should tell Aaron, but regarding your mum, that's up to you two."

"I certainly don't want to tell her this over the phone. That would be so wrong," I said. "I don't get it. Why didn't she tell us about losing a baby? We don't keep secrets from each other; at least, I didn't think so." I pondered what Mom's reason would be for not telling us. "Knowing Mom, I think it was too hard for her to talk about, even after all these years. Like, what's the point? We'd never meet our dead brother, right? It's all so bizarre.

"Hey, wait! Remember when Aaron showed up at my door that night after I had that violent vision? He must have felt my extreme emotions because we're siblings. I wondered why he came over, looking so confused and worried. He had no clue why he'd been drawn to my apartment, either. Poor guy…I guess we'd better tell him that as well," I explained quickly.

"I'd been wondering about that too, Mara. You're probably right. That would explain his troubled arrival that night," Jonas agreed.

Finn nodded, rose from the sofa, and said, "I'll leave you two alone to discuss this. It's up to you how you want to approach giving your mum the news. However, I feel we should tell Aaron as soon as possible. He's already lost so much time not knowing you and your mum; sadly, he'll never meet his father. He needs to know he has a good, loving family waiting with open arms for him, aye?" he asked.

We agreed wholeheartedly, and Finn left the apartment so Jonas and I could digest all the information he'd provided about Aaron and his life. *But how would Aaron take the news, and even worse, how would Mom?*

CHAPTER 17

inn called me the next day and said he needed to meet with me, Jonas, and Aaron. He also advised this should be done before the upcoming mission, so time was of the essence.

When I arrived, Aaron, Jonas, and Finn were already at the meeting table. They must have been talking about something funny because they were chuckling as I walked into the room. Aaron was fidgety and unsure about this meeting, so Finn started immediately.

Finn told a story about a woman who grieved after the loss of her son and what she did to replace him. He withheld everyone's name from the story until he'd finished. Finn looked at Aaron and said, "Aaron, the kidnapped boy was you. The stolen baby belonged to Mara and Jonas's mother. These two are your brother and sister, Aaron. I'm so sorry about throwing so much at you at once, but we didn't know how else to tell you. I have all the corroborating evidence within this folder for you to review when you feel the time is right."

As we watched Aaron's expression, many emotions moved through his face. We gave him time to process the information, and he sat there thinking for several minutes.

"So…I have a family I didn't know about," he stated as he peered at

Jonas and me. I gave him a warm smile and covered his hand in mine, and Jonas patted him on the shoulder in reassurance.

"Yes, you do, Aaron. It's such a great pleasure to know you finally. It's been way too long," I said assuredly.

"I agree," Jonas concurred.

"I have to say, I wondered why when I met the two of you, I felt like I'd known you forever. It explains a lot," Aaron said.

"We felt the same way. There's an instant connection that families have. We both hope in time, you'll feel comfortable enough to meet your mom—that's not to say that you'll ever put your other mother aside. I wouldn't want that to happen," I stuttered.

"Mara, don't worry. My mother was—well, as you know, not a good one. Oh sure, I loved her in my own way, but she wasn't a nurturing, loving woman. I only cared for her because I felt I had to, but that was it. We never had any genuine connection." As he sat there, he relaxed, and a genuine smile lit up his face. "I have a real family," he whispered and grinned from ear to ear.

"Yes, you do," I assured him.

Jonas and I stood and hugged him, and Aaron's eyes filled with tears.

"Welcome home, brother," Jonas said warmly.

I explained to Aaron why he'd felt compelled to rush to my apartment the night of my terrible vision and that we have a powerful bond as siblings and Chosen Ones. Aaron took the information in stride and wasn't fazed by this strange phenomenon. He seemed relieved to have an answer for why he woke so terrified that evening and how he was miraculously guided to my apartment.

We said goodnight to Aaron, and then Jonas and I spoke to each other after we left the meeting. We still had no clue how to discuss this with our mother and tried to assess our options. The details would have to be laid out at a later time.

That evening, I received another call from Finn. Another emergency meeting was scheduled, and he said to be there in thirty minutes.

When I arrived, several people were already seated at the table: Finn, Jonas, Aaron, Edison, Basheer, Jasper, Chuck, and two others I hadn't met previously.

Finn said, "Mara and Jonas, I believe you know most of the people here. But I don't think you've met Xavier Grayhawk and Billie Archer. They're military through-and-through and experts in military tactics, explosives, and extraction. Chuck will join us again for the next few missions, as he needs a little more field experience under his belt."

Xavier was an older gentleman in his early forties with a full head of long graying hair kept in check by a ponytail. He had big dark eyes, heavy brows, and a clean-shaven square jaw. He was a distinguished-looking man of Native American heritage.

Billie was a tall, strong-looking woman in her late twenties, with hair colored a shocking dark blue cut in a short butch style. Her face was attractive, although her features were hard and sharp, and she wore no makeup. She looked like she could take on anyone and win with minimal effort. It was obvious from her greeting that she was from New York because of her distinct Brooklyn accent.

I liked them instantly and greeted them in return with a smile.

Finn started the meeting and updated the group on the latest intelligence. "All week, Mara's been meeting with Brianna to hone her psychic skills, and as of two days ago, Mara was able to pinpoint Isabella's hideout. It will be a bear, my friends, to complete this mission. It's in a horrible location with very little intel, and we have only four locals who can provide support. Edison, please put the Venezuelan topographical map on the screen."

Edison pushed a few buttons on the computer and the map appeared. There were several moans and a few mild curse words spoken by the group.

"Good Lord, Finn, this is ridiculous. This plan will take an act of God to pull off. Good thing He's on our side," Xavier replied incredulously.

Finn raised his hand so he could continue speaking. "Look, I said it would be difficult, but we *can* do it. As you said, Xavier, we have God on our side. It'll also take everyone in this group for the mission. There's a brief in front of you outlining everything we know at this point. If you'd take a few moments to review it, then let me know if you have questions."

After several minutes, Jasper spoke in frustration, "Y'all got to be kidding! It's underground, the myrmidons have no pattern to their patrols, and we have to walk several miles up and around a mountain to get to this place. I hope y'all aren't barking up the wrong tree."

As I sat listening to the discussions, something in my mind told me there was a problem. *But what was it? What was I missing?* I stood, walked over to the map, and put my finger on the spot identified as the hideout.

"What is it, Mara?" inquired Finn.

Everyone looked up from their reading.

I concentrated intently on the map, turning my head this way and that. "Something differs from two days ago. I need a few moments."

The vision of the hideout appears once more. There's Isabella, and I see her as I did before, but someone's missing. The room changes to a different scene. The chair that Jake Mathison was tied to is now empty. Isabella stands there, and a man I've never seen before is viciously interrogating her.

"Where is he, you troll?" The man's voice is loud as it echoes in the small cement room. He strikes Isabella with his fist, and she falls to the ground. The man's eyes are black, and his expression is contemptuous. "You let him go? You stupid demon, how could you let her gain control, even for a second? You'll pay for this later, you imbecile!" He storms out of the room, and Isabella stands up again. Her face changes from stoic coldness to bitter fear and anguish, then back again.

The scene ended and I turned to the group. "Jake Mathison is no longer in the hideout. Isabella must have had a lucid moment because she let him escape. I don't know where he is now, but I'll try to find him because they *will* search for their escapee. There's a new player. But who he is, I don't know, and he's possessed by evil. He's a Latino man in his forties with a heavy South American accent. He's bald, heavyset, and about five foot nine. That's all I can say for now, but he's in charge at this bunker."

"Bloody heck! We now have an injured young man on the loose. I hope you can locate him, Mara. He can't have much time before they find him again," Edison growled.

"She will," Jonas said.

"Finn, do you have a photo of Jake? I don't have a good sense of what he looks like. Or maybe a personal item of his; that would work too," I suggested.

Finn went to one of the file cabinets, thumbed through a drawer, and found the file he needed. He pulled out an eight-by-ten photo and handed it to me. "I hope this will help."

As I was about to try and locate Jake Mathison, Finn dialed his satellite phone and spoke quietly with someone.

I nodded to him, sat back down, and cleared my mind. As I blocked everything and everyone else in the room, I concentrated on the photo and started my search for Jake.

JAKE IS SITTING *behind an enormous tree trunk, visibly hurt and bordering on exhaustion.*

"I SEE HIM, but he's in a large area of jungle, and there aren't identifying landmarks, not yet, anyway. He's nearing exhaustion and is pretty beat up, but he has a destination in mind. I need another moment, please."

SCANNING MY VISION AGAIN, *I try to gauge Jake's vantage point.*

"I CAN SEE where Jake's looking: he's seeing a small break at the top of the tree line. There's an edge of a bell tower, an ancient, broken-down one. It's worn away at the top left side, and the bell was barely hanging on. If I can get a sense of what direction he's looking…I've no idea. From what I'm seeing, there's no clue as to the sun's position. I'm sorry." I gave my team a look of defeat.

"Mara, don't worry. What you saw should be enough for us to find him. I'm on the phone with one of our assets, and his team is within five miles of the hideout. I gave him your intel, and he said there's an old abandoned monastery with a bell tower about two miles north of the hideout. That puts our asset only a couple of miles from him. They'll find Jake," Finn said with relief.

Everyone smiled, hoping we'd find our lost Chosen One before the myrmidons discovered him.

Speaking a few more words on his phone, Finn hung up and said, "Our asset will contact us as soon as he has more information or has found Jake."

Edison ordered coffee, tea, and sandwiches because no one wanted to leave until our lost Chosen One was discovered. It was a quiet meal with a few whispered conversations, and after about ninety minutes, Finn's phone vibrated.

"McKenna here." We watched Finn's face for any telltale signs, good or bad, that they had found Jake. His face was expressionless, but suddenly his smile lit up and he gave us a thumbs-up.

Everyone hollered and patted each other on the back. I sat watching everyone's jubilation and was thankful that the Lord worked through me to save the young man.

"Okay, everyone, we need a quick break. Let's take fifteen minutes, then afterward, we'll review the extraction plan and everyone's assigned roles. Thank you, my friends," Finn said sincerely.

Everyone thanked me, and I graciously replied, "You're welcome."

Billie stopped beside me and said, "Girlie, you've got quite a shtick. I don't know how you do it, but I look forward to seeing what else you can do. Later doll." She walked out with the rest of the group as they chatted up a storm.

Finn was about to exit when he saw me still seated at the table, immersed in my thoughts.

"Mara, are you alright? You did great, sweetheart."

"Thanks, Finn. I'm concerned we can't save Isabella. We have to pray the Lord gives us the time we need. We're running out of it, and it scares me." As I looked at him, he eyed me with worry. "I'm sorry, Finn. I guess I'm simply tired. These visions tend to exhaust me." He walked over and took me into his arms, holding me until I relaxed and leaned into him.

"It'll all work out, Mara. Don't be so hard on yourself. Only God knows what's meant to happen, and we're merely here for the ride." Finn looked down at me and said, "Now, go throw some water on your beautiful face or whatever you need to do, and then we have to get this show on the road. Aye?"

I smiled at him and hugged him. "Okay," I replied and left the room.

We reconvened fifteen minutes later, and everyone was ready to take notes or record the meeting on their phones.

"Let's get started," Finn said. "Everyone within this room will be part of the rescue and combat team. We'll take one of our planes to Colombia, where I have a friend there who will loan us a Huey helicopter. Basheer will be our pilot, and Xavier will be his backup. We'll fly to a site about five miles outside Isabella's hideout. Basheer, Xavier, Billie, and Chuck will wait at this location until we radio them to extract us. This is after we take out the demons at the site, then tranquilize and bring out Isabella. Just be prepared in case you get ambushed while waiting for our call. Billie and Chuck will man the door-mounted M60 machine guns if we get into trouble during the chopper extraction. We also have a couple of rocket launchers on the Huey that Basheer will use once we're all on the heli-copter and bugging out. I want that hellhole obliterated from the face of the earth.

"Now, the sticky part. Our four assets will wait for us at the drop-off location with horses and pack mules, which will be our transportation for our five-mile hike to the compound. I won't lie to you, it'll be a hellish trek—we're going through dense jungle, a river, and up and around a mountain, with lousy weather, extreme heat, and bugs as thick as thieves. Then, add the myrmidons and anyone else they may have with them. You can bet that through glimpses of Isabella's communications with Mara, the Devil can see bits of what Isabella may think we're doing to rescue her. This is always a possibility and a very serious threat. We have to hope we'll always be a few steps ahead of them. This is in God's hands, as you know.

"This trek may take us at least a day and a half, barring any run-ins with the enemy on the way. Once we're within one mile of the compound, we'll take cover. Since we're going into these tunnels blind, Jonas will do his psychic astral projection, sometimes called spirit walking, and take a trip into the compound. We're hoping he can get the intel we need—the compound's layout, the number of enemies we must face, where they're all located, and where Isabella is being held. Without this information, we'd be going in blind, and the odds of completing this mission would become infinitesimally small." Finn looked at Jonas and gave him a nod.

Finn continued, "Once we've neutralized the enemy forces, we'll grab Isabella, contact Basheer, and he and his team will fly into the compound and land. Then, we'll return to the airport base in Colombia, where our team will board the plane and get the heck out of Venezuela and Colombia as fast as possible. We'll take Isabella to a neutral, safe location in Panama, where two priests will be waiting to perform the exorcism. When that's complete, hopefully quickly, we'll head home on the same plane. Questions?"

We looked at each other, and most of us shook our heads, but Edison said, "Finn, I don't mean to cause a problem, but how do Mara and Aaron fit into this? No offense," he said contritely, as he looked at the two of us. "They're new recruits with little military training and no combat experience. We can't be fighting the enemy and protecting them at the same time. Will they be up to it? Is there a reason they're coming along?"

"I'm sure they take no offense, Edison," assured Finn. Aaron and I gave Edison a thumbs-up. "They've been working their butts off since they arrived here, far exceeding what we could have hoped for. God gave them the gifts they'll need to excel on this mission. They're excellent at hand-to-hand, weapons, ops, and maneuvers. They'll do fine. However, I think you should all be aware that the Lord advised us that Mara, Jonas, and Aaron must be part of this extraction, especially inside the compound. We don't know why, but it's not up to us to question Him. Any other concerns?"

We shook our heads, and Finn said, "Okay, we're ready to proceed. Mara and Aaron, since this is your first military mission, you'll need to be at the armory and supply at zero-five hundred tomorrow morning. I'll have staff waiting for you at both places to assist you.

"We'll leave by the elevator banks in the carpool garage at zero-six-thirty, so you'd better get what beauty sleep you can when this meeting concludes. I expect everyone to be in full combat gear and ready to go. May God be with us, my friends. Get some rest and I'll see you in the morning." Finn nodded to everyone, asked if there were any questions, then concluded the meeting.

Many of the team were talking to each other as they walked from the room, and Finn asked Aaron and me to stay behind.

"We've sent a small equipment supply bag to each of your rooms for you to use for essentials on this trip." We thanked Finn, and Aaron left the room ahead of us, saying he'd see us early in the morning.

Looking at Finn with doubt, I said, "This is going to be the most difficult thing I've ever done, and I hope I don't let the team down. It's such a long trek, plus carrying the extra weight of a pack; I hope I'm ready for this, Finn. The team, but most of all, Isabella, is counting on me. I'll pray in earnest tonight in hopes of our success. Finn, I want you to know how much everyone appreciates everything you do for us." I gave him a warm embrace.

"Mara, you'll do great. You've proved you're more than capable. I believe in you and need you to know I'm falling in love with you. If anything goes wrong down there, I just had to get that off my chest." I turned and gawked at him, and he gazed at me with sincerity and love.

After hearing his declaration of love, I was stunned, overjoyed, and giddy. With tears in my eyes, I burst out in response, "Finn, I love you too, so very much. I know we haven't been able to pursue our relationship because of our duties to God, but I know in my heart that we'll be together when this mess is over. You can count on it." Walking back to him, I pulled his head down to mine and kissed him passionately. I hugged him close, not wanting to let him go. After a few minutes, he gently put his finger under my chin, kissed me deeply again, and stepped away.

"Wow, we better not do much more of that, or I'll break one of God's laws." He was joking, yet he had a serious expression.

"You're right, but I had to do that, Finn." Being close to Finn was intoxicating and I wanted to stay near him. I couldn't believe how drawn I was to this man, and delight danced through me that he also felt the intense connection we had with one another.

"Goodnight, my sweet Mara." He gave me a tender smile and caressed my cheek.

"Goodnight. I look forward to seeing you in the morning." I smiled and left the room. Trying to contain my happiness at Finn's declaration, I almost skipped back to my apartment. Except trepidation nagged at me too. Tomorrow's mission would be the most important test of whether I was good enough to carry out God's war against evil. Can I do this, and will I be able to actually kill demons? I'll guess I'd find out.

CHAPTER 18

The next morning, I packed the small bag with essentials as Finn had requested, had a light breakfast, and sat down for a long prayer with God. Afterward, I was ready to go to the armory and supply.

The base's first level teemed with personnel, which I surmised was due to the harrowing mission we were about to attempt. I found the armory, and they gave me many choices for a weapon. Finn wanted me only to carry a handgun on this mission, so I selected a Sig P320. They handed me four fully loaded clips and a thigh rig holster for the gun.

My next stop was supply. The woman in attendance assisted me in selecting an appropriate size of fatigues as well as socks, underwear, t-shirts, a belt, a Kevlar vest, a boonie hat, and an LBE vest. She explained that the LBE stood for load-bearing equipment and said the pockets already contained everything I'd need. I looked in all the compartments, and they held a full canteen, first-aid kit, compass, maps, MREs, and a sizable knife. All I had to do was add my weapon magazines to another set of pockets. Figuring the LBE would be heavy, I hoped I'd get used to it.

The last thing she handed me was an earbud and battery for communication between our team members. She instructed me on all the clothing and equipment and assigned me a locker and key to store my civilian clothes.

With my hands full, I headed to the women's locker room. There was only one other person there: Billie, with her short, shocking blue hair. She was geared up and pulled a nasty-looking knife from her locker. She slid it securely into a sheath outside of her left thigh.

"That looks lean and mean," I said, indicating the knife.

"This stabber has saved my life more than once. It's still a Ka-Bar combat knife like yours, but just a lot bigger. I never go on a mission without it, even though it's bulky to schlep around during long-distance maneuvers," she answered and slammed the locker door shut with a bang. She also had a semi-automatic rifle slung over her shoulder and several large clips stuffed into her massive pockets.

As I changed my clothes, I hoped to remember how to put everything on correctly. I struggled with the LBE, so Billie gave me more instructions. "Thanks, this is my first time—can you tell?" I asked jokingly.

Billie snorted and quipped, "Nah, hadn't even noticed." She gave me a hard slap on my back which knocked me forward a step and left the room.

I strapped the thigh gun harness on my right thigh and secured my handgun. When I grabbed my boonie hat and earbud and started to walk, the sheer weight of the gear almost dropped me to the floor. It was like I had a truck attached to my body.

Geez! How am I supposed to walk through a jungle, around a mountain, or even fight with all this weight bearing down on me? I sat down on the bench and took a few moments to pray.

"Dear Father, I pray You'll help me bear this pack with the same strength and grace You had when You carried Your cross to Calvary, my dear, sweet Jesus. Amen." I stood up again and the pack felt immensely lighter. After giving thanks to the Lord above, I left the room to find the others.

Upon searching for directions to the motor pool, I spotted Jonas standing with the beautiful brunette he'd been dating. Jonas said excitedly, "It's about time the two of you meet. Mara, this is Dr. Poppy Matthews. Poppy, my sister, Mara." We shook hands and exchanged smiles.

"It's such a pleasure to finally meet you, Mara. I feel like I know you already. Jonas speaks highly of you." Poppy spoke with a cultured British accent and had confidence that radiated high intelligence. Her eyes were a bright hazel color, and her dark hair was in a short, layered cut that perfectly framed her heart-shaped, delicate face. Poppy was a few inches taller than me and had a thin yet curvy figure.

"So, he talks about me, does he?" I asked, poking Jonas lightly in the ribs.

"Every once in a while, pipsqueak."

In response, I stuck out my tongue at him, then turned to his girlfriend. "Are you helping us with our mission, Poppy?"

"Yes, I am, but I work behind the scenes. I'll be stuck staring at computer screens for the entire mission."

Jonas said, "She's being modest. Her official title is SAT-COM—Satellite Communications Specialist. She keeps us off the grid when we're on missions and even switches our transponder identifications when we fly from country to country. She's amazing at what she does and even has another Ph.D. in Aerospace Engineering, and designed the entire system within this room."

I looked through the window. It was a large area with many high-tech computers and several wide monitor screens with satellite images of several parts of the world. There were also enough technicians in the room that NASA would envy.

"Oh my," I replied. "This is way beyond my comprehension, Poppy. You're amazing. How did we get so lucky to have you on our team?"

"We stole her from MI6. Of course, they've no clue we have her, thank the Lord," Jonas said.

Several team members were assembling in a large area farther down the hall, and I motioned to Jonas. "Sorry, Poppy, we have to go. Our team is gathering. Can we meet again soon? I'd love to get to know you better."

"Definitely. Now you two go and save the world." She kissed Jonas and entered the SAT-COM room.

The others greeted Jonas and me, and we walked down a long corridor with signage that said, "To Motor Pool." We followed Finn to the garage and then to a military vehicle. He lifted the rear flap of the truck, and everyone stowed their gear in the back. We climbed into the vehicle, drove to the large, old military airbase, and up to an airplane that would take us to Colombia.

The jet appeared to be a little dilapidated and had seen better days, but Finn whispered in my ear, "It looks battle-worn, but that's the point. The inside is another story."

We stopped on the tarmac near the plane, and Finn stated it was time for prayer before we boarded. After forming a circle, we held hands. Finn asked God for His help, guidance, and protection as we each embark on this holy mission to save one of His flock who had lost her way and had been deceived by an evil one's empty promises. We each took our turn in thanking God for everything He'd given us and made a promise to do His will and to protect and defend all His children with our lives. Finn concluded with an "Amen," and we boarded the plane.

Finn had been correct. The inside of the jet was opulent, and I couldn't help myself and joked, "Does the Commander-in-Chief know we have his airplane?"

Everyone chuckled as we sat down and buckled in. The seats were large and plush with plenty of leg room, and they swiveled around and even reclined. Near the front was a meeting table with another set of leather chairs and a computer with a large screen. I happily sat next to Finn, hoping to get more details on the mission and spend time with him.

"How long is our flight to Colombia, Finn?"

"Around eight hours. They'll provide us with a meal and beverages, and restrooms are in the back."

"Nice."

The flight was comfortable and everyone took a well-deserved nap. Afterward, we enjoyed a meal and beverages.

It was a little over eight hours by the time we landed. The airport wasn't large but accommodated our airplane, and I eyed the impressive Huey sitting on the tarmac. After we stopped on the runway and taxied near a large hangar, three men stood nearby, waiting for us to disembark. Two males held automatic rifles, and the third had no weapon. However, he appeared even more dangerous than the first two. As we stepped off the plane, the third man's face lit up with a charming smile.

"Finn, you son of a monkey, it's about time we meet again, eh?" he said in a thick Spanish accent.

"Jorge, you've got that right! It's been way too long, my friend," Finn replied, and they gave each other a brotherly hug.

"I wish we had time to visit, *amigo,* but I know you're in a tight time crunch. The Huey is fueled up, the armaments and missiles are loaded, including the missile's holy fire; it's ready for battle."

"You're a loyal friend, Jorge. I hope you know what this means to all of us. We thank you sincerely for your generosity." Finn gave him another hug and a pat on the back.

Finn grabbed something from his pack and handed it to Jorge.

"Ahh, you remembered! I shall treasure this until I finish the bottle." Jorge laughed heartily. "Be safe, my friends. You will have no issues returning here when you've finished your mission. Your plane will be refueled and restocked for your next destination. May God be with you." He lifted his hand in farewell, and he and his men departed.

As we walked to the Huey and our equipment was transferred from the plane to the chopper, I asked Finn, "What did you give him?"

"It was a bottle of the most expensive Macallan Lalique, fifty-five-year-old single malt scotch. I spent one hundred eighty-eight thousand on that bottle. But it's his favorite, and it got us the use of the Huey and this airport."

"Nice job, Finn," I said proudly.

Our team climbed into the helicopter, buckled in tight, and put on the headphones. I was nervous because the doors were wide open, allowing for the M60 machine guns. *This was some mean chopper.*

About an hour later, we landed in a small clearing amid a huge, plush jungle. The terrain was dense with trees, brush, and mountains that looked impossible to navigate. Finn said rebels created this landing pad a few years ago but abandoned it a year later.

Basheer powered down the Huey and we climbed out and unpacked our gear. As we finished, four men with several horses and three mules approached. A few team members drew their rifles forward, but Finn raised his hand and said, "They're our assets. Lower your weapons."

The men were welcoming, kind, and informative. Introductions were made, and Finn reviewed the plan again with us, then said, "Everyone take a quick 'relief' break, and then we're going to saddle up and get moving. We want to arrive at our designated campsite before darkness falls."

After everyone returned, Basheer, Chuck, Xavier, and Billie set up camp. We spoke with them briefly, told them to stay safe, and hoped they remained under God's protection. Finn said he'd radio them when it was time for their grand entrance. Basheer replied they'd be fine and would be ready when they were needed.

Before we mounted up, I watched the group pull out their insect repellent and camo sticks and then add their earpieces. Finn explained to me how to use each one and said to put the repellent on first, then use the camo stick so the hard paint would glide on easier over the skin. I thanked him and we were ready to get on the horses.

The mounts were a combination of bays, chestnuts, and two dark red roans. They appeared calm and well-trained. However, Jasper was nervous and didn't want to approach them. I slowly walked from horse to horse, touching their noses and looking into their big brown eyes.

I walked back a few steps to the group and said, "Jasper, the larger bay horse on the far right is the one for you. These horses are Paso Finos and tend to be smaller than other horses but are strong and sturdy. Don't worry, their ride is smooth and elegant. You'll do well on this fine gelding."

Jasper's eyes widened, and he said, "They don't look small to me! I rode a horse years ago, which wasn't a pleasant experience. That nasty nag was fixin' to dump me in the drink—and he did. Are you sure, Mara?"

"Positive. His name is El Marron. He's protective of his rider and is confident and sure of himself, but not to the point of arrogance. He'll take excellent care of you."

Jasper swallowed hard, wiped his sweaty palms on his pants, and reluctantly moved toward the horse. One asset helped him to mount and adjust his stirrups. He actually smiled when the horse stood perfectly still. I felt the animal was being careful so he wouldn't startle his rider.

One of the assets said to Finn, "The *señorita* knows her horses, eh?"

"That she does. Anyone else nervous about riding a horse?" The rest of the crew shook their heads and selected their mounts.

I chose a dark red chestnut with a star on her forehead. It was a mare, and I read from her that her name was Alegría, which meant joy in Spanish. I found communicating with these amazing animals comforting and hoped this was a gift I could retain once this war was over.

The mules were packed, everyone was mounted on horseback, and one of the assets began leading us into the jungle. We were told his name was Miguel and he was the leader of the assets.

In the beginning, the trail was relatively clear, so we rode abreast two-by-two and stayed alert. I rode next to Aaron, and a few group members made short, quiet conversation, but their eyes continued to scan left to right and back again.

"You can read animals too, Mara?" Aaron asked.

"Luckily, yes. Aaron, did you meet a strange and friendly animal after your return? Because I did. It was a huge white wolf I named Spirit."

"I did, actually. While staying at a friend's cabin in Vancouver, I encountered a large, mature bald eagle. Initially, I noticed her circling above me whenever I went outside the cabin. She eventually landed near me, simply staring. Eventually, she walked up to me, put her foot on top of mine, and stood looking up at me. It was the weirdest thing. Then she followed me into the house, always on my heels when I went from room to room. I fed the eagle raw meat and we became friends. She was protective of me as well.

"When a myrmidon came around, she viciously attacked and killed him, and believe me, that left quite an impression. I named her Charlotte. It was something I remembered from childhood when I was very young. I've no clue why I recalled that name, though."

I smiled at him and we continued in silence. Everyone constantly scanned our surroundings, prepared for any possible dangers. The heat was oppressive, and the bugs never let up; they were relentless in their attempts to feed on our skin, as well as the hides of the poor horses and mules. The animals continued to shake their heads, swish their tails, and kick at their bellies in a futile attempt to swat away the offending bugs.

We'd been riding for over three hours when an eerie feeling came over me. Even the horses stomped and fretted in agitation. Jonas, who rode ahead, turned around and peered at Aaron and me. "You feel that Mara?" he whispered through the headset. I replied quietly that I did, and Aaron said he felt it too.

"Finn, something's wrong. We need to get off this trail immediately," I advised quietly but urgently.

Finn directed the team to move deep into the forest. We dismounted, pulled our horses and mules farther into the woods, ground-tied them, and then hunkered down with our weapons ready. I tried to communicate to the livestock to remain still and quiet. They seemed to respond as I had asked, not moving a muscle. Then I told the horses and mules to go down on their haunches and stay there, and to my delight, they complied. Everyone gaped at each other, astounded. I nodded at them and signaled that the livestock was fine. We stayed this way for several minutes, not hearing anything but the noise of the insects, wildlife, and our breathing. We faced outward, waiting for whatever spooked the animals.

That smell hit us first—the cloying, undeniable putrid odor—and it grew stronger by the minute. We could hear the myrmidons coming down the path we'd just abandoned. Finn motioned for Jonas, Aaron, Edison, and Jasper to get ready to ambush the demon's servants and was instructed only to use their knives. Finn told me to stay back and control the livestock.

The assets remained behind to protect me and the mounts. I waited quietly. My heart pounded loudly, and I feared everyone could hear the constant *thump, thump, thump*. I prepared my pistol to fire if the need arose. I had no fear of killing those evil predators.

It wasn't long until I heard scuffles, grunts, and groans, and after several minutes, it was quiet again. A moment passed, and then another, and I desperately wanted to run and assure myself everyone was safe.

Finally, Finn and the other team members returned. They placed their knives back in their sheaths, and myrmidon blood spattered their clothes, faces, and hands.

"We annihilated those heinous monsters and dragged them off the trail to the other side," Finn whispered. "Do you sense any more of them?" He looked at the horses and me.

"No, not at the moment. We're safe for now," I assured the team. I directed the animals to stand and relax, and they complied.

"I've got to say, that was some magic act, Mara," Jonas commented. "How did you think of it?"

"I don't honestly know. But I was afraid they'd give away our position. Since I could sense their thoughts, why couldn't they sense mine?"

As I glanced at the assets, they stared at me, then at the horses and mules in amazement. They made a sign of the cross, and Miguel said, "You're definitely God's warriors, yes?" We smiled, mounted again, and started back up the trail.

Several of us moaned in pain when we reached the spot where we would camp for the night. Riding horses for several hours was quite painful when one wasn't used to it. Our team gingerly dismounted and stood around, trying to relieve our aching glute muscles.

It was a decent location; there was a small clearing for us to bed down and a secluded area in the trees to secure the livestock. I could hear trickling water nearby, and Miguel said we were near the old monastery where they'd found Jake.

We led our horses and mules to the creek so they could drink their fill of water and we could replenish our canteens. I looked forward to cleaning off the sweat and grime of the day and was sure the others felt the same, especially those on the team covered in myrmidon blood.

Miguel and his men used a long, thick rope to make a corral for the livestock, then unsaddled and unbridled the horses and removed the packs from the mules. They gave them a good rubdown, cleaned their hooves, and let them rest for the night. The livestock had plenty of fresh grass to eat, so they were happy.

"Now that the horses and mules are fed and watered, it's time for us to partake, yes?" Miguel asked.

We nodded and our stomachs rumbled. I'd assumed we'd be eating our MREs, but instead, Miguel retrieved several cans of beans, corn, and rolled-up tortillas from one bag that a mule had carried. We smiled and couldn't wait for Miguel to start cooking. He made a small campfire which gave off minimal smoke and started warming the food and coffee. The rest of us prepared the camp for the long night ahead.

I asked Finn if I could return to the creek, and he said we'd go in pairs and always have weapons handy. Grabbing my small bag, I replied I'd like to clean up before dinner, and Jonas volunteered to accompany me.

When we returned, Finn had set up a schedule for a guard to be on watch during the night. I asked for the time of my assigned shift, and he said they were all covered. After a meaningful glare, I told him I'd take a shift, asking firmly which one he'd like me to have. He smiled, gave in, and assigned me one. I thanked him with a grin, and we sat down to dinner. The food was delicious and we enjoyed quiet, humorous banter while we ate.

It would be dark soon, so the rest of the team took turns going to the creek. We laid out our sleeping bags and I placed mine next to Finn's. He gave me a cheeky wink, and I tried to hide my blush behind a friendly smile.

Darkness descended, so we had our red flashlights and weapons handy in case we needed them during the night. Everyone crawled into their bedrolls, and Jonas took the first watch. He sat quietly while he scanned for anything out of the ordinary. I watched as he often glanced at the horses, using their instincts as alarms. We'd feel any fear or increased tension from them if danger was nearby. I listened to the comforting night sounds and thought about Finn and his handsome face as I fell into a deep, dreamless slumber.

All too soon, Finn jostled me awake. He whispered, "Your turn for guard duty, love." He gave me a quick kiss, moved toward his bedroll, laid his rifle within easy reach, and climbed into his bed.

Strolling to the designated guard spot, I took a seat. Holding my weapon loosely in my hand, I enjoyed the cool evening. I mentally checked the horses and they were all asleep and uncaring, so we were safe for the time being. Since I had a couple of hours to myself, I spent the time in prayer and gave thanks to Him for getting us this far.

According to my watch, it wasn't long before my shift was complete. I nudged Jasper awake as it was his turn to take watch. His response was a tired grunt, and I snuggled back into my warm bedroll. Sleep was slow to come as I dreaded the upcoming encounter with my first demon.

Can I fight such evil and win? How is this possible? A shiver slithered down my spine as I contemplated tomorrow's daunting task. I said an extra prayer and curled into a tight ball within my sleeping bag. Only God knew if I'd survive this upcoming battle.

CHAPTER 19

Snorting horses, hushed conversations, and the smell of food woke me the next morning. It was barely dawn and Miguel was already cooking us a quick breakfast. Most of the team was up and moving, except for Jasper and me.

I rose, placed my gun back in its holster, and packed my bedroll. Finn spotted me and grinned, "Good morning, sleepyhead." I smiled back and returned the greeting.

Finn gave Jasper a small nudge with his foot, and Jasper blinked as he tried to wipe the sleep away, giving Finn a thumbs up. I asked if anyone would join me at the stream for a few minutes so I could freshen up. Finn volunteered, and we hiked toward the water. I washed as modestly as possible, and Finn did the same. He had a shadow of a beard coming in, giving him a swarthy look. It was becoming, giving him a more dangerous countenance.

"You know, Mara, you've done well on this mission, and I want you to know how proud I am of you."

"Thanks. That means a lot coming from you." I smiled as I unwound my hair from its braid, brushed it well, and reworked it into a new one. I walked over and gave him a big kiss. He returned it, caressed my face, and we looked at each other for a few minutes, then returned to our team.

Before we left camp, Finn said it would take about two hours to ride a quarter way up the mountain. We'd then turn left and head ninety minutes around the mountain to the other side. The trek would be steep, and we'd need to be extra careful and stay on the path.

Luckily, we hadn't seen any more myrmidons, but there was always a chance we might as we neared the compound. We were back on the horses again, and it took a while for our bodies to limber up during the ride.

As we rode along, Finn said, "Once we get around the mountain, Miguel has a location selected for us, about a mile from the hideout. This is where you come in, Jonas, and we'll need you to do your thing. Your spirit walk will hopefully provide us the full layout of their base, exactly how many people or demons we're dealing with, and where they're located."

Finn hadn't been kidding. The ascent up the mountain was steep and frightening. It started to rain, so we donned our slickers as we rode. Luckily, the horses knew exactly where they were going. They never lost their footing, even as they walked over muddy and slick terrain.

Everyone was more vigilant than before if that was even possible. It was slow going, but Miguel finally led us near the top of our ascent, where we'd turn left and start heading around the mountain.

At this point, the rain stopped, and we took a quick break but soon started once more. It seemed to take forever, but we finally came around the far side of the mountain.

After another half-hour, Miguel raised his hand, and we stopped, taking in the view. This area was well-secluded, but there was a small, flat area of plush grass. There was enough room for the horses and mules to graze and get water from standing rain puddles. We dismounted, stretched our legs, and prepared for the next step of our mission.

"Jonas," Finn explained. "We'll put down a bedroll for you to lie on, so you can start traveling to the compound. Can you talk to us while you're doing this, or do we wait until you're finished?"

"I'll be in a deep trance, so it'll have to wait until I'm done. Someone should take notes on everything I relay back," Jonas said.

"Will do," Finn answered. "Aaron, would you mind?"

"No problem," Aaron replied, pulling out a small black book and pencil.

Two of Miguel's men took watch around our perimeter as we prepared for Jonas to take his spirit walk. He'd be vulnerable, and we had to protect him in case of an attack.

Jonas laid down and began his relaxation exercises, allowing his body and mind to drift and calm. Finn and I knelt beside him and watched as his breathing slowed, then seemed to stop. It was pretty frightening for me to witness. I put my finger on the pulse at his wrist and had to wait a moment to feel a beat. His face turned pale, but I knew he was entering his unconscious state.

The two men standing guard at our camp came to attention, and the horses snorted nervously. Finn gave them the signal to check out the possible threat and sent Jasper and Edison to assist them. Miguel and one of his men stayed behind to protect us as Jonas continued his spirit walk.

Jonas was out for approximately twenty minutes, and we waited patiently as we listened to the jungle noises, birds, insects, and snorting horses. Finally, Jonas's pulse and breathing returned to normal, and he opened his eyes. He related what he'd seen, and Aaron took studious notes.

"Where did our men go?" Jonas asked as he looked around for our missing people.

"They're investigating a possible threat. Hopefully, they'll be back soon," Finn said, with a look of worry on his brow.

We heard a rustling and then a whisper that said, "All's well" as our men emerged from the dense jungle. They were drenched in that sickening stench of myrmidon blood, but they grinned from ear to ear.

"We discovered a hive of twenty myrmidons about a mile due west of here, but we took care of their sorry arses," Edison said as he wiped his blade with a cloth.

Jasper's smiled with satisfaction as he replied, "We need to get this stench off of us—we smell bad enough to gag a maggot."

We laughed at Jasper's comments, and the four men found a large area of fresh water and washed off the gooey stench.

"You think we're clear for now, Edison?" Finn asked.

"My demon skank radar is quiet for now, and the horses are also content, so I'd say we're relatively safe at the moment, mate."

Finn nodded and turned back to Jonas. "Go ahead and continue your assessment."

"Just so you know, all the myrmidons I've seen at the hideout are carrying semi-automatic rifles and bowie knives. They're well prepared to guard this place. This is new since we've only seen them kill with their bare hands.

"Luckily, this isn't a large compound—we have this on our side. There are two tunnels, one facing east and the other north. There are two myrmidon guards outside each one, and one more just inside. Both tunnels are relatively straight but turn towards the end, as they lead to stairs that descend to the lower level. I'd advise we take the north tunnel to enter. It has a straighter landscape, and the stairs are easier to descend and are closer to the living quarters and office. There are more guards at this stairwell, but they appear lazier and less alert. I suggest we take out the guards on the north tunnel and post two of our team just on the inside, one facing outward and one inward.

"There are two more myrmidons at the top of the north tunnel stairway and two at the bottom. Once we take them out, we can traverse the hallway from the bottom of the stairs that lead east or left. Isabella is in her quarters in this hallway in a room two doors down, on the right. I have to inform you she's in terrible shape. She's been beaten severely but still appears possessed. I don't know if she'll make it out of the compound alive."

"What have they done to her—why would they beat her up? Isn't she supposedly one of them?" I asked.

Jonas said, "I think—and this is just an educated guess—that since she hasn't fully succumbed to the possession, the continuous conflict between good and evil inside her has taken its toll."

"Sounds plausible," Edison agreed.

"Wait, I haven't finished." Jonas continued. "The man or demon that Mara saw is there too, in the room one door down from Isabella, but on the left. This guy is going to be a big problem. He appears to be strong and won't be easy to kill. This creep isn't a myrmidon as we know, but he isn't human anymore either—I'd say he's a higher-level hellion. Two other men are with him, and I believe they're lower demons. I don't like this, Finn. These three may be a real issue for us."

"Are there any others in the compound, Jonas?" Finn asked.

"No. No one else."

Finn rose from his kneeling position next to Jonas and paced. Everyone but those keeping guard duty followed Finn with their eyes, wondering how he would proceed with this extraction. He asked everyone's opinion on how they'd approach this scenario. After receiving our input, he paced again for a few minutes, then asked Edison to join him. They talked for over twenty minutes, then turned back to the group.

"Alright, this is how we'll proceed," Finn said. "Miguel, we'll assist you and your men with taking out the guards positioned at the entrance of each tunnel. Once that'd been accomplished, your crew will then guard the entrances.

"Jonas: you, Jasper, and Mara will take the east tunnel and help Miguel and his men take out the guards. Then, make your way to the lower level, neutralize the stair guards, and proceed to meet us.

"We now have Miguel and his men guarding the tunnels. Aaron, Edison, and I will move down the north tunnel, eliminate the myrmidons on the stairs, and wait for Jonas and Mara. We pray that the three men don't come out of their office. Jonas, we'll need you to spirit walk again when we get closer to the hideout. We have to be sure of everyone's position in the compound. When we all meet on the lower level, Mara, Jasper, and Jonas, will need to subdue and tranquilize Isabella. Aaron, Edison, and I will deal with the ones in the office," Finn said, finishing his instructions.

"This plan is a good one. However, I know my brothers and I must take care of the men in the office first. I know Aaron and Jonas feel this also," I said as I glanced at them, and they nodded in agreement. "We have to be the ones to kill the major demon."

Finn looked at the three of us, noted the resolution in our eyes, and knew we were correct. He considered my comments, clenched his jaw, and said, "I believe you're right. I feel it too. We'll go after Isabella last, but she may try to enter the room and fight. Even though her body may be in poor shape, she's still possessed and strong."

The plan was now in place. We gathered together, prayed to the Lord for his guidance and protection, recited the St. Michael prayer, and mounted again. Our team continued to the last stop on the mountain before our final descent to the compound.

After leaving the horses and mules on the other side of the mountain ridge, we gathered our extra gear from the mules and reviewed the plan once more. We traipsed through the thick trees and dense brush; it was rough going, though it made excellent cover. Miguel said we'd reached our last stop, so we halted, dropped our packs, drank water, and ate another power bar. We remained vigilant for possible dangers.

Finn told Edison, "You'll need to find a viable yet well-hidden vantage point of the compound and scan the surrounding area. Report back with your findings."

Edison nodded and replied, "Copy that." He silently headed off to find the perfect location for his recon.

Jonas laid on the ground again and conducted his quick spirit walk. After coming to, he replied they'd moved little, but one of the lower demons had left the office and was grilling Isabella. This wasn't good news, but we hoped she'd continue to resist her demon possession until we arrived.

Ten minutes later, Edison returned, but he wasn't happy. "You missed something, mate," he said as he peered at Jonas.

"What?" Jonas asked.

"The sniper, my friend. He's approximately five hundred yards northeast of the compound, about twenty feet up a tree in a hunting stand."

"This *is* a problem. Even if we take the sniper out with a rifle, the shot would alert the guards in the tunnels. Our mission would be over before we ever reached the compound. Does anyone have any ideas?" Finn asked.

The team offered a few suggestions, but there weren't any workable solutions.

"We should gather together, hold hands, and ask God to guide us on this dilemma. That's my suggestion," I said.

Everyone agreed, so we prayed for the Lord's guidance. We were in prayer for several minutes, but we didn't receive any answers until Jasper said, "All y'all don't move, not unless you want your throat torn out and fed back to y'all."

I turned slowly, then quietly whooped for joy. "Spirit! I've missed you, my friend." Hustling over to him, I gave him a warm embrace. He huffed and licked my cheek.

A few feet from Spirit, Jonas approached a cougar and joyfully greeted him. The beautiful, large, and intimidating mountain lion must be Phantom. Then we heard a short screech, looked up a few feet in the nearest tree, and saw a majestic bald eagle. Aaron approached her, and she flew down to his arm. He made a slight wince as her talons dug into his jacket sleeve. This must be Aaron's friend, Charlotte.

"Everyone, I'd like you to meet Spirit, my white timber wolf, and that gorgeous cougar with Jonas is Phantom. And last but not least is Aaron's friend, Charlotte. This is how we solve the problem of the sniper." I said to my team.

None of the team said a word; they gawked at the seemingly wild beasts.

"I believe these animals are our spirit guides, sent by God," I said, trying to help them understand and not be afraid of them.

"Okay..." Finn replied skeptically. "Mara, can you tell us how this works—I mean, what can they do to help us?"

"Sure. The three of us have experienced these animals appearing and disappearing at will." I looked at my two brothers, and they nodded. "If we communicate what we need from them, hopefully, they'll take care of the sniper." When I finished, I watched my team for any reactions, good or bad.

They pondered my suggestion, and I waited for Finn to respond. He moved toward me, looked me in the eye, and said, "You think they'll do this for us? We have to be sure about this. If that sniper gets wind of anything in the least bit suspicious, our mission would be in serious jeopardy."

I nodded my head and smiled. "Well, let's try, shall we?" I looked at my brothers and they both agreed. We communicated with our spirit animals, and they entered the woods, then vanished.

Everyone grabbed their binoculars, and we quietly made our way to the vantage point that Edison had located, staying well hidden in the underbrush. Edison pointed to the sniper's location; we spotted him and waited to see what would happen. We observed for quite some time, and I think the team thought my brothers and I were a bit daft.

Finally, we saw large movements at the sniper's location. He flailed his arms, trying to scare a gigantic bald eagle away who repeatedly dive-bombed him. Then we witnessed the man falling heavily through the branches of the tree and he crashed into the undergrowth below. We watched in awe as a white wolf and a cougar killed the demon, then dragged him deep into the woods.

Everyone crawled backward and moved to return to the clearing. "Slap my head and call me silly! That's the craziest thing I've ever seen," Jasper exclaimed incredulously. The rest of the team agreed with surprised comments.

"I guess a change of plan is in order. Jasper, you're now our sniper. Can you make it over there and up the tree in two hours?" Finn asked.

"Roger that." Jasper gathered his gear and started moving out. "I'll catch y'all on the other side, my friends," he said as he disappeared into the woods.

Finn stated we'd better get started. We rechecked our weapons and ammunition, then carefully and quietly descended the mountain. Jasper was already about a half hour ahead of us as we maneuvered to the compound. As we moved closer, the entrances to the tunnels were easier to spot. Broken tree limbs camouflaged a couple of vehicles. We split into our groups and moved into position.

Miguel and his men ran silently and expertly around the side of the tunnels' entrances. Jonas and I followed Miguel and his man to the east tunnel. I hoped Finn and the others made it safely to the north side.

We planned to use our knives to take out the two guards. The kills needed to be silent so we wouldn't alert the men at the stairwells or the demons within the hideout. Miguel and his man surprised the two myrmidons, and the kills were quick.

After nodding to Miguel, we made our way down the tunnel, our rifles were drawn, and we slinked down the long shaft. We came to the end of the tunnel, where it turned toward the stairwell. Jonas signaled me; we stowed our guns and pulled out our knives.

The smell of the evil ones was unmistakable, and they were obviously around the corner. We moved around the bend and attacked the myrmidons, taking them by surprise. After kicking their feet out from under them, Jonas and I slit their throats—the brackish blood oozed from their deadly wounds.

There should have been two more at the bottom of the stairs, so we carefully moved down the stairway, but only one guard stood watch. Jonas jumped on him and took him out with barely a sound. I looked at my brother with raised eyebrows, but he only lifted his shoulders and returned his gaze with a puzzled expression.

There were two hallways and each one went in opposite directions. Jonas pointed to the one we needed, which was northbound. As I followed Jonas, I sensed someone behind me. I twisted around and spied the second myrmidon who'd been missing, heading directly toward us. I thought he'd simply shoot us both, so I grabbed my handgun. But instead of shooting, he tossed his weapon aside and charged me. I returned my gun to its holster and sprinted toward him. Within a few feet of the myrmidon, I placed a double kick to his chest, which shoved him violently to the ground, knocking the wind out of him. Before he could recover and retaliate, I deftly drew my knife and sliced his neck open from ear to ear. The hate flowed through me at this evil monster, and I happily sent another demon back to Hell.

I jumped to my feet and returned to Jonas's side. He smiled with pride and gave me a big hug. After wiping my knife on my pant leg, we continued to the next corner, leading us to the rendezvous point.

We didn't feel the presence of a myrmidon but weren't sure about the upper-level demons. This was a problem, as we'd never been around them before, and we weren't sure we could detect their presence.

Jonas gave me the all-clear signal, and we traversed around the corner and spotted Finn, Edison, and Aaron. They were in a down-low position, covering each end of the corridor with their semi-automatic weapons. They lowered their guns that had been pointed in our direction and motioned for us to join them.

Finn whispered, saying, "We've cleared these few rooms and they're empty. There's the cell where they're holding Isabella." He pointed to two doors in the hallway. "Let's get the cretons in the office first. Edison, you stay out here and watch our six."

We were outside the office door. I put my hand on Finn's arm and signaled him to wait a moment. Looking at Aaron and Jonas, I knew they felt it too. The tattoo on my arm tingled, and the three of us sensed the intense evil on the other side of the door. A strange and powerful force moved through me, and my brothers' faces reflected awe and confusion as well. Finn watched us with a puzzled look like he knew something in us had changed.

I nodded to Finn, giving him the go-ahead. Finn opened the door, and there were two "things" in the room. Yes, they appeared to be two normal-looking men, but we knew different, and the evil oozed from their pores. They had no weapons in their hands and were unafraid. I recognized the man behind the desk from my vision, and another man sat across from him. The person behind the desk was the one in charge and a higher-level demon.

The lower demon turned and charged at us with anger and hate on his ugly face. Finn shot him several times, but it merely slowed him down and only made him meaner. Jonas charged the demon, firing as he went, then knocked him over with one well-aimed kick. Jonas pulled out his knife and sliced his throat; the man gurgled but still fought to live. Jonas drew his handgun and shot him in the forehead. He finally stopped moving and was dead.

We looked at the man sitting behind the desk with our weapons raised toward his chest. The demon merely sat there, utterly calm, as if he hadn't a care in the world. He tapped a pencil on the desk as he watched us and said, "Bravo! Well done. I must say, you're better than I'd hoped for being insignificant little humans."

Giving us a condescending smile, he continued, "I've been waiting for you for quite some time; it took you long enough." He gazed arrogantly at his fingernails, wondering if he needed a manicure.

What a haughty little jerk. I glanced into his mind and confirmed he was a mid-level demon. The higher their caste, the more insufferable their arrogance. I could see through his façade the ugliness of evil and hints of this demon's authentic form. It would shimmer now and again, but I could see it, and I knew my brothers noticed it too.

This monster was oppressively dark with thick, gritty, leathered skin, and there were three vertical sets of deeply recessed beady eyes. Over each eye was a large, protruding ridge that gave it a ferocious stare. This demon had two thick, large black horns that jutted out of each side of its huge oblong head which flared outward, then around to the back of its skull. The body was dark, massive, and full of slimy scales, and it had that same putrid smell as the myrmidons.

"You know, Mara, I want to thank you for reading our Isabella. It gave her demon a quick look at you, which he reported to me. So, I knew you and a group of your little Chosen would come looking for her, and all I had to do was wait. And here you are. An excellent tradeoff, don't you think? The three of you are special indeed. I'll delight in extracting the information I need from your feeble minds. It'll be the most awful, slow, and excruciating experience, and you'll do anything to stop the torture. You'll gladly give me the information on your bases and the names of all His special Chosen Ones." When he said, "His," he said it with disdain and disgust.

He stood up, stooped over, and put his hands flat on his desk, glaring into my eyes. "I'll especially have fun with you! Slowly ripping out your entrails piece by piece, then stuffing them into your mouth."

I gave him a condescending smile, then tilted my head as if looking at a tiny insect. "Really? Am I supposed to be scared? You crawl along your slimy little belly, hoping for leftover scraps that the higher demons may leave behind. Is this the best you've got, you pathetic little parasite? Come on, come get me." I said every word calmly and succinctly, filled with scorn and pity.

The rage built in his ugly face and his skin turned crimson red. He lumbered around the desk and called me vile names that would make a sailor blush, but I maintained a deadpan expression, untouched by his tirade of insults.

I felt Finn moving forward, but I signaled him to retreat. This wasn't his fight; it was for the Gatekeepers. Finn wouldn't survive a battle with this putrid and unholy entity.

Jonas and Aaron moved forward, and we stood together, waiting. I silently communicated with both of them and heard their internal response. We knew how we would send this monster back to Hell.

The demon stood before us and was about to attack, but I drove my mind into his. It was the most hideous thing I'd ever seen, but I assaulted him from inside his head—using visions of God, love, hope, joy, and faith—and then began tearing his mind apart, piece by piece.

FINN HATED STANDING THERE, doing nothing, as he watched all this happen without getting into the fight. But by all that was holy, he knew he was no match for this evil entity standing before them. The favored three had to send it back to Hell.

The demon advanced toward the three but halted in his tracks, grabbed his head, and screamed in rage. The sound was guttural, unnatural, and not of this earth. Then, Finn saw something come out of Jonas—just a flash of a gossamer white fog with a glimmering blue and silver coil attached to the back of it. Jonas's body stood unmoving, with the other end of the cord tied back to his physical body. This white entity jumped into the demon, knocking the ungodly thing to the ground. Aaron jumped on top of the devil, and Mara also moved into action. They flipped the monster onto its stomach and had him in such a tight lock that there wasn't any direction the beast could move to escape. Finn could have sworn he saw flashes of gossamer wings when the three siblings made sudden moves. *Were angels actually inside their bodies as the Gatekeepers fought this demon?* He really couldn't say for sure.

Mara yelled, "Jonas, get out of him now!" The filmy, white spirit pushed out and returned to Jonas, being drawn back into him by the blue and silver coil. Jonas took a few seconds to recover, then physically descended on the demon too. They pulled their knives, stabbed the monster in the back several times, and then chanted together in some unknown language Finn didn't recognize.

The siblings continued stabbing and intoning, and the screams from the demon were deafening, not just in the ears but through Finn's body. He saw a black, slimy ooze sliding off the demon's possessed human. It screamed one last time, and the dark, horrible mass rolled across the cement floor, then disappeared. The possessed human stopped moving and was finally dead, and they had exorcised the demon. Finn stared in shock and couldn't believe what had transpired.

~

"My Lord and Savior, and by all that is holy, what just happened?" This comment came from Edison, who had opened the door and had been watching the entire face-off.

I sat quietly for a moment, as did Aaron, and Jonas. We shook our heads, stood up as we struggled to catch our breath, then looked down at the eviscerated body. We tried coming to terms with what we'd done. As we stared at each other, I said, "Did we really do that?" My brothers both nodded, and we turned to Finn and Edison.

Out of nowhere, the minor demon guarding Isabella came up behind Edison, but Edison felt his evil presence, spun around, and shot him several times in the heart, then twice in the forehead. He dropped quickly, but Edison continued his attack and slit the demon's throat.

"Well done, my friend," Finn said to Edison and patted him on the back.

"Bloody hell, I should've been paying better attention," Edison replied.

We sighed in relief, cleaned our knives, and rechecked the ammo in our rifles and handguns. Jonas loaded a tranquilizer gun to use on Isabella, and we proceeded across the hall to where she was being held. We drew our weapons as we entered the room, and Jonas was ready to take the shot to drug Isabella.

We expected her to be armed and waiting to shoot us, but that wasn't the case. Isabella sat in the same chair where their previous prisoner, Jake Mathison, had been restrained. She wasn't bound but slumped, her head hanging down to one side. The poor woman was in terrible shape.

Hearing the commotion, she slowly lifted her head, and a weak guttural grumbled, "She's mine, and you can't have her."

We knew the body the demon had possessed was too weak to fight us.

Isabella's complexion had a pale gray cast, and she was emaciated, bruised, and cut.

There was no point in sedation and I moved toward her. I checked her pulse, and it was weak. "Isabella, talk to me. We're here."

She struggled to get past the demon but had a moment of clarity in her eyes. "Mara? I knew you'd come. Please save me. Cast this horrible thing out of me, I beg of you!"

Her eyes grew dark and glaring again, and the one possessing her said, "She's still mine, and I'm taking her with me to the bowels of Hell."

"No, you aren't, you pathetic, slimy monster," I snarled in a confident and defiant tone at the demon in Isabella. I looked hard at Finn. "We have to get her out of here. Is it safe to sedate her in this poor condition?"

"Mara, she won't make it—she's barely alive now. There's no saving her—I'm so sorry. You know I'm speaking the truth," Finn said as he put his arm around me.

"There's no way we can leave her here like this. We should at least exorcise her. There's a possibility she could recover if this beast is out of her body. We have to try, Finn," I pleaded.

Jonas said, "We *can* cast out the demon, and we must do this for her."

Finn thought for a moment, then agreed we should proceed. My brothers and I laid down our weapons, gathered around Isabella, held hands, and stood quietly for a moment in silent prayer. We started chanting again in unison in the language of the angels. The blessings continued, and we witnessed the apparent conflict waging war on Isabella's face. The demon wasn't happy, and it caused Isabella to punch herself.

"Finn, would you and Edison hold her down, please?" The two men lifted her off the chair and laid her on the floor, restraining her hands and feet.

We chanted again for several minutes and finally heard a torturous scream; the black ooze slid off Isabella and through the floor. I knelt beside her, cradling her upper body in my lap.

"Isabella, the demon is gone. You're free, so please wake up. You can now live in freedom from that horrible evil. Open your eyes, honey!" I demanded. She did as I asked and peered at me in desperation.

"Mara, you saved me. I knew you would. Thank you with all my heart, and especially, my soul. Tell God I'm so sorry. Ask Him to forgive me for allowing the demon access to my mind and body. It was all my fault, but will you please ask our dear Father to forgive me?" she begged.

"He knows what's in your heart, what you've been through, and that you didn't mean for this to happen. He loves you; you'll have the rest of your life to live in His love and forgiveness. We have to get you out of here and to medical care," I said comfortingly.

"No. There's no hope for this body of mine. It's dying even as we speak, and you must leave me here. You did what I asked and saved me. Now you must go because more demons will be here soon, and they want the three of you more than anything. They greatly fear the Chosen Ones and everything God has given them to fight them. Now go!" Isabella insisted.

"But you asked me to save you. So I won't let you die!"

"You *did* save me, Mara. I wanted you to save my soul, not my body. I've done too much evil with this vessel, and it's not something I can live with, so I'm happy it's about gone. If you hadn't expelled the demon and this body had died, I would've gone to Hell. I begged you to come so you could save my soul before that happened, and I'll be eternally grateful for that. Thank you, Mara. Now, leave me. You must go."

"But Isabella…" I pleaded. But I saw the look in her eyes, the love and thankfulness for her freedom from evil, and knew I had to let her go. This was incredibly difficult and my heart was breaking. Tears cascaded down my face as I bent over and kissed her forehead. Holding her head to my chest, I rocked her and stroked her hair.

I whispered to her, not knowing what I was saying, then she quietly died. "Fly to heaven, sweet, Isabella. Go home and be with our glorious Father."

Finn took my arm and whispered, "We must go, sweetheart. I'm sorry."

I laid her gently on the floor, grabbed my weapon, and rose to my feet. Turning toward the door, I strode stiffly from the room.

CHAPTER 20

Finn contacted the four assets through his headset as we neared the surface. He told them we neutralized the enemy, but the mission was compromised because the target was down. Miguel informed Finn the coast was still clear, but he needed to get up top and contact Basheer ASAP.

When we reached the outside, Finn called Basheer, who answered promptly. "Finn, thank God we finally connected. Unfortunately, none of us at the chopper base could contact you, and our assets also tried. Our phones and radios couldn't reach you in the tunnels, so we assume they have a jamming signal within the bunker."

Basheer continued, "I received a call from Poppy, and a large contingent of myrmidons is headed your way. They're approximately seventeen minutes out. We also have five choppers flying to your location as well. These helicopters have no designation, but Poppy assures us they're demons. You have only fourteen minutes before the choppers arrive at your twenty. Tell me you copy, Finn."

"Copy that, Basheer. There's no way we'll make it out in time. Can you arrive at our twenty before they get here?"

"Roger that, but it'll be tight. The Huey is ready for take-off in twenty seconds. Hang on and out of sight until we arrive. We're locked and loaded," Basheer replied.

Finn turned to us and said, "Alright, you heard him. Get ready for incoming, and we better hope he gets the Huey here before the enemy arrives. Basheer has only one place to land, so let's use that grove of trees to wait. Jonas, tell Jasper we'll meet him there and provide him the coordinates."

We ran to the area Finn had selected, and Jasper joined us as we waited for the Huey. Within nine minutes, we heard the chopper approaching: Basheer was coming in fast. We hustled out of the woods and stayed a safe distance away as Basheer landed.

"Move, people!" Finn yelled, and we piled into the chopper.

Basheer was about to take off when we heard more helicopters coming over the mountain. Billie and Chuck operated the M-60 machine guns, and Xavier sat near the left door with a semi-automatic rifle.

"Here they come. Hang on, team!" Basheer bellowed.

We lifted off, and one of the five choppers attempted to fly over the Huey to impede our ascent. "I got this!" Billie yelled. She fired the M-60 with sheer determination on her face. Her upper body vibrated with the rapid recoil of the machine gun. Ammo shells flew from the side of the gun down to the earth below. The ammo belt feeding the gun rapidly pulled from a metal box on the chopper floor. Billie's shots hit the side of the offending chopper's rotor, sending it spinning toward the mountain. It disappeared around the other side, and a large plume of smoke appeared over the top of the mountain peak.

Down below, we spotted over two-hundred myrmidon troops on the ground. They surrounded the compound. The evil lackeys fired their automatic weapons at us, and we heard the shots pinging off the Huey's fuselage. Basheer ascended higher to protect us from the barrage of gunfire.

Four more choppers sped toward us with demon-possessed men inside, and they fired directly at us. We heard more pinging, and a few shots made it through the right open door. They whizzed past us, but one bullet caught Chuck in the upper left shoulder, knocking him on his butt. Xavier immediately took over the machine gun and continued firing. Jonas and I attended to Chuck and packed his wound to stop the bleeding.

One asset had been shot through his head, bleeding profusely. Miguel held the injured man close to his chest. He returned my gaze and shook his head with immense grief.

I mouthed, "I'm sorry," and lowered my eyes. Everyone else saw the dead soldier too, and they couldn't hide their mournful despair.

Basheer spoke through the headset, "Finn, we can't take much more of this. Even though we're equipped with a bulletproof exterior and glass, it can only take so much. It doesn't help when their choppers are also bullet-proof."

"I know. Can you send the missile with the holy fire into the compound yet?"

"Negative. I can't turn because the choppers on our right are too close to us. We must get more distance from the compound, but we're boxed in."

Xavier and Billie were still firing at the other choppers and the troops below. There was an endless barrage of bullets coming and going. It was a nightmare, and we kept praying to the Lord to be at our side.

Aaron yelled, "I can help." He fixed his gaze on the chopper closest to us. His eyes grew dark, and they almost appeared black. The helicopter that held his gaze sputtered, spun uncontrollably, and went down hard, disintegrating into several pieces.

He turned his attention to another one, and the same thing happened. Aaron now focused on the helicopter to our left, and we watched it move rapidly toward the mountain. We could see the pilot trying to gain a hold of the controls, but he could do nothing. The chopper picked up momentum and hit the side of the mountain. The impact created an enormous ball of fire.

There was one enemy chopper left. "This one is mine," Basheer said with conviction. He turned the Huey to face the last helicopter, targeting and firing one of the two missiles mounted on the Huey. It hit them dead center, and the enemy's chopper blew up, sending shrapnel and body parts to the earth below.

Bullets were still pelleting our helicopter, but the impacts were few. We were too far away from the ground assault for their shots to reach us.

Basheer said, "Hold on folks, this is a firework display you'll 'ooh and ahh' over." He sent the holy fire missile down to the base and the myrmidons. We watched in amazement as the entire compound and all the demon troops blew up in a tremendous flash, and an enormous blue fire enveloped the enemy base and surrounding area. Nothing was left, but a giant crater where the compound had been, and not one body could be seen. They vanished within the blue flames, and the view was astounding.

"Now that's what I call holy fire," said Jasper. "Jiminy Cricket, what is it anyway?" he asked Finn and Basheer.

"We don't know. The monks said it was a gift from God. The Lord told them how to use it in missiles, grenades, and flamethrowers. That's all we know, but it's definitely a present from Heaven," Finn said with a huge grin. "Aaron, what did you do to those choppers?"

"I seem to be able to take control of anything electrical by using my mind. For some reason, I can see all the circuits, switches, and currents, decide what I need to do to take control, then make it do what I want," Aaron replied. We gawked at him in surprise, gave him high fives, and thanked him for saving our lives.

As we flew around the mountain's peak, Finn pointed out the left window and said, "Look!" We craned our heads to see what had his undivided attention. At the top of the mountain were three animals: a white wolf with an eagle perched on its back and a cougar standing next to him. They looked proud and brave as they watched us. We hovered for a moment, staring at their strength and beauty. After offering our prayer of thanks to the Lord, we sent them a wave. Then the majestic animals turned and leaped over the side of the mountain, vanishing into the heavy mist.

"Goodbye, for now, dear Spirit, until we meet again," I muttered.

Everyone praised God and gave Him thanks for saving us and defeating the evil ones. I also prayed for Isabella with a heavy heart and couldn't shake the feeling I'd failed her. I knew she'd go to Heaven, but I still should have been able to save her life. If only there had been more time to heal and repair what she thought she'd lost—her goodness and love of being alive. I felt Finn's eyes on me, but I wouldn't return his gaze—I needed to be alone in my grief.

CHAPTER 21

Finn asked Miguel where he and his men would prefer to be dropped. He said to take them to the first camp where the Huey had been parked. Miguel would take care of Luis's body and notify his family of his tragic death, but he'd need his horses and mules.

"Finn, take us near where we left the livestock. I can tell them to return to where we parked the Huey. At least, I think I can," I said.

Basheer flew us close enough to see the mules and horses, and the animals were startled. I quickly connected to their minds, and they settled as they gazed in our direction. They raised their heads as if listening to my commands. After a few moments, they turned and quickly moved down the mountain toward the camp.

"That's so weird," said Billie. "How did you do that?"

Turning to her, I replied, "I talk to them through my mind, but I don't know how it works. Only God knows the secret." Billie gave me a big smile and then a high five.

Basheer landed at the original waiting site and dropped off Miguel and his men. We helped him carry Luis to a nice, grassy, shaded area and laid him on his back. He looked peaceful, but we felt such a loss of a beautiful human being. Aaron, Jonas, and I knelt and touched Luis's body. We felt happiness emanating from him. A pale, shimmering light danced around us, gently lifting upward until it disappeared. My siblings and I smiled with joy.

Turning to Miguel, I said, "He's at peace now. His spirit is on its way to Heaven, and he thanked you, Miguel, for saving his life in Medellin, Colombia. If you hadn't taken him out of that miserable existence, he'd never have met his beautiful wife and had his son."

Miguel's face melted with both happiness and grief. He hugged my brothers and me and thanked us for the gift of Luis's message.

Miguel said, "I'll never forget these last few days, not only because my dear friend has died, but because I was blessed to meet all of you. Praise God for this special gift of seeing His works through His Chosen Ones. I pray you'll stay in touch and let me know how the war turns out, eh?" He hugged the rest of the team.

"We will, my friend. It's a promise," Finn said.

Fast hoofbeats approached as we strode toward the bullet-riddled chopper. Startled, we raised our weapons, but it was only the horses and mules running in our direction.

"How did they get here so fast?" Chuck asked as he rubbed his aching shoulder.

"Maybe I forgot to tell them not to hurry," I said and cringed. Everyone laughed. I communicated to the mounts to slow their gait, and they complied. Miguel and his men gathered and guided them toward the trees to cool down before taking them to water for a drink.

"But there's still no way they could get back here in such a short time. It took us a day and a half to get where we left them. I believe we have the good Lord to thank for getting them here so quickly," Jonas replied. We nodded and gave thanks to our Savior.

"Do I have time to say goodbye to my horse?" Jonas inquired.

Finn nodded, and everyone laughed again. "Only a few minutes, then we must return to the airport. Who knows what the repercussions will be after that enormous explosion rocked this land for several miles."

Xavier examined and re-bandaged Chuck's wounded shoulder. It was a through-and-through, and the bullet hadn't hit anything significant. Xavier gave him something for the pain, and we again boarded the Huey.

It was a quiet flight and everyone was engrossed in their thoughts. We spotted Jorge and his men waiting for us as we neared our landing area in Colombia, and Basheer received landing instructions. I hoped there wouldn't be any problems, but Jorge wore his customary grin as we exited the Huey.

"My friends, thank you for ridding me of that den of iniquity in Venezuela. Much evil was committed there for many years, and I give you my sincere thanks for blowing it back to damnation," he said, beaming and giving each of us a big hug. "Come, come. You're all invited to my *hacienda* for a shower, a change of clothes, and an elaborate dinner. Don't worry. I'll take great care of you. You may even stay the night, if you so wish, and return to your home in the morning. *Si?*"

His offer sounded terrific because we were filthy, hungry, and exhausted. Finn agreed, and we stowed our extra gear in the airplane and returned to a couple of limousines waiting on the tarmac.

His *hacienda* was a palace fit for a king. A drug kingpin, I assumed. We didn't ask; he didn't tell and did precisely as he'd offered. We were each led to our private suites, where they gave us several clothing styles in our sizes. We availed ourselves of long, hot showers, changed into the expensive clothing, and returned downstairs to the dining hall.

The meal was elaborate and delicious and included every dessert imaginable. Jorge was a gracious and considerate host, and we couldn't have asked for more, but we were dead on our feet, and he told us to return to our rooms and sleep the night away. A large breakfast would be waiting for us at seven in the morning, and then the cars would return us to the airport. We sincerely thanked him for his generous hospitality and turned in for the night.

The following day, Jorge wasn't home. We were told he had an important business meeting, but he sent his regards and wished us a safe return flight. Another fabulous meal waited for us, and I had to speak up about Finn's South American friend.

"Okay, Finn, you've got to tell us how you met Jorge," I urged, and everyone trained their eyes on Finn with avid curiosity.

"Ahh, Jorge..." Finn said, with a smile on his face as he stroked his chin. "We met several years ago when I took a backpacking trip through Colombia—when I was young and foolish. This was after I came to the

United States and finally started making a few bucks. Arrogant as I was then, I thought I knew it all and could handle anything. I hadn't been here long when I got lost in the jungle and happened along a field of poppies. It was beautiful, but I also knew it could be trouble, and I needed to get out of there fast."

Finn shook his head in memory and said, "But I wasn't quick enough. Three guys built like Mac trucks with automatic weapons and machetes found me. They bound and gagged me and transported me to Jorge's mansion. They dragged me to a nasty-looking room with dried blood all over the walls and floors. Needless to say, I figured I was a dead man. I said many prayers that day, let me tell you.

"After they left me to stew awhile, Jorge came in the room, looking mean and ready to kick my butt. He had the same three men behind him, and they carried the ugliest-looking torture devices I'd ever seen. You can imagine the terror I felt. Jorge turned to the three men and made them leave the room. He then grabbed one of the mean-looking tools and cleaned his fingernails.

"When Jorge finally spoke, he asked me, 'Do you know who I am, young *amigo*?' Of course, I shook my head, told him I had no idea, and begged him to let me go because I wouldn't tell anyone about anything. He stared at me momentarily, then replied, 'You're an Irishman, yes? Do you know what I love more than anything? Irish whiskey. You know, the expensive stuff. It's been hard to bring it into my country, even with my money and influence.'"

Finn continued, "Then he told me to scream in agony. I remember gaping at him in shock, but he repeated the demand, so I did. He told me to scream louder, and I did again. He shushed me, looked back at the door, and whispered. 'I have to keep up my reputation, my Irish *amigo,* yes?'

"Then he explained he'd seen the Holy Mother, and he no longer killed people, was involved in human trafficking, or gave drugs to little children. Jorge said he had to pretend to be just as vile as before because if he didn't, his people or the competition would kill him. He cut a spot on his arm and smeared his blood across my face and chest. Then he looked at me and said, 'When you wake up, you'll be back in the city of Bogota, and then you must return home. This is our little secret, yes? But, please send me a bottle of your best Irish whiskey and mail it to this address in Texas. It will get to me. This is not a threat; I would just love a bottle of your country's finest vintage.' He tucked a piece of paper with an address into my shirt pocket, then struck me. The next thing I remember was waking up in Bogota. I bought him the whiskey and I'd send him another every so often. We became good friends after that terrifying day.

"He's a good man and doesn't kill innocent people or sell drugs to children, exactly as he'd said. Jorge is careful about what he gets involved in and only has a few trusted men who know he's now a good Christian doing God's will. He does what he can to protect and care for the people of his country. His cartel tries to eliminate the evil that's destroying his homeland and his countrymen," Finn said, then leaned back with a smile.

After our meal, Jorge's staff chauffeured us back to the airport, where we boarded the plane and headed home. After we were in the air, Finn praised us for our excellent work and said we should be proud of ourselves.

We gave him an appreciative smile, but we were still exhausted. Most of us slept on the way back, and there was little conversation. We were relieved to return to the base and our apartments. Everyone said they'd crash for the rest of the late afternoon and evening.

After returning to my place and tossing my gear on the floor inside the door, I plopped onto the sofa. My body and mind felt numb. I sat there, unaware that I hadn't turned on the lights in the apartment. The only illumination in the room was the therapeutic lights, simulating late afternoon. Eventually, after curling into a ball on the sofa, I fell into a deep sleep.

I was jostled while I slept but only ignored whatever disturbed me. After mumbling a few times, I didn't bother opening my eyes, then the minor intrusion finally left me alone, and my exhausted body returned to a deep slumber. I needed to escape the intrusive and depressive thoughts, and sleep was my remedy.

CHAPTER 22

a strange sound kept interrupting my need for sleep, and I pulled the pillow over my head to block out the noise. *Buzz, buzz.* "Dang, it! Just let me sleep, you awful thing." After mumbling a mild expletive, I threw the pillow across the room and turned toward the hateful grating sound. I opened one eye, then the other, trying to focus. It was my cell phone on the bedside table. Sitting up, I reached for it and tried to read the name on the caller I.D. It was Jonas.

"What!?" I asked rudely.

"Well, good morning, or should I say, afternoon to you too," Jonas replied humorously.

"What time is it?"

"Just a little after noon. You were still sleeping, eh? It's time to get out of bed, grumpy pants, and join the living again."

I made another rude noise, then threw off the covers. "Geez, where are my clothes? And how did I end up in my bed? I distinctly remember falling asleep on the sofa last night. Did I sleepwalk?" I asked no one in particular.

"Calm down. Finn and I were worried about you last night. You wouldn't answer the door, which scared us to death, so he did an override, and we came in to check on you. That's when we found you on the sofa.

Finn carried you to your bed, and you called him vulgar names. You weren't friendly, I must say."

"Crap! Jonas, who removed my clothes? I hope it wasn't Finn…I'd be mortified."

"Don't worry, it wasn't. He left me to do the dirty work. You're still wearing your T-shirt and undergarments, so don't get all bent out of shape. Finn put your phone by your bed in case you needed it. I'm glad he did, or you'd still be counting sheep."

"Sorry, Jonas. I'm still groggy and not in a very good mood. Oh, and thanks."

"You're welcome. I'm calling to see if you've looked at the mark on your arm since we returned from the mission."

"Uh, no. Why?"

"You'll see. Mara, are you okay? I mean, it's been a tough few days, and you seemed different on the return trip."

"I'm fine. I just need some alone time to figure things out. You understand?"

"Look who you're talking to. Of course, I understand, and Finn's worried too. Would you like me to talk to him about it? I will, you know."

"That's sweet, Jonas, but I should probably talk to him myself. I'll call him later after I'm fully awake and have lunch. I'll see you tomorrow at church, okay?"

"You got it. You know where I am if you need anything. Love you, Mara."

"Thanks. I love you too, Jonas."

After I disconnected the call, I sat there for a moment, then decided to get up and rejoin the living. For some reason though, my heart wasn't in it. I rose anyway, took a long hot shower, and washed my hair. After drying off, I stared grimly at myself in the mirror. *The mark, huh?* Turning to gaze at my upper left arm, the tattoo was more visible now and interesting. *But what did it mean?* It was a triad with an open area in the center. There were four different, odd-looking symbols in the mark. The center one looked familiar, but I couldn't place it. I'd need to figure this out, but it was time to have something to eat.

After my meal, I sat at the computer and searched for anything on the internet that was close to what God had imprinted on my arm, but I didn't know what to ask. After looking for over an hour, I couldn't find any related data. I shut down the computer and decided I'd better call Finn.

The conversation was short but sweet. He was anxious about me, but I told him what I'd said to Jonas, that I needed some time alone. I also thanked him for carrying me to bed last night and was sorry if I'd said anything rude.

He chuckled and replied, "That's okay. I didn't know you had such a colorful vocabulary. Were you a sailor in your previous life?"

"Ha, Ha," I answered sarcastically.

"I just had to ask. By the way, love, would you attend Mass with me tomorrow?"

"That I can do. I'll see you at the usual time. And Finn, thanks."

"Any time, Mara." He disconnected the call and I already missed hearing his voice.

I decided to spend time at church today. Maybe being closer to God would help my melancholy mood. The church's pews were empty except for one woman near the back who fingered her rosary in prayer. I loved being in the church alone, the scents of the candles and incense, the echoes of the minor sounds reverberating from one end to the other, and the soft lights illuminating the beautiful crucifix on the altar. I found it peaceful being alone with the Lord.

Sitting quietly, I reviewed the last few days and how the Lord helped us and worked through us to try and save Isabella. A tear ran down my cheek as I reminisced about her. She was in heaven, so why did the death of her body upset me like this? It really shouldn't, not with every miracle I'd seen. It made no sense, and I should have been grateful for everything. I asked God to help me overcome my depression and move on to the next part of the journey He'd chosen for me.

After I sat in the pew for another hour, my mood hadn't improved. I said a rosary to our Holy Mother, then it was time to leave the church and return to my apartment. This was something I needed to work out on my own. I left feeling despondent but hoped that, in time, this feeling would resolve itself.

I spent the night watching television, reading, and eating a light dinner, then went to bed. The exhaustion still had a firm grip on me, so maybe I needed more sleep and would feel better tomorrow.

The next morning, though, I still experienced the same heaviness. I had to prepare for Mass because Finn would soon pick me up so we could walk there together. Seeing the glorious angels during the consecration would surely improve my mood.

It was so good to see him. Finn gave me a long, sweet kiss, and we held one another. He set me back from him, but kept his arms around me, then peered intently into my eyes. "Mara, I'm here if you want to talk about anything, and I mean anything. You know that, right, sweetheart?" I saw pure love in his eyes and how much he wanted to help me.

"Finn, I know that. It's just...I don't know what I'm feeling right now. I need to figure this out on my own, I guess. So please give me a little more time, okay?"

He leaned down and kissed me again, and we strolled to the elevator. I saw Jonas and Poppy at church, and Aaron was also with them. I knew Aaron was trying to decide which religion he wanted to join. However, after being raised an atheist, finding God was such an awe-inspiring event he didn't know which religion would best fit his new love of the Lord. Jonas and I told him that God would tell him when he found the one meant for him.

Finn and I waved at them and sat in one of the pews. There was a different priest today; he wasn't one I'd seen before. I asked Finn about it, and he said that our current pastor, Father Faraj, was on vacation for a week, and this priest was Father Ryan. We enjoyed the service and were waiting in anticipation of the consecration. When it started, I grasped Finn's hand, but the angels never appeared. I glanced at Jonas, and apparently, he didn't see them either. We found it disheartening, but I realized Father Ryan was going through the motions of the Mass. His face was blank, and he said the Mass by rote.

After church, Finn took me to brunch, and we discussed what happened at the Mass, but I knew I wasn't good company. It made me want to cry because I loved Finn, but I couldn't carry on a decent conversation. I apologized and said I needed to return to my place. Smiling back at him, I said I'd be okay, kissed him, and returned to my apartment.

I did nothing for the rest of the day but sleep. Finn, Jonas, and Aaron called to check on me, and I said I was fine and would see them next week. I wasn't being truthful and they knew it, too, but I didn't know what else to say. This was my problem, not theirs, though I loved them for trying.

The next day, I made myself shower and donned a comfortable t-shirt, sweat pants, and a pair of fuzzy slippers. I'd stay in my apartment and try to cheer myself up. Maybe praying was the answer, so I said my daily prayers and read the Bible. When that was completed, I watched several sitcoms on the television, but I was still miserable. I sat on the sofa, trying to figure out what to do next, but fell asleep again.

A knock on the door woke me from my slumber. I tried to ignore it and return to sleep, but the rapping persisted, and I heard Finn's deep, soothing voice. "Mara, open up. I need to see you, sweetheart."

"Okay, just a moment," was all I said, and I went to the door. After opening it a crack, I saw Finn standing there, one arm behind his back and a massive grin on his face.

"May I come in? It won't take long, I promise."

I opened the door and spotted a young man behind him with a luggage cart that held several boxes.

"Sure." I motioned him inside, wondering what he was up to.

As he entered, the young man followed and laid the boxes just inside the door; he turned around and departed.

"What's going on, Finn?"

"I know you told me how you loved your Maine Coon kitty that you lost several years ago and how much you missed him. Well, I think I found something, or someone, that will ease your loneliness in this apartment, love."

He brought his arm from around his back and presented me with the most beautiful Maine Coon kitten I'd ever seen. It was a gorgeous silver-gray cat with white on his chest, feet, mustache, chin, and whiskers. His eyes were a bright, startling gold color. He had enormous tufted ears, a long nose, a large muzzle, and a huge fluffy tail. This cat was magnificent and all Maine Coon.

Finn handed him over to me, and I took the kitten like he was a precious piece of antique porcelain. I held him to my chest, and he snuggled his face into my neck and purred so loud it was almost deafening. Burying my face in his soft, silky, sweet-smelling coat, I felt tears running down my cheeks. The sweet ball of fur lifted his head and touched my face with his paws and bumped my cheek with his nose. Sinking to my knees, the tears wouldn't stop. I sobbed and blubbered into the kitten's silky fur.

I felt Finn pick us both up in his arms and he carried us to the sofa. He sat with us on his lap and let me cry, giving me time to release my grief, fear, and frustration. He grabbed some tissues from the end table and tenderly wiped my eyes. I was calming down now, but I still rubbed my face on the kitten's head. The little fur ball loved every minute of it and only wanted to snuggle closer.

I couldn't believe Finn's thoughtful gift of this precious animal made me feel better. The heavy weight I'd been carrying had lifted. I thanked God for giving me such a fantastic man and this precious kitten.

The hiccupping finally ceased, and I blew my nose, wiped my eyes, and tried to dry off the poor kitten with another tissue. I was embarrassed about breaking down in front of Finn but was happy that the awful, oppressive feeling had vanished.

"Finn…"

"Hmm?"

"Thank you so much. I love him to pieces. Just like I love you to pieces."

"You're very welcome, my sweet. I didn't mean to make you cry, but I guess that's just what you needed. A good cry to let it all go. The experience of the last few days was traumatic and new for you. The rest of us, except Aaron, have been doing this awhile, but we still remember the first time we had a tough mission like this. Don't keep it all in when your friends and family love you and can help you through the trauma. Aaron's feeling the same way as you and doesn't know how to deal with it either. He thinks he still doesn't have anyone he can count on or confide in. Old habits die hard, so we need to help him through this too."

"You're right. My goodness, I had no idea about Aaron. It was selfish of me. I'll see him and let him know we love him and are here for him too."

"We all will, Mara. I'll speak with Jonas and we can all see him together. Will that work?"

I nodded in agreement and enjoyed being held by Finn and feeling the soft, warm kitten in my arms.

Finn leaned back and said, "These people you worked with on this mission, everyone except you, Aaron, and I, have been through hell and back. They're seasoned combat veterans and have seen the worst of war, violence, and hate that comes from a total disregard for human life. I chose them for my elite team because I know, deep in my heart, how much they value every person, and they no longer want evil to permeate the human condition. They trust each other and know by experience what that does to people. Only a combat veteran can understand another combat veteran, and they only trust one another in combat conditions. That, in turn, makes me trust them, and I know you and Aaron can also count on them.

"Those brave veterans trained me and took me on my first mission. It was a horrible, bloody thing for a first-timer, and I went through the same grief that you and Aaron are now experiencing. Those good people got me through it, and we'll get the two of you through it as well. Just remember, you can talk to any of them about anything, and that goes for me too." He kissed the top of my head and held me even closer.

"Thanks, Finn. What you said helps me understand it and makes me appreciate what a special team we have. They're a superb group of soldiers." I snuggled into Finn's neck and caught a whiff of his spicy aftershave.

"But, it wasn't just the death of Isabella...." I tried to continue—to explain, but I didn't want to tell Finn what else had been weighing so heavily on my heart since we returned from the mission.

"Mara, what is it? You've got to know you can tell me anything." I know he saw the fear and doubt in my eyes and tried gently coaxing me into confiding in him. "Please, love, tell me what's eating at you."

"Finn, it's not something I ever wanted anyone to know or that I'm proud of. I'd hoped I wouldn't ever have those feelings again. But after connecting with Isabella as she lay dying, she experienced so many emotions, which caused me to remember the terrible events from my previous life. When things became so bad, the awful feelings of hopelessness consumed me." Finn continued to hold me close and patiently waited for me to continue.

"All those years of being ill, it not only took everything from me physically, but it also stole everything I was...inside. Fear, anxiety, hopelessness, and anger overwhelmed me. I was terrified of how bad the next bout of illness would be and how long it might last; afraid I would die, but also scared I'd survive it. Knowing that I could live many more years and that the torture would probably keep getting worse tormented me as well. This intense anxiety made me afraid I'd eventually take my own life, and God would send me to Hell.

"I remember how much hate I felt for myself and my traitorous body. How could it betray me, keep me utterly miserable, and be so flawed? Sometimes I'd scream in sheer frustration and repeatedly punch myself until my anger was finally spent. I always prayed to God for His help, but He stayed silent. He was my only hope, but I never understood why He didn't answer. I still don't, even now, since my trip to Heaven. How bad must I be that I needed to be continually punished by God?" I cried into Finn's chest until I couldn't anymore.

"Good Lord in holy Heaven, I didn't know it was that bad, love. I'm so sorry you had to endure such hell. My heart breaks for you, and I truly wish I could've been there to comfort you in any way I could. I'd never have let you go," Finn whispered above me, and I felt his tears slide down my temple.

A little while later, I sat up, grabbed another tissue, and blew my nose. My face was red with embarrassment, and I looked away. Finn put his finger under my chin and turned my head as he peered into my red-rimmed eyes. "You're one special, amazing, strong, and beautiful woman, Mara Patrick. I'm very proud and honored to have you in my life and so close to my heart. I don't know why you had to go through such horror and misery, but one thing I do know is that you're a good, kind, loving person, and you weren't being punished. I wish I could tell you why you had to endure so much suffering and wish it had never happened to you. If I could have traded places with you, I would have done it in a heartbeat."

Finn's eyes again filled with tears, and I gave him a watery smile and mouthed, "Thank you." Finn pulled me close again.

We sat together for some time, but then the kitten wanted attention and voiced a loud and unusual squeak.

Finn said, "Now then, about this little guy here, I contacted a friend of mine named Sergei, who lives in Russia, and it just so happens his wife breeds Maine Coons. Her kittens are highly sought after and have won many awards. The one you have in your arms is five months old, has papers, and he's already been neutered, vaccinated, toilet trained, and walks on a leash. He's very smart. Hey, you don't need a litter pan for him, you only have to leave the lid up on the toilet, or there may be a surprise left for you somewhere in your apartment." I felt his deep chuckle under my ear through his chest. The fluffy ball of fur was asleep under my chin but was still lightly purring.

I laughed, lifted my head, and gave Finn a sweet, tender kiss.

"How do you feel now, Mara?"

"So much better." I nodded with a smile.

"I'm delighted my incredible woman is happy again." Then he kissed me back.

CHAPTER 23

Finn departed an hour later, and I felt like my usual self again. I had a fabulous new companion to keep me company, and I was blessed indeed. Finn brought me a new kitten and everything I might need to care for him. There were several boxes to go through, and I discovered cat toys, scratching posts, fancy plush cat beds, food and water bowls, treats, grooming supplies, and organic human-grade cat food. This kitty would be spoiled rotten.

After I unpacked the boxes and stored almost everything away, I played with my new friend. He started looking around, so I figured I'd better show him the bathroom. I picked him up, carried him to the toilet, and lifted the lid. He jumped right up, straddled the bowl, and did his thing. I'd heard about cats doing this but had never seen it before, and it was startling. I surmised he'd jump down since he'd finished his business, but he reached out and pulled down on the flushing mechanism. After I praised him, he squeaked a couple of strange meows and hopped down, and rubbed his body around my calves.

"I have to come up with a name for you, kitty. Any ideas?" I didn't get much as I tried to connect my mind with his. There were only a few images of snow, a big Russian gentleman, and a delicate blonde woman. They must be Sergei and his wife. I thought it odd I couldn't get more information from his mind. *Can't I communicate with cats?* Hmm. Looking back, I'd never attempted to read Spirit's mind either.

Sitting on the couch with my new kitty, he climbed onto my lap, snuggled down while still purring, and then bathed.

I tried again to make a connection, asking if he already had a name, but all I could get was a word in Russian. *I could understand and read many languages, right?* What I saw meant "gray." I asked the kitten out loud if he liked the name, Gray. He stopped purring and pinned his ears.

"Okay, not really. I know, how about Asher—do you like that?" He purred again and rubbed his cheek against my face. "Asher it is, sweet one."

It was late by the time I played with Asher and showed him around the apartment. I placed a few of his cat beds in strategic places and also put one on the end of my bed. "I don't know where you'd like to sleep, but you're invited to sleep anywhere."

Turning out the lights, I went to the bathroom to prepare for bed. Asher chased my bare feet like a game, making me laugh. I crawled into bed and realized I hadn't turned on the television to keep me company as I slept. However, I didn't need it now because I had Asher. He jumped on the bed and laid against me, and purred again. I turned out the light, said my prayers, curled my body around my soft and warm companion, and quickly fell asleep.

~

"MARA, IT'S ME. ISABELLA." *I'm dreaming. At least, I think I am.*

"Isabella, is that you?"

"Yes. I'm here. I hope you can see me. I'm not sure if I'll be visible."

I'm looking through a white haze, and then I see her standing before me. She looks beautiful. The sickly color, along with the cuts and bruises, are gone. God has filled her face with joy, happiness, and peace. She's wearing a gorgeous white gossamer gown, but her hands and feet aren't visible.

"You can see me. Thank you, Lord," she says and is looking somewhere beyond me. "I want you to know that I'm in Heaven with the Lord, and it's

all because of you and your team. You're feeling grief about my body dying, and I'm hoping that coming to you now will give you peace and happiness. I'm free, Mara, and in the loving arms of our creator, and I can't thank you enough for releasing me. I'll be eternally grateful and hope our dear Lord will let me watch over you."

She's looking beyond me again and continues, *"It's time for me to go, Mara. Again, thank you, and please tell your team how grateful I am, will you?"*

"I will, Isabella. Thank you for letting me know you're at peace and with the Lord. That's the best news." Then Isabella fades away.

~

I woke up with Asher sitting barely a few inches from my face, intently staring at me. His bright gold eyes wondered if I was okay.

"I'm fine, Asher. We can go back to sleep. All is well, my friend." I smiled widely at him and gave him a big hug and kiss. He snuggled into my neck and went back to sleep. After rubbing my face in his soft fur, I returned to a peaceful, dreamless sleep.

Something made the mattress jiggle as I tried to sleep the following morning. Then something jumped on me. I opened my eyes and found Asher sitting on my chest, staring at me. He moved closer and licked the end of my nose. "Asher, it's too early, baby; go back to sleep."

I glanced at the clock, and it was only six in the morning. Turning over, I felt the bouncing of the mattress again. *What's he doing?* I turned back and he stared at me. Pretending to close my eyes, I felt it again, then peeked through my eyelashes. He bounced up and down, twisting his body as he went, as though on a trampoline. I couldn't help myself and burst out in laughter. He stopped for a moment, then started up again. "Asher, you're a character." I grabbed him mid-leap and hugged him. He opened his mouth and squeaked loudly, then purred.

"Okay, I give up. You want breakfast, and I must say, you've earned it." After feeding him, I gave him another pet and returned to bed.

A few minutes later, he jumped up, snuggled beside me, and bathed again. "I need another hour, please, Asher." He gave me an intent yet innocent look as I fell asleep.

Asher gave me another two hours and I felt more rested. As I prepared for the day, Asher rarely left my side. During my morning meal, however, he went to the living room and played noisily with a catnip mouse. I could hear loud banging and his endless kitten chatter, and I watched his playful antics for the longest time as I drank my hot tea.

During the morning, I received a call from Jonas, who asked how the kitten was doing. Jonas had been in cahoots with Finn on getting me this feline. I told him he was a sly dog and had to meet our family's recent addition. Regaling stories of the morning, I told Jonas the name I'd given the kitty and that I was smitten. Jonas said he was eager to meet him, and I suggested we invite Aaron to have dinner at my place this evening. He agreed it was a good idea and would bring pizza and brownies. I told him to come around seven and said I'd call Aaron. After reaching my new brother, he happily accepted my invitation and was looking forward to having dinner with us.

Later that morning, I also phoned Finn and told him how much I loved his gift and hoped to see him today. He said he wished he could, but he had several meetings throughout the day and a dinner meeting with Edison and Helen. Finn commented we could spend the following day together if that would work for me. I said I'd love to, but I hadn't checked my schedule yet and didn't know if I had any training sessions on the roster. He told me he had cleared my schedule when we returned from the mission to give me time to recuperate. I thanked him for being considerate and said I'd see him tomorrow.

That evening, Asher won over Jonas and Aaron. The kitty was charming, funny, and loving, and he knew how to make everyone love him.

My brothers and I didn't want the evening to end. Each of us told stories of stupid things we'd done in our lives and recounted embarrassing events. I even told Aaron the story about Dad's one squeaky shoe. We laughed so hard we could barely catch our breath, and I'd never seen Aaron this relaxed and happy.

As Jonas and I looked at each other, we knew we'd found a gem in

Aaron, and were thrilled we had him for a sibling. We carried our wine into the living room and sat on the sofa while enjoying each other's company.

Out of nowhere, Aaron asked, "Do you think your mom will like me?"

"She'll love you—I don't doubt that, Aaron. I'm not sure, though, how we can have you meet her. Should we say you're a good friend and give you two time to get to know each other?" I inquired.

"That could work, Mara," Jonas said. "It would take the stress off you, Aaron, and ease you and Mom into a gentle introduction."

"We need to all meet at her house. Would Finn let us, you think?" I asked them.

"I don't see why not. We can't bring her here, so we should fly to her place and stay for a day or two. I think that would work," Jonas concurred.

Aaron agreed to this plan, but we must finalize the details. I told them I'd talk to Finn and would contact them once I had more information.

We talked, joked, and laughed, but it was getting late. Jonas and Aaron said they should go, I hugged them both, and they left for their apartments.

Early the following day, Finn called and said he'd spoken with Jonas and had heard that we wanted to visit our mom. I told Finn that we would eventually like to have her meet Aaron and then try to explain that he was her son.

"Mara, how about the three of you go this afternoon? If your mum is available. What do you say, love?"

"Today? We'd need to arrange a flight, transportation, and maybe even a hotel. I'd love for you to meet her too, Finn. I love you, and I know she'd also adore you."

"That's not a problem. This place can spare us for a few days, and I think your mum should meet Aaron soon. We can take one of our planes and have a vehicle waiting for us, and the hotel isn't a problem either. I can make all the arrangements. Telling your mum won't be easy, so we should bite the bullet and do it as soon as possible."

"I'll have to call her. I know she'd be thrilled to see us. We may be able to stay at her place since there are enough bedrooms. Let me call her and see what she says. Thank you so much, Finn. I hope you know how much this means to me. I wish I could give you a big kiss," I whispered flirtatiously.

"Ahh, you now owe me, love. I have an excellent memory and I won't forget. Now, call home and let me know what she says. If it's a go, we'll notify your brothers, and I'll make all the arrangements."

"That would be awesome. I'll call you back as soon as I speak with her. Bye, Finn, I love you."

"Bye, sweetheart and I love you too."

I spoke with Mom and she couldn't wait to see us. She also said she'd love to meet Finn and my new friend, Aaron. My mom wanted us to stay with her at the house, and the spare rooms were already made up for guests so that it wouldn't give her more work. I called Finn, and he was delighted and said he'd contact the three of us with the travel details.

It didn't take long for Finn to make all the arrangements. We'd leave in two hours; the flight was departing at eleven this morning. It was now after nine, so I told Finn I'd better start packing. At that moment, a grayish-white streak flew by me across the floor.

"Oh shoot! Finn, what do I do about Asher? He should be okay while we're gone, right?"

"Bring him along. There's a carrier in the plethora of items that came with him. It's our private plane, so we don't need permission."

"Yay! Thank you so much. I'll get him ready too. You do spoil me."

"I love spoiling you. I'll have someone come for your luggage at ten-fifteen, and I'll call your brothers and give them the itinerary."

I was ready and waiting when a young man came for my luggage; I had Asher in his comfy carrier and he'd already fallen asleep.

The plane was as luxurious as the one we flew to Colombia. We quickly boarded, and I kept Asher on the seat to my right, with Finn on my left. Aaron and Jonas settled in too, but Aaron seemed apprehensive. I gave him a reassuring smile and told him Mom would love him and he shouldn't worry.

I thought this was a good time to tell everyone about my dream of Isabella, that she wanted everyone to know she was grateful to each team member for trying to save her life. We'd saved her soul, and she was now with the Lord. I asked Finn to relay her message to the rest of the team when we returned to base. It thrilled Finn to deliver my message and thanked me for sharing it with the group.

We touched down a few hours later at a private airstrip. A large black vehicle with dark-tinted windows waited for us. Asher remained calm and well behaved and I set him on the seat next to me.

As soon as we drove onto the expressway, Finn made a phone call. He said, "We'll arrive at the house in approximately one hour. Our plate number is...." He finished his conversation, and I asked him if there was a problem.

"We haven't told any of you yet, but any time a Chosen One has close family or loved ones, we arrange a protective detail for them. It's imperative we either move them to a safe location or, if they insist on staying in place, set up a security perimeter. Your jobs are dangerous, and it would thrill those we're fighting to take one of your loved ones to use as collateral. We're a constant threat to the evil we're fighting and exterminating, and loved ones can be in grave danger and would be an excellent bargaining chip. I didn't tell you because it's one more thing you'd have to worry about. You had enough on your plates when you came in, learning, training, and everything else you had to deal with. I never tell new Chosen about this until they're more confident in their position, but loved ones are always taken under our care immediately."

The three of us stared at him in shock, but our expressions changed to understanding and relief.

"Finn, did one of your people talk to our mother about any possible threats she may encounter?" Jonas asked.

"Aye. I know you've probably been careful about what you've been telling your mum about your new lives, but she does know what your jobs are and what dangers you're facing. We can't lie to our families; they need to understand that their lives may also be in peril. Your mum said she'd move to a safe location but preferred to stay in her home and within her community if possible. If we made a few security enhancements, we found she'd be safe where her home is, on several acres in the country and far from town. We have a man who closely monitors her home and movements to keep her safe; she knows this and is fine with these arrangements."

"Thanks, Finn. I can speak for all of us when I say we appreciate you taking such good care of her," I said, and my brothers agreed.

We rode down the paved country roads that Jonas and I knew so well.

It was beautiful here, and we turned into our long driveway to the house; I was elated to be home. I watched Aaron and there was a big grin plastered on his face. He said he loved the country and always felt at peace when he could escape the big city.

I told Finn and Aaron that our place was just an old, renovated ranch home. It was a five-bedroom home, but two of the bedrooms were in the finished basement, including a full bath and a small kitchenette. It wasn't very big, but it was home to Jonas and me.

There were two large barns on the property, one was a workshop where Jonas and my dad did small projects, and we used the other for the horses. We hadn't owned horses in several years, and we kept the barn in good shape, but unfortunately, the surrounding fences had long since fallen into disrepair. Large maple and fir trees and beds of rosebushes, petunias, and marigolds surrounded our home.

Since our dad died, we tried to keep up the repairs on the property but only managed to take care of the major ones. Mom and I had been on a strict budget, so we didn't complete many minor repairs. This would have to change. I could now afford to fix the things we'd needed to put on hold due to lack of finances.

As we drove up to the house, Mom hurried out the front door and smiled from ear to ear. I'd missed her so much. Once the car stopped, I jumped out, ran to her, and hugged and kissed her. I didn't want to let her go and cried joyfully. Jonas hesitantly strolled up to my mother and waited for her to get a look at him. She hadn't seen him since his return as a young man.

"Jonas...you look fantastic. I missed you so much, baby," she cried, took him into her arms, and he fought tears as well.

"I love you, Mom," Jonas professed.

They finally stepped apart, and I told her, "Mom, I'd like you to meet the love of my life, Finn McKenna. Finn, my mom."

Finn took my mother's hand and kissed the back of it. He seemed a bit shy, and I found it endearing.

"Finn, I'm so thrilled to meet you. My daughter finally found a great man, and I must say, she has excellent taste. Hug me, you dear, sweet young man." He seemed relieved and gave her a warm embrace.

Then she turned toward Aaron. Her face looked surprised, but she still kept her smile in place.

"Mom, this is Aaron, our very good friend we wanted you to meet. Aaron, my mother, Faye Patrick."

"I'm so pleased to meet you, ma'am," Aaron uttered.

She still had an odd yet friendly look but gave him a big smile and a hug. "I'm delighted to meet you, Aaron. Welcome to my home."

I told Mom I had another little friend I wanted her to meet. Going to the car's back seat, I pulled out Asher's carrier, and we went into the house. She loved Asher immediately. When I took him out of the crate and passed him to Mom, he rubbed his nose on her cheek. Then he went around the house to investigate every nook and cranny.

We visited for a while, and Mom showed everyone to their rooms to unpack and get comfortable. I noticed she put Finn in the basement, and I smiled in response. She fretted that he and I may sleep together under her roof, and she would not allow it. I'd tell her later that God would not permit it either, so there wasn't any need for her concern.

Aaron was also in the basement next to Finn's room. They were both happy with their accommodations and unpacked.

Jonas and I were back in our old bedrooms, and it felt good to have everything still the same. Jonas commented on seeing his old high school sports trophies and that he'd forgotten about them.

Mom fixed us an old-fashioned pot roast dinner with all the trimmings; she even baked some apple pies. I loved this dessert with the crumbly crust and brown sugar. Everyone filled themselves until they felt about to burst, and we all helped clean up.

I finally saw Asher strutting into the kitchen with Mom's cat, Peanut, on his tail. They seemed to have made friends, which included the dog, Sadie. I fed Asher some of Mom's leftover roast beef, and he was ecstatic. We laughed at him because he cried in his unusual squeak of a meow and lifted his paws to Mom to be held. He wanted more roast beef—the little con man.

We sat down in the living room and chatted for quite some time. Aaron walked around during our banter, carefully examining the family photographs, which gave him a whimsical expression. Aaron talked as much as the rest of us, and I was thrilled he felt at home. I snuck a peek at Jonas, then Finn, and they gave me an "it's working" look.

The sun was setting, and I took Finn outside for a walk around the farm. I guided him through the old barns and around the rest of the property. We finally sat on a wrought-iron bench under an enormous maple tree in front of the house and watched the sun go down. Finn wrapped his arm around me, and I rested my head on his shoulder. Inhaling Finn's intoxicating, clean scent, I snuggled against his muscular body.

The night was sultry, and a gentle cool breeze smelled of green grass and pine. I peered at Finn, and I'd never seen him this relaxed and at ease. Pure contentment filled his expression as he gazed at his surroundings, then at me.

Smiling back at him, I said, "I love it here, Finn, and I see you do too. That's why I also adored the cottage. Both places gave me almost the same sense of peace, like when I talked with Jesus in the garden."

He smiled warmly and said, "My Nana had a place similar to this. It brings back the few wonderful memories I had as a child. Thanks for inviting me here, sweetheart. Your mother is something special, too. She loves everyone, and they love her right back. I'll never forget this, Mara. Never," he said, then gave me a long, lingering kiss.

Sitting back, Finn moved me away from him. "Your mum would have my hide if she knew what I was thinking right now. Abstinence is difficult, that's for sure. In my previous life, if I wanted a woman, I didn't have a problem finding one that was willing. I was no saint, Mara. But now, it's all so different. I'm truly in love for the first time, and the wait is hard but so worth it, love."

He kissed me again, and we sat there until after dark and watched the fireflies doing their mating dance as a three-quarter moon rose over the starry sky. We listened to the summer's night music of frogs, crickets, and katydids. It was getting late, and we knew it was time for us to turn in. This was a night neither one of us would ever forget.

CHAPTER 24

The next morning, I couldn't wait to start the day. It was a little after seven, and my kitten slept soundly on the pillow next to my head. He must be exhausted after the previous day's activities. I reached over and scratched him behind the ears, and he purred. "Good morning, baby. I trust you slept well." He gave me a wink, then fell back asleep.

I said my morning prayers, climbed out of bed, grabbed a pair of shorts and a T-shirt, and walked to the bathroom for a quick shower. When I returned to my room, Asher was nowhere to be seen. I heard some noise in the kitchen, and Finn was already up, feeding Asher his breakfast.

"Good morning, love," Finn said, and pulled me in his arms, bent me backward, and gave me a passionate good morning kiss. He'd obviously already showered and shaved, looking and smelling fabulous.

"Oh my, that was very nice indeed."

"Ahem." It was Aaron, who had just come up the stairs from the basement, his hair tousled, and his face unshaven.

Finn released me, but not before he gave me another quick smooch.

"Good morning, Aaron. I trust you slept well," Finn said in greeting.

"I did actually, thanks. I slept like the dead." He grabbed a doughnut from a plate.

"I think your Mom and Jonas are still asleep. Can I take a quick shower?" Aaron asked.

"Sure, go ahead," I replied.

Aaron headed back downstairs, and I giggled as I picked up Asher's empty food dish.

"What are you chuckling about?" Finn asked.

"There probably won't be any hot water left for Aaron. But he'll find out soon enough. This is an older house, and it takes a good half hour for the water to heat again." I snickered again at my confession.

"Why, you conniving, frisky woman. I didn't know you had it in you. I like it!" Finn laughed too.

As Aaron showered, we descended the stairs and listened outside the bathroom door. He did fine for a few minutes, but we heard a shriek.

"Bingo!" I declared, and we ran up the basement stairs in hysterical laughter like a couple of bratty children.

"I'll apologize when he comes back to the kitchen. But I couldn't help myself," I said with a silly grin.

I took the initiative in making bacon and eggs for breakfast, and Finn manned the toaster. He also set the table and breakfast was soon ready. Mom emerged from her room with Sadie, and Jonas and Aaron bounded up the stairs.

The look on Aaron's face was priceless, and I giggled again. I walked over to him and whispered in his ear. "Hey Aaron, was your shower refreshing?" I laughed, then said, "Sorry, bub, but I couldn't help myself. You've just been initiated into the family by a stupid prank." I ruffled his perfectly groomed hair.

Aaron stuck out his tongue, called me a gruesome name, then smiled with a devilish grin. "Don't worry, Miss Trouble-in-the-Keester; payback is headed your way. Of course, you'll never see it coming."

"We'll see, butt-nugget," I replied with a sneer.

Everyone sat down for breakfast; we held hands and thanked God for our food and bringing us together. The meal remained casual and everyone spoke at once—just like a typical family get-together.

After we finished the dishes, Jonas, Finn, and I knew we'd have to talk to Mom alone about Aaron. I privately asked Aaron to make himself scarce and take a walk outside. It was a lovely morning, and he said he'd be back in half an hour.

I asked Mom if we could talk, and she agreed, and we sat in the living room. Sitting beside Mom, I held her hand, hoping the contact would help when we broke the news.

"Mom...oh, how do I start this...." I said, talking to myself. I inhaled a large breath and started again. "Okay. Mom, when you and Dad first got married, were you pregnant with a child, and the baby was stillborn?"

She stared at me in shock, then said, "Well, yes, actually. It was a few years before Jonas was born." Tears swam in her eyes and I hated to put her through this. "I'm sorry we never told either of you. At first, you were both too young to understand, and we were still grieving our loss. You never get over losing a child—never. Then, when you got a little older, your father and I discussed it, but we decided there wasn't any point in telling you. Both of you were teenagers and had enough angst with your schooling and puberty. We decided to wait until you became adults, but we never got around to telling you. Then, your father died, and I didn't see any reason to tell you about a brother you'd never know or get to meet. We should have told you, and I know that now, but time flew quickly by, and we never got around to it. I'm so sorry."

Tears glided down her cheeks, so I gave her a tissue and held her close. Jonas sat on her other side and rubbed her back.

"It's okay, Mom. We understand and you've nothing to apologize for," Jonas murmured.

"He's right, Mom. We love you, and you and Dad did nothing wrong," I agreed. "But, we have some vital information that you need to hear. Finn, would you mind?"

Finn nodded and told the story he'd previously relayed to my brothers and me—about the nurse who worked in the delivery ward that day and all that transpired thereafter.

When Finn finished the story, Mom stood and paced the room. She suddenly stopped and gaped at us incredulously.

"My baby lived? My first-born son survived, and your dad and I never knew? Is he okay? Does he know about us? How do we find him? Oh, my Lord in heaven—I have so many questions, I don't know where to start."

She sat down heavily on the sofa, staring off into space. Many emotions moved across her face: pain, sorrow, confusion, regret, and contemplation.

I gave her time to process the startling information; her face paled, and she turned to look at us, simply staring with unbelieving eyes. She was at a complete loss and didn't know what to say.

"Mom, we've found him, or should we say, God brought him to us through this plan of His for the Chosen Ones. The Lord selected him too, and he returned exactly like we did. He's young again as well," I tried to explain.

I continued, trying to help her understand, "Mom, we've met him and he's an amazing man. He's been through a lot, as Finn has said, but he's wonderful, and we love him already." Finn had quietly stepped outside and brought Aaron inside the front door.

I looked up and said quietly, "Mom, meet your son, Aaron."

Finn brought Aaron into the room, and Mom rose to her feet, slowly moving toward her firstborn child. She stood there, staring in disbelief. "You're my son? My baby boy? I knew you looked so familiar, but I surmised it was merely a delusion of an old woman. At least, that's what I kept telling myself after I met you yesterday. Aaron, you're the spitting image of your father; it's uncanny. Please, may I hug you?"

Aaron's eyes filled with tears and he gave Mom a warm and loving embrace. Mom silently cried, and Aaron couldn't contain his tears either. She kept hugging him, unwilling to let him out of her arms. Her silent tears turned into sobs, and Aaron continued to hold her close, giving her his love, support, and most of all, an outlet for her to release her grief, regret, and pain.

After Mom's crying subsided, she and Aaron sat down together. She dried her face and blew her nose using several tissues, but she grabbed Aaron's hand again, probably in fear he may vanish into thin air. Even Aaron had a difficult time stemming the flow of his own tears.

Several minutes later, Mom asked me to retrieve two family picture albums. She showed us a photo of my dad when he was Aaron's age, and they could have been twins. Aaron stared at the image in amazement. He asked if he could look at all the pictures, and they spent over two hours talking and getting to know one another.

We left them alone and walked outside, taking Sadie along. She chased a chipmunk up a tree and danced around the trunk for several minutes until she grew bored with the game.

I still sniffled from the emotional scene between Mom and Aaron, and Jonas and Finn were emotional too.

"That reunion was incredible," Finn mumbled. "I must say, we approached it very well."

"I'm so happy for both of them," Jonas said, and I agreed wholeheartedly.

We returned half an hour later, and they were still conversing deeply. Mom looked at us and said, "I want to get something I'd like you all to see. I'll be right back." She went to her bedroom and returned a few minutes later with a thin, light blue photo album. She sat down among us and opened to the first page. The name Aaron Michael Patrick was written at the top, along with a photo of a headstone inscribed, "Here lies Baby Aaron Michael Patrick." Attached to the page of the photo album was a pair of little yellow knitted booties.

"I...don't understand," Aaron stammered. "Why do I have the same name? Did she know what you named your son, or should I say, me?"

"I recall talking to the poor dead baby in my arms. We'd named you months before, Aaron if it was a boy, and Vivian if it was a girl. I know I called the baby Aaron several times, so she must have kept the name." They both smiled and were happy that he'd been allowed to keep the name of Aaron by the mother who'd stolen him away.

They turned the page, and a small book was inserted inside called *Charlotte's Web*. Mom added, "Your father and I read this book to you repeatedly the entire time I was pregnant with you."

I gasped, and we looked at each other in awe. "Aaron, you said you remembered that name from somewhere in your early childhood. That's why you named your bald eagle Charlotte. Could it be possible?" I asked incredulously.

"Anything is possible, Mara." Finn gave me a big smile, and everyone also grinned.

We laughed and began talking all at once again. We spent the rest of the day together, sharing stories, taking photos, and making new memories, especially for Aaron. He and Mom went for a long walk together, arm in arm around the property. They spent a lot of time talking, learning about each other's lives, and asking each other questions. It was a beautiful sight and one that neither of them would forget.

That afternoon, we played touch football in the backyard, and Mom watched and giggled at our antics. The guys were far too competitive for me, and it went beyond "touch." I bowed out and said it was all theirs, and joined Mom in a lawn chair in the shade and enjoyed a tall glass of lemonade. This gave her and me some alone time, and I said how much Aaron fit right in with the family. Mom commented she already loved him dearly, and he was so much like Jonas and me, it was uncanny. She added the fact that since he was the spitting image of his father—it was the clincher that gave no doubt he was her son.

She asked about my relationship with Finn and how it was going. I became teary-eyed and said I loved him so much, it hurt. I feared losing him because I wasn't good enough for him.

Mom took me into her arms and said, "Oh, honey, you really have no clue, do you? A mother knows, and I can tell you, that Finn is head-over-heels in love with you. And you, my precious daughter, are too good for any man, but if I had to choose, I'd say Finn is near the top of being good enough. But then, I *am* your mother, and I'm very partial when it comes to my lovely daughter."

"Thanks, Mom. I needed to hear that." She gave me another hug, and I kissed her cheek.

I had misgivings about allowing Asher outside and was leery of him running off, so I tried communicating with him again. I still could see only flashing disjointed images in his mind, but I had a brief glimpse of his mental attention and quickly tried to explain that he must stay near us when he's outdoors. It was dangerous for him to go anywhere on his own, so he always needed to remain with us. I hoped he understood, and I began to see that since he was so young, he had a brief attention span and was still learning. That's why I had a hard time connecting with him mentally. When I took Asher outside, he did as I asked. He stayed near us and loved playing in the strange new green grass and chasing butterflies and grasshoppers.

The guys hollered again, claiming someone was cheating, and they all laughed. I don't know how they played with just three of them, but they worked it out. It was Finn against the brothers. Finn held his own for a while, but in the end, the brothers won, hooting and hollering in triumph.

Finn came over and pulled me into a big hug, and I wrinkled my nose and told him he needed a shower. "It's called the smell of hard work, love." He kissed me and grabbed some lemonade.

There were three incredible days at Mom's home; we had superb meals and many conversations. We were one great, happy family.

On our last night, we had a late afternoon dinner of grilled hamburgers and hot dogs with all the fixings as we sat at a large umbrella table. After dinner, the night was falling, and Finn and my brothers had strung beautiful lights around us. We made cocktails and sat under the stars in the peaceful, warm evening. Finn acted jittery, and I worried something may be wrong. We continued the banter, and then it became uncomfortably quiet. Everyone stared at Finn, then he cleared his throat and stood up in front of me. I ogled him with suspicion.

"Mara, I want you to know how much I love you, and I can't imagine my world, or any world, without you, and I want us to spend the rest of our lives together." He reached into his pocket and pulled out a small velvet box. "I pray, with all my heart, that you'll take this ring, and when the time is right, you'll marry me. Please say 'yes.' " He knelt, opened the box, and revealed a sparkling platinum diamond engagement ring. The center stone was cut to look like sparks were shooting off the diamond. There were several smaller gems snuggled around the larger one and more along the band. It was the most beautiful diamond ring I'd ever seen.

My eyes widened and my mouth dropped open, and I stared between Finn's handsome face and the exquisite ring.

"Mara, say something. Don't leave the poor man hanging!" Jonas barked.

"I...Finn, I..." I placed my hand over my mouth, and tears sprang into my eyes. I stared at Mom with a stunned expression.

"Mara, sweetheart, the man's been on pins and needles, waiting for the right time to ask you. Now answer the poor guy," Mom ordered.

"Yes! Yes! Yes!" I yelled and leaped on him. He was knocked on his back, with me on top of him. Giving him a huge kiss, I rained more kisses across his handsome face.

Everyone yelled in happiness, and Finn and I struggled to get up off the ground. Sadie jumped up and down, wondering what was so exciting. Finn pulled the beautiful ring from the box and slid it on my finger. It fit perfectly and gleamed under the string of lights around our chairs. I kissed him again and held on as he tightened his hold.

"Hey, congratulations, my man! Welcome to our family," Jonas cheered, and Aaron congratulated him too.

Mom came over, hugged us both, and welcomed Finn to our brood. Finn's eyes brimmed with tears as she embraced him. It was evident by the look on his face that my answer filled him with joy and he was also gaining a loving family.

"Mara, I wish we could marry immediately, but we have set rules, and I was one of the rule makers. The regulation is that no married couples can go on missions together. It never works and should never be done. We already broke one major one in allowing immediate family members to go on the same mission, but we knew the three of you being together is part of God's ultimate plan. People *do* know we're dating, but that's all we want them to know. I knew you understood me on the last mission and how I kept you at a distance. So we must keep the engagement a secret for now and marry when God says it's time. If your brothers even hint at our relationship, I'll have their heads." Finn glared menacingly at Aaron and Jonas.

My two brothers both put their hands up in surrender, and Jonas made a sign of locking his mouth and throwing away the key.

"I understood when you kept me at a distance on the mission, Finn, and I agree. You can count on me to behave myself in public, and I won't wear the ring until we officially announce the engagement. Finn, you're the love of my life, and I can't believe you fell in love with me too. God gave me such a blessing when he brought us together." I took his face between my hands and kissed him sweetly. I pulled back and stared into his eyes, communicating my understanding and agreement.

"Let's leave the lovebirds alone for a bit, shall we?" Mom said. They went into the house to give us privacy.

Holding hands, we walked to the front and sat on our favorite bench.

Our only light to guide us was the full moon overhead. We sat in each other's arms, enjoying the quiet evening and watching the stars and fireflies, savoring the warm, pine-scented summer's night breeze.

As we sat under the stars, a vision rudely interrupted my peaceful contentment. I gasped as I witnessed something terrifyingly dark, dank, and evil. Some type of entity was attempting to climb out of a fiery hole in the ground, and I clutched Finn's arm in desperation.

"What is it, Mara?" Finn squeezed my hand and the vision vanished, but the remnants of terror remained within me.

"I saw…something dark and evil coming through some sort of gateway or portal. Oh, Finn, it was horrible, and the only thing that came to mind during the vision was that it had to be stopped. And the smell of it was so atrocious." I wrinkled my nose in disgust as the remnants of the odor still lingered within my nostrils. Luckily it quickly dissipated, and I could again smell the sweet scents of the night air.

Finn stared at me in worry and pulled me close. "You don't know who it was or when it happened?"

"No. But it's terrible…and I mean dangerous to everyone on Earth as well as the planet. I believe that it's supposed to happen in the near future. I wish I knew more." I bit my lip, and Finn hugged me again.

"Love, we will deal with it when and if it comes to fruition," he kissed my temple.

I snuggled close to his warmth and thought about what this vision could mean and what it had to do with me.

Did God want me to stop this horrible thing, and if so, how was I supposed to accomplish this monumental task? What a pickle!

CHAPTER 25

*W*e said our tearful goodbyes and gave Mom several hugs. I told everyone I'd forgotten something in the house, ran back in, and put an envelope on the counter that said "Mom" on the outside. The least I could do was give her some money to help her with the household finances. I had to leave it discreetly because she'd refuse it if I tried to hand it to her. It was such a blessing that I could now afford to help her out for a change. Returning outside, I hugged and kissed her, then climbed into the car.

She said she'd continue to pray for us and that God would keep us under His loving care. Tears were in her eyes; it frightened her that her children may die in one of those dangerous missions, but she also knew we had no choice. It was God's will. As she hugged Aaron, she told him to call her as often as he wished. She's just found him and didn't want to lose her firstborn again.

As we traveled down the driveway, Finn and Aaron kept looking back with melancholy, and it made me smile. I was elated that they felt they also had a home here.

On the return flight, I continued glancing at my beautiful diamond ring, and I'd have to take it off before we landed. Finn saw me gazing at it, clasped my hand, and kissed it in understanding. "It won't be long before you can wear it permanently, love."

"I know. I want to look at it on my hand, so I have a picture of it in my mind. Finn, I love you so much and I love the ring. You selected the perfect one. But I'd better take it off now—it's such a shame." I pulled the jewelry box from my carry-on luggage, laid the ring in the lovely velvet bed, and returned it safely to my bag. I kissed him, rested my head on his shoulder, and dozed.

I woke up when Finn's phone vibrated. He answered it, and the joy and contentment disappeared. "I see....Aye, Edison, we'll meet as soon as possible. I'll bring the favored three with me....I agree; they need to meet her. Did you find an ancient language specialist? I see....You're right, maybe she can help us. What about the DNA sequencing search and results? Okay, we'll see you then."

He put his phone away and turned to the three of us. "The demons are ramping up their activities around the globe. We'll meet in Room A on the secure floor at one o'clock, and I need you all there."

I asked Finn if it was bad. "Bad enough, love. Bad enough," was all he said.

Precisely at one, I arrived at the meeting room. Finn, Jonas, Aaron, and Edison were already there, and we settled into our seats.

"Okay, let's get started," Finn stated. "Would you like to give us an update, Edison?"

He nodded and turned on the large monitor and played a recording. "This is the news regarding the impact of the last mission." Edison turned up the volume, and we listened to the news item.

"In Venezuela today, citizens reported what they assumed was a minor earthquake. However, upon further investigation, the Venezuelan government stated a large explosion caused the vibration, reaching as far as five miles in all directions from ground zero. Here is the video of the location where it took place. At this time, it's unknown as to what or who is responsible for this devastation. The area is still burning with some type of blue fog, and our scientists have never seen any substance that would cause this phenomenon. We'll keep you advised with any new information as it becomes available."

We viewed the enormous hole and the blue fog was dissipating. There wasn't any evidence of bodies or signs there'd been a compound within the location. It looked like a meteor crater with a haze of blue floating over the area.

Edison turned off the video and said, "Our team of specialists did well blocking the satellite footage of our mission, and there wasn't a scrap of evidence that we were ever there. Our team did an excellent job, my friends." We sighed in relief that there weren't any repercussions from our military operation.

Finn stood and commented, "Mara, Jonas, Aaron, in a few minutes, I'll introduce you to someone vital to our cause. She's our eyes, ears, and voice in communicating between our great Father in Heaven and His Chosen.

"Her name is Kaiko, and she was born in Japan and sold into slavery as a baby to a very nasty, evil man. The deviant abused, raped, and tortured her until he killed her at the onset of puberty when she turned eleven. God returned her to her body at the same age, but that was three years ago. She's now fourteen. The Lord sent her back as a liaison if you will, and Archangel Gabriel speaks to her, and sometimes through her, to us. Through her communication, we receive vital information on how to kill myrmidons, the making of our weapons and ammunition, and other instructions the Lord feels we should know."

The three of us sat at the table in shock and didn't know what to say. I finally spoke up and said, "Finn, that's awful. Does she remember everything that monster did to her?"

"Thanks to the Lord above, no. She has no actual memory of that time, but she *does* know this man abused her; she's aware of who he is and has forgiven him. We try to provide her with the best life we can, and she now has an amazing family within this facility who takes excellent care of her. She's a sweet, kind, and forgiving young lady, and I know you'll love her as much as we do," Finn stated.

"Does she always communicate with St. Gabriel, or just when he has information to provide?" Jonas asked Finn.

"He only speaks to her when she's needed. She keeps a regular, normal life of a fourteen-year-old—as much as possible, that is," Finn said.

"Why are you introducing her to us now? Has something changed?" Aaron inquired.

"Actually, she wanted to meet you. Apparently, she has some information that you now need to know. She also said you weren't ready for it before, but now the time is right," Finn replied. "Shall we bring her in?"

We replied "Yes" simultaneously. Finn nodded to Edison, and he opened the door and ushered Kaiko into the room.

She was a stunning child: petite and graceful, and her features were delicate and blissful. She had short, beautiful jet-black hair and seemed happy and at peace. Finn gave her a chair and she sat directly in front of the three of us.

Finn made the introductions, "Kaiko, I'd like you to meet Mara, Aaron, and Jonas. My friends, this is Kaiko."

"I'm so very pleased to meet you," she replied in a sweet and gentle voice.

We said we were so happy to meet her too.

"I know you're wondering why Finn brought you to meet me. I have a couple of things to tell you, but I'm sure more will be forthcoming," she said kindly.

"The marks on your arms were given to you by our Lord and Savior, Jesus Christ, when He laid his hand on you in the garden in Heaven. This mark represents the Holy Trinity; the Father, Son, and the Holy Spirit." She stood, walked around the table, and moved closer to Aaron. "May I?" she asked him. He nodded, and she had him stand and roll up his shirt sleeve.

"This symbol in the left lobe means the lamb or the sacrificed one; on the right lobe is the dove or spirit of God. The one at the top represents our Father. Now the center one symbolizes the center of all, God, the Alpha, and Omega. The language is ancient and one that came long before Adam and Eve and is only understood by the Holy Trinity, the angels, and those God has selected to understand it. I know the three of you already knew the center represented God, didn't you?" We nodded in agreement.

She thanked Aaron and returned to her seat. She then said, "The three of you are the most powerful and gifted of all the Chosen. When you enter into battle against powerful evil ones, you'll feel a force come over you: it may be the Father, Son, or Spirit, but it may also be any powerful angel from Heaven, including any archangel. The highest angels, such as seraphim and cherubim, do not engage in earthly affairs since they serve only God and his throne, but if God wills it, they may also assist you. Only He knows who He's selected to aid you in a specific battle.

"Now, to the task at hand, you must be told what and who you are to battle in the very near future," Kaiko continued. "A dominant demon came to the earth decades ago. He's been biding his time and has been placing his legions in many powerful positions around the globe, not only within governments, but inside other influential positions too: within our military regimes, high-ranking professions within pharmaceutical companies, major banking institutions, leaders within our churches, and yes, even the Vatican. It's sad but true. They are many indeed, and the power the demon has given them is strong but never as mighty as his own. They can all be destroyed, but only by the Chosen and by the weapons God has instructed the monks to fabricate.

"As I said a few moments ago, you must take out as many of his closest legions as possible before you attempt to slay this dominant demon. His loyal legions' evil exploits feed his power and also the souls they've possessed. This will weaken him enough for you to destroy him. Sending him back to Hell will be a significant undertaking, and it'll require many Chosen to assist you in this task.

"I know you're wondering what this powerful demon wants. The more souls he corrupts, the more power he collects; thus, the gates of Hell are opening, allowing all evil to step onto the Earth. They will massacre God's loyal children, leaving Hell to reign on this planet. This is why you're called the Gatekeepers. Your goal is to seal the portal closed and any others who may try to open one in the future. God will tell you how this must be done when the time is right.

"There will be a large summit or meeting of this demon's most loyal subjects. It'll take place somewhere on the west side of this country very soon. This massive event would be the best opportunity for the Chosen to eliminate many of his followers in one fell swoop. This would cause a crippling blow to this major demon and would lay the foundation for taking him down, as well as closing the portal. Many young, innocent lives may be at stake at that time, which is another task the Chosen must address.

"I'm also to remind all of you to remain in good standing with our Lord. Stay chaste, loving, and committed to Him and His commandments. If you fall, be sure to quickly atone and ask for forgiveness. He knows you're human and have cravings of the flesh, but hold firm and steady and do as He asks. Substantial rewards will await you in Heaven.

"I'm at your disposal if you require any clarification or if you seek moral or angelic counsel. Thank you for meeting with me; I look forward to seeing you again. God is with you in your war and will remain at your side no matter how difficult it may become." She concluded her counsel, gave us a polite nod, and walked from the room.

We sat quietly for a few minutes, feeling stunned and thinking about everything she had said.

"Wow, that was the strangest thing I've ever experienced. Wonderful, but strange," Jonas said.

"I agree with you, Jonas. There was a divine electric energy coming off that precious girl," I replied.

"I can't get over the fact that we have the Holy Trinity stamped on our bodies, and I feel a bit unworthy. You know what I mean?" Aaron asked incredulously.

We nodded and then looked at Finn and Edison.

"You've known about this amazing little girl and never said a word to any of the Chosen?" Aaron asked gently.

"We can only tell those she requests. We call her our Prophet since we didn't know what other title to give her," Finn admitted. "And yes, she's awe-inspiring."

Edison said, "Kaiko told us where we're to begin, and I must tell you what our next mission will be and why it's critical. Since the COVID-19 disaster, the antichrist, I guess we'll call him, has been aggressively spreading his evil across the world faster than the Chosen can manage. We've been lucky our right to bear arms is still in place in forty-two states, but many more state legislatures are beginning to cave under Satan's anarchy. But the worst thing is that California's government recently introduced a bill to take away everyone's religious freedom; their strategy is to make the people despair, live without hope, and add the fear of imprisonment for worshiping God. The antichrist's favorite pastime is hating God and destroying the faithful and their churches. This new anti-religion bill, if passed, will spread like wildfire from state to state. It'll be illegal to practice any God-loving religion, and the punishment for disobeying this law will be severe, anywhere from two years in prison to a lifetime sentence. According to our sources, their legislature will pass this heinous bill when it's voted on in twelve weeks. Since his legions have infiltrated almost every state government, this could spread quickly, and our goal is to stop them."

Finn added, "We're not the only Chosen Ones having to address the anti-religious regime. All of our other bases have reported the same laws attempting to be enacted in their countries. They're also gathering their teams to make advanced strikes on their demon-controlled governments. We're in constant contact with them, and we'll coordinate our efforts with each other.

"All that being said," Finn continued, "This team's next goal is taking out the demons in the California hierarchy. We must figure out where and when this large event will occur."

Edison spoke again, "Finn, I've been busy researching all large forums, summits, meetings, and events on the west coast, and I think I may have found the location. There's a grand gala held every year for the California Legislature, judges, lawyers, bureaucrats, and the like—and it takes place in nine weeks. This event is three weeks before their legislature will vote on the anti-religion bill. The location is the Hotel Demente in California, which is generally open only once a year for this gala. According to my trusted sources, this event was the main stage for the exchange of inside information, drug deals, white slave trade negotiations—you name it. However, this year a large auction will take place at the hotel. It's very hush-hush, and at this time, I'm unable to obtain any additional intel on this private, highly illegal sale. I'll keep digging and let you know if I get any logistics on this auction."

Edison took a deep breath and continued, "But right now, we focus on identifying the guests. Now, if we can finagle our way in, our three gifted Gatekeepers should be able to tell us who the innocents are and who are the ones with pitchforks and tails. This has to be what Kaiko warned us about."

Finn thought for a few moments and paced around the room. "That has to be it, Edison. Please continue your research and see if it pans out, then we can begin our plans. If this is the correct event, and I believe it is, we'd need excellent covers and fake I.D.s. I think my friend Jorge could help with that score. Our exit plans would have to be in place too. We'd also need discreet communication devices and someone nearby to record our identifications. We know they'll have everyone scanned for weapons and devices, so we'd have to find a way to get past their scanners."

Finn looked at the three of us and said, "All of you would have to learn and memorize every person attending this gala. You'd have to be able to properly identify who is evil and who isn't, which could take some time. Could the three of you distinguish friend from foe and those who may be on the precipice of evil, as well?"

My brothers and I nodded, and I replied, "Definitely. Their stench is unmistakable. We can even feel if one is more powerful than another."

Edison turned to the three of us. "Once I receive the information, I'll send you the dossiers on the gala attendees. Then I'll have it downloaded to your apartment computers, and you'll have to memorize each face and the corresponding name. If you have questions, ask us. I don't envy you, my friends."

"Excellent," Finn said. "We need to see if the logistics of this plan will work. In the meantime, do you have questions or something you'd like to discuss?"

"I do have one thing to ask both of you," I answered as I glanced at Edison and Finn. "I strongly sense that Aaron and I will need more extensive sniper training. Why? I've no clue. But the feeling is strong. Is this doable?"

Finn replied. "It's definitely doable. Edison, sniper training is your expertise. I'll leave it to you to complete their training."

Edison nodded, then said, "Tomorrow is Sunday, so we'll start the following day. But I'll need to take them offsite. They'll need longer distance practice, so I'll take them to the usual area across the mountain."

"Sounds good. Make it so, my friend," Finn replied with a wink.

Edison looked at my brothers and me and stated, "Jonas, I'd like you to accompany us as a refresher course. The three of you will need to meet me at the motor pool at seven-thirty in the morning. Wear your camo gear, and I'll have the rifles already at the range. I'll see the three of you then."

The meeting was over, and when everyone started leaving the room, Finn touched my arm, detaining me. Once the remainder of the team left, he turned to me from his chair and said, "I hope you're attending Mass with me tomorrow."

"Of course, Finn, I'd love to. Do you have time for us to spend the day together after Mass?"

"Try to stop me." He leaned over to give me a long kiss. "I think this waiting is going to kill me, Mara." He leaned back in his chair and ran his hand through his hair in frustration.

"It won't be much longer, Finn. We can do this."

As we departed the room, he turned to me with a hopeful look on his handsome face. "I'm going to my office to finish up some paperwork. How about dinner tonight?"

I nodded, and he said he'd pick me up at my place around six. We kissed each other again, and I left for my apartment.

As I unlocked my door, Asher squeaked from the other side. I walked in, and he weaved his body around my legs, chirping and purring, then reached up to be held. "I missed you too, baby." He rubbed his head on my cheek.

Dropping my briefcase by the door, I saw a large, beautiful tropical ocean painting hanging on my wall. I stared at the gorgeous artwork, and my eyes filled with tears. The colors were vivid and breathtaking. The ocean's color was bright turquoise, and the sky was incredibly blue but had mixes of yellow, gold, and orange as the sun was setting on the horizon. There were three seabirds in the distance flying over the ocean on their way out to sea. A palm tree was placed along the right front edge containing a few coconuts, and a small area of sand grass was at the tree's base. There were two chairs with a couple of beach towels thrown over them by the water under a large, thatch-covered umbrella. The sand looked so realistic I could remember the feel of the soft grains beneath my feet. I peered closer, and two sets of bare footprints were imprinted in the sand. They began near the chairs, then ran parallel along the incoming gentle surf. One set was slightly smaller than the other.

"Finn..." I whispered. Sitting in my desk chair, I turned around to gaze at the painting. It looked so real, I thought I could feel the sun's warmth on my face as I stared at its beauty. Asher jumped in my lap and squeaked at me again, and I figured he was hungry.

As I walked toward the kitchen with the heavy cat in my arms, something in the bedroom caught my attention. On the bedside table, an object had been placed beside the lamp. It was a picture frame with a large photo of Bo, my favorite cat I had as a child. Looking around the room, I noticed several images beautifully mounted and framed on the wall beside my dresser. They were the ones I'd taken at the cottage, each of the lake, the woods, and the front and back of the cabin. Then I saw the spectacular photo of Spirit. He looked ethereal, his coat glimmered a startling white, and his eyes were the color of emeralds. The images were incredible. *My old phone had been destroyed, so how did Finn get them?*

Asher squirmed in my arms impatiently, so I told him I'd feed him immediately. We went to the kitchen, and I fed the demanding little man, and he was happily eating his kibble. Grabbing my phone, I called Finn but only received his voicemail, so I hung up.

"I guess I'll have to thank him tonight, right, Asher?" He looked back at me between bites of his food and squeaked a reply. Laughing, I gave him another pet and gathered my dirty laundry. "Finn, you're incredible and I don't know what I did to deserve you," I murmured aloud.

Later in the afternoon, I took extra time to prepare for my date with Finn and put on one of my new outfits. It was made of chiffon with an ankle-length skirt and matching sleeveless blouse in a gorgeous burgundy-colored floral print. Adding silver-colored high heels and delicate jewelry completed the outfit. I took extra time with my makeup and fluffed my hair to give my curls extra bounce.

Precisely at six, Finn arrived at my apartment and my heart jumped in anticipation. I opened the door and threw my arms around him, snuggling close to his warm, muscular body. I inhaled that intoxicating, sensual fragrance that was exclusively Finn.

"What's this, love?" He held me briefly while burying his face in my hair, then reluctantly stepped back. I gazed at him in his handsome dark suit, pale shirt, and dark tie and enjoyed staring at the attractive man I loved so much.

"Good Lord in heaven, sweetheart, you look even more stunning than usual." He admired me for a minute or two. I thanked him sweetly as I blushed from the compliment, then guided him into the apartment.

"Finn, I don't know how you did it, but I can't thank you enough. I love every one of them." I pulled him into the living room by his arm and led him to the front of the painting.

"Oh, that." He was contrite in his answer and smiled with pleasure.

"How did you find this? It's perfect and I love it so much. Then the photos—I don't know how you found them, but they're stunning too. How can I ever thank you, Finn?"

"I know an artist who specializes in seascapes and relayed to him exactly what you described to me. It took a couple of sketches to get it right, but you've seen the final result, my sweet. As for the photos, my talented staff in I.T. had them saved on our secure mainframe within this facility. When we destroy a cell phone, we usually delete everything from the phone's memory, including all the data and such in the cloud. But my team is ingenious and conniving. They aren't supposed to, but they've secretly kept copies of personal photos from our Chosen One's phones. I was angry at first but then relieved, and we recovered and printed these pictures. They downloaded the rest of them to your computer here in your apartment. I'm so glad you love them. By the way," he said as he walked closer to the painting. "Those footprints are from you and me."

I glided up to him, wrapped my arms around his strong, muscled body, and kissed him passionately. He moaned as he returned the kiss, then turned me toward the sofa and laid me down, with him closely following. He was now lying over me, kissing me again. Every thought left my mind, and I let myself enjoy these new, intense emotions. I sighed with happiness as he deepened the kiss. All I could think about was getting closer to him.

We sighed in satisfaction, then—*wham!* He was pulled off of me and thrown across the room, landing near the apartment door on his butt. I quickly sat up and stared openmouthed at Finn. He seemed a bit dazed as he sat on the floor against the door.

I got up and ran over to him, saying, "Oh my goodness, Finn, are you alright?" After helping him off the floor, he gingerly tested his limbs, making sure nothing was broken.

"I think so, just a bruised ego and bum." He chuckled, and I couldn't help myself either. We laughed so hard that we ended up sitting on the floor again, with tears streaming down our faces. "I'm lucky God didn't turn me into a eunuch." That comment started us laughing again. Asher came over and checked to assure himself we were both okay.

"I'm so sorry, Finn. You received the major brunt of the punishment, and I started it. It's really my fault."

"It's okay, love. I didn't do anything to slow it down and I'm the experienced one."

We apologized to the Lord, prayed He'd forgive us, and then made our way to dinner. It was an elegant restaurant, and Finn was a perfect gentleman. We still giggled occasionally, especially when Finn squirmed in his chair every so often to ease the pain in his backside. He said he was thankful it was a padded chair, or he wouldn't be able to sit for long. We both chuckled again as we savored the delicious cuisine.

Finn brought up the subject of the wedding and what I'd like as a venue, guests, and everything else that brides usually dream of for their special day. I told him I didn't want anything significant. As for guests, I wanted my mom, my brothers, and the friends we'd made here at the base. I'd be happy to keep it small and simple, and he agreed wholeheartedly.

After finishing our entrée, we topped the meal with a luscious strawberry cheesecake and another glass of wine. We discussed the honeymoon location, and I said I hadn't thought about it but would leave it up to him. I'd be happy if it was only the two of us and we had our privacy. He smiled with a gleam, and I could tell he'd already had the perfect place in mind.

When we returned to my apartment, I asked him to come in, but he politely declined. "I don't think that's a good idea. I need to soak in my tub and ease my painful burden." He rubbed his bruised behind. We laughed again, but I still gave him a gentle kiss and a warm hug.

"Sleep well, Finn, and enjoy the soak in the tub. I can't wait until we can share a bath." He gave me a huge smile and a wink, then headed down to his room with a little hitch in his gait.

CHAPTER 26

I was looking forward to Mass with Finn and couldn't wait to see the holy angels. It gave me strength and hope every time I saw them, and they reminded me that everything we were doing was worth all the sacrifices.

Finn arrived and we made our way to the worship floor. As we walked into the church, I spied Jonas, Poppy, and Aaron. I asked my brothers if I could speak with them for a moment. We left the church, talked for a few minutes, and returned. Finn and I sat in our usual seats on the left side of the pews, and Jonas and Poppy sat on the other. Aaron had moved back a couple of rows behind Jonas.

Finn looked at me questioningly, and I whispered, "Just wait; you'll see."

It was good to see Father Faraj back from vacation. He looked happy and well-rested, but then again, he always seemed to be good-natured and friendly. Finn sat close to me and held my hand through most of the Mass. When the consecration was about to start, I looked at Jonas and Aaron, and we nodded at each other.

"Finn," I whispered, "please take the hand of the parishioner on your side and ask them to take the next person's hand, and so on. Please, my love?"

He did as I requested, and Jonas and Aaron did the same.

Everyone in the church gave us a puzzled look, but they all participated. Father started the consecration and we heard gasps and several "oohs and ahhs" from the parishioners. Father glanced up to view the congregation. The entire parish gaped with awe in his direction, and many cried joyfully. He paused for a moment, stumbled a bit during his prayers, but continued.

After Mass, everyone talked loudly with elation about what they'd witnessed and the miracle of the angels. Father Faraj came back in and asked what was so exciting. Everyone gushed and gabbed at the same time again, and Father raised his hands to bring silence to the room.

Finn walked up to him and said, "Father, we have three of God's favored Chosen Ones who can see holy angels descend on each side of you during the consecration. When they hold everyone's hands, they can see the angels too. Everyone here witnessed the miracle today."

"The three of you can do that? You can see the holy angels beside me? Then share your sighting with others simply by holding their hands? My dear Lord in heaven, how can this be?" he asked us in his cultured Sudanese accent.

"We don't know, Father. But it has to be a gift from God and such a blessed one too," I said. "Father, may I speak with you somewhere in private, please?" He nodded, and I took Finn's hand, and Father guided us to the Sacristy for some privacy.

We sat down and I related the story of the first time I saw the angels. My account mesmerized him and he was beside himself with joy.

"Father, my concern is the angels didn't appear last week when we had the substitute priest. Is Father Ryan having some issues with his faith, maybe only going through the motions, so to speak?" I asked.

"I've known Father Ryan for many years. He's the one who encouraged me to become a priest when he came to South Sudan so many years ago. I was just a boy, but when he taught us about God and Christianity, the idea enthralled me. You know how destitute my country was and is, and this gave me hope for my people. He sponsored me so I could finish school, attend college, and train to become a priest. After being ordained, I returned to my country and stayed to help my people for several years. But when my health declined, I came to the U.S. to retire. That's when Finn found me and asked me to join this group. I was fascinated and immediately accepted the position.

"At that time, I asked Father Ryan to join me, but he no longer felt a connection to the faith. He didn't know what to do because being a priest was the only thing he'd ever known. But if he could see what you and the parishioners saw today, I believe it would renew his faith and bring him back to the Lord. Would you mind if I ask him to attend Mass next week, and you can take his hand so he can see the vision?" he asked in desperation.

"I'd love to." It gave me hope that if Father Ryan saw the angels, he'd be again filled with love for the Lord.

Father spoke again, saying, "I have another favor to ask of you and your brothers. After speaking with many other religious leaders on this base, they've shown great interest in what the three of you can do. Now that you tell me you can see the angels, I was thinking maybe you could visit each of their worship sites during their services to discover if you can also see angels there. And, if so, would you also share your visions with their devoted worshipers? I'm sure even the Jewish and Muslim leaders would love for you to attend their worship. Would you and your brothers be willing to do this?"

"I'd be happy to visit them during their worship services, and I'm sure my brothers would help too. We can't guarantee we'll see angels, but we're willing to try. Let us know if all of the religious leaders agree, then I'll speak with my brothers and let you know if they'll do it—though I'm sure they will."

"Thank you, my dear. I'd be most appreciative," Father said.

Father thanked us repeatedly and we said we'd see him the following Sunday. As we left the church, Jonas, Poppy, and Aaron waited for us and asked if we'd join them for lunch. We were happy to do so and made our way to the restaurants. When we entered the dining floor, we saw Billie with some friends and asked them to join us. They happily agreed.

We selected American cuisine and ordered burgers and fries. The food was delicious, and we spent over two hours talking and laughing. After our meal, Jonas said we had better let the restaurant have their table back. We chuckled at his comment, left the establishment, and decided to go bowling.

We split our teams and it was the boys against the girls. Finn cared little for bowling but was having a good time anyway. During one of my turns, I ended up with a seven-ten split. Jonas made several teasing comments that I could never take those two pins down. I merely turned my back on him, wiggled my butt as I approached to throw the ball, and took down the split, giving myself a spare. I swaggered back to him and ran my hands back and forth through his perfectly groomed hair until it stuck straight up in the air. Everyone laughed, including Jonas, as he tried unsuccessfully to return his hair to some semblance of order.

"Very funny, shrimp!" Jonas said in reprimand.

"Don't pick on your little sister, butthead. I can still kick your fanny," I retorted with a grin, then blew him a kiss. Billie and the other girls gave me fist bumps, and we hooted and hollered in triumph.

Finn laughed out loud and whispered in my ear as I sat down next to him, "That's my gorgeous, frisky woman." He then whispered something to me that made me blush.

"Shame on you, you dirty old man. But that does sound intriguing." I poked him in the ribs and he winked in return.

From then on, it was a game of war, and we had a great time. The girls lost, but we didn't care and just teased the boys, saying we let them win. We informed them that the male ego could never take losing to females.

After our two games of bowling, we said our goodbyes, and everyone went their separate ways.

Finn and I spent the rest of the day together, talking about what we wanted for our future, which included what our dream home would look like, the location of our house, and even children. It was good to know we had so much in common and had the same ideas of home and family. We agreed that once we were married, it was up to God when we'd have children. The Lord above would know when it was the proper time to raise a family.

He walked me to my room and kissed me, but I knew not to take it too far again. Finn didn't want to repeat the mistake of yesterday. I giggled at his comment, then told him I loved him and would hopefully see him within the next couple of days. He said he wasn't sure because Edison could be a hard taskmaster. I'd be tired after the training and would probably want to sleep. Agreeing he was probably right and then said I'd keep in touch to let him know how the sniper training progressed.

We kissed each other again and said goodnight. I closed the door, and a big grin was plastered on my face, then reality set in. Being in love was amazing, but would we live long enough to enjoy it? The tasks ahead of us seemed impossible, but we'd have to pray we'd live through this nasty war between good and evil. *Good usually won, right? But there was always the chance that any one of us might not survive.* It was a daunting and disheartening thought.

CHAPTER 27

My brothers and I were ready for our target practice to begin offsite. We met with Edison and Jasper at the motor pool, piled into a sturdy, all-terrain military vehicle, and drove over to the mountain. It took us an hour to drive a well-traveled, one-way road until we reached a clearing site where three sniper rifles were already set and waiting. They were aimed toward another mountain across the valley.

Edison said, "You've already had your trigonometry class and have all the formulas and charts you'll need to figure your angles. But remember, wind speed factors are learned by experience. You did well on the shorter distance target practice, but this is where you'll need to excel. The rifles are there, but they're not zeroed or ranged. Jasper and I will assist you until you know what you're doing. Let's get this show on the road."

I began setting up my rifle, and I needed to gauge the exact distance of my target across the mountain. Pulling out my rangefinder binoculars, I raised them to my eyes and assessed the distance. It took me several minutes, but I had the numbers I needed. I found the information required from my sniper's bible, then adjusted my rifle accordingly. Calling Edison, I said I was ready for my first shot. He glanced at me, did a double take, and looked at me again. Edison laughed boisterously, which caught the attention of everyone else.

"What?" I asked as I turned to gaze at my sniper group. They were all hooting and hollering, and I had no clue what was so amusing. I sat up and faced them again, and they laughed even harder.

"What's so funny, you hooligans?" I demanded, giggling now but unaware as to why.

"Your eyes...Mara," Jonas said, still laughing hysterically.

I touched my eyes and felt something greasy around them. Pulling a small military mirror from my range bag, I looked at my reflection.

"What the...?" There were dark black rings around each of my eyes. It made me look like a sickly raccoon who'd been drinking tequila all night long from a filthy garbage can.

"Okay, who did this?" I asked as I laughed with glee while trying to appear serious and accusatory. Even though I stared pointedly at Jonas and Aaron, they shrugged their heads in denial while they continued hooting with gales of guffaws. I wasn't convinced of their innocence.

"You dweebs. I'll get you for this. Just wait." I still giggled, then tried to remove the offending black grease from around my eyes. Sticking my tongue out at my two brothers, I resumed my spot at my rifle.

"Okay, everyone, the fun is over. We have to get back to work," Edison said, still snickering as he turned away from me.

Jasper worked with Aaron, and when Aaron laid on his belly and took his spot at his rifle, Jasper kicked at Aaron's feet. He told him to open his legs and rest his feet outward so they were flat to the ground and not to rest on his toes so his heels pointed up.

"Never give the enemy any more to see when you're in a sniper position, my man. Remember, you're a reptile and flat to the ground," Jasper said. Aaron smiled when Jasper flicked his tongue in and out while flapping his palms along his ears like a frilled lizard.

We worked for a few hours as we figured and re-figured our calculations. We did our best to hit the targets, which were only around one thousand yards away, straight across the mountain. Jonas did well because of his years of experience in the military, but Aaron and I had issues with accuracy.

We took a lunch break, and Aaron said, "I had no idea this would be so difficult. Mara, you and I did very well in our other target practices, but we can't get this right. What gives?"

"I think we're going at this all wrong," I commented to Aaron.

My team looked at me and started laughing again. Unfortunately, I couldn't remove all the black grease from around my eyes, so I still looked like the character from "Where's Waldo."

"Oh, stop!" I reprimanded but giggled again at my predicament.

I became serious and said, "We're trying to do this by ourselves, not using what God gave us. At least, that's how I feel about what I'm doing, or should I say, *not* doing. When I'm shooting, I feel like something is trying to push its way into me, trying to take over. Are you feeling it too?" I asked Aaron. He agreed he felt it as well but was also pushing it aside.

We finished lunch and returned to our weapons. "Okay, Aaron, let's wait and let the feeling take over, then make the shot," I instructed.

I went first, felt the warm rush, and took the shot.

"Direct hit!" Edison yelled. "Way to go, Mara. Now you try, Aaron."

Aaron also had direct hits in the center of the targets. We fired several more shots, and each one was perfect.

Edison seemed confused but said, "Now, move down the mountain. The next target is two-thousand yards."

We didn't have any issues hitting our objectives. Edison had us fire several more shots without a miss.

"Okay, that's enough for today. We can start again tomorrow at one-thousand yards," Edison ordered.

"Wait a minute, I want to try a longer distance target, Edison." As I looked through my high-powered binoculars, I pointed to one way down the mountain at a harrowing angle. "That one."

"Mara, I think you're getting too cocky. That target is thirty-two hundred yards, and the angle alone is impossible. None of us as seasoned snipers can make that shot," Edison said.

I just stared at him and waited.

"Okay, let's give it a try. Set yourself up, Mara," Edison replied, giving in with a sigh.

I set up my weapon and after several minutes, I calmly looked through the scope and waited. I found it amazing that, at first, I could only see a blurry spot which was the target, but it was crystal clear after I calmed down and let God take over. I inhaled deeply, made another adjustment, exhaled, then fired.

Edison looked through his binoculars and swore loudly, then apologized, "Oops, I mean, well done, Mara." He turned to me and stared, then looked to the heavens and said a few words to the Lord. "Jonas, Aaron, you two blokes might as well give it a go too."

My two brothers each hit their targets. It surprised Jonas because he'd never attempted a shot at this distance.

We packed up the guns and gear and returned to base. Edison and Jasper looked at us and scratched their heads in confusion. I finally confessed, "It was the man upstairs, not us doing the shooting."

After we returned to the garage, Edison pulled out his phone and told someone on the other end of the line that we'd returned to base and no longer needed satellite interference. My brothers and I said we'd help return the gear to the armory, but Edison replied they would handle it.

Edison advised us to take a soak in the hot tub because we'd probably be sore after laying on the ground all day. He wanted us back in the garage tomorrow morning for more shooting across the mountain.

We thanked them, and my brothers and I walked to the mission locker rooms on this floor to change out of our field gear. After we left our instructors down the hall, we glanced at each other and chuckled.

"Those poor guys, I feel so bad," Aaron began. "They worked hard to become excellent snipers, with their calculating, practicing, and putting notes in their shooter's bibles. Then we walk in and just start firing and hit every target, and over three-thousand yards, no less. I mean, I feel really bad."

"I know," I agreed. "But God gave us this gift because we're going to need it. It didn't hurt their feelings, they were simply surprised. Those two men are excellent shooters and will be needed too."

We arrived at the locker room doors, and Jonas said, "How about we meet by the swimming pool after changing our gear? We can return to our apartments, get our swimsuits and then enjoy a few hours at the pool. I'll bring us some pizzas and beer. I know I could use the hot tub. Edison was correct, my back does hurt. What do you two think?" Aaron and I agreed, and my brothers and I entered the locker rooms.

After sitting on the bench to unlace my boots, I heard a loud yell from the men's locker room. I hurried over and threw open the door. Bright orange ping pong balls were tumbling from Jonas's locker, and hundreds more cascaded from the ceiling above him, pelleting him relentlessly on the top of his head. Jonas stood there in shock while being assaulted by the raining projectiles. The *boing, boing, boing* echoed through the locker room as the balls continued to pummel Jonas and everything around him.

Aaron was still in the room, as well as Jasper and Chuck, and they laughed so hard they were doubled over in pain. I couldn't help myself and guffawed in complete abandon. I felt someone behind me, and it was Finn. He was about to ask what was happening, but then he saw all the balls still dumping on Jonas, which were now bouncing unchecked into the hallway. Finn entered the room, and he gibbered with glee, and finally, Jonas came out of his shock and joined in.

"Okay, who is the son-of-a-gun that did this?" Jonas finally asked as the laughter ebbed. He glared at Aaron, and Aaron shrugged his shoulders and shook his head. Jonas then looked pointedly at Jasper and Chuck, who were in complete denial.

"I *will* find out who did this, and they *will* pay dearly." Jonas stared accusingly at the three men but chuckled again.

I closed the door and left the men in private, as Chuck was only dressed in his underwear. Several balls were still bouncing down both directions of the hallway, and people were kicking them back and forth in playful fun.

Finn looked at me and laughed hysterically again. Once his chuckles receded, he asked, "What happened to you?"

"Ha, ha!" I replied sarcastically. "Someone's been playing practical jokes around here, and I believe something's afoot." I had to giggle again at the look on Finn's face. He seemed so happy and it was good to hear his laughter. I made a funny woodchuck face using my front teeth over my lower lip, crossed my eyes, and clicked my teeth. Finn chuckled in earnest again as I ambled away, mimicking a waddling duck. I kicked up my heels and entered the ladies' locker room. Finn still roared with laughter after I closed the door behind me.

After changing, I departed the room, and as I strolled by the men's locker room, I heard Finn say through the door, "Okay, gentlemen, you better clean this mess up before someone trips on one of these things, and that includes all the balls that are bouncing up and down the hallway."

Upon opening the door to my apartment, Asher had been waiting for me. I looked down at him, and in return, he hissed and pinned his ears. He raised himself on his hind legs and smacked my upper thighs with his massive paws like a well-seasoned boxer. *Whap, whap, whap!* The fur on his back and tail stood on end, which made him look like a hilarious cartoon caricature. My angry cat ran like a speeding bullet into my bedroom and hid under the bed.

Feeling baffled by his reaction, I finally remembered I still had the black rings around my eyes. Walking to the bed, I crooned Asher's name, told him it was me, and that it was safe for him to come out. I heard another low growl and a hiss, then he cautiously peeked from under the bed; he peered up at me and blinked several times. Asher scuttled out from his hiding place, and his fur returned to normal, except for the gigantic tail. He appeared embarrassed, then rubbed his body around my legs. I picked him up, told him I was sorry, and carried him to the kitchen to feed him his dinner, trying my best not to giggle.

Afterward, I went into the bathroom, viewed my reflection in the vanity mirror, and laughed again at my raccoon face. After repairing my makeup, I changed into jeans, a t-shirt, and sandals, then grabbed my already packed gym bag, plus bottled water. Locking the apartment door behind me, I strolled to the elevator and went to the gym floor.

As I was about to enter the women's locker room, I changed direction and moved to the door which led to the swimming pool area. I peered through the glass entry doors and saw only one person in the pool, swimming laps. The swimmer was the only person in the room.

As I was about to turn and walk back to the women's locker room door, I discovered the man swimming was Finn. Fascination took over, and I couldn't tear my gaze away as he swam from one end of the pool to the other. It was an enormous pool, but he kept swimming for four more laps. With smooth strokes, he turned toward the steps and climbed out of the water. *Oh, goodness gracious…*I'd never seen Finn without a shirt, much less in only a pair of swimming trunks. I felt like a voyeur, but I couldn't look away. Watching intently, I swallowed hard, and heat filled my cheeks. His physique was terrific; he was all muscle and had a fine sprinkling of hair down his forearms and legs. His chest and abs were magnificent, and I swallowed hard again as I watched him. I was jealous of the pool water that was running down his chest.

Stop! I told myself. *Get a grip.* He ran his hands through his thick hair to squeeze out the excess water, strode to a chair, picked up a towel, and dried off. Turning away, I leaned my back against the door. *Come on, Mara. You're a middle-aged woman, not a young, innocent schoolgirl.*

The elevator doors opened, and Jonas and Aaron stepped out and strolled toward me, carrying the beer and pizzas. They were already wearing their swimming trunks, t-shirts, and flip-flops.

"Uh...hey," I said, trying to cover my embarrassment. "How did you two clean up all the ping pong balls so fast?"

"Luckily, we had a lot of help from everyone in the hallway. You're not in your suit yet—are you going to join us in the pool?" Jonas asked, but he gave me a funny look.

"Yeah, sure. I just have to change. It'll only take a few minutes," I croaked as I walked back toward the women's locker room.

I changed, stowed my bag in a locker, and then returned to the hallway. After taking a deep breath, I entered the pool area. Finn still stood by the chair while he chatted with my brothers. Throwing my towel onto another seat, I greeted Finn by giving him a brief kiss, but he grabbed my hand and said, "Jonas, Aaron, you two go ahead and swim. I need to talk to your sister for a moment."

Jonas and Aaron yelled, ran, and jumped into the pool as water splashed everywhere. I looked at Finn, and he had a mischievous twinkle in his eyes. He pulled me close to his wet, well-muscled body and whispered, "Did you enjoy the view, love?" I stiffened slightly; he chuckled in his low timbre, then continued, "Aye, I saw you watching me. You also know how much I love being near you, Mara." He gave me a deep, loving kiss that made my knees weak. I thought I'd end up on my behind on the wet tiled floor.

He put me away from him, and I recognized love and mischief in his bright green eyes. Finn smiled, turned, strode towards the men's locker room, and started whistling a song and I couldn't place it. I swallowed hard when it came to me. It was "I Can't Get No Satisfaction" by the Rolling Stones. *The butt-head!*

I sat down hard into the chair that held my towel, waiting for my heart to stop racing.

"Hey, Mara, what's taking you so long?" Aaron yelled to me from the pool.

"Coming!" I bellowed, got up, walked shakily to the pool, and dove in. The cool temperature did little to ebb my heated skin, but I figured a few laps would burn off my excess frustration. *The rat*, I thought, and then smiled. How was I going to behave until we finally tied the knot? At least I knew that both Finn and I would suffer together. *That handsome, dirty rat!* The thought had me grinning from ear to ear.

CHAPTER 28

The sniper training lasted throughout the week, and our instructors, my brothers, and I felt we were ready for any long-distance shooting that may be required. We also spent many hours memorizing the gala photos and their corresponding names. Working together, we grilled each other and finally had them drilled into our memories.

At the end of the week, we assembled our entire mission team, and the large screen was up and ready for viewing.

Finn started the meeting and began, "Thank you, everyone, for coming to this emergency meeting. We have some concerning developments that can be solved if we put our heads together.

"Given our latest intel, this gala mission will be much larger than anticipated. We hacked into the guest list, and everyone from the California legislature, except for one Senator who's very ill, will be attending. It was also discovered that several high-ranking officials from our U.S. allies will also be there. That being said, we're making a joint effort from our other international bases to assist us. They're better informed of these allied officials and are more adept at identifying and taking out these demons from their own neighborhoods. I'm bringing the principals from the other locations on the screen, and we can devise a plan to complete this difficult and dangerous mission."

Finn selected some buttons on the keyboard before him, and several people appeared on the overhead screen. He made introductions and we began our brainstorming session.

Edison said, "Since we'll be identifying so many demons, and in basically two days, we need all the help we can get. But the difficulty in this mission, once the monsters are identified, is deciding when, where, and how we will proceed with the elimination. This plan must be well-coordinated. We must take them out within a very close time frame. If any demons get wind of our mission or have any idea they're being targeted, they'll scatter to the four winds, and our job will be even more difficult.

"The trick is knowing when we should commence our attack, and that has yet to be decided. A conglomerate of unknown origins owns the Demente Hotel. It's in a large California valley, surrounded by mountains on three sides, with only one access road coming to and from the hotel. I would suggest our Chosen become the staff at this hotel during this event. The conglomerate will interview people for the staff positions, so we'd have to get our Chosen Ones on the list of interviews. They must be hired for the majority of the openings. This place is so big that it can hold a few thousand. The gala will be held on the first night of our stay, and we've been told they'll hold the auction the next afternoon at the reception."

The principal from the Western European base replied, "The tough part of this plan would be identifying each hotel room of each demon. As you say, if they put our people in place at this hotel, they would have to participate in staff training. This would give them time to attain the hotel room list and distribute it to everyone on the team. Should we initiate our assassination plan before the reception?"

Everyone considered this, then Finn said, "I think we may have to hold off on that decision until we know exactly what's being sold. That's an unknown at this time."

The teams liked this plan and agreed we should try to fill the staff positions with as many Chosen as possible.

"Aaron, I hear you've been doing well on your psychic testing. You've successfully manipulated anything electrical simply with your mind, as you did with the helicopters on our last mission. You're also talented with computers. I'd like you to be one of the applicants at the hotel, possibly hiring into a security monitoring position or computer networking." Finn looked questioningly at Aaron, and Aaron agreed with his suggestion.

"Good. Aaron's infiltration would be a great asset when we begin our strike. Unfortunately, time isn't on our side. I'll leave it up to the principals of our subsidiary bases to select the people applying for the hotel staff positions. Many of the Chosen must be on the inside. The problem with this plan is ensuring they get hired," Finn commented with worry furrowing his brow.

"I think I can solve that problem," replied a young woman from the eastern European base. "We have a powerful psychic who can influence other people's minds and decision-making processes. He's quite amazing, and this Chosen One is well-educated. Of course, we can give him an excellent hotel management résumé with coordinating references. As long as he gets an interview, he would influence management's decision to employ him immediately, then he would assist in the hiring of the remainder of the staff."

"Excellent. God has thought of everything, I see," Helen admitted with a relieved smile. "When are they starting the interview process? Does anyone know? We have eight weeks until the gala."

"We only have nine days before they start the interview process," Edison said. "Nadia, can you get your man's résumé, work history, and interview in place before then?"

"I sure can, Edison; it won't be a problem. We'll start as soon as this meeting has concluded," Nadia replied.

"I'll need every principal to review their Chosen Ones and assess which ones would best fit the hotel staff positions. Let's meet again in two days. We can finalize the remaining Chosen staff employees, give them excellent résumés, and place them on the roster to be interviewed by the hotel. We'll also continue working on the rest of the mission details. I'll inform you of any information or updates as they develop. Please contact me if you have questions or if you have ideas that would ensure our mission's success. Thank you, everyone," Finn said to the other principals on the screen and disconnected the links.

"Finn, is this plan even feasible? It's getting so complex and involved," I said as I chewed nervously on my fingernail.

"I agree, Mara. This mission will be a pain in our behinds, but we'll ascertain all the required logistics. We've many smart minds working on it, and with God's assistance, it'll all come together," Finn replied.

"Guess what, Mara and Jonas? Now, you'll have to memorize more faces and names. Since you've completed your sniper training, and I must say, far surpassing our expectations, your goal now is memorization. We're counting on you to be quick and accurate when identifying our targets at the gala. The undercover guests who will attend the gala have been decided; it'll be Jonas with Poppy and Mara with me." Finn conveyed.

"That sounds workable, Finn. But how are we getting invitations to the gala? We know this is a highly exclusive group, and outsiders would not be permitted," Jonas said.

Finn replied, "That's where our good old friend Jorge comes in. You met him on the last mission; he still has excellent connections with the criminal world. He'll give the four of us outstanding recommendations for this function. Our profiles are currently being developed in coordination with Jorge and will be provided to each of us. We must commit to memory every detail of the profiles and be convincing to all the other event attendees."

Finn glanced at Jonas and me, then said to Jonas, "Poppy was unable to attend this briefing because of a satellite issue. However, she's been apprised about everything regarding the upcoming mission."

Edison chimed in, "We'll have a meeting with every Chosen One in this facility, and we'll determine which of our people should apply for the hotel staff positions, excluding you, of course, Aaron. Then we have to devise a plan for the extermination of the demons, and that may get complicated. We'll notify all of you when a meeting time has been scheduled."

Finn said, "Once this briefing is completed and the potential hotel staff has been selected, everyone must study and memorize every inch of the hotel and surrounding areas. We'll also have to study every road or trail to and from the hotel and possible sniper locations. We have a lot to figure out, learn, and coordinate in a short timeframe. Any questions?"

We shook our heads and Finn said the meeting was concluded. He also told us he'd forward all pertinent details to everyone via their computers and phones.

Most people exited the room, but I stayed behind with Finn. He was cleaning up the table and I assisted him. He was exhausted and I wanted to help him however I could.

"Mara, you don't have to do this. I can handle it," he said kindly.

"Finn, you don't have to. Do you realize how everyone on this base admires, supports, and loves you? You allow us to lean on you, but you've got to start leaning on others. I'm here, and you can rely on me." Strolling over to him, I gave him a warm embrace.

He returned the hug, letting my energy and support flow into him. "I needed that." He gave me a big yet tired smile.

"Finn, you're exhausted, it's late, and you need some downtime. So come to my apartment—I'll fix us spaghetti, and we can relax and veg in front of the television. What do you say?"

"You know, that sounds fabulous. I'm going to accept your invitation and will be happy doing nothing tonight. But I need to take this paperwork and computer to my office, then I'll meet you upstairs." Finn pointed to a couple of boxes and a laptop.

"I can help, so lead the way." I grabbed one of the bins.

He smiled in agreement, picked up a box and laptop, and led the way to his office, which was a few doors down from the meeting room. It was decorated in Finn's tasteful style. The office had a minimalistic flair but had warm colors, a leather sofa, a beautiful antique desk, and an oversized, comfortable leather office chair.

As I placed the box on a small table, I noticed a photo on his desk that couldn't be seen from the doorway. I went around the desk and found a picture I'd taken at the cottage. It was a selfie of me with my arm around Spirit on the dock, with the lake in the background. I never looked at the photo after I took it, but it was terrific. The ethereal glow from Spirit seemed to surround me too, and it looked almost as if the photo had been retouched. But I knew it hadn't: it was merely the luminescence emanating from Spirit and encompassed me as well.

Finn said, "It's wonderful, isn't it? We recovered it a few days ago, and I couldn't resist it. I have another framed copy on my bedroom dresser. It's incredible, and I love having it around me because it reminds me of how special you are and why we're going through all this. The love of God shines off that amazing animal and radiates around you, too." Finn's voice was thick with emotion. Putting the photo down, I wrapped my arms around him.

I gazed at him with a big smile and said, "Let's get some food, then get comfortable. Okay?"

Finn agreed, and we walked hand-in-hand to the elevators and up to my apartment. He removed his jacket, kicked off his shoes, and said he'd help me with dinner. I told him it wasn't necessary, but he insisted, so I had him prepare the salad.

After I fed Asher and gave him a new catnip mouse, I browned and drained the hamburger, started cooking the pasta, and opened a jar of sauce.

Finn laughed and asked, "Your special recipe?"

"You got it, and this tomato concoction is excellent. It's organic and has tons of vegetables and mushrooms. You'll love it."

Finn *did* love it and had three helpings. I had no clue where he put it all because there wasn't a single ounce of fat on his body. After dinner, we put the few leftovers away and loaded the dishwasher.

Finn, Asher, and I snuggled on the sofa and watched old sitcom reruns. When I glanced at Finn, he'd nodded off, and I gently slid his body along the couch, then went to my room and grabbed one of my pillows, putting it under his head. I covered him with a quilt, turned off the TV, and went to my room.

As I prepared for bed, I didn't see Asher under my feet, which was his regular routine. He wasn't on my bed either, so I tiptoed into the living room, and Asher was sound asleep next to Finn's head, with one of his big fluffy paws around Finn's neck. Even Asher knew the man needed affection and support. After kissing them both, I turned off the lamp and returned to my bedroom. I left the door ajar and it made me happy having Finn nearby as I said my evening prayers and fell into a deep sleep.

The next morning arrived all too soon and I craved sleeping the day away. Then I bolted upright because I remembered Finn was asleep on my living room sofa. I quickly rose, cleaned up, and dressed, then quietly opened the door and saw Finn still asleep with Asher lying on his chest. The cat saw me, jumped down, and strolled to the kitchen, where I fed him his breakfast.

I quietly returned to the living room, walked over to Finn, and watched him sleep. Morning stubble darkened his jaw and he still looked amazingly handsome. I decided to let him doze a while longer and turned away, but Finn grabbed my arm and toppled me over so I was lying on top of him.

"Good morning, sunshine. Your man needs a good morning kiss." He growled and laid a hot one on me.

I giggled and murmured, "Finn, you know what happened last time, and I don't think I want to be thrown across the room this morning."

"You're right, love. But it's so dang frustrating. We have to get married soon before I blow a gasket."

"I love you, but you must let me up," I said quickly, pushing against his chest.

He gave me a quick kiss and gently assisted me off of him. "Sorry about falling asleep on your sofa. That wasn't my intention, love, but you took care of me, right?" He asked as he adjusted the pillow and blanket. "By the way, why do I have cat hair stuck in my morning beard?"

"That was Asher. He insisted on staying on the sofa last night to look after you. He likes to sleep against your neck. You'll get used to it."

Finn chuckled, sat up on the sofa, and responded, "You don't say?" He glanced at his watch and said, "I have a meeting this morning, and at this rate, I'm going to be late."

"Oh, Finn, I wanted to fix you pancakes and eggs for breakfast. You sure you don't have time for me to feed you?"

He thought for a moment, then smiled. "I'm the boss: I can postpone the meeting for an hour, just this once, right?"

I smiled back and gave him another kiss. "Then I'll start breakfast."

"Let me return to my apartment to clean up and change. It shouldn't take me long and I'll be back soon." He caressed my cheek and went out the door.

Finn returned a short time later, had changed clothes after his shower, and was freshly shaven. I had the table set and his breakfast was ready and piping hot. "Ahh, it looks delicious, love. Almost as scrumptious as you."

He came over, pulled me into his arms, and gave me a proper good morning kiss. I moaned, then buried my nose in his chest to happily drink in his masculine scent.

"Trust me, my sweet, I'd love to stay this way all day, but I don't think my colleagues would be too happy." I stepped away, caressed his jaw, kissed his dimpled chin, and sat at the table.

Finn loved my pancakes and eggs and ate a good helping of both. He told me of his plans for the day, and I said I'd be working on memorizing the new faces, as well as the hotel layout and surrounding areas. I would meet with the other snipers today to plan our ideal spots for us to set up.

Finn said he'd help with the cleanup, but I told him I could handle it so he could get to his meeting. We took a few moments for another heated kiss, then I had to let him depart.

"That man is intoxicating and addictive," I commented to Asher, who had watched the entire goodbye scene. "Okay, silly boy, after I clean up the kitchen, I'll have time to play with you for a while, then give you a good brushing. How does that sound?" He squeaked in approval, and I lifted him in my arms, and we went into the kitchen.

As I cleaned up the breakfast dishes, a flash went through my mind, and I grabbed the countertop so I wouldn't drop to the floor. It was the same vision I'd had when visiting my mom's house—a horrifying demon climbing out of a hole in the ground. Flames had also been shooting out of this portal, and the stench of this place made my stomach turn.

Why was I seeing this monster again? The brief image scared me to death, and what did it mean? Crap!

CHAPTER 29

Over the next several days, I received many more photos with matching names from Edison and spent hours memorizing them. It was monotonous but necessary, and I worried I'd never remember everyone. I knew the hotel building by heart, as well as the surrounding areas and corresponding roads and trails.

As I drilled myself on the photos and recited their names that evening, I kept pausing at one man in particular. I didn't like looking at it or touching the picture, but I didn't want to delve into why I felt this way.

His name was Maksym Yurchenko, and he was a high-ranking government official from Ukraine. I then scanned his wife's photo, whose name was Kateryna, and the same feeling of dread surfaced. Even after I put the two images aside, my eyes kept returning to these two people. I did my best to ignore them, so I turned their snapshots upside down and tested myself on the next group of people.

Sighing, I put the balance of the pictures aside and grabbed the two photos that were driving me crazy. I placed them in front of me, concentrating on Maksym's face, and my stomach started to roll. Running to the bathroom, I stood over the commode, but the feeling passed. My reflection in the mirror showed my sickening pale face, so I splashed cold water on my skin. Asher swaggered into the bathroom, jumped onto the counter, and rubbed against my arm as he looked at me questioningly.

"I'm fine, baby. It's just a bit nausea."

After my stomach settled, I returned to the desk where I'd been working. The faces in the two photos stared back at me, and I felt dread again. I turned away, walked to the sofa, and sat down, wondering what to do next. Something was eerily wrong, but I didn't know what to do, so I called Finn.

After dialing his number, he answered quickly, "Mara, I'm so glad to hear from you. How are you?" By the business-like tone of his voice, I knew he wasn't alone.

"Finn, I wasn't sure I should call you about this, but I didn't know what else to do." My voice was etched with frustration.

"You *should* call me if there's a problem. I'm finishing a meeting with Helen and can meet you at your place in thirty minutes. Can it wait that long?"

"That would be fine, Finn. Thank you. I'll see you in half an hour."

"I'll see you soon, Mara."

A short while later, there was a knock on my door, and I let Finn into the apartment. He pulled me into his arms, then studied my face. "Something's wrong. I'm sorry I couldn't get here sooner." He gave me a long kiss, then held me close for a few minutes. When Finn did that, I always felt strength and warmth returning to my body, which improved my mood.

"Mara, I'm sorry about my unaffectionate conversation on the phone. Helen was sitting directly across from me, and I had to be careful."

"That's what I figured. So don't worry about it."

He released me, kicked off his shoes, and I asked if he'd eaten dinner. Finn shook his head, so I led him to the kitchen, where I had half a dozen BLT sandwiches, a bowl of chips, and a plate of sliced watermelon.

"Oh, Mara, that looks heavenly. Thanks for thinking about me and my stomach." He kissed my cheek and we sat down and ate dinner. I dropped a few pieces of bacon on the floor for Asher, and he went to Finn, hoping he'd get more, which he did.

I inquired about his day and he asked about mine. He finally stopped me and said, "Okay, love, you're avoiding the subject. What's the problem?"

I told him about my reaction to two of the photos, and I wasn't sure if I'd be able to delve into what caused my discomfort.

"Mara, I'm sorry to say, I think you'll have to. If this Ukraine diplomat is creating this reaction from you, it must be vital to this mission. Will you show me the photos?"

I nodded and guided him to the desk in the living room. Finn picked them up, then scanned the names on the back. He shook his head and said, "I've never heard of them, but let's take them to the sofa—you can review them again and tell me what you're feeling." I agreed, and we sat on the couch. Finn held my hand, then had me look at the pictures.

"I feel a little sick to my stomach when I study them, but it's worse when I see *his* face," I admitted as I pointed to Maksym. "Finn, I'm afraid to focus on him. There's a sense of dread, and I won't like what I see."

I gripped his hand tighter and he pulled me close to him. "I'm here and won't let anything happen to you, love."

"I have the feeling it'll be something hideous. Just give me a few moments, and I'll start."

He rubbed my back and patiently waited for me to begin.

I FOCUSED on the man's face and peered into his eyes. Feeling myself floating, I was pulled into darkness—it was ugly, violent, and evil. So many children of every age and race were being kidnapped and drugged. Then I saw several adult faces twisted in rage and evil as they abused and repeatedly assaulted these precious children.

I PULLED OUT; tears ran down my cheeks, and I couldn't stop shaking at the horror I'd seen. Finn pulled me onto his lap, then rocked me and whispered words of comfort and reassurance. I could feel each of the children's terror and pain.

"Mara, it's alright, and you have to stop now. You're safe. Focus on me and look into my eyes." His voice grew harsh as he grabbed my face. "Mara, look at me!"

Finn finally pulled me out of it. I saw his handsome face and focused only on him, and I returned my mind to the present and out of my despair. "Finn?"

"That's my girl. Aye, it's me. You scared me to death."

"It was grotesque! This man, or should I say, monster, is selling children to the highest bidder. So many precious, innocent children were being abused, tortured, assaulted, and killed. I've never seen this much horror in my life," I blubbered again. Finn held me close and I could feel anger seeping through him.

"You saw all this, sweetheart? Oh, Lord in Heaven, I'm so sorry. No one should ever have to see such a vile thing." He continued to hold me close until I finally calmed.

Pulling away, I returned to sit beside him. "Finn, we have to stop this monster! I know from what I saw and felt that two hundred children would be up for sale the weekend of the gala. That's why this event is so large this year. It's all about the children. These reprobates are coming that weekend to buy these babies for their own sick and twisted needs. We have to stop it!"

I focused on Finn, and his face turned ghostly white, his lips pulled into a thin line. I'd never seen him this angry. He abruptly stood and began pacing the room. He then returned, stared at the two photos, and asked, "Is his wife involved?"

"Apparently, yes, but how much, I'm not sure. But she's part of it."

"Is he a demon? Could you tell?"

"Undoubtedly. There was intense evil and darkness when I probed his face, and his wife is one too."

"We must discover where these children are being held. I'll call an emergency meeting, then contact our other principals, especially the ones in our Eastern European facility. We need to get eyes on him and his wife immediately. We must track their movements and find out if he has anyone working closely with them. You don't need to attend this meeting, love; I would prefer you didn't. I want you to step away and leave it up to my staff and me." He gazed at me with protectiveness and concern.

"I'd appreciate not being part of this meeting tonight. But I'll insist on being involved in everything stepping forward. Deal?"

"Deal." He pulled me back into his arms. "I'm going to call your brothers. It would be best if you weren't alone right now. May I take these two photos?"

"Please do. I'd prefer never to set eyes on them again." I grimaced at the memory. "Thanks, Finn, you're so good to me. Thanks, too, for calling my brothers because I'd love for them to keep me company for a few hours."

"You're very welcome. I have to call everyone in tonight, then contact you in the morning with the meeting results. You'll be okay?" He looked at me as if checking to see if I was falling apart.

"I'm good now and you don't need to worry. You can go and solve the world's problems." I smiled, kissed him again, and pushed him out the door.

I looked back into the living room, then down at my feet. Asher stared up at me, then reached up to be held.

"You know I need a hug, don't you, baby? You're good to me too." He answered with a loud purr and nuzzled my neck. I carried him to the sofa, and we snuggled while I waited for Jonas and Aaron to arrive.

My brothers were at my door within minutes, and I was relieved to see them. I recounted the afternoon's events, and they were appalled at what I'd seen. They agreed they'd love to have a turn at taking out these evil monsters.

We changed the subject and played a couple of games of Canasta, which our family used to play to pass the time. Jonas and I were thrilled that Aaron knew how to play. I supplied snacks, beer, and wine.

"Aaron, I hope you know how happy we both are at finding you. I'm sorry you fit in so well—we're such a motley group." I threw a piece of cheese at him, and we laughed.

"Now I know where I got my bizarre sense of humor. The woman who stole me had no witticism and never understood mine. It all makes so much sense now. I want you both to know that I've never been so happy having you as my siblings," he said with a hitch in his voice.

I reached over, squeezed his hand, and replied, "It's a good thing because you're stuck with us." I smiled and crossed my eyes. He laughed at that and was a little embarrassed.

After squeezing his hand, I said, "By the way, Aaron, I hear you've fixed and built several types of vehicles, including sports cars. Do you think you could keep an eye out for a 1967 Ford GT500 Shelby Mustang Coupe, preferably in cherry red, fully restored? Finn told me when he was living on the streets in Ireland, he saw this exact car, fell in love with it, and always wanted one. I asked him why he never bought one when he made it big, and he only said he never got around to it. I'd love to give him this car as a wedding present. Do you think you could find one?"

"I most certainly can. Let me know your price range because they're not cheap." I gave him a number, and he nodded. "I have plenty of contacts who are into classic cars. Don't worry, Mara, I can do this for you."

"You're a gem, Aaron. This would mean so much to me. I've been wracking my brain, trying to figure out what to get a man who has everything, and it's next to impossible."

"It shall be done, my lady." We all laughed at him as he mimicked a British accent.

I mentioned to my brothers what Father Faraj had asked of us: if we would attend worship for the other religions on the base and see if we could see the angels.

Jonas answered, "I'd be more than willing to do this. Do you think we could start this Friday? I could take the Mosques, and Aaron, could you attend the synagogues?"

Aaron spoke up, saying, "Definitely."

"That would be great. Then we can finish with all the other religious services on Sunday. I believe that would take care of them," I said.

My brothers agreed, and I said I'd notify Father, and he could contact all the other religious leaders.

"By the way, I've decided to join the Catholic faith. I know it will take some time, but I'm excited," Aaron confessed.

We told him how happy we were that he was joining the faith, but we wanted him to be sure that we weren't pressuring him into becoming Catholic. Aaron assured us that we hadn't influenced his final decision. It had been from a recurring dream he was having about being ordained into the priesthood.

"What?" Jonas and I exclaimed together in shock.

"Yes, a priest. I'm not sure how I feel about it yet. Is it an omen or simply a dream? I guess time will tell," Aaron replied.

"Whatever you decide, Aaron, we're one-hundred percent behind you," Jonas commented, slapping him on the back. This response made Aaron happy, and the joy on his face was contagious.

We played another game of Canasta. I'd won the first game, then Aaron the second. After his triumph, he danced around the room, and Asher followed him as though it was a parade. Aaron picked him up, perched him on his shoulder, and marched again. Asher was in heaven.

I was thankful my brothers kept my mind off the awful vision. Jonas and Aaron were special to me, and I also knew they loved me. They stayed for another hour, and I finally told them to go home and get some rest. My brothers looked at me questioningly, but I convinced them I was fine, thanks to their kind company.

I smiled as they left my apartment, picked up Asher, and prepared for bed. As I laid there trying to fall asleep, the faces of those two demons from the photos flashed through my mind. How were we supposed to kill these terrifying monsters? God gave us everything we needed for this task, but the thought of fighting something so heinous sent shivers down my spine.

CHAPTER 30

Finn called the next morning and said the Eastern European base was handling the investigation and surveillance of the diplomat, his wife, and his people. Finn thought this was a good start, and he trusted the people at their facility.

"Mara, you'll need to purchase an evening gown for the gala and something for the outdoor reception. I'll send you a link to a website for you to look at several gowns, select a few that may work, and they'll forward them to the boutique in the shopping center. They can make any required alterations. You should also purchase accessories or whatever ladies need for such an event. The base will pay for all the expenses."

"I can afford to pay for whatever is needed. The base doesn't need to cover my expenses."

"Sweetheart, these are designer dresses and the costs are exorbitant. We have to portray a filthy rich couple who wants to buy a child, and only designer clothing and genuine diamonds and gemstones will do. Don't worry, we can afford it."

"Oh, Finn, that's awful, but I know you're correct. We're supposed to be a disgusting and corrupt couple. Okay, I'll do as you ask and make sure I buy a gown with sleeves to cover my mark. I worry that someone may recognize what the tattoo represents, and we'd be up a creek."

"Good thinking. What are your plans for the rest of the week?"

"My goal is to memorize more attendees, continue my sniper target practice, and work out at the gym daily. This body must be in the best shape when we go on the impossible mission." I hummed the music from *Mission Impossible*.

Finn chuckled on the other end of the line and said, "You nut, you sure have a way of always cheering me up. I have a full day today, so how about dinner tomorrow night at around seven?"

"It's a date. I love you so much, Finn, and please take care of yourself. You're working too hard and it worries me."

"I love you too, my beautiful Mara. I'm fine, and I'll eat right and get plenty of rest." He said goodbye and disconnected the call.

THE FOLLOWING FRIDAY THROUGH SUNDAY, my brothers and I attended all the religious services, and indeed, we saw many holy angels. We held hands with everyone at each religious gathering, and it astounded the worshipers at seeing the glorious beings. It was joyous that our fellow God-loving brothers and sisters could share in the stunning visions of Heaven's wondrous beings. God's worshipers now had a renewed fervor in worshipping Him, and they also gave Him splendid praise with tears of joy. It was a glorious and heartwarming sight to see.

JONAS and I continued working on the photos for the next few weeks, trying to get any psychic connection to the faces. Luckily, we could designate whether they were evil or could be saved, and we completed over seventy percent of them. We crossed referenced with each other on the designations because we had to be sure we were correct. These people's lives depended on our accuracy.

The interview and hiring process of our people at the hotel was a success. The psychic who could influence someone's mind and decision-making processes worked, and they hired him as the staff manager. This gave him access to most of the interviews, and they hired all our people, including Aaron. This was a big win for us and would give us significant control of the hotel. Our people were being trained in their hired positions.

According to Finn, the child trafficker had been challenging to surveil. He had many bodyguards; at times, he'd have several blackout-window sedans leave a parking garage, and each car would drive in a different direction. This man was careful and paranoid about his comings and goings. Unbeknownst to this demon, they'd hired two of our Chosen Ones as additional bodyguards, finally giving us an edge. Although he never seemed to go to any location where the children were being held, they were able to gain intel from other bodyguards. They learned about warehouses, abandoned buildings, and other out-of-the-way places that may lead to the children.

Unfortunately, each site was carefully monitored and searched, and they hadn't found any children—there weren't even any signs they'd ever been there. We were getting down to the wire, and we had to find these precious babies.

Finn called a meeting and the remaining Chosen Ones from our facility were in attendance. I'd never seen this meeting room on the training floor. It was a huge auditorium.

Finn stood on the stage in front of a microphone and gave an update on the information which pertained to the gala, its attendees, and the hotel. Every Chosen One had a task, whether on-site or at the base. So many areas had to be covered and manned, and Finn stressed the importance of everyone's participation. He said our people staffing the hotel were given their assignments, and communication with them would be limited. We had to be cautious that nothing would give away our plans or our people's involvement in this mission. Many lives would be at stake, and we were to protect one another and all the innocents and kidnapped children.

There was a question-and-answer session, and after we prayed for God's guidance, love, and protection, the meeting concluded.

Finn approached Jonas and me and said, "I'll need the two of you to come to another meeting in Room A. Our team is assembled there, and we need to review a few other plans. I also have some information for you I think you'll find interesting. The meeting is in one hour—I'll see you there."

It was good to see most of our mission team in attendance at the meeting, and Poppy was also there. We greeted each other, gave hugs, and sat in our usual seats at the table.

Finn greeted everyone, said a group prayer, and started the meeting. "I'm glad you're all here because we have some logistics to work through. As of yet, we haven't found the location of the children. I believe they may have been on U.S. soil all along. We also haven't been able to find any large transports from Yurchenko's companies or subsidiaries, so we have to assume the children are already somewhere near or on the hotel grounds. We're still working diligently on this problem, and we *will* find those babies."

I frowned in concern and asked, "Would it be feasible for me to try and connect with the children? I wouldn't need to psychically gain access to all of them. All I need is one. But I'd need a photo of one of the kidnapped juveniles or maybe a personal item. Do we have any information on any child he may have taken?"

Edison replied, "Mara, there are so many missing children in this world, I wouldn't have a clue where to look. Does anyone have any ideas?"

There weren't any suggestions, so I replied, "I can start by reviewing missing children in Ukraine. They must have a database."

"Mara, it'll be a long and tedious job, but we're behind you if you think it may produce any information. We'll get access to their database today and forward the information to your computer. Thanks, Mara. We'll take your offer and pray it'll be fruitful," Finn said. "Edison, do you want to address the sniper situation?"

Edison nodded and replied, "We have a tricky problem regarding the hotel's location. The surrounding mountains, which are extremely rugged, have been assessed, and the only good landscapes for setting up sniper sites are haphazard at best. There's nothing workable directly across from the hotel, where vehicles will be arriving and departing. Same with the rear of the hotel where the large outdoor reception will be held. Our only optional sites are at extreme angles and not optimal for firing accuracy."

I saw Finn's brain working to solve the sniper location problem. He shook his head and said, "I think we should nix the idea of using the mountain. It would take too much time to get up the mountain, and the odds of hitting a target that far and at extreme angles aren't worth it. To that end, our people must cover all the exits from the parking ramp and the outgoing roads. We don't want our targets to leave the hotel before the reception. None of those demons are to escape—not on our watch."

Xavier said, "I agree. But, on another subject, do we have any of our people staffed in security positions?"

Finn nodded and replied, "Aye. Aaron is in place as well as Billie and Jasper. They're already at the hotel and are assigned to security. They'll keep us covered at the resort during our mission. Billie and Jasper will also place the explosives.

"After they've secured that station, Aaron, Billie, and Jasper will keep us apprised of the positions of all our targets immediately before the attack," Finn said. "The rest of you already know your assignments, but keep reviewing them and make sure you're all in sync."

Edison spoke up, saying, "As to the weapons you'll need at the hotel, our people who have already infiltrated the facility received our shipments of weapons under the guise of groceries for the kitchens. It's their job to get the weapons to each of your rooms. Trust me, your fellow Chosen won't disappoint you, and your munitions will be there."

Finn stood, picked up some small gadgets in his hands, and passed them around. "These are our new communication devices while we're at the hotel. They're virtually invisible and their mic range is phenomenal. You still need to wear a small battery pack, but it's undetectable if you get scanned. Pick one up as well as the charger on your way out after this meeting."

"Mara, Jonas, and Poppy—the gala invitations, the fake identifications, and bios will be ready by tomorrow. They'll be delivered to your apartments by the afternoon," Edison said.

"We're done for today unless any of you have questions," Finn commented, paused, then said another prayer to the Lord. He thanked everyone and concluded the meeting but asked Jonas and me to remain.

"Since you've been at this facility, we've been perplexed by your marks and why your family was specifically chosen as the Gatekeepers. Not that we question God's choice or your abilities to fight this war, it's just our human nature that made us wonder why you were selected. We've been asking our Prophet, but she answered in parables and kept us in the dark. But today, she's shone the light on God's choice of the Patrick siblings." Finn stopped speaking, and we waited on the edge of our seats for him to continue.

Finn started speaking again, "Kaiko said, and I quote, 'These three Chosen are direct descendants of one of the twelve tribes of Israel.' She also said there are other descendants from the twelve tribes, and although this was a major factor in God's choice, there were many other contributing aspects she wouldn't share with us. She continued to say they weren't pertinent to the task at hand."

I looked at Jonas and raised my eyebrows at him. *How should we respond to this kind of information?*

Finn waited patiently for a response, and I said, "I'm sorry, Finn, we don't know what to say. It's interesting, and if I may speak for my brothers, we're honored to be connected to such an amazing bloodline. But Kaiko is correct; it doesn't change what we must do and how we must accomplish God's will. But we appreciate you finding this answer for us."

Finn smiled at my reply. "You're welcome, and I do understand. I don't think it would change how I feel about myself or what I must do. Now that we're done here, how about we eat lots of pizza?"

We all cheered, "Yes!" and piled out of the room to eat our favorite food.

CHAPTER 31

Our mission would begin in two days. The base was busy, and tension filled the air. Finn sent everyone an encouraging text, attempting to ease the nervousness and stress of every person involved in the upcoming battle. It made a difference because people were smiling again.

I was in my apartment quizzing myself on the attendees again but felt an instant emotion of despair, fear, and anger. It wasn't coming from me, so I concentrated on honing in on the source. It was Finn, and something was wrong. I dialed his cell, but it went directly to voice mail. Then I felt more intense emotions coming from another direction.

"What's going on?" I said out loud. I had to find Finn, then investigate the other person. Sitting for a moment, I concentrated on Finn and his location. He wasn't nearby, so he wasn't in his apartment. Rushing out the door, I hurried toward the elevators and stopped before them, but it wasn't quite right. Moving to the supply closet, I was getting warmer. Striding to the secured elevators, I used my security card, rode to the meeting floor, and followed my instincts. After getting off the elevator, I was pulled toward Finn's office. I ran down the hall and threw open the door.

Finn sat behind his desk, his cheeks were wet with tears, and he had a look of horror on his handsome face. "My Lord in Heaven, what is it, sweetheart?" I cried as I rushed to his side behind the desk. Upon hearing my voice, he grabbed his phone and flipped it closed.

I wrapped my arms around him and held his head against my chest, and I could feel his intense anger. After a few minutes, he pulled me onto his lap. Laying my head on his shoulder, I waited for him to tell me what had caused him such despair.

"Mara, their evil is so vile that I'm beyond angry at what they've done. I could kick myself for not anticipating this. But, oh, my Lord in Heaven, Jonas must have also received these images." Then a very explicit tirade of swear words spewed from his mouth.

"Finn, tell me what's going on!" I demanded.

He turned and looked at me, inhaled several deep breaths, then answered, "Jonas and I just received photos of the inventory for sale at the hotel. As part of our invitation, they required us to give them contact phone numbers, so we created encrypted and untraceable numbers. But apparently, they use these phones to send out their heinous catalog of the products for sale during the event."

"Finn, let me see what they sent you." I went to pick up his phone, but he grabbed it and placed it in his pocket.

"Trust me, sweetheart, you don't want to see it, and I wish I hadn't either. Mara, it's explicit photos of the children for sale; they are graphic. Some photos of the children are sweet and beautiful, but in the next ones, the children are naked, and the photos...well, you can imagine." Finn let out a shaky breath and shuddered.

"Those evil, disgusting, and depraved monsters," I said as I held him close. "I don't know what to say except I'm so sorry you had to see those awful things."

In the next moment, Jonas showed up at Finn's door. His face told it all —he was pale and looked sick to his stomach.

Finn said, "Aye, I got them too, and I'm sorry, Jonas. I should've expected this, but I was concentrating so much on the mission it never occurred to me they'd give us something like this as potential buyers. I truly apologize."

"What do we do, Finn? Do we respond, make bids to keep our cover going, what?" Jonas asked.

Finn nodded his head, then said. "I'm afraid we'll have to. I'll text you which children we should start bidding on and how much we should offer. We must maintain the charade and keep the bidding active. I'll contact a friend at the FBI and notify him that we hope to obtain intel on two hundred trafficked children. We'll ensure he has a safe place to take them once we rescue them from these perverts. Let's pray we'll be able to find their loved ones, at least those that have a family."

Jonas and I were concerned about Finn telling anyone on the outside about what we were about to do.

"Don't worry, he can be trusted. Keep quiet about these pictures for now, and I'll get back to you," Finn advised.

Jonas nodded, then said he'd see us later. He left the room, closing the door behind him.

"Finn, can you send me just one photo, and I mean a clean one? I'm going to try and track one of these children. First, we have to locate where they're being held," I explained.

"That I can do. But Mara, don't attempt this unless I'm with you, okay? Just in case you see something horrifying again."

"I will, I promise. Are you going to be okay?"

"I'll be fine, I just have these images stamped on my brain at the moment, and I have to somehow remove them. So, I'm heading to the pool for a vigorous swim. Maybe strenuous exercise will help. By the way, how did you know what I was going through, sweetheart?" Finn asked in puzzlement.

"I simply knew you were upset about something and began tracking you. Please don't ask; I have no clue how I do it. You and I are connected, so don't forget it, buster." I gave him a loving kiss. "Go take that swim. I'll imagine you in those swimming trunks with pool water dripping down your exquisite body." I wiggled my eyebrows at him, then gave him a suggestive grin.

Finn chuckled and gave me a thankful smile. "Ahh, Mara, you do have a way of cheering me up. Now give me one more kiss before you go." I did as he asked, then left his office, knowing he felt more like himself.

After I returned to my room, I heard a ding from my computer, and there was a message from Finn. It was one of the photos of the children. I was hesitant to open it; afraid of what I might feel once I looked into the eyes of the stolen child. Taking a deep breath, I opened the attachment. It was a little girl of about four years old, with big brown eyes, rosy dimpled cheeks, and dark brown, long curly hair. She was beautiful and I felt pain in my chest, knowing the possible fate of this innocent little child.

Finn told me not to try and see into the child's mind without someone being with me, but it was difficult to restrain myself from attempting to locate this little girl and all the kidnapped children. I struggled for a moment to gain my composure, then opened my mind and gazed into the precious child's face. This was only a test to see if I could get a connection with her.

I SEE IMAGES OF A WOMAN, probably the mother because her face is filled with love as she gazes at her child. Then I see a small stuffed brown teddy bear that's worn and has been restitched many times. The images are turning dark, and I quickly disconnect my mind from what I'm about to see next.

I KNEW FINN WAS CORRECT, and it would be wise to wait for support. Picking up my phone, I dialed his number to ask him to come to my apartment later this afternoon. After reaching his voicemail, I left him a message that I could briefly connect with the child but would wait for him before I tried to go further.

Putting the photo aside, I decided I'd better have something to eat.

Two hours later, Finn showed up at my door. By the smile on his face, he seemed to be in better spirits and must have just come from the gym after his swim. He was freshly showered and smelled of soap, toothpaste, and aftershave. Grasping his hand, I pulled him into my apartment and wrapped my arms around him. I loved being close to this man. He must have felt the same way because he merely stood there, holding me close, and buried his face in my hair. After a few moments, he put his finger under my chin, lifted my face to his, and kissed me with such tenderness it brought tears to my eyes.

"Finn, I love you so much that I just ache." I gazed deeply into his beautiful and intelligent green eyes.

"Mmm." He kissed me again. "The things you do to me, Mara. I never knew being in love could be this wonderful." He brushed the hair away from my face, then cautioned, "We have to stop this right now, my love, before I get an angel's halo up my behind."

We both laughed, then I invited him in and asked if he'd eaten dinner yet. He replied he hadn't. After receiving my voicemail, he figured he should come right over, fearing I'd decide to continue my psychic investigation of the child on my own.

"I have leftover lasagna from yesterday plus soft, buttery garlic bread sticks. How does that sound?"

"Great. I just realized I'm famished."

I reheated the dinner and brought him a large glass of sweetened iced tea. As I watched him eat, we continued talking about everything except the mission and anything about our war. It was nice to discuss trivial things and forget what was to come, at least briefly.

Finn offered to take his dishes to the sink, but I insisted he kick his feet up and relax. When I returned to the living room, Asher was lying across the back of Finn's shoulders and rubbed his cheek against Finn's ear.

I immediately laughed and told him I was sorry about Asher demanding his attention.

Finn chuckled and reached up to scratch Asher's head. "This cat appears to be psychic too. Does he always know when someone needs reassurance and affection?"

"Oh, yes. He always does and is very persistent about it. The only problem is, he's getting so big that he weighs a ton."

Asher looked at me with disdain and then gave me a rude meow. "Sorry, Asher, I didn't mean it as an insult. You're very handsome indeed, and I wouldn't change a thing about you." I kissed and scratched the top of his head.

"He understands what you're saying. It's uncanny." Finn shook his head, raised an eyebrow, and pulled me close. Apparently, three was a crowd because the cat made another rude squeak, climbed off of Finn's shoulders, and went to play with his catnip mouse.

"I guess I'd better start on the photo." Walking to the computer, I opened the file and sent the picture to the printer. I carried the printed document to Finn, sat beside him again, and concentrated on the child.

I SEE the same images as before—the mother, the stuffed toy, then darkness. But what I view next is her mother in a casket, and the little girl is sleeping in a sizable room with several other little girls. None of the children are being restrained or look afraid, and I then discover that it's an orphanage. I hear some of the girls talking, and they're speaking English with an American accent. This orphanage is in the United States.

I BACKED out of the vision, turned to Finn, and relayed everything I'd seen.

"Mara, is there any way you can tell where this orphanage is located? Maybe they're supplying children to these animals."

I told him I'd try and began again to connect to the photo.

I'M BACK at the orphanage, looking around at the surroundings, but nothing in the room gives me the information I need. Then I see a window. This little girl spends endless hours gazing through it. I try to visualize what she sees as she stares through the glass. I notice nothing unusual through her eyes—only trees, a small playground, and a tall fence. As she gazes to her right, there are more trees and fencing, but as she turns to look left, there it is. Now I see a massive church across the street and a sign with writing on it, but some of the letters are gibberish.

"I see a church." I'm speaking with Finn but still in contact with the child's view. "The church's name—give me a minute; the child doesn't know all of her alphabet, so it looks skewed. Write this down." I tell Finn

which letters the child can read and the order of the words from left to right. "Geez, I've no clue what that spells," I complain. "Wait, there's a fog over the horizon, and I see...come on, show me...Jiminy Cricket! It's the St. Louis Gateway Arch! Eureka!"

~

AFTER I YELLED, it pulled me out of the connection. When I turned toward Finn, he stared at me, stunned.

"What?"

He snapped out of his shock and smiled. "That was amazing!" He kissed me hard, then looked at what he'd written. I perused it as well, and we tried to ascertain the church's name by the clues we were given.

"I think the child only knows her alphabet through, let's say, R," I replied.

Finn started arranging the letters and deduced, "The Church of The Holy—then what?"

I yelled, "Veil! The Church of the Holy Veil, in St. Louis, Missouri, or a surrounding suburb. Finn, this is great! We at least know where she came from, right?"

Finn pulled out his phone, called his FBI contact, and gave him the name and location of the church. He spoke for a few minutes, thanked his friend, and disconnected his call. "My friend is going to get right on it."

"But now, we must find where they're all being held. I have to go back in and find this location. Are you with me?" I asked Finn.

"Most definitely. Just be careful. It may get ugly in there, so try to distance yourself and not go too deep."

"I'll try not to," I agreed and went in again. I did a fast-forward through everything I'd already seen.

~

I SEE SIX GIRLS, including our little child, being taken out of the building in the middle of the night to a large, black dark-windowed van. They aren't fearful as the children are told they're going on a nice vacation. I view a woman leading them into the truck. She's in her fifties with bleached blonde hair and brown eyes and is wearing a large sapphire ring. In the van, they give the girls something to drink, and after, I see blackness, so I assume they're being drugged.

There are more locations where they only stay for a short time. Moving forward, my vision rests on a large cement room with many small cots, portable toilets, and several sinks along one wall. More rooms are laid out in the same way, with many more prepubescent children. There are as many boys as girls, and I see and feel their fear and anxiety but also hope.

I continue to look around the giant room. There are no windows, and I notice guards with rifles outside the doors and at the end of a long corridor. Several cement steps ascend upwards, but I can't see to the top. I'm still looking through the little girl's eyes and scan the room again. As I gaze toward the wall that contains the sinks, I see a logo on several towels lying on the floor.

I JUMPED out of the vision, turned to Finn, and hugged him.

"Finn, they're at the hotel! I saw the logo of the Hotel Demente on the towels in the rooms where the children are being held. They've been at the hotel all this time, and we never knew. But the thing is, they must be in the basement—an immense one that's well guarded by armed thugs."

"Mara, are you sure? We've looked at the hotel's blueprints; there's no basement as you described. Our people have gone through every inch of that place, and the basement has only the usual items a hotel would have; laundry, boilers, electrical, and security rooms. Nothing as you've described."

"Finn, they're under the hotel or very near to it. I don't care what the blueprints say, but I know it in my bones. There's no doubt in my mind whatsoever. Even if our people scoured every inch of that place, these monsters would have hidden any access to where the children are, and I know you believe that, too. We have to find the entrance."

"I believe you. You haven't been wrong about anything yet. I'll contact our people at the hotel tonight, carefully and discreetly, of course, and they'll have to do a more thorough search. We suspect this location may be under the hotel or leading off the basement. Either way, we'll have them conduct another search for any hidden doors. I need to get going on this information, my love. Now, please don't do any more of the psychic voodoo that you do so well, and rest. Promise?" Finn looked at me with puppy dog eyes, and I laughed at his joke.

"I promise. I'm exhausted anyway and need to sleep." Walking Finn to the door, I added, "You need to rest too. It's been a rough day for you, and you need to take a break. It goes both ways, you know." I gave him a goofy smile and did a little jig. It made him laugh.

"I also promise that I'll take it easy." He kissed me and departed. I closed the door behind him, but there was an immediate knock. I opened it again, and there stood Finn. He grabbed me around the waist, pulled me against him, and kissed me passionately. Finn whispered goodnight and walked toward his apartment. I smiled as I closed the door again and strolled to my bedroom to turn in for the night.

Again, sleep eluded me. That nagging fear of the unknown reared its ugly head once more. This upcoming mission scared me to death, and I couldn't help but worry if we'd make it out of this mess alive.

CHAPTER 32

*A*t precisely 2:00 p.m. the next day, a currier arrived at my apartment and handed me my fake identification and biography for the upcoming mission. Also included was the actual invitation from the hotel for the entire weekend's events. My phony name would be Courtney Martin, and I'd be with my husband, Daniel, and we currently reside in Boise, Idaho. Courtney is twenty-five years old and loves everything money can buy. She's self-centered, shallow, a snob, and a bigot, and she only became rich when she married Daniel.

Her husband of four years became a self-made millionaire when he was twenty-five by conning rich women out of their fortunes. He spent some time in prison, but he was released after three years due to good behavior. However, he continued his inappropriate lifestyle even after prison. Daniel then met Courtney when they tried to con the same woman, and the two have been together ever since. Ten years later, he still enjoys the finer things in life and wants to expand into child trafficking to increase his fortune.

I must say, this was a very unseemly couple. I cringed and called Finn, thinking we should meet to review our profiles and ensure we were on the same page. He agreed to meet at his apartment for dinner, and we'd practice roleplaying to confirm we had our covers in place.

Jonas called and told me about the identities of him and his date, Poppy. They would be two British subjects, and their names are Archie and Emelia Walsh. These two have also been conning their millions from the rich and famous and enjoy many nefarious and illegal activities. They are a loud and gregarious couple who want to become rich by selling children to the highest bidder. He gave me more details and had me laughing out loud.

"Jonas, this sounds like it would be so much fun if it didn't involve the chance we could die."

"I agree. Poppy's been helping me with the accent and current slang. We need to keep working on this through the night and again tomorrow."

"All work and no play, huh? Right, Jonas—like, I believe that's all you're doing. I see the way you look at each other. But keep it clean because Finn and I have experienced the downside of going too far."

"We have as well, Mara, and it was terrifying. By the way, have you received your new luggage and the clothing for the mission? Geez, talk about over the top." I told him it hadn't been delivered yet but was eager to see what Finn had ordered and ended the call.

Immediately after I hung up, there was a knock at my door. Another courier was waiting outside with extravagant luggage and several garment bags on a rack.

"Miss Patrick, these are for you for the upcoming mission. Finn said not to argue and that you have to look the part." He brought everything into my apartment, set the luggage inside the door, and laid the garment bags over the sofa. I thanked him, and he gave me a kind smile and left.

The luggage was over the top—glistening gold with jewels covering the handles. *Yuck*, but I understood why Finn chose this style of designer luggage—it fit my cover to a tee. I picked up the garment bags and looked at each item. There were three more dresses, a couple of suits, and one skimpy bathing suit. A note pinned to the bikini said, 'Love, I'm drooling thinking of you in this bit of string. Finn.' *You dirty dog*, I said to myself and laughed out loud. I tried on the bathing suit, which was shameful and left little to the imagination. As I looked at myself in the mirror, I had no clue how I could wear such a thing in public. The color was neon orange, and the bra only had two tiny triangles, the bottom was even skimpier, and there was only a small piece of fabric that covered my private area. My hind end was bare, with one string across the top of my butt and down the crack. *Oh my, this is so not me. Finn, you've got to be kidding!*

When I prepared to meet Finn that evening, I decided to take the bathing suit with me. I had to tease him about it and would ask him how I would ever wear such a thing. Knocking on his door, I held the bikini so it hung in front of my face. The door opened, and I heard his surprised and exaggerated gasp. He invited me in and took the suit from me, then held it in front of my body.

"Oh baby, I can't wait to see you in this bit of a thing. Would you try it on for me now?" His smile turned lecherous, and his tone was positively slimy.

"You rat!" I blurted but couldn't help laughing. "You expect me to wear this…this tiny piece of string? It's awful, and I'd have to wax my entire body. Do you know how painful that is?" I was still giggling when he turned on his heel and picked up something from the coffee table.

"Look what I have to wear. You think yours is bad—mine is a couple pieces of string attached to a small-sized bag in the front. And I reiterate, a *small* bag. This is an insult to my manhood." His suit was worse than mine. The image of where the two pieces of cloth would go made me cry with laughter.

"Finn, that's most certainly worse than mine. Are we going to wear these horrible, disgusting things?"

Finn paused a few moments with a serious look on his face, then confessed, "No, I was just kidding." He laughed hysterically, and I along with him. We guffawed so hard we ended up with our rumps on the floor with tears streaming down our faces.

"Finn, that was darn right, genius! But you're still a handsome, conniving rat!" I laughed again. We were both on our knees now, and he reached across and gave me a heated kiss.

"Wow! That was—wow! We have to stop. If you keep kissing me like that, I'm going to catch fire." I reluctantly pulled away from him and rose to my feet. He gazed at me from the floor, then also stood.

"I have the actual suits we'll wear at the pool party." He grabbed a bag from the end table and pulled out two suits. The ones he showed me were more modest but still a little risqué.

"Better, but I'd still prefer more material for my suit. On the other hand, I quite like yours," I admitted, tapping my chin with my forefinger, then sent him a devious smile.

"Are you going to try your suit on for me, love?" he whispered.

"Not on your life." I playfully poked him in his ribs.

He laughed again, then gave me a wink. "Okay, now for the serious stuff." After strolling into his bedroom, he brought out a few jewelry boxes. Finn showed me the matching engagement and wedding rings. The center diamond was gigantic, and the smaller stones glistened like stars in their setting.

"It's awfully big. However, it's probably what my character would want and demand." He pulled out three different sets of matching jewelry, including rings, necklaces, earrings, and bracelets. One was made of diamonds, one of rubies, and the other, sapphires. "Oh, my goodness. These are real, aren't they?"

"I'm afraid so. But I think you can handle it." I reluctantly took the jewelry cases from him and set them aside.

"By the way, can I wear a small pistol while I'm at the hotel? I mean, not with the bathing suit, like—where would I hide it?" I looked at him, and he raised one eyebrow in suggestion. I poked him again in the ribs and he chuckled.

"Aye, you may. I'll have a small pistol with the appropriate ammo sent to your room. I can also send you an inner thigh holster that would work well with this weapon. Most of us will be packing too."

We sat down to dinner and had a relaxing evening together. Finn and I still laughed about the bathing suits and then spent time rehearsing the relationship between our two characters and how they might treat each other in public. It was an enjoyable night, but we still feared we might not survive this upcoming, dangerous mission.

CHAPTER 33

*I*t was time to begin our mission, so we packed our suitcases and went to the flight deck on the first floor of the base. We'd been to several meetings, grilled each other until every plan was in place, and reviewed every possible contingency that might occur. It was impossible to plan for everything, but we had to be prepared that something could and would go wrong on this mission.

Finn and I were taking a chopper to a private airbase near Boise. After landing, we'd take a limo to another airport, then board a private jet to California. The hotel would pick us up using their limo service.

We were dressed to kill in our couture suits, expensive jewelry, and designer luggage. Our characters certainly looked the part of two self-indulgent, conceited, and haughty rich people. When we rehearsed, we'd worked on appearing arrogant, bossy, and self-important to give the impression we were who we claimed to be.

Jonas and Poppy left the base a day earlier for their destination to a private airbase outside of London. They'd take a limousine to Heathrow Airport, where they'd catch a flashy yet private flight back to California, then another limo from the airport to the Demente. It was a roundabout way of getting there, but it had to appear they arrived from London.

The rest of our crew flew one of the larger choppers to an airbase fifty miles from the hotel. They'd stay at a nearby inn and wait for our signal to advance to the next step.

After a long journey, Finn and I arrived at the Demente, waited for someone to open our car doors, and acted like we were arguing.

"Well, I don't know why you must parade your endless line of hussies before me. That's all I have to say about your ghastly behavior. I'm now finished with this tedious subject," I said as I haughtily strutted through the hotel's front entrance with my nose in the air.

Finn's character looked at the doorman, rolled his eyes, and complained under his breath, "Women. Can't live with them, can't…well, you know the rest."

After checking in, they escorted us up one of the elevators to our suite. I looked around the room, turned to the bellman, and said snidely, "It'll do. You can go." Then I waived him off like I was swatting a pesky fly.

Finn gave the bellman a one-hundred-dollar bill and closed the door behind the poor sap, who was not one of our people. Finn signaled me to keep chatting as he pulled a gadget from his luggage and scanned every room for listening devices. He gave me the "all clear" sign, and I plopped down on one of the gaudy, ornate sofas.

"Finn, I had no idea being a rich witch would be so exhausting." I smiled and blew him a kiss.

"You did a fabulous job, my love. Unfortunately, everyone believed we were a couple of real jerks." He leaned down and gave me a peck on the cheek. "Let's get ourselves settled and search the room for our hidden weapons."

"Finn, I didn't see any metal detectors at the lobby entrance. Could you tell if the hotel has that type of security?"

"There was a very efficient one encasing the hotel's front doors as we entered. Luckily, our little jammers protected the weapons we brought with us." He removed his jacket, and I saw the handgun he had tucked into a holster at the right side of his back hip.

"Me too." I lifted my skirt and showed him the small weapon I'd hidden on the inside of my left thigh.

"Ooh, baby, let me see…."

I gave him a look of censure, strolled to the bedrooms, and said, "There are two bedrooms. This is a bonus since we can't have any hanky-panky going on."

"Sorry to tell you, sweetheart, but we'll still have to share a bed. We don't know if our maid will be one of our people or theirs'. We're supposed to be married, and we can't sleep in separate beds. How would that look?" He saw the surprise and worry on my face. "It's a California King bed. There's plenty of room to stay far away from each other. I'll do my best to behave, scout's honor."

I gave him a doubtful look. "Who said I was talking about you? It's me I'm worried about. I don't know if I can control myself." I gave him a flirtatious smile. He came over to me and whispered suggestively into my ear. My only response was a rude noise.

I liked our light flirtation because it distracted me from my fear, and Finn knew it too. The gala was tonight, so I made sure my gown was in good shape after the flight and set everything out I'd need for the evening. We also checked that the mics and earpieces were fully charged. Finn and I put them on and hid the small battery packs inside our clothing.

Finn found the additional weapons and ammunition but left them hidden for future use. There had been a problem with our phones before we arrived, and our people in charge of communications at the base said hotel security had been attempting to hack our phone satellite programs. Thanks to Aaron, Finn received a coded text they'd finally solved the problem, and they were safe to use. Finn checked his cell, and it was once again, secured.

We went downstairs to lunch, kept up the charade during our meal, and pretended to forgive each other for the previous argument. Finn and I were overly affectionate and acted as if we hadn't a care in the world. Jonas and Poppy hadn't arrived yet, but we expected them within the hour.

It was time to carefully and casually scan the room, looking for any targets and assessing if they were good or evil. I spotted fifteen of them, and Finn identified eleven others. Finn gave me time to concentrate on each one, and I said each target's name quietly and designated evil, salvageable, or innocent. Once this was completed, we finished our meal and returned to our room.

When Jonas and Poppy arrived, they'd also have a late lunch in public and would begin identifying the guests.

Each of our people who were undercover at this hotel had been assigned to be responsible for specific guests. Once we made the proper designations, they'd remain under surveillance.

Each designation of a guest or staff was vitally important to the final events of our mission. Evil meant the person was possessed and would have to be eliminated. Salvageable signified they were still human but had chosen to follow the wicked, and they still could be saved. Innocents were just that: innocent but happened to be in the wrong location at the wrong time.

Aaron was in place at security and was monitoring the cameras. He was also covering all transmissions between our people. This included inside the hotel and through our satellite communications to and from our people on the outside. Billie and Jasper were to assist Aaron in the security position and would also take his place when he was off duty.

About five miles away, down and around one of the service roads near the hotel, Basheer and Edison sat inside a small electrical service van. They received and recorded our target identifications and designations and compiled the information into a laptop. This information would be continually updated until everyone was targeted and designated.

After Finn and I returned to our room, he made another sweep for listening devices, then we sat down and discussed our next strategy.

"Finn, I need to locate the children, but I'm at a loss as to how we will find the doorway to where they're being held. If our people who have been on the inside couldn't find it, how can we? Any ideas?"

"I believe we should get you down to the basement and have you feel your way through the entire area. I'm hoping that through your psychic abilities, you may get a sense of what areas are close to, or far from, the children. Once we find the location, I'd like to get Jonas to do a spirit walk. We need as much intel as possible on who is also in this holding area, along with the children, including the number and location of any guards."

I nodded in response and bit my lip as I considered his suggestion. "I agree it's a good idea for me to go down there, but won't we look suspicious?"

"We would, that's why I need to talk to Aaron. I'll text him and find out if he can cover us while we're in the basement." Finn sent Aaron a message and waited for a response, and it wasn't long before Finn's phone vibrated with a reply. Aaron would give us cover in the basement, but we'd only get about an hour between two and three o'clock this afternoon. Most of the staff were to attend a meeting to review the gala assignments for the evening, so we should be free to move about. Aaron would also take care of the security cameras while we searched the basement.

When it was time, Finn and I put on casual clothes, made our way down the elevator to the second floor, and descended the stairs to the basement. We made sure none of the guests or staff would see us. I strolled around one end of the basement in the laundry area, which was noisy with all the machines running.

Unfortunately, I didn't feel any vibration or connection to the children. Since I received no data in this room, we moved around the rest of the basement. As we reached the farthest side along the west wall, I paused, backed up, and stood there momentarily. Luckily, I could sense the little girl. Although she wasn't very close, there was a small remnant of her. Kneeling on the floor, I placed my hand on the cold cement beneath me and closed my eyes.

They're below the basement, but where, and how do we get there? Where is the door? I told Finn what I'd discovered, and he scanned the room for any possible entrance while I did the same.

"There's nothing here," Finn said. "Mara, put your hand on the outside wall and tell me if you feel anything." I did as he asked, waited a moment, and I had the same feeling as when I'd touched the floor.

"I don't get it," I commented, perplexed. "She's here, yet she isn't. I'm sorry, Finn. I know it makes little sense."

Finn reassured me but asked that I give him a few moments to think. I waited for Finn to access something in his mind, and he said, "You memorized the blueprints too, correct?" I nodded in response. "Do you remember what's against the west wall of this hotel?"

"Yes, the parking garage. Do you think that's where they are, or maybe under the garage? Finn, that makes more sense. No one would notice several children being brought in and out of the parking structure. Isn't there a service entrance on the outer northwest side of the garage? It's where they receive large deliveries for the hotel. Oh, Finn, I think we may be closer to finding them." I grabbed his arm and gave him a big hug. "Now, what do we do? I know the structure has several cameras, especially in the delivery area. Do we need Aaron again?"

"I think so, but we don't have time to do this ourselves. Remember we have to get ready for the gala, and don't you have a salon appointment at four thirty?"

"Unfortunately, I do. I'd much rather be looking for the children. We need Jonas to spirit walk and find the exact location of the entrance to where they're being held." Finn agreed, and we returned to our suite.

Finn contacted Jonas and the spirit walk would soon begin. It was time for me to leave for my salon appointment, and I informed Finn I'd be back soon and would want to hear the results of Jonas's investigation.

I was at the salon for sixty-five minutes. Using the haughty tone of my character, I said they might be fast, but the results better be perfect. Being mean was awful, but I gave them a large tip and hurried back to the room.

Finn gave me a loud wolf whistle as I walked into our suite, and I smiled at him. "Okay, what's the news?" I asked.

"I'm waiting for him to return my call. He was with a few of our under-cover staff, going over the evening, and said he'd call me back." After a few moments, his phone rang, and Finn put it on speaker.

It was Jonas, and he'd found the entrance—it was at the back of the loading dock. The entrance door had security cameras, but they were on a separate system from the hotel's main feed. So, this explained why Aaron couldn't find the children's hiding place either. But now that he knew this, he found this separate camera feed and obtained access.

Jonas informed us that he discovered the door to where the children were being held, and it had a high-security digital code lock, so we'd need Aaron to get us in. There were two guards outside of the door, two on the inside, and two more at the bottom of the stairwell. According to the camera footage, Aaron told Jonas that six guards changed shifts every six hours. Jonas went on to say the kids appeared unharmed but were, of course, frightened.

Jonas said, "Mara, your two favorite people were down there checking on the children. Maksym Yurchenko and his wife, Kateryna. But, Mara, you had it wrong: the wife is in charge. Maksym is merely enjoying the show, the disgusting beast."

"Why, that devious reprobate," I exclaimed. "I can't wait to get my hands on her."

"You'll have to wait in line, my sweet." Finn continued, "The auction is still taking place, so Jonas, keep up the bidding and make it look real. The auction concludes at the reception tomorrow, so we better hope we have everyone targeted and designated by then. We can't remove the children until we've neutralized all the evil, and let's hope we'll have it completed before the end of the reception."

Finn said, "The reception starts at five and ends at seven-thirty on Sunday. Jonas, pass the word to Aaron and the rest of our team that we'll be going after the children at six-thirty, that's eighteen-thirty hours on the evening of the reception. This is immediately after the guard's shift changes, and the bidding will be about to close.

"Aaron will need to take care of the loading dock and holding area cameras before we begin our attack on the guards. Then, he'll join Mara, Jonas, Poppy, and me as we infiltrate the entrance, take out all the guards, hide their bodies, and replace their guards with our people. Jonas, please assemble six of our Chosen to take the guards' places." Finn still looked worried, and I could tell he wasn't sure the plan would be successful.

"Finn, it *will* work. It has to be because we've no other choice. These evil demons must be eliminated, and we're the ones God chose to do this." I said and squeezed his hand.

We finished preparing for the gala, which we both dreaded attending. I put on my evening gown, high heels, and the stunning diamond jewelry Finn had given me. After strapping on my thigh holster and weapon, I made sure my communication device was secure and out of sight, as well as the battery pack. I exited the bedroom and spotted Finn adjusting his bow tie in the mirror. He looked stunning in his designer black tuxedo, which perfectly hugged his exquisite masculine form.

"Finn, you're positively handsome! Or should I call you Bond, James Bond?" I grinned and wiggled my eyebrows at him. He laughed as he turned around until he laid his eyes on me.

His jaw dropped, and he stared at me in my evening gown. It was a form-fitting, dark purple dress with silky and slinky material that had tiny silver beading sewn throughout the gown, giving it a soft, sparkling quality. It was sleeveless with a high scooped neck. There was a V-panel down the neckline with a semi-sheer panel that showed a hint of cleavage. The back was open and very low with silver beaded crisscross straps. The lower half of the dress was also figure-hugging, and there was a long slit up the front of my right leg, hinting at bare skin. A fine, delicate diamond necklace and matching earrings completed the outfit.

"Mara, you look stunning, and that dress is…it's just…wow!" He came up to me and looked me up and down again. "You're so incredibly beautiful." He gently held me by my upper arms, and a look of realization came over his handsome face. "Wait, your mark—you said you'd have to wear something with sleeves. I didn't think about it when I bought you the bathing suit. We all have tattoos, and the guests will see them at the pool party tomorrow. Oh geez, I really screwed up." Finn paced the room with agitation.

"Finn, stop! We took care of it. You've been so busy, so the rest of us devised a good plan to disguise the marks. We have an excellent makeup artist at the base who showed us how to cover them perfectly. The plan is to use a small piece of special effects makeup material that easily adheres to the skin, and then we apply waterproof matching concealer to cover it up. Look, see how great it works?" I showed him where my mark was, and it was invisible. Finn looked closely, then ran his hand over the now camouflaged tattoo.

"Mara, thank the Lord above. I'm relieved my talented people are looking out for me. I figured we were screwed. We couldn't wear jackets to a pool party." We both laughed, and I was glad he let himself off the hook.

"I can cover yours tomorrow before the pool party. Now, let's get cracking. We have a plethora of people to identify tonight."

I grabbed my small clutch purse and we headed down the elevators to the gala, which was already in full swing. The music was loud, and there were many choices of appetizers, entrees, and desserts on ornately decorated tables. Several bars along each wall provided every drink imaginable. It would've been a beautiful, enchanting evening if we didn't know what "things" were attending this party. Every inch of the room oozed with evil.

I was slightly nauseated, and as I spotted Jonas across the room with Poppy, his complexion had an unusual pale color, and his eyes appeared glassy.

As we walked in, I first observed that every woman in the room had their eyes on Finn. Desire filled their expressions, and when their eyes lit on my face—were they wondering what such a handsome man would see in someone like me? The insecurities about my looks from my previous life crept into my mind again, and I felt undesirable and unworthy to be this handsome man's date.

Finn must have known what I was thinking and whispered that I was the most beautiful woman in the room. His remark made me smile, even though I knew it wasn't true. So many women at this event were stunning and much more attractive than me, but as I looked into Finn's eyes, I could tell he saw only me. I then scanned the men in the room and realized they were ogling me. Between Finn's sincere comments and the male stares, my insecurities departed, and I gave Finn a look of gratitude and love.

"Courtney, darling, would you like something to eat?" Finn asked me as his Daniel character.

"Daniel, I'd love a diet cola. I can get tipsy on that delicious champagne later." Finn looked at me with a raised eyebrow, so I whispered into his ear that I was nauseated because of what was in the room. He nodded his understanding and brought me a diet cola to settle my stomach.

He guided me to an empty table and held my seat for me. The location he selected gave us an excellent view of the entire room. Spotting several people I'd previously memorized, I rattled off each name and their designation. I'd already completed over a hundred guests and heard Jonas had finished just as many. Finn told me to take a break and we'd start again later, but I was afraid I'd get confused and not remember which ones I'd already identified.

Jonas and I continued for the next hour, and I whispered into the mic, "Did we get them all?" Again, I waited for a response from Edison.

He told me to wait a moment, then said, "We're missing nine more guests." I gave Finn a panicked look and he told me not to worry. We had plenty of time, and Jonas also gave a subtle hand signal that he'd received the message. He couldn't say anything because two guests had approached him and started a conversation. He and Poppy did a superb job of pretending to be shallow and carefree.

I told Finn I needed to use the ladies' room, and he stood as I departed the table. The restrooms were outside the ballroom and down a hallway towards the left side of the lobby. After walking into the bathroom, I noted there wasn't anyone else there, so I turned off my mic before entering the stall. After using the facilities, I washed my hands, turned my mic back on, and checked my makeup. Everything was still where it should be, but I applied more lipstick and stepped out of the restroom.

I bumped into a man and was about to apologize, but he grabbed me and pulled me through a doorway of a utility closet. Struggling to break his hold, I was about to grab my gun, but if I fired a shot, it would jeopardize our entire plan.

"Ooh, you are such an exquisite, stunning filly, yes?" he growled in a heavy Russian accent, gripping me painfully. "I have been watching you all night, and I know you will enjoy what I can give you, eh?"

"If you've been watching me all night, then you know that gorgeous man I'm with takes care of all my needs," I stated in my character's arrogant tone. *Come on, Finn, get me out of this.* "However, why don't we find a more suitable location than this filthy, little utility closet next to the restrooms? I think we can find a more comfortable place, then you can show me how much better you are than my man, yes?"

I was trying to buy us more time, knowing my team could hear every word I said. The creep attempted to shove his hand up my skirt. I was about to grab his hand, break his fingers, then shove him to the ground, but Finn barged into the room. He picked the man up by the scruff of his scrawny little neck and pushed him against the wall, knocking down several brooms and a mop. I'd never seen Finn this angry, and if looks could kill, this horrible man would be dead.

"Now, darling," I said, "this poor little schmuck just wanted a taste of your Courtney, but I knew you wouldn't be happy about it. Especially not getting it for free." I touched Finn's arm, still trying to keep up the charade and attempting to calm him down at the same time.

I felt Finn releasing his hold on the pervert, and he lowered the man to his feet and told him to get away from his woman unless he wanted to pay the high price. Like the little maggot he was, the pervert slithered away and quickly escaped down the hall.

When the door slid shut, I threw myself at Finn and hung on. "Thank the Lord you got here in time. I was afraid I'd have to kill the man, then what would have happened to our entire plan?" I said, trying to sound calm and unfazed by what had happened.

However, Finn knew me well and could feel me shaking in his arms. "Are you okay? That filthy monster didn't hurt you, did he? Jonas is outside, but I told him I wanted to handle the creep." Finn continued to hold me close and whispered comforting words.

"I'm just shaken up, but I'm fine now. Thank you so much for coming to my rescue." I pulled away from him, feeling stronger and ready to leave the room. "We can go back now, Finn. I need you to dance with me and help me forget this incident." I took his hand in mine.

We opened the door, and Jonas stared back at us, looking frantic, but I assured him I was okay.

After returning to the ballroom, Finn pulled me into his arms, and we began dancing. I needed to be in his embrace for a few minutes to absorb his strength and assurance. He pulled me close and we gently swayed to the lovely music. I could feel his resilience seeping into my body.

"Are you wearing anything under this dress?" Finn asked suggestively into my ear after we'd been dancing for about a half hour. "I'd like to know because my imagination is running away with me."

I gave him a stifled, unfeminine snort, which made Finn chuckle in my ear. "Finn, everyone on our team can hear what we're saying."

"I know that Mara, but we have to give those poor men in the van some entertainment," Finn said jokingly. I heard snickers coming through my earpiece.

"Well, if you must know, I thought about wearing armor-plated shorts but then changed my mind and put on a pair of burlap boxers—in other words, it's none of your business, bucko!" I stressed my last words by pointing a stern finger into Finn's muscled chest. "You boys out there, keep your imaginations P.G." I snorted again and heard more laughter in my ear.

"Yuck! You ruined every enticing dirty thought I'd been clinging to,"

Finn countered. "You know, you could've simply gone commando. I wouldn't have minded." I looked up at him and he had laughter in his eyes.

"You rat! I just bet you wouldn't. Now shut up and let me enjoy this dance." I gave him another smile and snuggled close again.

When the music was over, I heard Jonas say into the mic, "Heads up."

I looked around and saw more people entering the room. There were precisely nine. I uttered the names and designations for five of them but was drawing a blank on the other four. "Jonas, I hope you can remember the rest."

"Got 'em," he said and finished the identifications.

Finn said, "Mara, we need to eat. This part of the job is now done, so let's enjoy the food and drinks. Are you up to it?" I nodded, smiled, and we filled our plates with delicious food and grabbed a couple of drinks.

Returning to our seats, Jonas and Poppy joined us, but we pretended we were meeting for the first time. We enjoyed ourselves, despite the evil permeating the room.

Finn and I danced several more times through the night and savored a few cocktails. However, I felt something was wrong with me, which made me uncomfortable. I told Finn we needed to leave; he gave me a questioning look but agreed to take me back to our room. As we walked out, I spoke quietly with Jonas and noticed he acted like he had to leave the gala too. Jonas and Poppy moved outside to get fresh air, and Finn escorted me to the elevator.

As luck would have it, Maksym Yurchenko and his wife, Kateryna, walked into the same elevator. We found it odd they hadn't been at the gala, but it made us happy that we didn't have to deal with them. I smelled their stench as soon as they stepped next to us, and Finn also noticed it. Maksym stared rudely at my cleavage, then down the rest of my body, and he even tried to rub up against me. Finn quickly, yet casually, moved between us, blocking Maksym's advancement. The disgusting couple introduced themselves and began a conversation with us, and we had to pretend we were slightly tipsy but were having a great time.

Kateryna moved over to Finn and ran her hands over his chest, looking at him with blatant desire. "Ooh, you are a handsome and virile one, yes? I would love to have a go at you. I bet you would give me a wild ride, eh?"

she drawled in her thick Ukrainian accent. She suggestively rubbed up against Finn and pulled him against her body.

Finn arrogantly looked down his nose at her and smiled coldly. "I doubt you could handle me, but my gorgeous woman can—right, Courtney?" he asked me, pulling that demon's slimy hands off his body.

I slid my hands up his chest, kissed him deeply, and pulled his bottom lip with my teeth as I finished the lip lock.

"Hmmm," she replied, still devouring his body with her eyes. "I hope you'll attend the pool party tomorrow. It would be such a waste if you didn't come." Their floor dinged, and they exited the elevator.

As soon as the doors closed, I wanted to lean heavily against the wall but knew the cameras were on us. Finn held my hand and we kept straight poker faces until we entered our suite.

Finn scanned the room again, advised it was clear, and we collapsed onto the sofa after removing our communication devices and battery packs.

"Finn, I thought many of the gala guests were horrible, but those two demons on the elevator take the cake. I appreciate you intercepting Maksym's lecherous advancement. Are you alright after that barracuda came on to you?" I took his hand in mine and searched his face with concern.

He kissed my fingers and said, "I feel like I should take an extremely long shower and the slime still wouldn't come off me."

I leaned my head on his shoulder but moved away from him after a few moments. Finn looked at me with raised eyebrows, and I stuttered, "I had to leave the gala because, well...because I was becoming overwhelmed by...." I stopped talking, and my face turned red.

"Mara?"

"Finn, all those demons at the gala were thinking about what they would do to those children they were bidding on. It was ugly and vulgar, I had to pull myself away from everything in the room. Towards the end of the gala, it got better, but then, I could still feel their intense...desire...and it was affecting me and Jonas as well. Did you notice he kept placing Poppy in front of him to hide his...excitement? I was also becoming very...well, you know. That feeling was awful because their appetites are evil and have nothing to do with love and goodness, so why did I become, shall we say, overly heated? I'm humiliated, Finn." My eyes filled with tears.

"Oh, sweetheart, you're still human and have needs like the rest of us. You have to admit, being Chosen Ones and also being in love has been torture. We can't make love to our mates unless we're married in the eyes of God, and the stress alone will make you more susceptible to suggestion. Give yourself a break, love. There's nothing wrong with you, and it's a normal human reaction to your circumstances. Is it safe to hug you now?"

I nodded, and he pulled me gently into his arms and wiped the tears from my face. He then sweetly kissed my cheeks and held me again. There was nothing sensual in his embrace, and I was thankful for his gentleness.

"Thanks. You have a way of always making me feel better." I snuggled closer, enjoying his warmth and strength.

"I know, and you do the same for me, sweetheart." After a moment, he started to chuckle.

I moved back a few inches and gave him a questioning look. "I'm sorry, Mara. When I saw you squirming a few times in your seat, I thought you were having issues with your underwear. Now I know why you were wiggling." He chuckled again, and I lightly punched him in the arm.

He feigned injury and smiled at me. "I have to confess, love. I was feeling it too. Not as bad as you and Jonas, but it was becoming a problem. Why do you think I didn't ask you to dance anymore and wanted to stay seated at the table? I had to think about going to the dreaded dentist to get my mind off what my body was doing." I appreciated his honesty and grinned at him.

"Finn, I'm beat. I want to take off all this makeup, take a long shower, put on comfortable pajamas, and not think about any of these creepy monsters. Can we do that?"

"Most definitely, we can. Let's make it a date and I'll meet you back here on this gaudy sofa." We laughed, then headed to the bathrooms.

The remainder of the night was quite enjoyable, and Finn remained a perfect gentleman. We talked and laughed for quite some time, but I yawned incessantly, and Finn said we'd better get some sleep.

I was nervous about us sleeping in the same bed, but I was being silly and followed him to the bedroom. He gave me a reassuring smile, held his hand to me, and led me to the bed. After pulling back the blanket and sheets, he sat me on the mattress, kissed me lightly, and said, "Now go to sleep, my beautiful Mara."

He walked to the other side of the enormous bed, climbed in, and closed his eyes. "Mara, I can hear your eyes blinking. Go to sleep, love." He opened one eye to look at me, and I gave him a big smile and a giggle.

"Goodnight, Finn." I turned off the bedside light and climbed under the covers. Tomorrow would be a day from hell, and I trusted God and my team to get me through it. But it didn't stop that tiny edge of fear that knocked at the back of my mind. *We can do this, right?*

CHAPTER 34

*A*s I opened my eyes the next morning, I had to take a moment to remember where I was. I was lying on my side with a warm body pressed to mine. Finn was spooning me. I laid there, reveling in being close to him, but I sighed in resignation as I climbed out of bed. He grunted a quiet protest at my retreat and pulled me even closer. Darn, I thought, this was dangerous.

"Finn, you have to let me go," I instructed him reluctantly and heard him mumble an explicit swear word of frustration, and he shifted his weight away from me.

After rising from the bed, I turned to look at him. Oh, my goodness. With one simple glance at him, I groaned with frustration. How can a man look even better, half asleep, tousled, and needing a morning shave? He had one arm over his eyes and the other thrown carelessly where I'd been sleeping. He lowered his arm and opened his eyes to gaze at me. I knew he saw me breathing hard and biting my lip, and this gorgeous man smiled, knowing what he was doing to me. Sighing again, I grabbed my pillow from the bed and threw it at him.

"It's not funny, you handsome beast!" I smiled, groaned again, then turned on my heel and stalked to the bathroom.

"I love you too, baby!" he yelled at me as I firmly closed the door. I leaned against the bathroom wall and tried Finn's tactic of thinking about sitting in a dentist's chair while my teeth were being drilled. Hmm, it was actually working, and my hormones calmed down to a manageable level.

By the time I emerged, Finn had already used the second bathroom. He was shaved and dressed and had ordered breakfast. It looked like he was going to feed an army, not merely the two of us because every breakfast food imaginable sat on the table.

We spent the morning reviewing the day's plan, and Finn checked in with the rest of our people. There hadn't been any problems yet, but today was D-day, and anything could, and probably would, go wrong. He gave everyone a pep talk, reviewed the plan a few more times, then disconnected the link.

We decided to have a lazy morning, and then we'd attend the pool party, which would begin at one this afternoon. I was nervous again, and Finn was agitated as well. After covering Finn's mark with makeup, I packed a bag for the pool party and slid my weapon into a padded and secured side pocket. The communication earbuds would be useless since we had no place for the battery packs in the bathing suit. Finn said we probably would only be there an hour or two, so we hoped the mics wouldn't be needed.

As the time drew closer for us to prepare for the party, everything seemed to cause delays. First, one of the bathroom sinks backed up with water. We had to call the front desk to have someone make repairs. Our hotel phone kept ringing for some unknown reason, but there wasn't anyone on the line. We worried one of our people couldn't reach us through the cell phone, so Finn contacted everyone again, but no one tried to call. Then, one of my bathing suit straps broke, and I had to borrow a maid's sewing kit to mend it. Jonas called us to say he and Poppy ran late because of several delays. Finn and I looked at each other, shrugged our shoulders, and said we'd meet them in the lobby before heading to the pool.

I waved at Jonas and Poppy as we reached the lobby, and we strolled to the doors that led to the large and extravagant pool area. We moved through the doors, then under a protected archway, until we reached the clearing that led to the pool. Finn grabbed my arm and stopped me from walking any farther. Giving him a strange look, I was about to ask what the problem was when I immediately saw why Finn had stopped me. I'd seen some horrible things these last few months, but what was around and in the pool didn't compare.

The pool party was an orgy. So that's what that disgusting, evil she-demon had meant in the elevator last night—she'd wanted to have sex with Finn at the orgy. At first, I noticed many people having perverted relations together—which was bad enough—but then I spied the true appearance of the things engaging in these disgusting acts. Their actual visage came through, and I only saw their demon forms—ugly, scaly, dark, and deformed. I could hear them grunting, hissing, and swearing. That horrific decaying odor of demons permeated the air and mingled with the stinging chlorine scent from the pool water. The sight, noise, and smells consumed every part of me, and I swayed on my feet.

Finn said something into my ear, but all I could hear was a loud ringing. He must have realized I couldn't hear him because he quickly ushered me out of the pool area and back into the lobby. Jonas and Poppy followed closely behind. Finn led us to the back stairwell; we went through the door and stood where we were out of view of the cameras. My hearing was returning, and the terrible smell dissipated. Finn spoke to me, trying to get me to understand him. Poppy was doing the same with Jonas as well.

I finally muttered, "I can hear you now, Finn, but please get me to our room because I think I'm going to hurl." Jonas's face had lost all its color, and Finn told Poppy to get him to their room. Finn guided me up one floor, checked the hallway, and led me to the elevator. He advised me again to act normal until we returned to our suite.

When we finally reached our room, I dropped my bag and ran to the bathroom. I made it to the commode just in time before becoming violently sick. Finn had rushed in behind me; he doused a washcloth and sat behind me, supporting my body. Finn pressed the cold compress on the back of my neck as I repeatedly vomited into the toilet. He continued to talk soothingly until I finally sat back against him, unable to support myself. After he wiped my face, he held and comforted me until the nausea finally passed. I'd never felt so tired and I couldn't move. Finn asked me if I was done with the toilet and all I could do was nod.

He rose to his feet, lifted me in his arms, and carried me to the bed. I leaned back against the pillows; I only wanted to sleep. Finn gently pulled my suit straps down enough to slip my arms out of it, then dropped my nightgown over my head. He pulled the gown down over my body, slipped his arms beneath it, and carefully removed my swimsuit. Feeling him pull the sheets back over me, he left for a few moments, returned with a cold washcloth, and wiped my face, neck, and arms.

I heard him say everything would be fine and I'd feel better after a couple of hours of sleep. Hearing him close the blinds, I peered back at him, and he'd changed out of his suit into a pair of sweatpants. He climbed into bed next to me and pulled me close. The horrific odor of those monsters still permeated my nostrils when I tried to sleep, but the exhaustion finally won out over the nauseating stench.

CHAPTER 35

"*M*ara, wake up now, my love." Finn jostled me awake. "There you are. How are you feeling?" He brushed the hair away from my forehead.

"Okay, I think. How long have I been out?"

"Just under two hours. I wish I could let you sleep longer, but we have a full schedule. I'm not sure if you or Jonas should take part in any of it. You must feel like you've been sucker-punched. Although, you look much better now."

I sat up slowly and was back to normal. "I feel great now, believe it or not. Is Jonas okay? Have you talked to him or Poppy?"

"Yes, I have. Jonas went through the same hell you did. But he's doing fine now as well. I didn't know witnessing a giant orgy would affect the two of you as it did."

"Finn, it wasn't the orgy—I mean, not really. Jonas and I saw, smelled, and heard what I'd call their satanic mating. We actually witnessed their true selves as they participated in that heinous act, not the people they pretended to be. It was hideous and disgustingly overwhelming to all our senses that it made us violently sick. Oh, my goodness, Finn, I just realized that our problems before the pool party were God's way of protecting us. I don't know what may have happened if we'd been there when it all started.

We might not have been able to get away. Thank you, my Lord and Savior."

"Jonas and I thought that too; we simply weren't listening. It's not a good thing to do when we're doing the Lord's work, right?"

I hugged him and he was about to kiss me, but I covered my mouth with my hand and said, "Vomit breath. Let me brush my teeth." I scooted off the bed, entered the bathroom, and brushed my teeth twice, finishing with mouthwash. It was then I realized I was in my nightgown, and I remembered how Finn helped me retain my modesty as he changed me out of my swimsuit.

I dressed in the clothing I'd left in the bathroom this morning and entered the living area. Finn had ordered more food and looked at my expression to see if the smell and look of it made me nauseous again. I gave him the all-clear sign and sat down to eat.

"Are you sure you're up to this next part, Mara? It won't be pretty, and you'll have to deal with those monsters again."

"I'm sure. I'd do anything for those children, especially that precious little girl. I'm ready when you need me."

"I'm relieved you're okay, sweetheart. You scared me to death again." He picked up my hand, kissed my palm, and we finished our late lunch.

Would our lives always be this dangerous, and would we have to worry about what our next mission would bring?

Finn and I were prepared for the reception in record time. He looked handsome in a casual yet elegant summer suit, and I wore a black sleeveless cocktail dress with matching heels, a beautiful emerald necklace, and earrings. We looked dressed to kill, and, unfortunately, that's exactly what we were going to do. As we strolled through the doors leading to the outdoor reception, I was apprehensive, afraid it would be a repeat of the pool party. Luckily, all the attendees were fully clothed and on their best behavior. Many were clicking on their phones since it was the last few hours for placing bids on the children. Finn and Jonas also kept up the charade of the auction process.

"Finn, here comes Godzilla. Gird your loins, my love," I whispered in his ear as Kateryna slithered up to us.

"You handsome piece of flesh, I missed you at the pool party. I was so looking forward to sampling you," she growled as she ran her hands down his chest and moved them down his body.

Finn grabbed her hands and stopped them from reaching her intended target. "We had our own private party in our room, isn't that right, my friends?" he asked Jonas and Poppy as they joined the conversation.

"Most definitely," Jonas said in a convincing British accent. "It was certainly the most satisfying foursome I'd ever experienced. These two were positively well-equipped and limber, I must say. All we needed was a trampoline." Jonas let out a loud snort and a snobbish chortle.

Finn, Poppy, and I struggled not to laugh out loud at Jonas's hilarious comments. I had to turn away so Kateryna wouldn't see me trying to contain my laughter. Finn's hand tightened on mine as he attempted to keep a straight face.

Kateryna peered at Jonas with a puzzled look. "Well, I hope you will invite me next time, yes?" She then continued to relay what she would do for the men, as well as the women, if she were to be invited into our four-some. Her husband called her over to him, and she gave us a goodbye wave and finally left us alone.

We turned away and laughed hysterically at what Jonas had said. "My goodness, man, your acting is quite inventive, and you do have a way with words," Finn admitted to Jonas, still chuckling. Poppy and I agreed as we wiped our eyes from laughing so hard.

"That barracuda gives a new meaning to the word lechery. Jonas, I think you surprised her with your comments," I replied. "Should we take her up on her offer?" I had a sinister smile on my face. We proceeded to make gagging sounds and guffawed once more.

We stopped talking for a moment and listened to what was being said in our earpieces. An unknown guest had arrived. The four of us walked over to an area that would give us some privacy, and I said, "We weren't expecting another guest, Finn. This could be a real problem. They haven't a clue who this person is?"

"Not yet. I think we should stroll out of here and sit in a private area in the lobby. It's imperative that we see this person before they see us, agreed?" Finn asked, and we nodded and casually strolled to the lobby. We sat on a sofa in a secluded area which also provided a good view of the hotel entrance. This location had large plants that we could use as cover since we didn't want to be seen by the newcomer.

The man we were waiting for sauntered through the door with his entourage. He was handsome but in an effeminate way. The new arrival was in his middle forties, with perfectly styled blonde hair and a thin frame. He walked with a confident swagger but with a slight limp. His entourage comprised three tall, voluptuous women who fawned over him and two young, pretty-looking men who walked closely behind. There were no signs of any bodyguards, but maybe they were still outside by the enormous white limousine.

Quickly drawing in a breath, I noticed Jonas felt it too. I'd never felt such intense power or evil of this magnitude, and he had to be the formidable demon Kaiko warned us about. Pulling Finn farther behind the plants, I shook my head at him, signaling him to stay out of view of this person. The four of us remained hidden as we heard several people running up to the demon, fussing and fawning over him. The voices dissipated as they joined the reception in the other room.

"Finn, that is *the* demon. Right, Jonas?" Jonas nodded in apparent agreement, and Poppy drew in a gasp.

Finn was shocked, and then he advised everyone connected on the link of who'd just joined the party. He subsequently said to us, "If he stays for the entire reception, our plan will be useless because we're not prepared to take him on at this time. This could throw a nasty wrench into our plans."

"I agree, Finn, but this is also a golden opportunity. We must discover who he is and where he resides; this would be excellent intel for our future plans. Let's mingle with some lower minions and try to get the scoop on him. But we mustn't get into direct contact with this high-powered demon because we don't know if he'll be able to sense that we're the Chosen," I said.

Carefully walking back into the reception, we stayed clear of the demon's view. We found a couple we'd been friendly with at last night's gala. Hopefully, these two people could provide information about the devil without becoming suspicious of our questions.

I asked the woman, "Who's that glorious handsome man who just walked in?"

"You don't know? Oh, yes, you're new to our group. That's the one and only Nicolas Drakos. He's the Greek tycoon who practically owns the planet. This handsome male took over the world's central banks after the COVID-19 fiasco. Nicolas connived, blackmailed, slept, and murdered his way to the top of the banking system, and now he owns everything. This is his hotel and he also arranged for the auction, lucky devil. I'd love to get into his bed and get a taste of that gorgeous man—he oozes sensuality. Everyone says so." The woman was positively smitten, and everyone else in the room was too. People gathered around this demon, hoping to get his undivided attention.

"Will he be staying long with us today?" Finn asked.

"Oh, I doubt it. He usually stops in to make his presence known, then departs as quickly as he arrives. Isn't he amazing?" She gushed.

"Definitely," I answered, trying to sound equally awed by him. "Does he live around here? I'd also love to get to know this stunning man." I still attempted to sound like I was smitten with the creep.

"I honestly don't know where he lives, but he has many homes world-wide. Excuse me, I want to see if I can speak with him." She strode over to join the crowd around the demon.

Finn glanced at his watch and said, "We better pray he departs soon, or our plan is out the window." He guided us back out of the room to the lobby, and we returned to the sofa behind the plants.

Just as the woman had said, the demon was already leaving and making his way to the exit. We sighed in relief, and Finn said into the mic, "Does anyone have eyes on this newcomer? We need to find out where he's headed."

"I took care of it, Finn. I put two trackers on his vehicle," Aaron said over the communication device.

"Nice work, brother," Jonas replied.

A few minutes later, Aaron spoke over the link again. "At the moment, I'm tracking him through the hotel cameras. I hate to tell you this, but he's going to the hotel garage and is heading toward the entrance where the children are located."

We panicked but waited to hear from Aaron. After ten minutes, Aaron's voice came through the com, "He's coming out now, and luckily, without any children."

We sighed with relief but wondered what he'd been doing with the children. Finn said, "We can't worry about that now because it's time to return to our rooms, change, grab our gear, and go to the parking garage. Let's get moving."

At approximately six-twenty, the security cameras outside the entrance to the children's location, as well as inside, begin looping their videos exactly as Aaron had planned.

Aaron, Finn, Jonas, Poppy, and I were waiting to start our attack on the guards outside the doorway. Finn gave the signal, and Jonas and Poppy quickly and efficiently took out the outer door guards. Aaron now stood in front of the door, staring at the security lock, and we heard a decisive click as he disengaged the lock with his mind. Aaron stepped back as Finn slowly opened the door, staying out of sight of the guards inside the doorway.

We waited until the guards walked out of the hallway to investigate who had opened the door. Finn and I eliminated them just as efficiently, and we proceeded quietly down the stairwell, our pistols ready to shoot the next couple of guards.

Aaron and the six other team members who would take the guards' places waited at the top of the stairs in case other demons came to the door from the outside. We encountered only one as we continued down the stairs and around the corner. This demon faced away from the stairs, so Finn deftly came up behind him and slit his throat. There should have been one sentry left, and we looked around the doorways to where the children were being held, but we still didn't see him. Then, a door opened to a restroom, and the last guard walked out, zipping up his pants. He was about to aim his rifle at us, but Jonas was faster, shooting him directly in the forehead.

After he fired the shot, we heard the children screaming in fear. We carefully raised our guns and waited a few minutes in case another demon exited one of the rooms that held the children. Finn gave a signal, and we carefully entered each room, scanning for other threats.

We yelled, "Clear," and found around two-hundred children in the dank, cold rooms. Lowering our weapons, we carefully and calmly walked toward the children. We explained they were now safe and that we would return them to their homes. Many of them cried, and it broke our hearts.

An older boy of about eleven years of age came forward with his little brother of about six and asked if we would rescue them. Finn crouched to his level and said he promised they would be taken from this horrible place. Finn saw a number on the smaller child's arm and asked the older boy why he was marked with a digit.

The boy said, "The pretty blonde man had come in and marked some of us with a number and said every numbered child would belong to him. A truck would deliver all the tattooed children to one of his mansions tomorrow."

We looked at each other and then examined each child for a number. The exact number of children who were marked was thirteen. "Did he have to be so predictable?" I asked Finn.

"The arrogance of these demons never ceases to surprise me. He probably figured using that superstitious number would be funny," Finn remarked, then spoke into his com. "Team, it's a go. Repeat, it's a go."

Finn told the children, "You're all safe now, I promise. But you'll have to wait a little longer until it's time for us to move you out of here. Our people will protect you, but I'll need you to do whatever they tell you. Do you all pinky swear you'll do as we ask?" The children smiled and said they would. They were bright and knew we were good people and could be trusted.

The six people on our team replacing the guards were now in position. We were about to depart from the children's area when a young voice yelled, "Mara, Mara!" The little girl I'd been connected to came running over to me with her arms outstretched. I picked her up and held her close. She cried joyfully and kept hugging me, raining kisses on my face. "I knew you'd come," she said in her sweet little voice and lovingly touched my face.

"Hi there, my sweet one. I'm pleased to finally meet you," I replied and gave her a big kiss and a hug. Finn looked at me with some confusion, but he merely shook his head in resignation. "I'm sorry, my love, but I don't know your name. Can you tell me?"

"My name is Gracie. They told me my new name was Mary, but I kept telling them it was Gracie. They were very mean." This little girl had a temper.

I smiled and told her I was delighted to meet her. Gracie also had a number on her arm, and it was number one. Finn and I looked at each other, assuming she must have been the demon's favorite. I then explained to her I had to leave for a while, so we could make sure the bad people would never bother her or any of the other children again, but I'd see her after she was moved to safety. She seemed to understand but was still reluctant to let me go. One of our guards took her in his arms and started chatting about his little girl and what cartoons she liked to watch. This seemed to ease her mind, and it was time for us to move back upstairs and finish our job.

When we reached the top of the stairs, Aaron and Poppy were waiting for us, and Billie and Jasper had arrived. Billie said the explosives were in place and handed Finn the detonator, which he slipped carefully into his pocket.

Finn said, "According to everyone's check-in, everything is going as planned. Our job now is to ensure all our targets are eliminated or secured. You have your instructions: now let's make certain your sectors are under control." Finn told all the teams to begin elimination.

Billie and Xavier walked through the garage to ensure this area was contained. Aaron and Poppy headed to the security room to confirm that all hotel floors were secured. Finn and I were responsible for the hotel lobby and reception area. We heard screams from every direction as so many gunshots were fired. It would have been gruesome if we hadn't known what was being killed. But these were full-fledged demons being eliminated, which was why God brought us back to life.

Finn and I made our way through the lobby doors, rifles raised, ready to shoot any demons who were still a threat. Our team of three hundred Chosen had done their job well. No monster was left alive except for the two we specifically wanted for ourselves. Our people were strategically placed over the entire area, and the only demons that should have been left alive were Maksym and Kateryna Yurchenko.

Finn nodded to our people and asked Marcus, who was in charge of this specific team, "Is everyone accounted for, Marcus?"

"Everyone but Kateryna Yurchenko. We're still looking for her, but we have her husband. Maksym is over there, nicely bound and gagged." He pointed his rifle toward Yurchenko, who was seated on the floor against the inner wall of the reception area. Maksym was livid. He was red-faced and his body shook with rage.

Marcus continued, "We have all the innocents in the Grand Marquis room down the hall. The salvageable are being detained in the ballroom."

We both smiled with satisfaction, and Finn praised Marcus. "Well done, my friend. Please explain to the innocents what has happened and why. Although, I'm sure they already know what evil beings they've been dealing with all weekend. Then, get them on the buses out front and off the premises. Remind them again what will happen if they breathe a word of this to anyone." Marcus nodded and left for the Grand Marquis room.

We knew these innocent people who had the bad luck of getting hired by this hotel must have witnessed the horrific activities of these demons. But they also saw the black slimy ooze from these monsters' bullet wounds and the noxious smell they emitted when they died. Their features and skin changed to something abhorrent a few minutes after their bodies expired. It was unmistakably evil and couldn't be explained any other way. Our team would inform the innocents if they told anyone what had happened there, God's holy angels would deliver swift retribution for their betrayal of God's Chosen soldiers. This was, in fact, true, as told to us by our prophet Kaiko before we left the base for this mission.

Finn approached Maksym, removed his gag, and asked him for the location of his wife. He swore at Finn and said he wouldn't tell him anything, even if he knew where she was. Finn pulled out his knife, ripped off Maksym's sleeves, then sliced one of his arms from shoulder to wrist. The metal on his blade was like acid to a demon and excruciatingly painful.

Maksym called Finn every foul word imaginable, but we saw fear in the demon's eyes. "I tell you, I don't know where she is. She took off as soon as the shooting started," he whined, clearly in great pain. Finn glared at the man, turned away, paced the floor a few times, then returned to face him again.

"You'd better hope you can provide at least some useful intelligence. I have a job to do and you're standing directly in my path. That's not a healthy place for you," Finn whispered into Maksym's ear.

As I looked at Finn, it dawned on me I'd never seen this side of him—the part that's God's Chosen One. The look on his face was fierce yet calm and utterly terrifying to someone who didn't know him. His green eyes appeared almost black with determination and resolve. His expression was cold and methodical. I felt a bit sorry for Maksym—almost.

"I don't know what you want from me. I'm just the middleman, and I'm told virtually nothing. You're simply barking up the wrong tree," Maksym explained shakily and was lying through his crooked, evil teeth.

Finn turned away again for a brief second, put his knife away, and turned back to the demon. He quickly pulled out his handgun and fired a shot into each of Maksym's kneecaps. The fiend screamed in agony as the putrid, evil blood and bone spouted from the two shattered joints.

"You want more?" Finn asked him in that same quiet yet deadly tone of voice. He crouched down so he could face the demon eye-to-eye. "Look, I can do this all day if that's what you want. There are many of your body parts I can shatter, one at a time, and still keep you alive to endure the endless agony. It's up to you." Finn stood, holstered his gun, and took out the knife again. He then put the deadly knife into the demon's groin.

"No! Please no! Okay, I'll tell you what I know." Maksym cried like a child, and Finn waited, his handsome face expressionless.

Finn grilled him about their child trafficking operation and wanted all the pertinent names and locations. When the demon faltered with his answers, Finn approached him with his blade again and cut off the demon's left ear. This action spurred Maksym into giving us the information we needed, and it was all recorded by Edison's computer in the van.

As Finn finished with the monster, we heard over our coms that four of our team members had found Kateryna in the basement. They were bringing her up in the elevators and should reach the lobby in a few minutes.

I looked at Finn and said, "She's mine." He saw the determination in my expression and nodded his head. Finn walked over to Maksym, pulled out his pistol, and shot him through the head, which killed him instantly.

The black slime oozed out of the large wound, and his face and body turned into the ugly demon countenance.

The elevator dinged, the doors opened, and four of our Chosen walked out; two were pushing a utility cart. They had tightly bound Kateryna to the cart with duct tape, which was a sight to behold. She was furious and was trying to wiggle out of her confinement. The four Chosen team members seemed a little worse for wear but only had a few cuts and bruises. They stopped the cart before Finn and me and returned to the elevators to continue their sweep.

I looked at her with disdain, and she continued to glare at me with her evil expression. She could have been pretty, dressed in that dark red chiffon dress and the giant ruby necklace, but the wickedness couldn't be disguised. Not from us.

"My, my, what have we here? I suppose you're quite happy since I expect you're into bondage too?" I asked her, using a sickeningly sweet tone. "Are you liking it so far, Kateryna? Is it good for you?" The duct tape that was wrapped several times over her mouth and around her head made it impossible for her to respond. Pulling out my knife, I raised it to her face; she flinched in response. Sliding the blade under the tape, I sliced it from her face. Once the gag was removed, she spouted a tirade of filth, obviously hoping her language would cause us embarrassment.

"Oh really? Daniel, do you think that it's physically possible? I mean, even if one was double-jointed?" I asked Finn as I continued to keep up the charade of our characters.

Finn looked at me, put two fingers to his chin, and thought for a moment. "You know, I suppose if there was a bungee cord, three tennis balls, and a pogo stick, I could see it happening." We laughed out loud, and Kateryna became so infuriated that she could no longer speak. She busted through the duct tape, fell to the floor, quickly rose to her feet, and took off through the doors to the swimming pool area.

"I wondered how long it would take her to do that. She's kind of slow and weak for a demon, don't you think, my sweet?" I asked Finn.

"I thought so too," he agreed, with a casual and bored expression.

"Remember, she's mine," I grumbled to Finn as the rest of the team watched the spectacle. Tossing my rifle toward Finn, which he deftly caught, I then trod through the pool area door with everyone following closely behind. Her getting away didn't concern me because there was no way out of the pool area. At least, not easily.

"Kateryna..." I said in a sing-song voice. "Olly, Olly, oxen-free." After reaching the pool, I stopped as I caught a whiff of her stench. She jumped out from behind an ivy wall, brandishing a long skimmer pool pole. She deftly broke it in two and threw the smaller half behind her.

"Come on, I thought you were a big, tough, evil demon. Show me what you've got, you filthy, little maggot," I bellowed, motioning her to fight me.

She started toward me as she swung the pole in circles with a devious smile. Her shoes were long gone—she'd probably lost them from the scuffle in the basement. She came closer, ready to impale me with the pole, as her anger overtook her reasoning.

Kateryna called me another name, then ran straight for me. The witch attempted to thrust the pole into my stomach, but I easily blocked her and twisted the rod out of her hands. I flipped the pole around, hit her several times around her head in rapid succession, and jabbed her sharply into her stomach. She let out a soft "oomph," staggered back several paces, and I thrust it at her again, but she grabbed onto it once more. The way I twisted the rod caused her arm to gyrate backward at such a horrendous angle that her bones snapped. She screamed in agony and grew even more enraged. I tossed the long pole over her head, and it went over the high ornate fence surrounding the pool area.

Out of the corner of my eye, I spied Jonas, Finn, and Aaron, and they had a look of sheer terror on their faces. Their hands were clenched into fists, and I knew it took sheer willpower for them not to interfere in my battle with the demon.

Kateryna turned back toward me with her broken arm dangling uselessly at her side. She growled, "You can't kill me, you vile little human, and I'm going to take my fill of all those sweet, innocent babies. After we've taken them every way that is physically possible, we will eat them. Do you know how sweet their flesh tastes? You should try it some-time." She licked her lips in anticipation, her expression hideous with egregious lust and hunger.

I restrained myself from revealing any expression as I faced this heinous creature. Kateryna approached me again, but I took the initiative and ran toward her. I jumped up and landed with my thighs around Kateryna's neck, pulling her down and flipping her over my body as I deftly somersaulted to the side and returned to my feet. The back of the demon's body hit the concrete hard with a solid *whack*. I hurried back to Kateryna, grabbed a heavy pool-side chair, and launched it at the demon's face. As the chair hit its intended target, I heard a couple of cracks as her facial bones shattered.

I waited with bated breath for the demon to return to her feet. Kateryna shook her head as if dazed, but she eventually staggered back into a standing position. The black ooze trickled from her badly broken nose, and one eye socket and cheekbone also appeared to be splintered. But she focused her attention on me.

The demon ran at me again, but I was ready. I picked her up bodily, throwing her over my shoulder and into the pool behind me. The demon sank but then struggled to swim toward the surface, using her legs and one good arm. Diving into the pool, I came up behind her and firmly grabbed the ruby necklace that was around Kateryna's throat. The demon struggled to get a grip on my hands to break out of the choke hold, but she couldn't find purchase on my slippery, wet skin.

The demon still fought me, but then I twisted myself around so I was now facing the fiend, and I sputtered into her ugly face, "I…am…done… with…you, you…ugly…bitch!" Still keeping a firm grip on the necklace choke hold, I pulled my gun up with the other hand and shot the demon twice, once in each eye.

I released the tight grip on her necklace as it finally broke under pressure. The sparkling rubies fell through the water and slid to the bottom of the pool. Then Kateryna's body followed suit. The black ooze and slime permeated the pool water, turning it black and putrid.

I swam to the side of the pool, and Finn reached down, grabbed both of my wrists and gently pulled me out. He drew me into his arms and held me close. I breathed hard, and my heart pumped rapidly, but Finn's strength calmed my frantic adrenaline. Pulling away, I whispered shakily, "I'm getting you wet, Finn."

He placed both hands on the sides of my face and replied, "What are you, Jackie Chan?" He chuckled, but I saw fear and relief on his handsome face.

"No, just someone with God's love on her side." I turned and glanced back at the pool, which now was a dark, ugly shade of gray, and I looked at my team members as they stared at me in awe. They clapped loudly and whistled their approval.

I smiled shyly at them, then said to everyone. "Let's finish this job and leave this horrifying place." They hooted and hollered and returned to complete their jobs.

Turning to Finn, I said, "I need some dry clothes that don't smell like demons. Do I have time to return to the suite, take a quick shower, and change?"

"Yes, you do. Billie, will you escort Mara back to her suite?" Finn asked. Billie agreed, gave me a huge smile, and slapped me on my back as we strolled toward the elevators.

"Goodness, Mara, you're wondrous to behold when you do that shtick. You've got a lot of chutzpah, doll!" Billie commented in her Brooklyn accent and squeezed my arm as we entered the elevator.

After Billie and I returned to the lobby, Finn nodded to us as he spoke with Jonas and Aaron. He told them to confirm with all other team members that every floor was secured and cleared.

"Edison, bring in the last buses, and let's get those poor children out of here," Finn ordered.

"Copy that. They're on the way: we'll get them out as quickly as possible," Edison replied.

As Finn and I entered the reception area again, we realized most of the dead demons were naked, and some were in explicit positions. We looked questioningly at our team members, and one woman named Alyssa said, "After that major demon left the room, they started going nuts, stripping off their clothes and doing the nasty with each other. It was disgusting but made our job much easier. They never saw it coming."

"It had to be that major demon. I have the feeling he uses sex to control his underlings to keep them in line. They're so addicted to him they can't help themselves and will do anything to please him." I said, shaking my head. "We'll have to talk to Kaiko about this—maybe she'll tell us more about this monster."

"I agree. We'll need as much information as possible when we go after that fiend. Jasper informed me they've been tracking him, and he's headed to LAX. We'll have our people continue to monitor his movements. Until then, let's finish this disgusting job," Finn replied, and we moved to the ballroom to speak with our salvageable.

They were huddled on the floor but not restrained in any way. Our team members had their guns trained on them in case they attempted to flee.

"Well, well, well," Finn said as he looked at his watch. "All of you will have a difficult decision to make, and you'll have approximately ninety minutes to make the correct one. We'll take you by large semi-trucks to another secure location, which will take about thirty minutes. At this other site, you'll have one hour to decide if you want to continue to follow evil or change your ways and follow God. I'll tell you now that choosing God will save your life and soul. But that's totally up to you and whether you truly want to live. If you cause us any problems during or after the move, we'll kill you as swiftly as we killed the demons you've been pursuing and serving. This is also your choice."

Finn nodded to several Chosen, and they began moving the large group to the semi-trucks. One man became violent with one of our people, and they shot him with no remorse. It was only a bullet to the leg, but this warning made the rest of them understand that this was a serious situation, and whether they lived or died was their choice.

God and his angels would handle the salvageable. Kaiko told us to take these people to a specific abandoned church, take them inside, and have them sit in the pews. Then our people would close the doors, depart the site, and never return. We had no clue what God or the angels would do with these people, but we figured they were now in the best of hands. We prayed these people would make the right choice and begin living their lives dedicated to God, but we'd never know.

More buses came up the road, and these vehicles were for our people. Finn would detonate the explosives that had been set in place once everyone was cleared from the hotel.

Finn nodded to me, and I called in Jonas and Aaron. We each took a third of the hotel, centered ourselves, and scanned every inch of the large estate for anyone who may have been missed or hiding. I felt nothing alive; no demon or human remained on the premises. Giving the all-clear over the mic, I heard the same from Aaron and Jonas.

The three of us met with Finn at the front of the hotel, where one bus remained to take us away from this place. We did one last psychic scan, climbed into the bus, and drove to an area around the mountain. Finn held the detonator and looked at us one last time; we nodded, and he pressed the button. We heard and felt the sonic boom from the explosion, and waited for several minutes, then drove just to the mountain's edge. As we looked back to where the hotel had been, nothing was left but an enormous crater and an intense blue fire. Tears were in our eyes as we thanked God for being with us, guiding us in our tasks, and keeping us all safe. The driver turned our bus around, and we left this Godforsaken place.

CHAPTER 36

The return flights were a quiet affair, and our people were relieved to be returning home. My team was the last to leave California. We wanted to be sure our precious Chosen warriors were treated for any injuries from the hotel battle and were safely on their way home. Finn was gracious to every individual, thanked each one, and said prayers for them as well.

After landing at the base, we unloaded our gear and changed out of our military clothing, then returned to our apartments. We didn't have luggage because, before the hotel trip, our team decided to leave our belongings in the rooms and depart with what we had on us. Finn was kind enough to see me to my home, so I invited him inside, and he accepted. After entering my place, I stood for a moment, thankful to be back. Finn came up behind me and pulled me against him, and I turned around and hugged him close.

I missed seeing Asher as I entered my place, but he'd been staying with Father Faraj while we were on the mission. He'd kindly offered to cat-sit because Father missed his feline, who passed away a year before. I'd pick up Asher in a couple of hours after I showered, changed, and ate dinner.

"Oh, I almost forgot," I replied, backing away from Finn and digging into one of my deep pockets. In my hands was the expensive jewelry he'd given me to wear at the hotel.

"Seriously, you brought them back with you?" He laughed as I handed the gems to him. "You should keep the jewelry, sweetheart, because you earned it."

Finn tried to hand them back to me, but I shook my head in refusal. "Oh, no. They would only remind me of that awful place, so I want nothing to do with them. I merely wanted you to have the gems back. You can return them, give them to a charity—it doesn't matter. I didn't want to see that much money go up in smoke."

"I know what we can do with the jewelry: we'll put it in an auction and use the money for the children we rescued."

"Oh, Finn, what a great idea. Thank you!" I reached up and gave him a fierce embrace.

The children were being flown to an area thirty miles from our facility. Finn's contacts at the FBI would reunite them with their families. The remaining children who were orphans would be placed in proper foster facilities until permanent homes could be found. Our people would take excellent care of them.

"I plan on visiting the children tomorrow to make sure they're settling in," I said.

"Mara, please be careful and don't get attached to them. I know it can be difficult, especially after everything they've been through."

"I know, but we're responsible for following this through. Gracie is expecting me to visit her."

"You're walking a fine line with her; I hope you know that. You can't let her get attached to you, sweetheart. It'll only become more difficult for Gracie when you can no longer see her. Our people will find her a loving, permanent home," Finn said in a warning tone.

"I'm well aware she needs parents. But I promised to visit her after she left that hellhole, and I won't disappoint her." I was angry at Finn's comment.

Finn sighed in resignation and replied, "I'm sorry. I have several meetings all day tomorrow, so I can't go with you, though I wish I could." He kissed me, then stepped back. "Will you be okay tonight?"

I sighed in resignation and exhaustion. "I'll be fine. But first, I want to get this evil stink off me, then retrieve Asher. He's waiting for me and I missed that handsome boy." After returning his kiss, I escorted him to the door.

After Finn's departure, I took a long, well-deserved shower and scrubbed the remainder of the disgusting demon smell off my body and hair. With a towel wrapped around me, I wiped off the foggy mirror, and the face that returned my gaze was ghostly. I was pale with weariness and noticed a few bruises on my arms from the fight with that she-demon. After drying my hair, I dressed, reapplied make-up, and retrieved Asher.

The next day, I took a car and driver and visited the children. They looked happier with their new toys, a vast playground, and lovely rooms to sleep in. Several adults were tending to them, and they were treated well. When Gracie spotted me, she ran over, yelling my name with pure glee. We visited for over an hour, and she asked when I would take her home with me. I couldn't answer immediately because I never expected that question and had no clue how to respond.

"Gracie, honey, you can't come with me. I don't even have a permanent home, and you wouldn't like where I live. It's no place for a young child and I'm hardly ever there. It would be best if you had a great place with a giant backyard, and two wonderful parents, a mommy and a daddy. We're going to find you the best home ever. I promise, sweetheart." She stared at me for a few moments, and I thought she would cry. I gave her a big hug and could hear her sniffling. As I glanced at her arm, the number one was still visible, and I wondered why it hadn't washed off.

"But, I want to live with you. I'll be good, I promise. I don't take up much room and I can sleep anywhere. Please, Mara, take me with you. Please." She hugged me close and didn't want to let go.

How do I get out of this mess and not break her heart? "Sweetheart, if I could take you, I would, but that's not how it works. I'm so sorry and I know it isn't fair." There were tears in my voice as I continued to hold her close. I finally set her away from me, looked her in the eyes, and said, "Gracie, I'll try to keep in touch and ensure you get the most wonderful new family. I promise, my precious. Okay?" Her little face was wet with tears, but I had to be strong for both of us. "Oh honey, you're never alone, you understand?" After giving her another hug, I felt her nodding against me. "That's my girl."

Before I left, I spoke with Gracie's caregiver, Margaret. I asked if any of the children's marks had come off, and she said they had, except Gracie's. They would try other non-toxic substances to see if they would remove the ink. She said she'd keep me posted, and I gave her my cell phone number. I thanked her for taking good care of Gracie.

After my visit, I climbed into the car's back seat for my return trip to the base. As we pulled away from the estate, my eyes watered, and I grabbed a tissue from my purse. The driver asked if I was okay and said I was fine, but I continued wiping my face as I stared out the window, trying to stem the tears.

Finn called later that night and asked about my visit. Keeping my tone light, I informed him the children were doing well and settling in. I didn't want Finn to know how much that precious little girl affected me. That beautiful child already stole my heart and I wanted her as my own, but it could never happen. Our current lifestyle was no place for her, and I wondered if it ever would be. I'd probably have to face the fact that children may never be an option in this lifetime either.

I dreamed of Gracie that night, but it wasn't pleasant. It was filled with darkness and sadness, but I surmised it reflected my negative feelings, worrying that I may never have children. A dark, threatening voice echoed in the back of my mind, and I could have sworn it was calling to the child. Evil was after that precious baby, and I wouldn't let it win. Not if I had anything to say about it!

CHAPTER 37

Finn and I had dinner together the next night, and he escorted me to one of the elegant French restaurants. I wore another cocktail dress with high heels and thanked him for taking the time out of his busy day to have dinner with me. We enjoyed our usual teasing conversation, but he eyed me thoughtfully. I finally asked him what was wrong; he said it was nothing and that he enjoyed looking at me. But there must have been something else. He took me dancing, and I was happy to be held close to him as we glided across the floor.

When the night was over, I was reluctant to part ways. Finn kissed me passionately inside my apartment door and held me close once more. He was about to leave but returned to me and murmured, "Mara, are you alright, sweetheart?"

Smiling brightly, I replied I was great, only a little tired from the mission. I told him to go home, get some rest, and I'd see him at tomorrow's meeting. Giving him another kiss, I shooed him down the hall. After I closed the door, I went to my bedroom to prepare for bed. As I said my evening prayers, I asked God if he would bless Finn and me with children when the time was right, and I fell asleep.

I STARTED DREAMING ABOUT GRACIE, but this one is different. It's dark, and I feel a great, ominous presence coming after her, but I can't determine who or what it is.

~

I JERKED awake and yelled Gracie's name. Asher yowled at me in concern. Pulling him close, I rubbed my face in his sweet-smelling fur. "I'm okay, my boy. I pray it was only a nightmare and not an omen."

The next day, they called a meeting for our team. We were all in attendance and reviewed everything that had transpired on the last mission. Finn and Edison wanted any recommendations on what we could have done differently or if there were any apparent mistakes in the planning or implementation. We reviewed the entire mission and discussed everything at length, and then the conversation turned to some recent information.

Edison said with satisfaction, "Since we eliminated the evil part of the California legislature, the remaining legislators are scrambling to reassemble what's left of their government and are attempting to find replacements for the newly empty seats. The few attendees who were 'on the fence' about turning evil are trying to fill the vacated positions with good people, and the proposed anti-religion bill has been put by the wayside. Once their legislature is reassembled, this atrocious bill will be vetoed and will never be introduced again. Our trusted sources have given us assurances that we can rely on their intel. We should be proud of what we've done to save our fellow, God-loving worshippers. You should give yourselves a pat on the back."

It thrilled everyone to hear the fantastic news. We'd made an immense difference in saving the right of religious freedom in California and, hopefully, in the rest of the country and the world.

We continued discussing the past mission for twenty minutes, but I had difficulty concentrating on the meeting. Something was pushing at the back of my mind, and I did my best to block it, but whatever it was persisted.

"Gracie…" The voice drew out her name, which was loud, clear, and malevolent. I heard it again and felt Gracie's terror.

"Excuse me," I said to the team, quietly leaving the room, then walked rapidly down the hall to Finn's office. Thankfully, it was unlocked, and I sat on the sofa. Pulling out my phone, I called the children's estate. Finn walked in and stared at me with concern. Holding my hand up to him in a halting motion, I said into the phone, "I need to speak with Margaret, please. It's urgent." I breathed heavily and felt sick to my stomach. "Come on…come on…," I muttered to myself.

"Margaret, is Gracie okay?"

She spoke rapidly, saying something upset Gracie, and the child repeated the words, "The voice won't stop," and kept placing her hands over her ears.

"Margaret, I'm coming right over. Please hold her and tell her she'll be fine and Mara is coming. Will you please do this for me?" She agreed to my request, and I hung up.

I was about to rush out the door, but Finn stopped me. "What's going on?"

"Finn, there isn't time. I have to leave immediately because Gracie's in trouble."

"Wait, I'll tell Edison we're leaving and to finish the meeting without us." He grabbed my hand, apparently afraid I'd go without him.

After advising Edison of our departure, Finn called ahead for a car and it was waiting for us in the motor pool garage. Finn told the driver to step on it, and we arrived at the estate in under forty minutes. Margaret met us inside the door.

"She's still upset but calming down," Margaret explained.

"Is she still hearing the voice?" I asked.

"I don't think so, but she's stopped talking to us."

I ran up the stairs and into Gracie's room, and she was huddled into a ball on her bed. "Gracie, honey, it's me, Mara. Can you hear me?" I sat on the bed next to her and touched her gently. She twisted around, cried out to me, and wrapped her arms around my neck. Pulling her onto my lap, I held her close. As I glanced at Gracie's arm, the number one mark was still as vivid as the day we found her. I looked at Finn and he noticed it, too, shaking his head questioningly.

"I'm here, baby, and I promise I won't let anyone hurt you." She was still crying, but not as loudly. Finn rubbed her back, and I saw the pain in his eyes as he felt for the child.

"Margaret, pack her things for me, please. She's coming with us," I ordered, and she looked at me, then at Finn, clearly seeking his approval. Covering Gracie's ears, I barked, "Don't look at him, this is my decision and I'm responsible for her. Now move!" That got Margaret's attention, and she immediately did as I ordered.

They packed a bag for Gracie, which included her favorite stuffed kitty, and Finn took it from Margaret and placed it in the car. The sweet child was now asleep, and I carried her out to the vehicle and sat her in my lap. I suddenly realized we didn't have a car booster seat, but Margaret brought one out for us, Finn installed it, then securely buckled Gracie in. I thanked Margaret, promised to call her later, and we drove back to the base.

Finn looked at me and whispered, "You have some explaining to do." This was all he said, and we finished the trip in silence so Gracie could sleep.

After we arrived at the base, Finn carried the child to my apartment and put her into my bed. I gave her the stuffed kitty, but Asher came in and pushed the stuffed animal out of his way. He snuggled against the little girl and wrapped his paws around her neck.

"Thanks, Asher, she could use you right now, and you know it, too," I replied, kissing Asher and Gracie.

Finn smiled and followed me out of the bedroom to the kitchen. I fixed us both a glass of iced tea and sat down with him at the table. He waited patiently for me to explain what had just happened.

"Finn, I have little to tell you, except the past few nights, I've been dreaming that some dark entity was after Gracie. Then, at the meeting, I heard the entity's voice talking to her—it was calling her name repeatedly. I assume that's what she heard in her head as well. Also, they haven't been able to remove the number the demon put on her arm. The marks he placed on the other children had washed off, but Gracie's didn't. I don't know what to make of it unless the major demon who placed the numeral tattoo has some hold on her. We couldn't protect her at the estate, which would only endanger the other children. I had to bring her here, but I don't have a clue what we do now. Do you think Kaiko could shed some light on this problem?"

Finn sat there a moment, digesting the information, and he answered, "I think she could because I, like you, don't know what else to do. In the meantime, I'll search for an appropriate bed for a four-year-old and find space for it in your bedroom. We'll also purchase whatever we need to care for a young child. I'll look into it immediately." Finn took my hand and kissed my palm.

I also asked Finn if he would take my handgun and place it somewhere safe. It shouldn't be in my apartment with Gracie being here because I couldn't safely lock it away. He said he'd see that it was secured in my locker in the armory.

"Have I told you lately how much I love you?" I asked and kissed him soundly on the lips.

"I believe so, but you can tell me again." He leaned in and gave me another kiss. Then I quietly retrieved the box from my bedroom closet that held my handgun and handed it to Finn. I hugged him and thanked him again; he gave me a reassuring smile and left my apartment.

Two hours later, Gracie was still asleep with Asher curled against her. There was a knock at the door, and it was a courier with a cart full of boxes. He entered and stacked all the items in the living room. I thanked him and he left with a smile and stated, "Enjoy."

Opening the boxes, I discovered everything a little girl might need. I heard another knock at the door, and two young men delivered a youth bed. They said they'd assemble it for me and would also move my bed over to make room for it. I asked them to wait for a second and moved Gracie to the sofa. She woke up, and I felt bad for interrupting her sleep, but she gave me a big smile and a hug. The men then went into the bedroom to take care of the beds.

Asher sauntered from the room, obviously in a huff at being disturbed from his nap, but strolled over to Gracie and sat in her lap. It thrilled her that the fluffy cat was sitting with her and purring loudly. She seemed to have forgotten what had happened earlier or didn't want to discuss it.

When the men finished, I thanked them profusely; they said it wasn't a problem and departed. I escorted her back to the bedroom and she loved her new bed. It was a pink toddler bed with a removable rail, and the design was made for a princess. Gracie helped me make the bed, using the new princess sheets, blanket, and pillow.

An hour later, Finn called and asked how Gracie was doing. I replied that she was great and hadn't said anything about the attack from earlier in the day. Then I thanked Finn for the items he bought for her and told him she was thrilled with everything. He said he was happy she was doing well.

"Mara, we have to meet with Kaiko. We have an appointment with her in about an hour, but we need someone to stay with Gracie."

"Yes, that could be a problem. How about I ask Jonas and Aaron? I'm sure they wouldn't mind, and I think they could help block any attack that may happen when I'm not with her. Of course, I don't even know if I can block the demon either, but I'm sure Kaiko can tell us if it's possible."

"That's a great idea. Please call them and I'll see you at the meeting." I phoned my brothers and told them about everything that had transpired regarding Gracie. They said they'd love to watch her and would be at my place in forty-five minutes.

When my brothers arrived, I introduced them to Gracie; she was polite and hugged them both. "There's macaroni and cheese, hot dogs, and chicken in the refrigerator, as well as some green beans. I'm not sure what she likes, so I guess you'll have to ask her. There are plenty of toys, books, and videos for entertainment. Finn thought of everything, thank goodness. I don't know how long this meeting will take, but I'd like to get dinner afterward. I love you two for doing this." I hugged them and left the apartment.

I met Finn in the meeting room. Kaiko hadn't yet arrived, so we had a few minutes to talk alone. "Finn, do you know who can care for Gracie when I have to be away from her?"

"I'm afraid not. We can ask around, though, and find a suitable babysitter."

There was a knock on the door, and Kaiko entered and took a seat. We exchanged greetings, and I told her what had transpired at the hotel, including the arrival of a major demon. I also mentioned Gracie and what was now happening to her.

After digesting my information, Kaiko closed her eyes for several minutes, opened them again, and announced, "This is the evil beast who must be destroyed. Archangel Gabriel says this demon's name is Asmodeus, and he's one of the worst of the archdemons. This monster is one of the seven princes of Hell and is also called the prince of lust. His outward appearance is that of a pretty young man, and he spreads his lechery to others just by his touch or even suggestion, but his actual countenance is quite the opposite. He has three heads: one human, the second is of a sheep, and the third, is a bull. The ultimate goal of this demon is to bring his seven legions of followers up through the portal and take over the earth."

She stopped briefly, then continued, "But, there's a caveat regarding his plan. He's trying to overthrow Lucifer in Hell, then gain control of the Earth. We don't know how or why the archangel Lucifer hasn't interfered in Asmodeus's endeavors. But we have a supposition that Lucifer is letting Asmodeus do all the work in opening the portal. Then Lucifer would come through, defeat Asmodeus, and take the earth for himself. That's why you must destroy this major demon and close the portal before this happens."

"That's quite a battle, Kaiko. We don't even know where this fiend is or where the portal's located. How do we find them both?" I inquired.

"Where you'll find one, you'll find the other," Kaiko said. "He'll stay close to the door, especially now that you eliminated so many of his followers. Their evil fed his power and now that they're gone, he must stay closer to Hell to maintain his strength. I'd advise you to look for any recent weather or supernatural anomalies. He'd have to quickly escalate opening the portal before he loses this advantage and has to return to Hell. However, I believe you'll be given more information about the gateway, Mara, through your dreams or possibly visions."

"But what about Gracie? What hold does he have on her, and why?" I asked.

"Gracie is someone he greatly desires. Her innocence and beauty fascinate him, and he merely wants to possess her. Out of the thirteen children he marked with a number, she was the only one who'd been tattooed by his demon blood. The only way to break the connection between her and this monster is by destroying him. You did well by bringing her here because she's safer by being amongst the Chosen, especially the Gatekeepers.

"Asmodeus still has a connection with her, even here, and you'd be wise never to let her leave this facility until we eliminate the demon. I must warn you, Mara, and please tell your brothers when you attempt to block this evil one from entering Gracie's mind, be sure that yours are protected as well. If you don't, he can invade and take control of all your minds too, so be vigilant and safeguard yourselves."

Kaiko closed her eyes for another moment, then continued, "I'm sorry I don't have more for you, but that's all the information I can impart for now. I'll let you know if the great angel speaks with me again." Kaiko gave us each a hug and turned to leave but stopped.

"I know you'll need someone to care for Gracie when you're unable. My home is open to the precious child, and we'd love to care for her when we're needed. You have my number, Finn, please give it to Mara." Finn nodded, and she quietly departed.

Finn and I decided to get some dinner, discussed Kaiko's valuable information, then returned to my apartment. My brothers and Gracie were playing a game of cards on the living room rug. She was laughing hysterically when we entered the room, and Jonas and Aaron were making goofy faces at her.

Jonas had the inane talent of making one of his eyes turn in the opposite direction of the other. When we were kids, he always made me laugh when he did his "eye trick." But apparently, Aaron had the same hysterical skill. Finn and I also couldn't help ourselves and joined in the laughter.

When Gracie saw me, she ran over for a hug, and I picked her up in my arms. "I see my brothers are sharing their googly eyes with you, sweetheart."

"Yes. Aaron and Jonas are so 'filarious,'" she answered giggling, which made her dimples visible. I smiled at her fumbled word, kissed her cheek, and she returned to my brothers and their game.

Finn and I went into the kitchen, I poured us both an iced tea, and we sat down at the table. Keeping my voice low, I whispered, "I hate to say it, but we better look for the portal as soon as possible. I don't like his hold on her and how much danger she could face."

"I agree. I'll speak with Poppy tomorrow, and she and her team can begin looking for those anomalies Kaiko mentioned. I'll also inform everyone about the information she divulged this afternoon."

Just then, my brothers and Gracie walked into the room, and Jonas said, "We'd better go. I have a late date with Poppy, and it's Aaron's bedtime."

Aaron snorted and pretended to strangle Jonas. Gracie laughed loudly, but I could see how tired she was, and it was past her bedtime.

Finn replied, "I'll see the two of you to the door." He looked at me, signaling that he'd update my brothers on the latest information from Kaiko.

"You, young lady, should bathe and get into your pajamas." She smiled and didn't argue with me, which I found surprising.

The bath didn't take long, and I finished preparing her for bed. She climbed under the sheets, and Asher jumped in bed with her, much to Gracie's delight, and they snuggled together. I asked her if she ever said prayers, and she said she did, and I had her lead a blessing to the Lord.

I found this child to be highly intelligent and articulate, and she seemed well-educated about God. She thanked Jesus for caring for her today and asked Him if I could become her new mommy. She finished with an "Amen," and then gave me a hug and a kiss.

Finn walked in and told Gracie he hoped she'd sleep well and have happy dreams. She motioned for Finn to come to her, which he did, then she asked him to bend over so she could hug him as well. Finn smiled with such pleasure that my heart melted.

I turned on the nightlight and told Gracie to sleep well. I reassured her I'd return in a little while and would go to bed too. That made her happy, and she put her arms around Asher and went to sleep.

Strolling with Finn to the door, he turned to me with a warning, "Mara, be careful, will you? You know what Kaiko said, that you could be in danger too if you try to block him from connecting with Gracie."

"Trust me, I definitely will. I don't want that monster in my head either. Will you call me tomorrow and let me know if you get any information regarding the demon or the portal?"

"Of course, sweetheart. You'll be the first to know as soon as I hear anything. You'll call me if you need me, right?" He put his finger under my chin, raising my eyes to look into his.

"I will, I promise. I love you, Finn, with all of my heart." I wrapped my arms around him.

"I love you too, my sweet. I'll talk to you tomorrow." He moved away and closed the door behind him, but I could tell by his expression he was worried about leaving me and Gracie alone.

After preparing for bed, I knelt by my bedside and prayed to the Lord to help and guide us with whatever we had to deal with next. I then climbed into bed and went to sleep.

~

I'M DREAMING AGAIN, but this one is different. Isabella is off in the distance and her finger is pointing toward something. There's a dense fog and I strain to see what she's trying to show me. It slowly clears, and there's an ocean, a large river, and a dense jungle. I'm coming to a clearing with several wooden buildings, some trucks, and machinery, but then, I view close to one thousand people lying on the ground. There are men, women, and children, all obviously deceased. Their faces are frozen in horrible grimaces from their excruciatingly painful deaths.

Looking beyond the bodies, I spot what appears to be a pavilion, and one man is sitting in a wooden chair in front of the pews. He looks familiar to me, but then his face becomes distorted, filled with evil satisfaction, his eyes glowing a fiery red. The righteous smile on his face turns into a painful grimace as he dies in agonizing pain, like the other poor people in the village.

Now, the scene changes. I can see an old signpost that had once been over some type of entrance. The writing is faded, and I can't focus on it enough to discern the lettering. Beyond the old signage, I also see a few dilapidated small buildings and pieces of old machinery, but most of the area is overgrown by dense jungle foliage.

I hear several loud cracks as a giant storm cloud hovers over the area, and the lightning bolts strike the ground, then return to the enormous cloud. The earth is shaking, and I see a hole forming in what used to be the pavilion. A hideous black ooze spews from it, and now I hear torturous screaming echoing from the cavernous pit. Many monsters of every shape and form climb out of the hole, slithering through the dense foliage and across the jungle floor. Finally, a hideous dragon struggles to emerge from

the gaping crevasse; he turns to look at me, his eyes blazing, and his sharp
teeth are gnashing on something. He finally spits out a large mass of flesh,
and it's Gracie, or what's left of her.

I'm about to scream, but Isabella appears again and says, "The
Chosen can stop this. But it'll take the faith of every believer to weaken the
dragon enough for the Gatekeepers to destroy him, then close the portal. I
know you can do this, Mara, and He does as well."

WAKING IN BED, I glanced at the clock; it was only two in the morning.
Asher was sitting next to my head, staring at me with huge, bright eyes. I
quietly told him I was fine, but he knew differently. He curled into my neck
with his paws touching my face as if to say, "You'll be okay."

But would I be?

CHAPTER 38

The next morning, I woke up and felt my bed bounce up and down and suspected it was Asher, but then I heard a giggle. It was Gracie. I pretended to still be asleep but then grabbed Gracie, rolled her on her back, and tickled her belly. She giggled even louder, then Asher decided to get in on the action. He also jumped up and down on the mattress, making Gracie roar with childhood glee. Her laughter was infectious and I had to join in.

My phone rang, so I grabbed it off the bedside table, and it was Finn. "Good morning, handsome." Gracie was still laughing and Finn could hear her over the cell.

"Good morning, love. It sounds like the two of you are having a good time. I guess I don't have to ask if you're both doing well this morning," he said in his deep and sultry voice.

"We're doing great." I walked from the bed to the bathroom, slowly closing the door. "Finn, we need to meet this morning. I had a dream last night and Isabella tried to show me something. It might give us some insight as to the demon's location, but we'll need to brainstorm using the information God gave me."

"I can put our team together, let's say, in about two hours. Call Kaiko's parents and see if they can watch Gracie." After agreeing, I said I'd call them to see if they were available. It so happened they were, and they gave me their apartment number.

When I delivered Gracie to Kaiko's apartment, I found her parents delightful. Their names were Gloria and Marshall Riley; they were friendly and kind, and Gracie loved them. It also thrilled Kaiko to meet this new precious girl. She clasped Gracie's hand, and they went into the living room to watch television. I gave Kaiko's parents Gracie's bag and said her stuffed kitty was inside, and I informed them I'd be back in a couple of hours. They said not to worry and were pleased to take care of her.

My team was already in the meeting room when I arrived, and we sat in our usual seats. Finn began with a group prayer, and then he wanted to update us on the child trafficking ring. "According to my FBI contact, they've apprehended over five hundred people worldwide. They accomplished this because of the information we retrieved from the demons at the hotel."

Phbbbt!—A strange noise interrupted Finn, but he continued, "There are more who are still under investigation and will soon be brought to justice." We were elated to hear we could stop so many of these deviant criminals and put them behind bars.

Finn continued, "Regarding the children, we've found most of these children's families and are being careful—and diligent—with finding wonderful homes for those kids who have no relatives. I'll keep you updated—as I get more information." Finn kept stopping because the strange noises continued during his update.

Then Finn continued, saying, "Mara, would you like to tell us what transpired last night?" *Ppppprrrrrrrrrrttttt!* Everyone in the room snickered but tried to ignore the sound.

I nodded to Finn, related everything I'd seen in my dream, and then asked if anyone had any idea where this place might be. "My guess would be that it's a tropical location, near a major ocean and a large—river. I wish I could provide—you with more information, but that's all God has provided so far," I chortled. "What *is* that noise?" *Phbbbt!* "There it is again!"

"So, all we know so far is that it's in a tropical location," Aaron asked. *Phbbbt! Ppppprrrrrrrrrrttttt!* "Oh my gosh, it's coming from under my chair!" Aaron squawked, stood up, turned his chair over, and found a remote-controlled fart machine taped to the bottom of his seat. "Okay, who has the remote for this thing?" he yelled in accusation.

By this time, everyone in the room was hysterical with laughter. The look on Aaron's face was priceless, and we couldn't stop howling. Aaron stared at our grins and joined in, cackling as loudly as the rest of us.

"Okay, Jonas, I know it has to be you, bucko! You still think I pulled the ping pong ball stunt on you, and it's payback, right?" Aaron squeaked.

Jonas said, "It's not me, really," but his denial certainly didn't sound sincere because he was still doubled over with glee.

"Okay, everyone, the fun is over, and we must get back to work." Finn said in a reprimanding tone, but we were still giggling and chuckling, so Finn finally said, "Why don't we take a fifteen-minute break? Be ready to get serious and back to work when you return."

After the break, Finn commented sternly, "Now that everyone is back into working mode, let's begin again. Mara, what can you tell us about the poor people who were dead? Were they of any specific ethnicity?"

"Not that I could tell. But I'd say mostly Caucasian, and the leader was as well. He seemed familiar to me, but I still can't place him. I'm sorry. It was definitely in the past because I saw two specific scenes: one from a while ago, then a second from the present or the not-too-distant future. In the second vision, there weren't any dead or decayed corpses or skeletons. I'm assuming someone discovered all of the bodies."

Jonas added, "I doubt they've kept this event quiet, not with that many dead at one time. It could be a natural disaster or maybe a mass murder. Edison, let's start by searching the Internet for a large number of dead from a natural disaster."

Edison typed on his keyboard, and it displayed the results on the overhead screen. We could watch as he scrolled through different files on the web. He displayed several photos of different locations, but nothing was familiar to me. I shook my head, and he continued his search. After several minutes, he typed in "mass murders" and scrolled through several files. I shook my head again with frustration.

Rising to my feet, I paced the room. "I've seen that man from somewhere, but where? It seems like it was from an old memory...." I walked some more, stopped, and looked at the large computer screen. After a few moments, I concentrated on the dream and what I'd seen.

I had a hunch and said, "Edison, please look up mass suicide." He did as I asked, and it didn't take but a moment to find "Jonestown mass suicide in Guyana, South America." He displayed the photos of Jim Jones, and I replied, "That's the man I saw in my dream, and this is the place."

Everyone in the room talked at once, then became silent. We remembered how horrible this event was back in the seventies and how so many innocent lives were taken, all at the instruction of this diabolical monster.

I felt sick; I told everyone I needed a break, rushed from the room, and hurried to the bathroom. Finn found me sitting on the floor in the restroom with my head between my knees. Jonas and Aaron followed closely behind him.

Finn grabbed a few paper towels, wet them with cold water, sat next to me on the floor, and put them on my neck. I leaned into him and waited for the dizziness to pass.

Jonas sat on the other side of me and gave me instructions. "Mara, put that block up inside your mind. You were taught how; now I need you to do it." He rubbed my back as he reminded me how to add the barrier. I did as he asked, started my deep breathing exercises, and began to feel better.

"Her color's coming back," Aaron replied as he crouched before me.

"Okay, boys, I think you have the wrong bathroom. She appreciates each of you being a mensch, but skedaddle now and let me take care of her." It was Billie, and she shooed them from the room. I thanked them weakly and said I was returning to normal, but they still hesitated to leave.

"Wait outside, boys. I'll send her out when she's ready. Now stop hovering and schlep yourselves out of here, will ya?" Billie ordered. I couldn't help myself and chuckled at her pushy mothering tactics.

After the men departed, I said, "Thanks, Billie. I love them all, but I needed some air." She lifted the paper towels from the back of my neck, doused them in cold water again, and returned them to me.

"Look, Mara, I've been there. I happened upon one of the worst massacres I'd ever had the misfortune to see when I was in the Peace Corps in Rwanda. These monsters would come through, and, well, I'd rather not repeat what I saw. But I can guess what you're going through, being psychic and all. Jonas is correct, you have to block it for now. We have a job to do. It would be best if you stayed focused, so we can stop this beast from bringing even more beasts to this planet. Here, take a swig of this, doll. It'll shock you down to your toes." She pulled out a small flask, opened it, and handed it to me. I inhaled a whiff, took a sip, and gasped, followed by several coughs.

"Ya see, that'll do the trick every time. Nothing like a swig of good ol' single-malt whiskey."

I was still hacking up a lung but then laughed. Billie helped me off the floor; I hugged her and thanked her for her kindness. She seemed embarrassed and said, "No problem," and left the restroom.

After cleaning myself up, I returned to the meeting. Finn approached me and examined my expression, ensuring I was alright. Giving him the thumbs-up sign, I sat again at the table. Finn brought me a large iced tea, which I accepted gratefully.

"I'm sorry for running out like that, but I felt the death of all those poor people, and I couldn't pull myself out fast enough. I appreciate your patience. I'm okay now and can continue," I offered apologetically.

Finn said, "I have Poppy on the link, and she's accessed satellite images from that area. Poppy, have you found anything?"

Poppy answered, "Regarding anomalies and strange weather patterns, the area where Jonestown took place has shown significant lightning storms over the last few months. The lightning seems to only strike near one place where the pavilion was located. We also heard through the locals that odd things had been occurring in and around Jonestown. People reported strange, demon-like creatures who would appear, then disappear. They've also experienced eerie noises, strange smells, and ghostly apparitions. As a result, the locals are staying away from this area."

Poppy continued, "Regarding the demon, we finally tracked him to a large estate about one mile from the Jonestown location. His home is well-guarded, gated, and electrified. We've seen him going to and from Jonestown, but he doesn't stay at the site for long. They've also reported that he's limping badly and needs help getting around. After he spends time in Jonestown, he seems stronger for a while. From what our prophet said, we assume that our latest assassination of many of his demons has weakened him significantly. We deduce he needs to spend time at the camp to regain his strength. How he's doing this, we're unsure. This is all the information we have at this time."

"Thanks, Poppy," Finn replied and disconnected the link.

I spoke up, saying, "I'm assuming he's using energy from the portal that's slowly opening, or maybe even the souls who'd been left at the site. I don't know how many Jones may have been trapped in that camp. Even in death, he could still have control over them. We'll need to see if our prophet has information regarding the souls of Jones's victims."

"Until we get more intel, we're unable to develop any strategies for taking this demon down or finding a way to close the portal. Let's meet again tomorrow morning at nine, and I pray we'll have more data by then. Time is of the essence, my friends, so let's be prepared that we may need to leave for South America at a moment's notice. Thank you," Finn said, and everyone departed except for Finn and me.

Finn strolled over and enfolded me in his arms. I leaned into him, soaking up his strong, quiet energy. "Thanks, I needed this," I whispered into his shirt, breathing in his sensual, clean scent. He kissed the top of my head and held me a while longer. Eventually, I pulled away but then reached up and kissed him soundly on his lips. "I needed to do that as well."

He smiled and said, "How about we make it a date night? Just you, me, and Gracie, of course. We'll have dinner and have the meal catered to your place, followed by a night of dancing. I'll take care of the ordering, and you wear something stunning. What do you say?"

"That sounds wonderful. I'd love to forget this mess, at least for a little while. Gracie would love it too, but we'd have to order something simple for her. I still don't know what she likes to eat. What kind of guardian am I? I need to get to know her better, so I think I'll spend the afternoon with her. Can you join us?"

"I have some paperwork to finish, but I should be able to stop by after lunch, maybe around two this afternoon. We can have a fun day with Gracie, then have dinner and dancing tonight." Finn took my hand and walked me out of the meeting room.

"I'll see you this afternoon. Don't work too hard, Finn." I reached up again, kissed his dimpled chin, and turned toward the elevators. He stopped me from moving away as he grabbed my hand, pulled me close, and kissed me so passionately that it made my knees weak.

"Whiskey?" he asked, licking his lips. He said goodbye, and I only nodded because I was too giddy to reply.

I heard him chuckle as I walked away, so I turned and joked, "Just you wait, buster, you'll get what's coming to you."

As he walked to his office, I heard him mutter, "I sure hope so, love, I sure hope so."

After Finn arrived that afternoon, we spent the day getting to know Gracie. She was as smart as she was funny, and one couldn't help but adore her. A couple of hours later, Finn went to his apartment to change, and Gracie and I also donned our Sunday best. I put on a dark blue, low-cut cocktail dress with matching high heels, and Gracie wore a pink lacy dress with matching patent leather shoes. She enjoyed looking at herself in the mirror and danced in circles.

After we ate our delicious catered meal, we returned to the living room. We sat on the sofa and talked for a while, then Gracie climbed into Finn's lap, curled up against him, and fell asleep. I pointed to the bedroom, and he carried her to bed. I changed her into pajamas and tucked her in. Finn brushed the hair off her face, leaned down and kissed her cheek, and said in Gaelic, "Sleep well little one."

We tiptoed from the room, and I turned up the music I'd been playing through the stereo, kicked off my shoes, and asked Finn to dance. He pulled me close, and we moved slowly to the romantic music and relished being in each other's arms. Finn eventually pulled away, and I understood why because I had the same problem.

"Is it getting hot in here?" I asked, fanning my face with my hand.

"Exactly." Finn tried adjusting his pants, which had become a bit tight, and gingerly sat on the sofa.

"I'll get us some refreshing iced tea. Hopefully, that'll cool us down a bit." I giggled at my comment as I strode to the kitchen.

"You sassy wench. It'll only help if I pour it down the front of my pants." He chuckled, and I couldn't help myself and snickered as well.

We spent another hour sitting on the couch and talked the night away.

Finn had long since removed his shoes, jacket, and tie. We watched an old rerun of *Happy Days,* and I snuggled against him.

I started to doze off but then heard a scream in my head and from the bedroom. Both of us ran to check on Gracie. She was sitting in bed with her hands over her ears, and tears were running down her face. After pulling her into my arms, I entered her mind.

"Mara, don't let him into your head. Remember what Kaiko said," Finn warned as he wrapped his arms around us. I nodded, put up a wall around the outside of my mind, and tunneled into Gracie's.

The voice was still calling to her, *"Gracie...You're mine, and you can't get away from me. Gracie..."* I put up a giant cement wall and the voice stopped, but it tried to direct itself toward me. But my barrier was solid, even though I could feel the demon trying to break into my mind. The fury he directed toward me was terrifying, and he tried repeatedly but couldn't push through. Even though his anger and frustration were apparent, he finally gave up and departed.

"It's alright, Gracie, the bad man is gone. You're safe, sweetheart, I promise," I replied and gave Finn a look confirming that the demon had stopped, for now, at least. Gracie was calming down and her tears slowed.

"Why does that monster talk to me? What does he want?" she begged, sniffling against my shoulder.

Finn replied, "My pet, we don't know why, but what we can tell you is that the monster will never get you. He knows that as well; that's why he only talks to you in your head, but Mara can stop him from getting to you."

Gracie turned from me to look at Finn. He brushed the hair off her tear-stained face and kissed her cheek. "I promise, little one, that soon, Mara and I will make the monster go away, and you'll never be bothered by him again."

Gracie moved from my lap and climbed into Finn's, replying sternly, "That's a really bad monster, and I believe you, Finn." He held her for a long time until she fell asleep, and we tucked her back under the blankets. Asher diligently curled himself around her, protecting her in the only way he knew how. I kissed them both and left the room.

"I'm so sorry, Mara, that was not how I wanted our evening to end," Finn apologized and took me into his arms to hold me close.

"I know, Finn, neither did I. But we had a great time tonight, and that monstrosity doesn't get the satisfaction of ruining it for us." I smiled at him, and he grinned back.

"That's my girl. Do you mind if I spend the night on the couch? I don't want to leave the two of you alone. I'll return to my apartment to change, then come back and sleep on your sofa. I won't be much trouble. Scout's honor."

"I'd love it if you could stay. But I doubt you were ever a scout." I snorted loudly, and he laughed and gave me a playful pat on my behind. He went out the door and said he'd be back shortly.

I prepared for bed, then made up the sofa for Finn. He returned wearing an old, well-worn t-shirt, sweatpants, and slippers.

"Finn, I'm apprehensive about my ability to block the demon, not only for Gracie but for me. Can you access a stronger psychic to help me hone my skills?"

"I know some good psychics are at our other facilities. Let me make some calls tomorrow, and I'll see if any of them can help. If this is their expertise, I know they'd be more than willing to fly in and assist you. Don't worry, we'll figure this out and get what you need. Now, go to bed, my love. I'll be fine out here, and you know where I am if you need me. Goodnight, Mara." He gave me another kiss, then pushed me toward the bedroom.

"Goodnight, Finn, and thanks so much for being here for us."

CHAPTER 39

The following day when I woke, I heard laughter coming from the living room. Climbing from the bed, I slowly opened the door and saw Finn, Gracie, and Asher sitting on the floor at the coffee table, having a tea party. I quickly hid behind the door to secretly enjoy their adorable playtime. Finn sat cross-legged with a tiara on his head and daintily held a tiny teacup. He spoke in a high, feminine voice, pretending to be a lady and discussing the latest in women's fashion. I took another peek and witnessed Asher sitting on the other side, a teacup in front of him and a big pink bow perched precariously on the top of his head. He seemed perfectly comfortable, licking water from the little cup. I grabbed my phone to take photos and recorded their tea party. This was the most precious thing I'd ever seen in my life. Quietly shutting the door to give them privacy, I walked into the bathroom to prepare for the day with a giddy grin on my face.

When I entered the living room twenty minutes later, they had finished their party. Finn returned to a standing position, trying to get the kinks out of his long legs, and Gracie came over and hugged him. He lifted her into his arms and spotted me entering the room.

"It's about time you got up, sleepyhead. We've been up forever," Finn said.

"Good morning. I see you two have been busy. Gracie is already dressed, with her hair in a beautiful ponytail. Nice job, Finn."

"Thanks, my love. But I have to get going. I must shower, change, and then make a few phone calls before our nine o'clock meeting. Kaiko's mother said she'd take Gracie for the day. Both of us already had breakfast, including Asher." Finn came over to me and kissed me sweetly, scratching my cheeks with his morning stubble, and handed me Gracie.

"Thanks so much, handsome. By the way, you look gorgeous in that tiara, and our team will think so, too. It's so…you."

He felt the top of his head, and by the look of surprise, he hadn't realized he was still wearing it. "It *does* go well with my sweatpants." He laughed, slightly embarrassed, placed the tiara on my head at a cockeyed angle, and walked out the door.

After I ate a quick breakfast, I dropped Gracie off at Kaiko's place and spoke for several minutes with Gloria. She said not to worry because a full day was planned for her. They would work on her letters, numbers, and even a little American history. I smiled when I left, knowing Gracie was in capable hands.

I walked into the meeting room a few minutes early, and Finn was finishing a phone call but was wiggling in his seat.

He spotted me and said, "Ahh, you're here. I just spoke with the principal at our African location, and they have an accomplished psychic who can help you. Her name is Sizani, and she's South African and apparently, a powerful psychic. She's kindly agreed to fly here and give you extensive training. She'll be here tomorrow evening and will assist you and Gracie."

"That's wonderful. I hope you told her we're most grateful for her help and for coming so quickly."

"I already did, and she's quite a charismatic woman. You'll like her. I have a few more things to discuss, so let's talk again after the morning meeting." Finn made a painful face and wiggled again in his chair. Raising my eyebrows at him, he shook his head in return.

Everyone arrived. I teased my brothers, which was my job as their sister, and my team sat down to start the meeting. It pleased me that Poppy was joining us, and she took the lead on the computer, so I assumed she had more information for us.

Finn started the meeting with our usual prayer, then told everyone about the demon entering Gracie's mind again and how I had hopefully stopped him for now. He next turned to Poppy for any new information she may have obtained. Finn squirmed in his seat repeatedly, and his odd behavior mystified me.

"Thank you, everyone," Poppy began. "My team has obtained new satellite images of the demon's estate and the Jonestown site. It took a lot of unscrambling because whoever the demon hired knew their stuff. But luckily, we're better," she said proudly, then posted the images on the overhead screen.

Poppy continued, "This is his estate. As you can see, it's large and impressive. Several cameras are placed strategically around the entire property, along with electrified wire fencing. He has guards on every side of the estate's roof, plus two on each side of the guest house. This one-story building off to the north is the guard barracks, but there are no shooters on the top of this building. The other rooftop security teams could be a problem because our snipers' only clear line of sight is from the surrounding low-range mountains. However, each mountain is over three thousand yards away. I'm assuming he chose this location because there are only two roads in or out of the estate. Of course, these are protected by cameras and gates as well. As you can also see, he's cleared all the dense jungle within twenty-five hundred yards around his home. The only possible coverage for nearing the property is this line of trees along each side of the main driveway to the estate. But the guards on the rooftops would have to be taken out first. It's a real mess."

Everyone reviewed each photo she showed us and we shook our heads in frustration.

"Poppy, does one of the roads lead to the Jonestown location?" Finn asked as he wiggled in his seat as if trying to get comfortable.

"Yes, this one here. He created this road to get back and forth from the Jonestown camp. There are only two guards at the entrance on this private one-lane road," Poppy answered, pointing to the track that headed west from the demon's home.

She continued, "You can see guards everywhere in these closer satellite photos. This little bugger doesn't lack security, that's for sure. They're consistent with their routine, which is in our favor. Plus, they keep to a strict schedule, and each sentry makes the same rounds, like clockwork.

"We believe the demon's quarters are on the second floor, where this large balcony is located. We've seen him wearing a robe several times, so we concluded it's connected to his sleeping quarters."

Basheer interrupted, asking, "Poppy, do we know how many guards he has and if they are all demons? And do we know if he has any myrmidons protecting the surrounding area?"

"There are at least thirty sentries around the outer perimeter of the estate. It's unknown at this time as to how many may be inside the buildings or if they are all demons. Our psychics would have to make that determination. We haven't seen any myrmidons on any satellite images on or around the demon's property," Poppy replied.

"Now, on to the Jonestown camp: this is where the myrmidons are located, and at least one hundred of them surround the outer camp perimeter. They're only armed with knives and seem to have no pattern to their guard duty. However, they appear to stay within ten yards of the outer perimeter fence that surrounds the camp.

"We tried to zoom into the site for better pictures, but the jungle is incredibly dense, so we haven't been successful. Then we tried infrared and thermal imaging and had better luck. As Mara said, the hot zone appears to be the location of the old pavilion. There's an opening that grows larger every day, but only by a few centimeters. As you can see here, we used layers of thermal imaging to estimate how deep this crevasse is, and so far, it's approximately ten feet below the surface. It doesn't go straight down into the earth but at a forty-five-degree angle. At this time, the hole at the surface is just large enough for a dog to fit through. We estimate that the opening should be large enough for a man to enter in roughly eight to ten days. This is gauged by the number of lightning strikes throughout the night that hit near and at the opening. That's what we have so far, my friends," Poppy concluded.

It was several moments before anyone spoke, then Finn finally replied while adjusting his seat, "Thanks, Poppy. We have a more complicated mission than before." Everyone murmured their agreement.

Finn wiggled in his chair again and stood up quickly, his chair toppling behind him. He adjusted his pants angrily and yelled, "Son of a...! Who freakin' did this?" His face was red, and he was obviously in extreme discomfort.

"Holy fire and brimstone...what's the problem, mate?" Edison demanded of his good friend.

"Someone must have put itching powder in my shorts! It's driving me insane!" Finn retorted as he scratched urgently.

Everyone in the room responded with gales of laughter. We couldn't contain ourselves. Finn's expression changed to a bit of a smile, but he tried to retain the look of reprimand on his face.

"Okay, that's it! I can't stand it anymore. We're taking a thirty-minute break. But, let me say this, I *will* find out who did this, and they *will* pay dearly." Finn turned on his heel and stalked to the door while he scratched everything in his nether regions. The door slammed behind him.

Everyone in the room hooted even harder, and tears of laughter ran down our faces.

Billie spoke up and said between giggles, "Someone got him good in the tuches. I've never seen him schvitzing like that before."

"That's the first time I've witnessed him lose his temper. That stunt really dilled his pickle!" Jasper said, still quaking with humor.

Everyone guffawed in earnest again.

Thirty minutes later, Finn returned and was obviously in a much better mood. His expression was contrite, and he even had laughter in his eyes.

"Okay, let's continue our meeting. And, before you ask, I'm feeling much better. However, the prankster dumped the itching powder in my dresser drawer, covering all my underwear."

"Oh mate, you're going commando!" Edison hooted as he roared with laughter all over again. The rest of us joined in, including Finn.

Once we calmed down, Finn began the meeting again. "Now, where were we? Oh, yes. Regarding this upcoming mission, we'll need a lot of help on this one. We'll require our best minds to plan this next op to the minuscule detail. I'd like to bring in our A-team from our Eastern European facility again. They were a great asset on our last mission at the hotel, and I think we'd be wise to take advantage of their expertise."

Our team provided their thoughts, ideas, and possible strategies for the next two hours. Finn said it was time for lunch and we'd meet again afterward. Everyone left the room, but Finn asked Jonas, Aaron, and me to stay behind.

Finn said, "Why don't we go to lunch together? I have a few things to discuss with all of you, and we might as well enjoy a good meal at the same time."

We arrived at the restaurant and placed our order, and Finn stated, "Jonas and Aaron, I know you heard my announcement about a seasoned psychic coming to assist us. I hope you'll both take advantage of her expertise, especially given what we will face within the next few weeks."

Jonas said, "Finn, I know I can speak for Aaron too, that we would very much appreciate the opportunity for more extensive training. It can only help when we have to deal with these monsters and in protecting Gracie as well. Thank you for doing this." Aaron nodded in agreement.

"You're welcome," Finn replied and continued, "Mara, I have a proposition for you, which I hope you'll accept. Now that you're caring for a child, I'd like to move you to a different, larger apartment. It's a three-bedroom, two-bath suite that's roomier than where you're currently living. It's on the same floor as Kaiko's home, so this location would also be more convenient when you need a babysitter. The move can take place tomorrow, and professionals will handle it. You wouldn't have to do a thing. Just make sure Asher is somewhere safe, and you'd have to be out of the apartment while everything is packed and moved. The furniture would stay, except for Gracie's bed. Everything else will be relocated to the new residence."

I gaped at him and didn't know what to say. It sounded great, but it had a significant drawback. "Finn, I appreciate what you're offering, but I don't think I'd be comfortable being that far away from you. I know it may sound selfish and maybe a little childish, but I have great comfort knowing you're down the hall from me."

Finn reached across the table, clasped my hand in his, and explained, "I've already considered that, and I'll also move to the same floor. I don't need the larger apartment, but I'd feel better staying near the two of you as well."

I smiled brightly and said, "In that case, I'd very much like to take you up on your generous offer. Gracie and Asher would also love more room."

Aaron and Jonas agreed it was a good idea and said they'd help however they could.

"One other thing," Finn continued, "I don't think you should leave your engagement ring in your apartment tomorrow. Not that anyone would steal it, it's just they'd probably know exactly what it's for, and I don't want to compromise our positions."

"I agree. I'll be sure to keep it on me tomorrow. Don't worry, I'll store it in my briefcase and no one would be wiser." Our server arrived and delivered our food. We spent the rest of our lunch enjoying the company and the delicious food.

CHAPTER 40

*T*he next afternoon, we spent several hours in a meeting, devising viable ideas to safely and successfully complete our upcoming mission. There were a few plans in place, but it would take several more sessions to prepare for our operation.

The movers took the entire day to transfer our belongings to the larger apartments. Asher was staying with Father today, and Gracie was with Kaiko's family, and we were blessed they delighted in watching her. She'd also receive a nice education, as Gloria did prekindergarten lessons with her.

The psychic Sizani was arriving this evening, and I asked Finn if she could stay in my spare bedroom in the new apartment. He mentioned she'd also suggested this so that she could work more closely with me. She'd also be near to help to protect Gracie when I couldn't be with her.

Sizani was also a Chosen One and had returned as a young woman. In her previous life, she'd been a mother of six children and a grandmother to fourteen, so she had plenty of experience with youngsters. She'd also been a teacher in her community. I looked forward to meeting her and was glad I'd have help to protect Gracie. It was such a blessing the demon hadn't contacted her again, but I knew it would happen soon.

We finished our meeting seventy minutes before Sizani was due to arrive on the base. I barely had enough time to pick up Gracie, return to my new apartment, and hopefully get somewhat organized. Finn would pick up Asher and bring him to our new home.

Gracie was overjoyed being only a few doors down from Kaiko and her family, and I used my new security card to open the door to our apartment. I was surprised at how big the place was, and the movers did an excellent job putting everything in its proper place. My seascape painting fit beautifully in the living area of the suite. The kitchen was large, with a table, an island, and a separate dining area with an exquisite dining room table and chairs. The primary suite was also impressive. It had a large ensuite bathroom with a double sink vanity, jetted soaker tub, and a separate walk-in shower. The second bathroom was between the second and third bedrooms, with access from the living room.

Gracie's bedroom was delightful, and I surmised Finn had it fixed up exclusively for her. Everything was fit for a princess, and Gracie twirled around her room in great pleasure.

There was a knock at the door, and I found Finn on the other side, with Asher riding on his shoulder. I invited him in and thanked him profusely for the beautiful accommodations. Finn scanned the place and said they'd indeed done an excellent job.

"Finn, I hope Sizani likes cats, and I pray she isn't allergic. I never considered that possibility."

"If there's a problem, Asher can stay with me."

Asher jumped down from Finn's shoulder and strutted around the suite, intently checking out every nook and cranny. His tail was up and he squeaked every time he found something of interest. He made sure his cat beds were accounted for, and his toys were still around.

"Where's your apartment?"

"It's only two doors down to the right, on the same side. I'm closer to you now. We need to get some dinner, but I wondered if we should wait for Sizani. How about I order a variety of food, and we can use your new dining room table? We can place the meal in warmers to stay hot until we're ready to eat."

"That sounds great. I'll go ahead and set the table."

Once everything was prepared for the upcoming dinner, we went to

Finn's new home. It was beautiful and painted in the soft earth tones that he loved. The place was laid out like mine, but the furniture had a more masculine feel.

Finn received a call that Sizani had arrived. We returned to my place and waited for her at the door. A tall, beautiful woman strode down the hall, followed by a young man pushing a luggage cart. We introduced ourselves and I welcomed her to my home. Gracie ran over and wrapped her arms around my legs.

"You must be the lovely Gracie. I'm so pleased to meet you. My name is Sizani, but you can call me Si." She pronounced it like the word "sigh." Gracie loved her.

"Hello, Si. I'm also pleased to meet you," Gracie answered, shyly pulling on the ponytail at the back of her head.

"Si, I hope you'll be comfortable here, but we forgot to tell you I have a cat. If that's a problem, he can stay with Finn while you're here," I replied.

"That's not a problem. I never really had much exposure to cats until I moved to the United States for college. But fell in love with them after a small gold kitten kept showing up at my college dorm. I took her in and had to hide her, of course, and we were together for over eighteen years until she died of old age."

I loved listening to her cultured South African accent, and I couldn't stop looking at her because her beauty was astounding. She had large amber-colored eyes, a straight aquiline nose with slightly flaring nostrils, and a full mouth. Her complexion was a dark ebony color with a beautiful glow of health and vitality. She kept her curly black hair short, accentuating her lovely, striking features.

She gave me an odd look, and I finally said, "I'm so sorry for staring, but you're a stunning woman. Men must follow you around like puppy dogs," I chuckled.

She also laughed and replied, "You're very kind, but no, I think they find me intimidating. Being psychic has been a real problem when trying to date. It makes them nervous, and they're afraid I'm reading every thought in their heads."

"I guess that could be daunting for prospective dates. Now, we need to show you to your room. We're having dinner delivered in about twenty minutes, so I hope you're hungry." She nodded, and I showed her around and let her settle in.

The food arrived and Si emerged from her room, having changed into something more comfortable, and we sat down to eat. We said grace, then had a relaxing, pleasurable meal. It felt like Si was part of our family. She was friendly, engaging, and had a great sense of humor.

Later in the evening, Finn announced he was going to his place for the night, but I should call him if I needed him. We went into the outer hallway, and I kissed him warmly and said I'd see him tomorrow afternoon at the meeting. He returned the kiss and walked down the hall. Stopping for a moment before entering his apartment, he sent me a charming smile. "Goodnight, Mara."

After entering my new home again, Si and Gracie were still sitting on the sofa reading one of the children's books. Asher crawled into Si's lap and purred loudly, enjoying his new companion.

"This is some cat, Mara. You didn't mention he's the size of a puma." She laughed, then added, "By the way, you don't need to hide your relationship with Finn from me. I feel your intense connection and deep love, and I find it exquisite. It's also obvious the two of you have a symbiotic strength that compliments both of you and if you need that strength, you draw it from each other. This is quite an amazing gift, and God specifically chose the two of you to be together. I pray I'll find such a match in my near future."

"Thanks, Si. We're so in love, and we can't do anything about it. At least, not yet. I pray that eventually, we can marry because it's driving us nuts that we can't be husband and wife."

"You will—just continue to be patient. Now, Gracie, I need you to entertain yourself while I talk with Mara. Would you please read to Asher?"

"Okay. I'm almost five years old," she announced, holding up her hand with all five fingers displayed, smiling proudly.

We thanked Gracie and went to the kitchen to sit at the table. She trained me to block and protect my mind from any intrusion and keep it in place.

"You'll need to perfect this exercise before you help Gracie. You're in grave danger by not protecting your own mind first. Until you have this practice firmly in place, I'll need to provide the block for Gracie. I'll help her as soon as I finish with you, and I'll see how well you can do this tomorrow morning."

I thanked her and said I'd work on it this evening. She told me that tomorrow, she'd try to intrude into my mind, and I should attempt to block her.

She went over to Gracie, sat with her, talking quietly, and then asked Gracie to continue enjoying her book. I observed Si watching the child, but I could feel her reaching out to Gracie with her mind.

Si returned my gaze and said, "You're strong, Mara. I felt you instantly; your ability will be an excellent asset in your fight. I'm excited that I may keep training you to discover what other psychic skills you may have. You may continue to observe what I'm doing for Gracie."

I monitored Si as she worked carefully within the child's mind. She remained just beyond Gracie's consciousness as she placed a powerful wall around her. I felt her leave the child, but I had no clue how the wall would stay in place or for how long.

She turned to me and replied, "You'll learn, trust me. There's a difference in every wall's feel and look, and I'll show you what they are. The barrier you put around Gracie was strong, but it had a few minor holes and was only temporary. That's enough for tonight, and I'm ready for bed."

I couldn't help myself and gave her a big hug. "Thank you so much for all your help and it's a relief to know she's safe. Praise God for sending you to us. You must be exhausted; that was a long trip, and you must rest. If you require anything, please let me know."

"God told me you, your brothers, and Gracie needed me and that it was urgent. I'll be fine, Mara, but thank you. I wish you a blessed and peaceful goodnight." She turned and kissed Gracie, wished her sweet dreams, and went to her room.

I bathed Gracie, put her in pajamas, and had her brush her teeth and hair. As I put her to bed, Asher climbed in beside her. She put her arms around him and said, "Will the monster come again tonight, Mara?"

"No, he won't, sweetie. You're safe, and I'm certain you'll never hear from him again. I'll leave the nightlight on, but if you need me, you know where I am, right?" Gracie nodded, and we said our nightly prayer; she hugged and kissed me. She fell instantly asleep, and I was thankful she'd now be safe.

I prepared for bed, said my evening prayers, and practiced building walls around my mind. It took a couple of hours before I felt I'd done it efficiently, and I'd see if Si could penetrate the barrier tomorrow. But for now, I removed it in case Gracie needed me during the night. I turned out the bedside lamp and fell into a deep slumber.

A few hours later, there was an intense interruption to my sleep. It was evil, and I knew it was meant for Gracie. Jumping out of bed, I ran to her bedroom. Stopping quickly, I saw Si standing near her bed, and she motioned to me to remain quiet. I waited and realized the demon couldn't enter Gracie's mind. His rage fueled his determination to enter her psyche, but after failing, he retreated as quickly as he had come. We both left her room and closed the door.

"Oh my, that scared me to death, Si. But you did it; you stopped him. Thank you!" I squeezed her hand and blinked back tears.

"I had to make sure the block was successful. He's a strong demon, and he'll try again. In the morning, I'll build a second wall around her. I didn't know he'd be a major demon—he'll attempt it again if he can gain more strength. The harder he pushed to gain access, the weaker he became. That is definitely in our favor. But if he gets stronger, my single wall may not hold. Don't worry, we can successfully protect her, and she's safe for tonight," Si whispered, reassuring me. "You can go back to bed and get some sleep. We have much work to accomplish in the morning." She hugged me again.

The following day, I woke up with Gracie lying beside me, her face only a few inches from mine. She gave me a big dimpled smile and said, "Good morning, Mara!"

"Good morning, my sweet. How are you this fine day?" I asked, reaching over to tickle her. She laughed joyously, and we got out of bed and readied ourselves for the day. Si was already up and joined us in the kitchen for breakfast. After our meal, I ushered Gracie down to Kaiko's place, kissed her goodbye, and returned to my apartment.

Si told me she'd already placed the second wall around Gracie before the child woke up this morning. We spent the entire morning working on my walls, and after a few tries, I finally had a solid barrier that Si couldn't penetrate. She showed me how to keep it in place, put another one around her mind, and how to build a third. We continued to work until the early afternoon, and my accomplishments pleased Si.

"You've done well, Mara, and are also a quick study. The important thing to know is when to use these different types of walls and how long you should make each one last. These decisions will become natural to you once you use them daily. Keep practicing, and you won't have any problems."

She continued, "When you face the demon, you'll still have to keep a barrier around yourself but be open enough to connect to your siblings. I'd recommend you practice this together before you embark on your mission. You'll also have to be open enough to keep your other senses working, which is vital to your survival. Apparently, you did this when you encountered the demon in the underground hideout. But this new devil is much stronger, so plenty of practice is vital."

"Thank you, Si. Will you continue to instruct me until we leave for our mission?"

"You can count on it. I want to be sure you all come out of this alive and without mental damage. If this demon enters any of your minds, even for a few seconds, he can easily cause insanity and even death. Now, I must spend the afternoon with each of your brothers. I hear they're quite gifted as well, though in different ways. I look forward to seeing what the good Lord has given them."

I had a meeting with Finn and Edison that afternoon, so I left Si and said I looked forward to seeing her in the evening. But, no matter how hard I tried to fight it, the sense of doom remained in my thoughts. How would my brothers and I fight and kill such a powerful entity? It seemed a daunting task and one that wouldn't end well.

CHAPTER 41

*W*hen I arrived early for the meeting, I stopped by Finn's office to speak with him. I provided an update on Gracie and Si, and he was pleased everything was going well. Edison knocked on the door and said he wanted to get started.

In the meeting room, Finn informed us the opening leading to the portal was widening faster than predicted. We'd only have a few more days because the lightning was occurring more frequently, and according to Poppy, tremors were also taking place in the area. More unearthly activities were occurring at and around the site, which were also concerning.

"Finn, were we ever able to obtain better photos of the Jonestown camp? If so, I may be able to provide more information about what may be causing these strange anomalies," I said.

He nodded and replied, "We've obtained clearer images using a high-tech drone at the camp provided by one of our assets. Needless to say, he had to work quickly to get these new pictures. He barely stayed ahead of the myrmidons who were guarding the site."

Finn called Poppy and asked her to bring the new photos of Jonestown. She arrived within twenty minutes and provided several clear pictures.

As I scanned them carefully, I noticed hundreds of white and gray wisps within the photos. Clearing my mind, I created a minor wall in case of potential danger to myself and gazed intently at one specific picture. I concentrated for several minutes before pulling out.

Turning to Finn and Edison, I said, "This is exactly what I suspected. These wisps in the photos are the spirits of the dead from the Jonestown massacre. The minor demon who possessed Jim Jones is keeping these poor souls trapped within the spirit realm. These souls are angry yet frightened and want help. I think I can work with them when the time comes to close the portal. They would be beneficial too if Asmodeus is at the site when we begin our attack."

"Poppy, does the demon visit the camp at the same time every day?" Finn asked.

"Generally, yes. However, this morning, he visited unusually early for some reason. But normally, he arrives about an hour before nightfall."

"I know why he visited this morning. He attempted to contact Gracie but couldn't break through, though he kept trying. Si's barrier around Gracie stopped him, but this caused a drain of his power. So, he had to return to the portal to regain his strength," I surmised. "Maybe he draws power, not from the portal, but from these poor souls, or maybe a combination of the two."

Edison inquired, "Should we attack him at the Jonestown site or his estate?"

"That's a dilemma; he'd be weaker at the estate, which would be in our favor; however, we could use the restless spirits to help us destroy him at the camp. I'm concerned about Jim Jones's demon as well. It's difficult to tell how strong he is or if he has much power, which is a great unknown. I think it would be a good idea for me to try to gauge if he's a threat to us. I'd prefer to have Si with me when I attempt this, but we'd need to do it before we make any additional plans. It's all contingent on Jones's demon. We wouldn't want to deal with two evil monsters and the portal at the same time," I said.

The team agreed it was a good idea to ask Si to aid me in accessing Jones's demon this evening. I'd speak with Si this afternoon, hoping she'd help with this endeavor.

That evening, Si assisted me in evaluating Jones's evil spirit. She could aid in my blocking, but this also allowed me to stay open enough to get a sense of his powers. Finn was in attendance because Si agreed Finn should hold my hand to strengthen my connection to this plane. Jones's demon was a minor one, but he was strong enough to hold the poor souls at the camp. He attempted to enter my mind but wasn't strong enough to knock on my walls. Pulling out, I told Si and Finn what I'd discovered. I wanted to contact one of the trapped souls to see if they could be an asset in our upcoming fight. Finn held my hand again, and I waited until I felt a connection.

~

THE FIRST ONE is a young child, and he can't communicate much of anything, so I move on to another. I find a young adult woman, and she's angry yet hopeful. Touching her briefly, she eagerly reaches out to me.

"Who are you?" The young woman demands of me.

"My name is Mara, and I'm here to help you and all the trapped souls within this camp. Please don't be afraid and take the gift I'm offering."

"How do I know you aren't Jones and trying to take me farther down the rabbit hole?" She rages at me, yet I can feel a twinge of hope in her rant.

"You know I'm not Jones. Just as I know, you have a good heart and want to be saved from the hell that has kept you trapped inside this place. Have faith in what I'm telling you. I hope to destroy Jones and free all of you, so you may ascend to the Father—where you're meant to be." She is doubtful again, but I surround her with peace and the love of the Lord, and her anger ebbs.

"You'll really do this for us? Destroy this awful person and allow us to journey to the Heavens?" I sense her hope, and she says she'll do anything to leave this awful place.

I continue to reassure the young woman, saying, "This is my goal. But I'll need your help and that of the others to accomplish this enormous task." I ask her to communicate with the other souls to see if they'll help us. She agrees, and I reply I'll connect with her soon and will need everyone's answers at that time. She'll have to stay open to me so I can find her again.

≈

I TOLD Finn and Si what the young woman said, and I'd wait until later tonight to receive their answers.

Gloria agreed to keep Gracie overnight after I told her I'd have to work late. Finn, Si, and I went to dinner, then returned to the meeting room to contact the young woman's spirit again. She was openly waiting for me to answer my request.

≈

"MARA, we all agree to help you if you promise to free us from the clutches of Jim Jones. There are a few within the camp I couldn't reach. They seem to be lost and almost on the verge of insanity. What should I do?"

"My dear, don't attempt to contact them again, as their souls may be beyond saving within this realm. Thank you for all you've done, and I'll contact you again within a few days once my team and I arrive physically in the camp."

≈

I DISCONNECTED WITH HER, and thankfully, we had a valuable ally with the ghosts of Jonestown.

The next day, we met with the entire team, including the group from the Eastern European facility. We now had a viable strategy and would begin the final phase of assignments, transportation, and satellite blocking.

The training with Si was complete, and my two brothers and I were ready to face whatever may happen on the upcoming mission. We wondered if Si should come with us because of her talents, but we decided it was better that she stay on base to watch and protect Gracie. It was time to face the monster from Hell.

CHAPTER 42

*T*he team was prepared to leave for Guyana. Everyone knew their assignments and was ready to start the mission. We'd use our planes to travel to Puerto Rico, then take a commercial flight to the national airport in Guyana. Our group would arrive on three separate aircraft. Some of us pretended to be tourists, others botanists, and the rest archaeologists. Our completed passports, plane tickets, and other identification were in our hands.

We had the usual nine people from our team for this mission. Although Basheer would remain behind so he could pilot one of our planes into Puerto Rico. He would then wait for our arrival to take us home after we completed our mission.

The other five team members were from our Eastern European facility. We called this sister base group our Omega Team, whose leader was Goran. This group was already in Guyana, and they'd handle our transportation needs and receive the equipment we had sent previously to the location. They were also dealing with any needed bribes and would ensure there weren't any complications. Our advanced team said everything was in place and ready for the mission.

Finn, Jasper, and I were on our way to Guyana, and Aaron and Edison were on another flight. Billie, Jonas, and Xavier took the third. I asked

Finn if our faithful had been notified and if they would be ready to start once we gave the signal. He said they were, and he'd call Poppy to initiate contact when we needed the faithful's help.

The third flight team wouldn't arrive until late the next morning, so we didn't plan our strike until that afternoon. The attack on the demon would happen at his estate, and it had to be before he went to the Jonestown site to gain more power.

We landed in Guyana, grabbed our luggage, and went through customs. The hotel we were using was a low-end inn that was small and clean, with no security cameras. We must remain low-profile and unremarkable, with no trace of us left behind. After grabbing a cab to the hotel, we checked in and went to our rooms. We settled in and left our large bag inside the hotel room door, which contained random clothing that would be left behind. We wanted to give the impression we were staying for an entire week, not simply one night.

Late tomorrow morning, two of Goran's team would come by, collect the large bags, and dispose of the contents and the cases. Our carry-on bags contained only a few essentials for an overnight stay. Everything else we would need, including our fatigues, weapons, and a change of clothes before and after the mission, would be waiting for us at the meeting site the following day.

Finn and I went to dinner and Aaron's group arrived at the hotel. We were wearing our links, and Finn answered, "No problems," as if he was talking to me, and Aaron nodded in agreement. We returned to our rooms because the fewer people who saw us, the better.

Finn contacted our Omega team and verified there weren't any issues. They confirmed we were all set, and they were ready to meet at fourteen-hundred hours the next day.

I told Finn I'd need a few minutes for my psychic connection. He nodded, smiled, and said, "Let me know how that works for you."

I gave him a look of censure and began concentrating while I sat at the head of the bed. The first connection was successful. I found it pleasant, and I received a positive response and compliance. After giving Finn a thumbs up, I tried my second connection: this one wasn't easy. It was chaotic and primal, and it took a while to understand my target's thought processes. I must have made a funny face because Finn chuckled. While staying in contact, I threw a bed pillow at him. He laughed again but then let me concentrate on the task at hand. I finally understood what I needed to do and made the connection. It took much more time to get through, but my instructions were finally understood and confirmed.

I withdrew and told Finn I needed to brush my teeth and gargle with something strong, so I went into the bathroom. Chuckling at my comment, he checked the mini-fridge. He found a small bottle of whiskey and came into the bathroom to hand me the liquor.

Finn was still laughing, and I said, "You rat," and giggled too. "I swear, I can still taste blood in my mouth." The whiskey did the trick. We had a leisurely evening on the balcony and watched the sun go down.

The next morning arrived too quickly, and Finn woke me up by pulling me into his arms and kissing the back of my neck. "Oh, Finn, I wish we could stay in this bed and do the hanky-panky. But we can't." I turned around, we locked lips again, and quickly climbed out of bed.

Finn smiled, then sighed. "I know, sweetheart, me too. You can go ahead and use the shower while I wait until I can get out of bed without embarrassing myself." He smiled deviously.

"Like that would ever embarrass you, my love." I swayed my behind back and forth provocatively, then shut the bathroom door. His laughter followed me, and he called me a sassy wench.

When I emerged from the bathroom, Finn had already ordered brunch for us, which should be delivered by the time he finished his shower. He was correct in his timing; we ate the delicious food, and Finn contacted everyone on the team afterward. Jonas arrived with his group, pretended to check in, and would meet us at our rendezvous point. One of Goran's men came by our room and picked up our disposable luggage.

Before leaving our hotel room, Finn and I meticulously cleaned the room, removing any traces of our DNA or fingerprints. We left the hotel and walked down the road to catch our ride. Our Omega team members drove several random vehicles. Each car used different routes out of town, so we'd remain inconspicuous, and it took about thirty minutes for us to reach our destination. It was in an out-of-the-way area, down an old beaten track, and well-hidden from the main road. Our off-road vehicles were camouflaged and waiting for us. An Omega team member would drive each one of the vehicles. They knew where we needed to go and had already surveilled the area. Finn and I were in one, Jonas and Edison were in the second, and Aaron and Jasper rode in the third. Chuck, Billie, Xavier, and the rest of the Omega group were to wait with the primary vehicles until we returned.

We changed into our fatigues, and I relayed to my team that the LBE vest wouldn't be needed as it only slowed us down. I placed two extra handguns and ammo into my gun belt, plus the large Kabar knife, into a sheath on my left thigh. The SAT phone and compass were stuffed into my pockets. A small backpack would suffice for carrying a canteen, first aid kit, binoculars, sniper bible, and a map. The rest of my team agreed, and they also ditched their LBEs.

Our team reviewed the plan and how much time we had to complete it. We also made sure our links were working and there weren't any communication issues. The three vehicles drove off in separate directions, each group going to a different mountain.

Finn and I reached our destination in about twenty minutes. We knew it would take Jonas and Aaron's teams longer because their low-range mountains were farther away. Grabbing the sniper gun bag, we started the strenuous climb. Finn insisted on pulling the weapon case, which weighed a ton, and it was rough going. Finn kept checking his GPS and said we'd finally reached our appointed area. We crept through the trees and brush and found the site chosen for our sniper location. Using the high-powered binoculars, we spotted the roof guards on the demon's estate.

Finn texted Poppy, and she gave him the distance between me and my first target using the closest satellite data. I set up the sniper rifle, checked my figures from my bible, loaded the gun with fifty-caliber ammunition, and made the adjustments for my intended target. Finn and I laid on our stomachs on the ground, checked our watches, and waited for Jonas and Aaron to give us their ready signal. Before we would strike, Jonas would conduct a spirit walk and scan each building. He'd identify the guards and their locations and pinpoint Asmodeus.

Finn vigilantly scanned the estate through his binoculars and gave updates through his link as to the whereabouts of the outside guards.

"Finn, waiting is always the worst part of these missions. Do you ever get used to it?"

"Nope, you never do." He peered through his binoculars again.

We heard through the earpiece that Edison was setting up the rifle, and Jonas started his spirit walk. Aaron and Jasper were ten minutes from their location. We continued to wait, and I took these few moments to sense the demon and gauge his current power.

"The demon is only at half strength, at least by my quick scan of him. We won't know for sure until we get closer," I said.

Finn commented this was at least some good news.

Jonas was on the link, giving us the number and positions of all the guards inside the buildings. They were definitely all demons. There weren't as many as we had feared, but enough that it would take all of us to eliminate them.

Finn and I received the signal that Jonas and Aaron were ready for the strike. We asked for the yardage, and Edison said Jonas's distance was three thousand, two hundred and fifteen. Jasper replied that Aaron's was three thousand, three hundred and eleven. Finn gave my sniper distance again, and it was still three thousand, eight hundred and nine yards.

Jonas croaked, "Mara, you've got to be kidding. We've never practiced at these distances before. We better pray the good Lord will make these shots for us."

"Let's hope that using these new silencers and the long distances suppresses our rifle fire. We don't want them to know we're coming," Finn warned. "Okay, ready...mark. Let's get this party started." Each team member responded with a quick prayer, and we took out the guards.

Finn, being my spotter, gave me the exact distance of my first target again. Checking my adjustments, I looked through the scope and waited for the Lord's angels to guide me in my first shot. I felt the warmth come over me, and my vision of the first target cleared, and I fired.

"Direct hit," Finn praised. "Now, there's the one more on the west side of the estate roof, then the one on the southwest side. The last target for you is the one on the west side of the guest house."

We heard a "direct hit" from Jasper and Edison, which meant two more guards were down.

Finn gave me the distance, and I calibrated the rifle for the next guard. I adjusted again for angle and distance and checked for wind speed and direction once more. Waiting for the calm to come over me again, I fired. This shot was louder, and I cringed.

"That's another perfect one, Mara." Finn put on gloves, removed the used suppressor from the rifle, and screwed on another. Our blessed monks made these suppressors to the Lord's specifications, but they'd have to be changed after two shots.

There were more thumps and two more "direct hits" over the link.

"Don't think about it, Mara. Just move on to the next demon," Finn said. He gave me the distance, and I adjusted the rifle, aiming for the guard on the southwest side of the estate roof. It took me longer because it was farther away and had a harsher angle. I calmed myself and waited for the target to clear, but it wouldn't come into focus, and I told Finn my current adjustments must be incorrect. After rechecking my sniper's bible, I had Finn repeat the distance, noted my mistake, and adjusted the rifle again. Looking through the scope, I waited; this time, my aim was ready. Once I fired, I heard Finn say, "You got another one."

Finn scanned for movement or excitement anywhere around the estate using the binoculars, and all was quiet. Moving on to the roof guard on the west side of the guest house, I set up and fired again. "Another excellent shot. Great job—you're now done, Mara. We have to get packed up and out of here."

Jonas and Aaron completed their hits and said they'd meet us at the rendezvous point. The estate remained quiet, so they were unaware the roof guards had been neutralized.

Moving as quickly as possible, Finn and I made it down to the vehicle in record time, although we had the cuts and scratches to prove it. He promptly loaded the rifle, and we returned to our meeting site.

Upon our arrival, we had to wait for the other two teams. Once they arrived, we assembled into our assigned groups, then traveled toward the estate. Our Omega team was now watching both entrances to the site, and they'd notify us if any demons arrived or departed.

Billie and Xavier were already bound for the road that led to the Jonestown camp. They'd hide their vehicle, walk through the jungle, and take out the two guards on the drive that led back to the estate from the camp, but they'd have to wait for our signal once Aaron put the gate cameras on a loop.

We drove until we were approximately half a mile from the main driveway's entrance and hid our vehicle in the jungle. We met up with Goran and two of his men, and he said there'd been no new arrivals, and no one had left the estate either.

Aaron set up his laptop using the closest satellite and began hacking into the estate's security cameras. It only took him a few minutes, and he was in. Once he looped the gate's cameras and turned off the electrified fence, we could proceed. Aaron would stay and operate the cameras for the estate. Once we were ready to enter the building, he'd join us.

Finn told Xavier and Billie they were clear to continue, and the rest of us made our way through the jungle toward the estate's main driveway. We came upon the guards at the driveway entrance. They appeared bored, which was good for us because two were leaning against a couple of trees off to the side. The other two were looking at some magazine and boasting about who had the better car. My problem was these four guards were huge men.

Finn signaled to us, and Edison and Goran went to the other side, behind the two arguing guards. Finn and I came up behind the first two, waited until Edison and Goran were ready, and began our attack. The guard I had to take out saw me, gave me the typical "come get me" look, and smiled. I had my knife before me but put it back in the sheath and moved toward him.

He expected I'd come at him with the knife, so he gave me a puzzled look. I lowered my head, charged toward his legs, grabbed him around both knees, and flipped him backward. He landed hard on his back, loudly grunting as I knocked the air from his lungs. I straddled him, but he flipped me over so he was on top, then grabbed me by the neck, trying to choke me. I anticipated this move and had learned from experience to grease my neck before a possible hand-to-hand fight. He couldn't tighten his grip, so I grabbed his thumbs and twisted them back against his wrist. I then moved my thighs up and wrapped them tightly around his neck. Releasing his thumbs while choking him with my legs, I grabbed my knife and stabbed him in the eye. He fell to his side, and I slit his throat.

The four guards were dead; their faces and bodies quickly turned into that ghastly demonic appearance. We dragged them into the jungle and covered them with foliage.

"Finn, it's time to start the prayers of the faithful. Please begin the chain." Finn contacted Poppy, and she'd initiate the chain of calls that would notify all the faithful in the world to start praying. They wouldn't stop until we called them again. This is what Kaiko had meant about the faithful being needed during our battle. Millions of people would pray as we attempted to destroy the demon and the portal. They were essential in strengthening the Chosen and weakening the evil.

Finn nodded and asked, "Is it time for the myrmidons' downfall?"

I smiled and replied, "Yes, I believe it is. Once Asmodeus realizes he's in danger, he'd likely call upon them to come to his aid at the estate, and this can't happen. I'll connect with our helpers, and they'll do what we could never accomplish alone."

Standing still, I closed my eyes and contacted the same beings I connected with yesterday at the hotel. The Jaguars were the first group in the area who received my message, and they remembered me from the previous day's psychic link. They would attack the myrmidons and could easily find them by their putrid smell.

The second group was the Black Caiman alligators, which were harder to communicate with. They were driven by instinct, and I could taste raw flesh and blood when I touched their minds. They received and understood my communication now, and they made their way to the myrmidons, who were closest to the river's edge along the jungle. I could feel their intense hunger as I showed them the minions who would provide them sustenance.

"The myrmidons will be taken care of," I told my team. Finn handed me a flask of whiskey, which I gratefully accepted; I rinsed with a tiny sip and returned the flask.

Taking another few moments, I contacted the poor souls in the Jonestown camp. I could reach them but was unable to find a way for them to come over to the estate.

"Finn, we have to make sure that Asmodeus escapes to Jonestown. The poor souls can't leave the confines of the camp, and we need their help in destroying him. We may as well use our guns when taking out the outer perimeter guards and the ones inside," I replied.

Finn spoke up, "Did everyone get that? When we reach the estate, use your firearms. Billie and Xavier, make yourself scarce when Asmodeus heads your way." Our team confirmed the order and we were ready to continue.

Two of the Omega group would stay at the main entrance if anyone attempted to arrive or depart the estate. The rest of us moved swiftly, yet quietly, behind the tree line along the driveway toward the buildings. Jonas, Aaron, and I asked God to send our spirit animals to assist us in the next part of our mission, and I explained what we needed from them. We heard a roar, a howl, and a screech and watched the guards run to the back of the estate. Rushing ahead, we pulled out our automatic weapons as we covertly ran to the main house.

Four members of our team moved toward the guest house. The guards returned, shook their heads in confusion, and we started our attack. Spirit and Phantom were also killing sentries, so it didn't take us long to eliminate the thirteen demons who'd been patrolling the perimeter.

The sound of gunfire would surely send Asmodeus on the run to the camp, but we didn't know which exit he'd use. Xavier and Billie had long since taken out the two driveway guards and were hiding in the brush near the entrance to the camp.

Jonas, Aaron, and I took a few moments, placed mind blocks on each of our team members, and scanned the inside of each building. The guard house only had two demons inside, and Chuck and Edison went to take them out. After I psychically scanned the guest house, I didn't find anything, so that left the estate itself. We counted eight on the first level and seven on the second.

We tracked the location of Asmodeus and discovered he was still on the second floor. He panicked and had to decide which exit to use as an escape. We felt him move to the back balcony as he descended the outdoor trellises. Our team would stay away from him and let him run. Two guards followed the demon.

"Finn, a couple of his men are with the Asmodeus, and they're going down the trellis in the back. We must take these two out before they reach the camp because he's drawing power from them."

"We'll get 'em." This reply came from Billie and Xavier, and Finn gave them the go-ahead.

We slowly opened the front door but stayed behind the exterior wall. Automatic gunfire spewed out the entrance, so we ducked low. Finn put his gun in the doorway and fired inside the building in a random pattern. This distraction gave Jonas and Jasper the time to cover the side French doors, and they fired at the inside guards. Jonas said the two sentries were down, but two more had moved from the back of the house.

We now had six of us entering the estate, and Aaron followed behind us. Staying low, we hid behind heavy furniture while waiting for the other six guards to come into view. It wasn't long before they ran in from three different directions, but we continued firing, and Jonas threw a small holy fire bomb. It went off with a loud bang, and two more hellions went down.

I rolled across the floor to a better position behind a large marble sculpture. It made me jump when I heard the pings as the bullets hit the artwork.

"Two on the stair balcony! Eleven o'clock from your position, Mara. You're clear to shoot," Finn ordered. I moved swiftly around the sculpture and fired at the two on the balcony. They died and fell to the marble floor below. I hid behind the statue again and heard a lot more gunfire. "You're trapped, Mara, so stay put." I heard endless shooting, so I couldn't tell who was firing or what direction it was coming from.

"Mara, two o'clock. Two more guards are on the upper right balcony. I can't get them from here. I'll make sure you're covered. Go!" Finn yelled.

I snuck out from the right side of the sculpture and fired at the two to the upper right. Two more down, and I hid again. More shots rang out, and then silence.

"Everyone, sound off," Finn ordered. Every team member reported in.

Then he asked, "Did we get them all?" We cautiously emerged from behind our cover.

Jonas answered, "We missed one. Jasper and I will make sure he's eliminated."

They moved through the main floor, reported they found no one, and proceeded upstairs. The rest of us made sure the guards we'd shot were dead. The estate reeked of gunfire and the putrid smell of dead demons.

We heard shots fired upstairs, and Jonas reported, "We found him and he's been neutralized."

"Billie, has the demon made it to the camp, and are the two guards eliminated?" Finn asked.

"Affirmative and affirmative," Billie replied.

"Okay, team, we'll meet at the entrance of the camp to regroup." We moved cautiously out the front door, weapons still drawn, and we proceeded to the road which led to Jonestown.

I stopped briefly, tilted my head, and ordered, "Wait." I looked at the guest house and something caught my eye. "Everyone, stop for a minute." The team moved into a circle, crouched down, and faced outward with guns drawn.

"It's okay. I don't sense danger or demons—it's something else. Jonas and Aaron, I need your help. Please be ready to place a wall around me if I've made a mistake, but I have to lower my barrier enough to figure out what has been pressing into my mind. It's not evil, of that I'm sure. We need to move toward the guest house," I said.

Finn replied, "Be prepared for anything, but I need Mara protected."

We advanced toward the guest house, then stopped ten feet away. I nodded to Jonas and Aaron and lowered my block. Several young children stood around the guest house, their faces and bodies were difficult to see clearly. They were apparitions, and there were nine of these spirits.

"Oh, my dear Lord in heaven," I stammered, with tears in my eyes. "Children, there are—were children in this guest house. Their spirits are here and they don't know what to do or where to go. Lower your weapons, please. We've frightened them." I moved forward, approaching a young boy of about nine years old. His image was the clearest, and I knelt in front of him.

"Hello, my name is Mara. Can you tell me your name, sweetheart?" He said he was Milo Christenson, and he wanted to go home. They all wanted to return to their families.

"Finn, please take down this information," I asked each child for their name, and Finn recorded them. They were of varying ages and both male and female. One little boy was only about two and didn't know his last name. He said he was Noah, like Noah's ark. I asked the older boy if he knew Noah's last name, and he told me it was Martinez.

I motioned to Finn to come to me and take my hand, and the rest of the team also joined hands. Everyone was shocked, as well as in terrible grief.

"Can you help us go home, Mara?" The older boy asked as the children gathered around me.

"I can do better than that. There's a place of no pain, grief, or evil— only love, joy, and happiness. Your families will join you there later, I promise. Would you let us help you get there? This is where God, Jesus, the Holy Mother, and all the angels live. These are my brothers, Aaron and Jonas. We'll help you get to this wonderful place if you let us," I offered.

They talked to each other; some weren't so sure, but they finally agreed to let us help. I nodded to my brothers, and we joined hands and prayed. We chanted in the ancient language of the angels and asked the Holy Trinity's assistance to take these precious children to Heaven.

The sky above us changed as swirls of every color moved in unison, then descended to the earth. The iridescent hues were filled with what I would call bright stars. We realized they were angels who would escort the children to the Heavens. The air was filled with the sweetest scents, and a warm, living breeze surrounded us. We heard music that made the most joyous sound—almost like thousands of chimes ringing in harmony to God's glory. The myriad of colors and stars encompassed the children's transparent bodies and lifted them toward the sky until they disappeared into a giant ball of opalescent heavenly light.

My team and I stood in awe, enchanted by the miracle the Lord allowed us to witness. This astounding spectacle dropped us to our knees. No words were said, and we silently thanked our heavenly Father.

After several minutes, we finally stood, and I said quietly, "They're now in God's loving embrace," I released my brothers' hands. "We need to check out the building, Finn." I moved toward it, but Finn stopped me, shaking his head.

"You're not going in there, Mara. We'll take care of it, not you," he said firmly, then nodded to Jasper and Chuck to follow him.

The rest of us waited outside, and the three exited the building ten minutes later. Their faces said it all, and their grief broke my heart. I pulled the three men into my arms and held them, giving them my strength. They eagerly accepted it and eventually pulled away.

Finn said, "We have a job to finish, my good friends, regardless of our despair. It's time to take this monster out, so he can't hurt another child again. Are you with me?"

"Dei Bellator! Warrior for God!" we announced together.

We replied we were with him and said another prayer for God's assistance as we strode toward the Jonestown camp and the demon from Hell.

CHAPTER 43

As we neared the camp, I asked everyone to stop and wait. I needed to find the locations of the Jaguars and alligators to confirm they'd killed every one of the myrmidons. After psychically scanning for these disgusting lackeys, I discovered about a dozen left. They weren't in good shape, but they were still alive.

The Jaguars were moving away from the camp, and I told them how grateful I was and wished them much food and plenty of fresh water. I moved my thoughts toward the Black Caiman alligators. They were still feeding but were by the river again as they had dragged their recent kills to the water's edge. I didn't notice any of them near the camp, which was a blessing.

I told the team what I'd discovered but that we still had to eliminate twelve myrmidons. Goran said he and his team would take care of the remaining monsters. We'd wait at our current location until the Omega team had finished this task. Goran and his men moved off into the jungle and began tracking them.

This gave me time to contact the poor, trapped souls in the camp. Finn and the team remained alert, with weapons drawn, while I connected. Finding the same young woman I'd spoken with before, she said everyone wanted their freedom. I promised it would happen, but they'd have to help us first. Then I asked if the human demon had entered the camp, and she told me he was in the pavilion. He was trying to use their souls again to gain strength. I told her they'd have to stop him from using them and instructed her on how to accomplish this task. Once she understood, she said she'd tell the others how to block the demon from draining their energy. After instructing her to start quickly, I said I'd reconnect with her soon.

"I think we're set, but I won't know our success until we enter the camp," I advised my team.

We waited thirty minutes until we heard the Omega team through our headsets. "We got them all," he said in his strong Slavic accent. They emerged into the clearing, and we reviewed our next strategy.

After reaching the gate to the camp, the team entered Jonestown. We surveyed the area and it was eerily quiet. No sound could be heard: not a bird, frog, cricket, or anything you'd typically hear in a jungle. It was hauntingly unnatural, and I felt my team's extreme unease.

Raising my hand, I gestured for them to wait and opened my mind to my surroundings. Jonas and Aaron moved next to me in case I needed their help re-securing my wall. For a brief moment, intense pressure was trying to take me over. Easing my wall up more, I concentrated on who or what was trying to connect with me. I felt all the lost souls, but I couldn't gauge without lowering my protection as to their exact location. Then I felt something evil moving about the camp. It was definitely to my right, and I motioned for the team to move in that direction. They kept me in the middle since I was unable to maintain a mental connection and defend myself physically at the same time.

I motioned for them to stop as a dark shadow appeared over a small rusty tractor tipped over on its side. It was Jim Jones or the minor demon who possessed him. He wasn't interested in us but was furious and frustrated. Apparently, he'd lost control of the majority of the souls. I watched the dark shadow as it jumped a few feet, but then a small piece of metal flew across the camp and landed in the undergrowth. Signaling my team, I instructed them to back away slowly, move to the left, and I put my primary wall back in place.

"Jim Jones's spirit is here, and a minor demon possesses him. He's enraged and that's why that piece of metal went flying, but I don't see him as a threat to us. He's only focused on the poor souls and is trying desperately to regain control," I whispered.

"Asmodeus is our priority now, then the portal. I'm sure he's at or near the gateway to Hell, which, according to my information, is about thirty yards in that direction. That must be the location of the pavilion," Finn said as he glanced at his phone's GPS.

"I'll contact the lost souls and ensure they're no longer being used by Asmodeus. I'll need a couple more minutes, and then we can proceed," I replied.

Finn nodded, and I attempted to find the young woman. It took several minutes, but when we connected, she was hysterical, and I couldn't comprehend what she was saying. I instructed her to slow down, and she advised me that Jones and the demon had been desperately trying to use all the souls' power. She said they'd been fighting them off, and most of them had been successful, but some had given in. I told her this wasn't a problem but to keep up what they were doing and that we were now at the camp and would deal with Jones and the demon. Instructing her that all the souls needed to stay near the devil, I added we were headed her way. I would give her more directions when we arrived at her location.

I signaled to the team to proceed to the pavilion. The camp was heavily overgrown, so getting through was rough, and the visibility wasn't great either. Jonas, Aaron, and I abruptly stopped, and the team also halted. The demon was straight ahead but below the surface, and my brothers and I felt him.

Jonas whispered, "His location is directly ahead but below ground. This is concerning because this means the entrance to the underground area is now wide enough for a man to enter."

Finn nodded, and several of our team surrounded what was left of the pavilion. The building was demolished, and random pieces of wood were strewn about. We spotted where the entrance had formed, and the surrounding ground was black and parched from the lightning strikes. The smell of ozone still hung in the air from the previous night's electrical storm. The hole was just large enough for a man to climb through, and Finn pulled out his night vision glasses to peer into the pit.

Finn motioned for us to move away and quietly said, "There's just enough room to climb down into the entrance. We've no choice, my friends: we must proceed down into the crevasse. Everyone must wear their night vision glasses because it's black as hell down there. No pun intended."

Finn continued, "Mara, I need to know he's the only one below. Can you or your brothers tell if there are any other demons, guards, or myrmidons with him?"

"We can. No, it's only him, and I also feel the poor souls fighting him off. Asmodeus is weak, but he's trying to draw power from the portal. He hasn't been successful so far," I answered.

Turning to my team, I said quietly, "I need to remind everyone that even though the three of us put shields around your minds, this demon is still powerful and will try anything to gain control over you. You must remain stoic and resolute and keep praying to the Lord and the angels to protect you. Don't let him in. Also, and I'm adamant about this, none of you are to approach or attack him. If you try, you'll lose, and he'll kill you. Aaron, Jonas, and I are the ones who have been given the tools to defeat Asmodeus. I pray we'll be successful." I motioned to Finn that I included him in my instructions. He nodded in understanding and took my hand to give it a reassuring squeeze.

"Let's go and kick some demon butt," Finn ordered. We repeated a group prayer and began our downward climb. The descent team consisted of Finn, Aaron, Jonas, Billie, Edison, and me.

As Finn said, it was pitch dark, and the rocks and mud made it a hazardous course. We traveled downward at a sharp angle for about ten minutes. As we progressed forward, the opening narrowed, and I feared we wouldn't be able to fit in the small space. Finn dumped his backpack at this point, and we followed suit. He squeezed into the small area, then crawled through the narrow fissure on his belly. A few minutes later, he said it was much larger on the other side and told everyone to come through. I followed behind Finn, and as I came out the other side, it had turned into a large underground cavern. There was the sound of dripping water, and I smelled the dampness and decay, and two tunnels led in different directions.

Finn looked at me and asked, "Which way do we go?"

I stepped toward one tunnel, concentrated on it for a few minutes, then turned to Finn and pointed to the other. "That way."

We moved forward but had to move carefully, so it took us longer than expected. The ground was still slick and uneven, and we had to rely on our glasses to find our way. We continued through the tunnel for another fifteen minutes, then Aaron, Jonas, and I called a halt simultaneously. "He's directly ahead," Jonas said.

I whispered to my brothers, "I need to open my mind, so the two of you have to protect me again." They moved to my side, and I searched for Asmodeus. He was there and was furious and frustrated, but he was also weak. I could feel the portal, too, and sensed evil and darkness. There were also horrific odors, and I was being pulled in. Then I sensed my brothers as they pulled me back, and Finn had a firm hold of my hand. Luckily, I could retreat enough to evaluate the demon and the portal.

Asmodeus was still attempting to extract power from the doorway, but it hadn't finished opening. Many of the poor souls could still block the demon's control over them and continued waiting for my instructions.

I pulled back out and whispered, "He's still weakened but by no means vulnerable. The portal isn't fully open yet, so that's also to our advantage. Many souls are inside waiting for our directions, so it's now or never. My brothers and I will enter first, then everyone else should follow. Remember to always protect yourselves, and don't let the monster penetrate your minds."

My siblings and I gathered together, held hands, prayed fervently, and gave ourselves to the Holy Trinity.

FINN WATCHED as the three siblings gathered together and said a prayer and a flash of light emanated around them. Their countenance altered briefly as their bodies shimmered. Eventually, they looked normal again, but their expressions had changed: they appeared calm, strong, and filled with holiness, yet with fearless determination. He waited until they moved through the doorway, then he, Billie, and Edison followed behind.

～

As MY BROTHERS and I crept through the opening, the smells of sulfur and evil overwhelmed our senses. The heat was intense in this room, and I could hear tortured screams, moans, and heinous and vulgar language as it spewed from the deep, hellish hole. I thought I heard something ominously dark and threatening intoning my name, then it felt like unearthly critters were crawling over my skin.

As I eyed my team, they heard and felt the same horrible things. They shook their heads and attempted to brush off whatever they thought had been creeping over their bodies. My brothers and I had to block everything distracting us from our task. We turned to face the demon, who stood on the other side of the portal. He ignored us at first but soon raised his heads to face us.

The hellish monster was no longer using his human persona but was now in his demonic form. He had three heads, just as Kaiko had said. A human-like face was in the center, but no humanity existed in its expression. It had grotesquely twisted features and a perpetual sneer to its mouth. The head on the left was a bull, then to the right of the human was a ram. Each mouth had several rows of razor-sharp teeth, and I could see flames down each throat. The upper portion of his body resembled a human man, but his left appendage was that of a lizard, and his right looked like a giant scorpion claw. Scales covered his lower body, and his right leg appeared to be a ram's leg, yet his left one was ostrich-like. He was tall, ten feet at least, and stooped over to avoid hitting his head on the cavern ceiling.

The demon finally spoke. His voice was gritty and dark, but his words were slow and sounded like a snake's hiss. "So, you had the gall to come here. I felt your presence in my mind, but you're nothing to me or what is happening here. Be gone with you, or I will send you to the great fires of my dark kingdom where you will suffer greatly for eternity." He waved his claw in our direction, dismissing us as if we were gnats hovering over a rotted piece of fruit.

"We're not leaving; we *will* destroy you and your precious portal," I growled. "You'll die a horrible death and will never return again, you disgusting maggot."

"Don't you dare insult me! You are pitiful little humans and are unimportant to me or my purpose here! Your insolence offends me and I am done with the lot of you!" He sputtered in anger, but his words were difficult to understand, as he was talking from three mouths simultaneously. Then lumbering around the portal, he moved closer to where we stood, hitting his heads twice on the ceiling, which angered him further.

"Ahh, I know you," he snarled, looking at me with his human face. "You are the one with the precious little morsel of a child. How dare you think you can interfere. She is mine, and I will thoroughly enjoy taking her apart, piece by piece, just like I did to the others.

"I see. You saw the fruits of my handiwork, didn't you?" He hissed his words directly to Finn, but Finn tried to shield his mind from the demon. "Did you enjoy what you found, pretty man? I bet you wished you could have had your turn at poking them too."

Finn grew enraged, and I yelled, "Don't let him get to you! It's what he's after, and getting angry opens your mind and lets the demon in. Stop it now, Finn." I felt Finn follow my instructions, and his wall closed up again. But then, Asmodeus focused on Billie and Edison.

"You two are pretty as well." The demon hissed, then taunted us, his tongues flicking in and out of his three mouths. "How does that feel? Good? You want some more?" I turned momentarily, and they both had fallen to their knees. They moaned, squirmed, and desperately tried to fight the demon in their minds. I had to do something to distract the monster, so I looked at Jonas and Aaron, and they nodded and placed the walls back up for Billie and Edison.

I jumped into the demon's psyche and filled it with God's love and compassion, and he screamed at me, telling me to get out or I would pay dearly. I still pushed my thoughts into his, and he tried to enter my mind and take over my body. It was like getting punched in the head by a grizzly bear. Going down on one knee, I saw a brief glimpse of intense evil but pushed at him with an enormous blow, which shoved him back out of my mind and body.

Glaring hard at his evil human face, I punched him violently in his mind with a massive blow of energy. Aaron and Jonas felt what I was doing and proceeded to strike the demon with two more attacks from their minds. Asmodeus staggered back and shook his three heads; this gave us time to prepare for the next step.

My brothers and I held hands and prayed in the language of the Lord, our God. The demon bellowed in rage and tried to swipe his vicious claw across our heads. But as the talon neared us, it instantly flew back as if he had struck a lead wall.

I stopped my prayers for a brief moment, contacted the souls, and told them to attack the demon's mind. We continued praying again, and the monster screamed in undeniable rage. His bellow filled the cave with such noise that the cavern tremored slightly from the loud reverberation. He moved closer, and the three of us broke apart but continued chanting our prayers. Asmodeus grabbed at his heads and tried to cast the souls from his mind, but they persisted in their attack.

FINN WATCHED in horror as the love of his life battled with the most disgusting thing he could have ever imagined. He'd also grown to love his future brothers-in-law and wanted nothing more than to protect them. It took everything he had not to interfere, but he knew he didn't have the skills to fight this demon, just as Mara had warned.

Intense dread filled him as the demon approached the three. The siblings released each other's hands, but their prayers continued. A bright light surrounded the three but disappeared as quickly as it came. Now, however, the three held magnificent swords that were large, ornate, sharp, and glowed with a blue aura. Mara moved a couple of steps closer to Asmodeus and swung the sword in patterns of expertise that he'd never seen before. Jonas and Aaron also approached and carried their swords similarly, yet in alternating motions.

For some reason, the evil monster had problems with his coordination and thinking, and he shook his giant heads. He moved to attack Mara, but she swiftly dodged his advance, swung her sword high and wide, and hit him fiercely across his chest. The demon screamed in agony, and the smelly black ooze poured from the gaping wound. Jonas and Aaron also attacked, slicing the monster several times across the front and back of his body.

The gashes were deep and gushed enormous amounts of the demon's blood. Asmodeus then attempted to use his claw again, but Mara leaped against the cavern wall and kicked off the hard surface with her feet, giving her leverage to jump high in the air. This maneuver elevated her enough to give her access to the demon's heads, and she chopped off his left one, which was the bull. He grabbed his neck where the head had been and cried out in agony, frantically swinging his claw back and forth, attempting to hit anything he could reach.

Jonas took advantage of this opportunity and removed the clawed arm with one swift swing of his sword. Aaron removed the right lizard leg cleanly, and Asmodeus dropped to the cavern floor, howling with one earth-shattering, hideous scream. Then the Chosen attacked him in earnest and never eased their onslaught. They cut, sliced, and hacked until the demon was in so many pieces that bits of putrid flesh and scales littered the cavern and the siblings. The three stood up and said several more prayers in that beautiful, haunting, ancient language. The white light appeared again, briefly blinding everyone, then it vanished, and the swords disappeared as well.

I WAS BREATHING hard and fell to my knees. My brothers were also kneeling on the ground, gasping for air. Our minds returned to the present and to what we'd accomplished. We prayed in English now and thanked the Holy Trinity and the archangels for their help in defeating the demon. Finn came up behind me as he said reassuring words, and I turned around so he could hold me close. Finn's body shook violently, and I realized he feared losing me. Leaning into him, I whispered the Lord wouldn't have let me die. I pushed my strength into him, and his shaking subsided. Holding him until his trembling stopped, I released him, looked him in the eyes, and smiled.

"Finn, we have to close the portal. It's getting larger, and demons are beginning their ascent to the surface. Lucifer isn't far behind them," I urged. "But first, we have to free the tortured souls. They've done what they promised and have suffered for many years; we must release them from their agony."

There was an insistent push against my mind, and the souls begged for their freedom. I told them my brothers and I would now cut the ties Jones's demon had on them. My brothers heard my message to the souls, and we held hands again, chanting in the ancient language.

We felt the souls being released from Jones's possession and sensed their joy, relief, and thankfulness. A few souls were at the point of insanity, but we helped them out of their madness. Slowly they responded and clung to our sanity, love, and faith in God. They reached to us in desperation, and we turned them toward the angels, and they too were sent to the glory of Heaven. My brothers and I hugged each other with relief, but we knew the portal would be the most troublesome part of this mission.

"The souls are free of the lesser demon's hold. Now that Jones's demon has lost his grip on them, he's also forfeited his place in our dimension. This catalyst has caused his re-entry into Hell. We must start on the portal now. Are you ready, brothers?" I asked. They nodded, and we said another prayer for God's help and protection. I told Finn, Edison, and Billie that everyone must pray and continue until the portal closed.

My brothers and I stood at the pit's edge, held hands, and chanted again. We prayed fervently, felt God's love and protection, and the angels surrounded us and gave glory to God and the Holy Trinity. We felt the portal growing more prominent as we chanted, but our prayers continued. We heard so many supplications that they echoed through the cavern. They weren't just our chants, or even Finn's, Billie's, or Edison's, but the prayers from all the world's faithful. They filled the chamber with such great love, devotion, and complete trust in God that the entire cave was filled with a bright light.

Several creatures of varying sizes began climbing out of the burning cavernous pit. The little demon monsters looked like dark, slimy, scaly lizards with several fire-filled eyes, and their mouths were encased with layers of razor-edged fangs which dripped with saliva. My team attacked each one, sending them back down to the pit.

More of these hellish creatures attempted to ascend from below, but my team continued their onslaught of firing their rifles and handguns, which kept them at bay, so we could continue our attempt at sealing the gate.

As my brothers and I prayed, I heard Kaiko's voice, and my brothers also heard her. "Three faithful spirits of God must enter the portal to complete the seal." Her voice repeated the same message, and we gaped at each other in absolute fear and misery.

I thought to my brothers as we chanted out loud, *Do we have to fall into Hell to close the portal? How can that be?* They gawked at me with the same terror, and we knew we had no choice. Her message repeated in our heads, and we moved closer to the edge. I told my brothers I loved them dearly and prayed Jesus would pull us out of Hell and into Heaven after our fall. We continued our prayers and moved nearer to the edge.

I desperately said to Finn's mind as loud as I could, *I love you, my dear Finn and I always will. You're my heart, and we'll meet again in Heaven, my love.* Finn yelled my name from behind me, and he tried to move forward, but something unseen held him in place.

We smelled it first. A stench that was so heinous, it can't be described, and I thought I'd vomit as soon as it hit my nostrils. To the left of Hell's gate, a malformed hand grasped the side of the portal's edge. This appendage was large, had nine fingers, and was a blueish-pink color. The veins throbbed with some strange brackish blood, and the nails at the tips were long, pointed, and also appeared to pulsate. The hand had scales, and as I watched, several tiny disgusting insects erupted from this creature's appendage. I screamed at Finn, and he and Edison moved from the right side of the portal to attack what was now trying to emerge from the fiery chasm. We heard a loud, angry, and fierce scream as the creature brought up one more of its hands to grab onto the edge of the abyss.

My team fired many shots into this colossal beast—it slowed the monster down, but it was determined to come to the earth. I then saw the top of a head: giant horns appeared, and they matched the hideous claws as they also oozed with bile, slime, and insects. Many of my team vomited from the intense, gruesome, deathly odor and had difficulty staying upright. We needed to finish this before the creature fully emerged, or my team succumbed to the overwhelming stench of this evil entity.

I messaged my brothers one last time, and as we were about to step over the side, our spirit animals appeared across from us at the other edge of the portal. It was Phantom, Charlotte, and Spirit. They stood perfectly still and gave us a look of pure love, thankfulness, and peace. I tried to say something to them, but the prayers were so loud in the chamber I could hear nothing else.

A bright glow surrounded our spirit animals, and they communicated their love for us and that they would take our place in the portal. My brothers and I tried in vain to yell. We waved our hands to stop them from doing what they were about to do, but they gazed at us lovingly, moved forward, and leaped into the fiery void of the portal.

I screamed, "No!" but they'd disappeared into the raging abyss. The entire cavern now trembled, and we felt ourselves falling forward toward the evil opening. We were grabbed from behind, and the portal began to collapse. The prayers of the faithful still echoed through the cave, and the shaking grew more violent.

The giant beast lost its hold on the edge of the pit, and his bellow of ferocious anger echoed through the chamber as it fell back into the fiery pit of Hell.

"We have to get out of here!" Finn shouted at us. He grabbed me and pushed me toward the doorway of the cavern. Our team scrambled to get out, but the shaking was so intense we could barely stay upright. Our team fell several times, but we forced ourselves through the narrow fissure one by one.

We were about to grab our discarded backpacks, but Finn ordered us to leave them. Pushing on, we finally reached the slope that led out of the cave system. We struggled, pushed, and clawed up the sharp incline toward the daylight ahead. Hands reached down from above and grabbed each of us: our other team members were pulling us out of the hole.

Goran warned, after he helped to extract us, "We have to get out of the camp. The entire area is collapsing."

We tried to run, but the earth was still quaking, and we helped each other until we reached the outer perimeter of the camp gate entrance. Once we arrived outside the grounds of Jonestown, the area beneath us was stable and sound. We looked inside the gate, and the ground was collapsing inward. God was taking the entire camp out of existence.

We watched in awe as an unseen force pulled the Jonestown camp deep into the earth. Everything was falling away into a vast nothingness; the noise was deafening, and we saw winds swirling what was left into vortexes and down into the abyss.

After several minutes, it finally stopped, and everything was still. We stared at each other, then into the camp. The hole was so immense there wasn't a bottom to the giant chasm.

The tremors began, the winds picked up again, and a blazing light emanated from the heavens. We had to look away because the brilliance of the glow was too bright for our human eyes.

I screamed above the intense noise, "Everyone, close your eyes!" My team followed my instruction and crouched down, facing away from the frightening scene. We could feel heat, wind, and intense power, and the earth shook violently once more.

After crouching for several minutes, everything grew still once again. Rising on shaky legs, we slowly turned around. The camp fence was gone, but the area that had been a gigantic hole was now filled with lush jungle foliage.

I stood for several moments, searching for anything dangerous or ominous, then said to my team, "God has restored this area and it's now safe and pure. Let's go look."

Jasper's smile was infectious as he said, "I can't help myself for grinnin' like a possum eatin' a sweet tater. This's…unbelievable!"

Billie also spoke up, with joyful tears in her eyes, "I agree with Jasper. After that insane kerfuffle, I'm totally verklempt."

After chuckling at their responses, we slowly stepped into what had been the camp and saw the typical jungle plants, trees, flowers, and grasses. This place was now filled with the beautiful sounds of the jungle again. We spotted all kinds of tropical birds, insects, and animals. All was well, and God had replaced evil with His grace.

We walked around for several minutes, and two giant gold and blue macaws landed before us. I told them I was pleased to meet them; they squawked twice in answer and flew into a tree. A swarm of brightly colored butterflies flew around our team, and we laughed in delight as they swirled and danced around us. A giant anteater came over, sniffed at our feet, then slowly moved away in pursuit of his next meal.

As we were leaving, a massive black jaguar moved toward us. My team raised their guns, but I told them to lower their weapons. It came forward and stood in front of my brothers and me. We crouched down; the gorgeous cat moved to stand beside us, and I offered him my hand. He licked me, which was quite painful because of his barbed tongue, and then he purred. The jaguar laid on his side and let us stroke his magnificent coat. I asked the beautiful animal if the others could touch him. He consented, and I motioned for the rest of the team to come over to stroke the magnificent creature. Tears streamed down my cheeks as I gazed at the Lord's glorious creation, and I thanked God for giving us the gift of friendship with this amazing cat.

The jaguar continued to drone in that strange sound, between a purr and a growl. Finn petted his belly, and the cat laid his massive paw over Finn's arm, then licked him. Finn's face lit up with a smile of pure joy, and it took my breath away. After a few moments, the cat gently stood and walked away.

As we gazed at where the jaguar was headed, we counted twenty more of them. Most of them were black, but there were also a few that were white. I knew these unusually colored jaguars were on the endangered list, and God was giving us more in the hopes we could save the species.

"*Querida Santa Madre de Dios!*" exclaimed Goran. "I can't believe it!" He pointed in a different direction, and we stared in disbelief.

"What in holy Heaven are they?" Jasper asked incredulously. There was a group of the strangest looking birds we'd ever seen. They were approximately three feet tall, with large bald heads, thick beaks, fat feathered bodies, and bright yellow legs and feet.

"I believe they're dodo birds. But how can this be? They aren't even indigenous to this area," Goran asked no one in particular.

"It must be God has brought them back from extinction. The Lord can put them anywhere he wants," Aaron replied and snapped several photos with his phone.

"If I see even a hint of a Velociraptor, clear the way because I'll be out of here faster than green grass through a goose!" Jasper exclaimed in a fearful yet joking tone.

"I think we can all agree with that statement," Finn said, snickering.

My team members were in a state of awe and wonder. After gazing at the stunning view of God's re-creation, we laughed joyfully and praised the Lord.

"It's time to finish the job and head home," Finn replied. Everyone agreed, and we walked out of God's new jungle habitat.

"Finn, it's time to call the faithful and thank them for their devoted prayers. Please tell them we'll be forever grateful for their assistance in sending that horrible evil back to Hell," I replied.

Finn nodded, then made the call to Poppy so she could forward our message.

"We must now dispose of the myrmidons before we set the explosives at the estate. Goran, lead the way to the disgusting things, or what's left of them," Finn ordered.

We followed Goran, and as we approached where he'd left several of their bodies, we discovered they'd vanished. All that remained was an enormous bed of giant, vivid blue orchids. We went to the next area, and the same orchids were present instead of the bodies. The fragrance of these flowers was intoxicating, and our lungs filled with their delightful scent.

Every myrmidon dump site was the same, so we proceeded to the estate. Billie, Chuck, and Xavier strategically placed the explosives around and under the estate and handed Finn the detonator. Goran and his men dragged the driveway guards near the house, so their bodies would also be destroyed.

I took a moment and warned any surrounding wildlife, informing them to leave the area. After a few moments, I told Finn it was clear, and we walked down the main driveway and returned to our vehicles. Once we were far enough away, we stopped the trucks, and Finn removed the cover to the detonator remote and pressed the button. We felt and heard the explosion and knew every molecule of Asmodeus's house, surrounding buildings, and demon guards had vanished from this planet.

As we drove back toward civilization, a horrific odor hit my nostrils, and it permeated the entire vehicle.

"What's the terrible smell?" I asked Finn.

"It's you, love, Jonas, and Aaron too."

"What?" I asked. Pushing myself up to look into the front seat's rearview mirror, I cringed at my reflection. My face and hair were doused in demon ooze. I looked down, and my entire body and clothes were in the same horrendous condition. "How utterly disgusting! I'm so sorry, everyone. I stink to high heaven."

Goran, who was driving, remarked, "Don't worry, Mara. We're headed to the safe house where everyone's carry-on bags are waiting. We can all shower and change into fresh clothing while waiting for our exit."

"Thank you, Goran. I'd hate to think my brothers and I would have to look and smell like this all the way home. I'm sure the rest of you agree."

They all said "Yes!" loudly, and we snickered and chuckled at everyone's obvious response.

"You're all crazy and I love every one of you," I blabbed. Finn gave me a jealous, dirty look, then laughed again. None of the team had escaped the demon ooze, mud, scratches, bruises, and bug bites.

"I would kiss you, Mara, but there's no safe, non-smelly place for me to touch," Finn whispered. I punched him lightly in the arm, and he pretended I hurt him badly.

"You rat." I clasped his hand in mine and squeezed it lovingly.

CHAPTER 44

Goran found a decent place for us to take showers, change our clothes and get sustenance. He said the vehicles we'd used would be destroyed, and no one would find evidence of our travel through the jungle.

After showering and washing my hair, my mind went to our three spirit animals, and I started to cry and couldn't stop. Grief overwhelmed me. I sat on the floor naked and sobbed. Someone knocked on the door, but I didn't want to face anyone.

"Mara, it's Finn. Baby, I can hear you crying your eyes out. I'm coming in."

I heard him enter and then he rushed toward me, obviously upset at my misery. He grabbed a bath towel, wrapped it around my body, then sat on the floor and pulled me into his arms. Holding me close, he waited until the crying slowed, then grabbed toilet paper and wiped my face.

"This stuff is only sticking to your skin. Sorry about that," he mumbled. Reaching for a hand towel, he wiped my face again. "That's better." He pulled me close again, and I finally stopped blubbering.

"I'm sorry, Finn. I started thinking of Spirit, Phantom, and Charlotte, then the tears started and wouldn't stop. The others are waiting to use this shower and I need to get out of here."

I looked down and realized I was nude under the skimpy bath towel. "Oh, my dear Lord in heaven, I'm naked under this tiny piece of cloth. I'm so embarrassed." I buried my face in his neck and my body burned with mortification.

"They can wait, my love. And, yes, you're totally 'bare-assed.' " He snorted at his play on words, and I playfully pinched him in the ribs. "Ouch!" he said in reply, then chuckled. "You'd better get dressed before the entire team ends up here, wondering what's happening." Finn set me on the floor next to him, and I did my best to cover up certain areas of my naked body. He kissed me quickly, got up off the floor, and strolled to the door. Turning to look at me, he smiled wickedly and added, "You missed a spot," then shut the door behind him. I looked down and discovered the towel had slipped down, revealing the entire right side of my chest.

"The rat. That gorgeous, funny, kind, handsome rat," I whispered as I blushed again, then smiled and blew my nose into more toilet paper.

After everyone had showered and changed, we had dinner, went outside to the backyard, and enjoyed the late afternoon weather. Finn, Aaron, Jonas, and I sat together, savoring an evening cocktail. The rest of our team was farther out in the yard, playing a competitive game of horseshoes.

My brothers and I were silent, and Finn understood we were mourning the loss of our spirit animals. We each reminisced and shared stories of our past experiences with our furry friends. With tears in our eyes, we gave a toast in their honor and prayed that they were back in Heaven with the Lord.

Our teammates playing horseshoes yelled at each other, claiming that someone was cheating, and they laughed. We smiled at their antics and agreed they were wonderful friends and soldiers.

It was time to head home. We quietly and discreetly departed the country under the guise of darkness, using connections, bribes, and boats. It took us two days by freighter to reach Puerto Rico, and there weren't any problems getting through immigration and customs.

Our gear with our weapons and ammunition was processed through a military base with the proper paperwork and loaded into our plane.

Basheer waited for us as we boarded our private jet to Idaho. He asked how the mission went and was elated that we were unharmed. Then, giving each of us a hug, he returned to the cockpit to fly us back home.

When we arrived at the base, we returned to our apartments. Finn accompanied me to our floor and walked me to my place.

"Mara, I think we need to have a serious discussion tomorrow about us getting married. It's time and frankly, I can't wait any longer. A person can only take so many cold showers; I'm sure you feel the same way." He pulled me into his arms and gave me a passionate kiss. I sighed loudly and my body melted into his.

"I fervently agree. This torture is more than anyone can take." I made a loud groan of frustration, then backed away from him. "We better get married soon, and I mean ASAP!"

Finn also grumbled with disappointment, then replied, "I'll call you in the morning, and I think it's time we meet with the other principals. We'll also ask Kaiko to join us in the meeting." He kissed me quickly, without our bodies touching, then said he'd see me tomorrow. I smiled at him, squeezed his hand, and said my goodbyes.

After entering my apartment, Asher came running over. It thrilled me to see him, so I picked him up and held him close. He purred in delight and repeatedly rubbed his face against mine. "I missed you too, you wonderful feline."

I saw a note on the kitchen table and it was from Father. *I heard you were returning tonight and knew you'd need your sweet kitty to welcome you home. Congratulations on a job well done, and thank you for what you and your excellent team accomplished. Father Faraj.*

There was a second note from Si telling me that Gracie was spending the night with Kaiko's family so I could have a good night's rest. She also said she was having an evening out, would be back late, and would see me in the morning.

I ambled to the bathroom to shower and get ready for bed. After saying my prayers, I fell asleep as soon as I mumbled, "Amen," with Asher curled around my neck.

CHAPTER 45

*W*hen I woke the following day, Gracie wrapped her arms around me and snuggled close. Giving her a big hug and a loud smooch, she giggled with delight. "I missed you so much, my beautiful girl." I looked to see if the demon's mark had vanished from Gracie's arm. To my great relief, the black number one had disappeared.

"I missed you too, Mara, so much!" she exclaimed and continued to hug me close. Si walked in and censured Gracie for waking me early, but she was kind in her reprimand and laughed when Gracie made a pouty face.

"Come on, Gracie. Let Mara wake up and I'll make breakfast." Si smiled at me, mouthing the words, "Welcome back," then took Gracie's hand and led her from the room. I stretched, looked at my phone, and Finn had left me a morning text. He said he loved me and we had a meeting at nine with the principals and Kaiko.

Ten minutes before the meeting, I entered the room and spotted Finn sitting at the table alone. He was nervous, which was not typical for Finn. I only witnessed it a couple of times, once on our first date and when he was about to propose marriage at my mother's home.

"Finn, you look handsome as usual." I walked up behind him, wrapped my arms around his chest, and kissed his neck.

"Good morning, angel. You look stunning, as usual." He turned around and pulled me into his lap, kissing me passionately. Finn put me back on my feet. "The principals and Kaiko should be here soon, and I must admit, I'm nervous. I'll start the conversation, plead my case, then you'll state yours." I agreed and sat down next to him.

Kaiko walked in and congratulated us on our successful mission. We thanked her for her kindness and help and hoped she'd advise the other principals and us during the meeting. She smiled and sat beside me.

Helen and Edison arrived and sat down, then Edison displayed each of the head principals from the other facilities on the overhead screen.

"Welcome, everyone," Edison said. "Finn asked for this meeting, and at this time, we've no clue what he wishes to discuss. So, I'm turning this meeting over to you, Finn."

Finn stood and cleared his throat. "At these facilities' inception, we all met, reviewed, hashed, and deliberated about how we should run these bases. We created strict rules which we put into place, then followed them like a religion. I'm here, along with Mara, to plead our case against one of the major rules we agreed to obey, including myself." Finn paced the room as he gathered his thoughts, then stopped and faced the group again.

"Mara and I have fallen deeply in love and want to be married as soon as possible. We've followed God's commandments, and believe me, it hasn't been easy."

We heard a few snickers, then Finn continued, "I know we've banned married couples from going on missions together, and I understand why, but I'm pleading with you to rescind this regulation for Mara and me. Then, in the future, if this happens again with other Chosen Ones, we can review this rule on a case-by-case basis. We've proven to ourselves and the rest of our team that we can remain professional on missions. Our relationship won't cause issues on our future operations either." Finn looked at me with a hopeful expression, then took his seat.

I stood up and began, "I agree wholeheartedly with Finn, but then, I know I'm biased." I smiled widely at him and continued, "I love Finn with all my heart, and I never thought it would happen to me. But God brought us together, and I know our Lord would agree with Finn's assessment of how well we work together on missions. I'm asking that you speak with our team members and consult with Kaiko before making the final decision. Thank you."

Edison asked Finn and me to leave the room and wait in Finn's office. We walked out the door, and our team members stood in the hallway. They congratulated us, and we stared at them in surprise.

Billie said, "We were eavesdropping, but we already knew you both were passionately in love. It was obvious, doll." Then she hugged us both.

We thanked them and walked to Finn's office. It was over thirty minutes before Finn received a text, calling us back to the meeting room.

The only people who remained in the room were Edison, Helen, and Kaiko. The other principals had left the meeting.

"Finn and Mara, we've made our decision. We deliberated for quite some time, and it wasn't easy to make," Edison admitted.

I took Finn's hand in mine and we figured they would deny our request. Edison's voice was sad and negative.

Edison continued, "Finn, you know we set these rules for a reason, and making exceptions is not normal business or military practice. The principals debated back and forth, and then Kaiko assessed the situation. Your team members also gave honest and forthcoming opinions, and everyone's voice was considered."

We lowered our heads, waiting for the other shoe to drop. Edison frowned, then spoke up once more, "That being said, it was by unanimous vote that we granted your appeal." Edison's expression changed to joy, and he grinned from ear to ear.

We both looked up in shock, then stood up, and Finn pulled me into his arms. "I honestly didn't think they'd give us permission," Finn admitted to Edison. "I was sure everyone would deny our request. So, what made you say yes?"

"It was because of everyone's statements of how well every mission was coordinated and accomplished. The two of you were always professional and never interfered in each other's duties. I don't know how you do it, but I sincerely hope you'll remain professional in every operation. Kaiko also had a large impact on our decision. Kaiko, please tell them what you told us," Edison said.

Kaiko smiled and answered, "I told them what Archangel Gabriel said. He informed me the two of you were chosen to be together by God, and splitting you apart would be a grave mistake. Combining your two souls is a major powerhouse in this fight, and you can accomplish great things together. That includes what's happening now and what will take place in the future."

"Really?" I asked Kaiko. She nodded happily, and I gave her a warm embrace.

Edison spoke up, saying, "I have to say, Finn, I also had a good idea what your response would be if we'd denied your request. I know how badly you love and want to protect Mara, and if you couldn't be on missions with her, you'd be a veritable nightmare. You can be a real son-of-a-gun, mate, when you're protective of someone. Seeing this first hand, I know you'd be a real pain in my, uh...bum." He laughed boisterously and continued, "Congratulations you two, and you'd better invite me to the wedding." He came over and gave us both a hug.

I was now crying, and when I looked at Finn, I realized I'd never seen him this happy. We thanked everyone again and walked out of the room as if we were on cloud nine.

Finn stopped, turned to me, and exclaimed, "We're getting married as soon as possible, and I mean right away! I've been thinking about this for a long time, and I know just the place. You need to buy a gorgeous dress and we have to get your mother to the wedding. Let's go to lunch and we can discuss our nuptials. What do you say?"

I nodded quickly, and I still had tears on my cheeks. Finn gently brushed them away, and we were eager to discuss our future. I insisted on going to my apartment, so I could finally put on my engagement ring, and we went to dinner to discuss our nuptials.

The wedding would take place on the island of Aruba and we'd leave in six days. Finn had several rooms reserved at a five-star resort, and we'd have our wedding on the beach. However, the reception would be held at the same hotel a week later. We hadn't been able to arrange the reception on the same day as the wedding because of a scheduling conflict at the resort. Our wedding and reception were short notice, so we understood and would make it work. We'd have the wedding, go on a honeymoon for a week, then return to the hotel, and the reception would be that evening. Our guests would stay the entire week and have a great vacation. They were invited to stay an additional week after the reception if desired.

We invited our entire team and they could bring a "plus one." Of course, my mother would come, as well as Gracie and Si. Edison would be Finn's best man, Si would be my maid of honor, and Gracie, the flower girl. Jonas and Aaron would give me away, and I couldn't wait for it all to become real. We also invited Poppy since Jonas said he'd love to have her come along.

Finn worked his magic, had me select several wedding dresses, and shipped them to the boutique. My mom joined me on a video call and was there as I tried on several dresses. But when I slipped on the fourth gown, it was the one. Only a few alterations had to be made, and the seamstress could do them immediately. I also selected a tea-length dress for the reception, accessories, and several unmentionables for the honeymoon. I couldn't wait to see Finn's face when he saw me in these skimpy outfits, which included a tiny bikini bathing suit and filmy lingerie.

Finn and I applied to become Gracie's adoptive parents. We hadn't told her yet, because we didn't want to get her hopes up if we were denied. Finn's FBI friend said it could take up to six months. However, he told us he had a lot of influence and was quite optimistic they would approve us.

Finn didn't tell me the location of our honeymoon and I didn't press it. He was as giddy as a little boy about his secret, and I didn't want to spoil his fun.

Asher would stay with Father again, and they were both happy with the arrangement.

The day before we were to leave for the wedding, I asked Finn to meet me at the elevators on our apartment floor. He was waiting for me and asked what this was about. I only said, "You'll see." We walked into the elevator and I pressed the first-floor button. Finn looked puzzled, but he waited patiently as we rode the elevator to the main floor. I clasped his hand and led him to the motor pool.

"Finn, you're always giving me so many wonderful things, and I racked my brain wondering what to get you in return. I wanted to find a wedding gift for you, and you must admit, you're impossible to buy for."

"Sweetheart, I don't need you to buy me anything. I love you, and you're all I want and need."

"That's sweet, but I wanted to do this. Aaron helped me find the perfect gift." I led him through the parking garage, around a corner, and then we stopped. Aaron and Jonas were waiting for us, and they stood in front of a vehicle with a large white tarp over it with a gigantic red bow on top.

"Okay, boys, lift the tarp," I ordered, and my brothers carefully removed the covering.

Watching Finn's face, I wondered if I'd made a colossal mistake. He appeared shocked, but then I thought I saw a pained expression in his eyes. Moving forward, he ran his fingers over the hood, down across the doors, and moved to the rear of the vehicle. The bright red color of the car was stunning, and the vehicle was in excellent condition.

I waited for Finn to say something, but he was quiet while gazing at the Mustang. Finally, he moved forward, opened the driver's door, and slid into the black leather seat. Aaron handed him the keys and Finn started the engine. The Shelby sounded like it was purring in a dark, rumbling vibration that echoed darkly from the cement garage walls. He sat for a while, gazing out of the windshield. I couldn't see his expression, only his profile, and I still wondered if this had been a mistake. After a few moments, Finn turned to look at me; a gigantic smile lit up his handsome face, and there were tears in his eyes.

"You did good, sis," Jonas said in my ear. Aaron agreed and squeezed my arm.

I moved toward Finn and admitted, "I was afraid for a moment that I'd made an error in judgment. I'm so glad you like it. It's a 1967 Ford GT500 Shelby Mustang Coupe, like you didn't already know. Just like the one you told me about from your childhood. Aaron found it for me and had it shipped from Florida."

Finn turned off the ignition, got out, and pulled me into his arms. He hugged me fiercely and I had a hard time breathing.

"Finn, too tight," I stammered, laughing.

He loosened his hold, gazed into my eyes, and confessed, "Mara, I don't know what to say except that I love it. You couldn't have done any better." He kissed me hard and hugged me again.

We walked over to Aaron, and Finn shook his hand. He then gave him a brotherly hug and embraced Jonas as well.

"We have to take it out for a ride, and my bride-to-be is coming with me," he proudly replied.

Jonas chimed in, "We already told security you'd be taking it out, so you're covered."

Finn opened the passenger door for me. Then he walked to the driver's side and slid into the seat like he'd owned this car his entire life. He expertly handled the manual shift as he made his way out of the garage. Once we hit a straightaway, he let the engine rip, and we flew down the road. Finn was exhilarated and I hung on as we roared down the highway. He finally downshifted as we approached a sharp curve, and we drove around the area for thirty minutes and eventually returned to the garage.

That evening, Finn treated me to a romantic dinner, and he couldn't stop grinning the entire night.

"Finn, I'm glad you love the car. I've never seen you so happy."

"My sweet, it's not just your wonderful gift. When I saw the car, I realized how much you truly love me, to give me such a thoughtful present. That's why I couldn't say anything at first. Since we first met, I couldn't figure out why such a beautiful, special, smart, and amazing woman would want to be with me and fall in love with me too."

"Finn, I've been feeling the same thing since we met. I know I'm not, nor have I ever been graced with beauty, and my limited experience with men hadn't been positive. When you started flirting with me and asked me out, I still wondered if I imagined your interest in me. Finn, you could have any woman on this planet. You're incredibly handsome, highly intelligent, charming, thoughtful, and generous. I figured you'd break up with me many times, but you didn't. So, I kept praying that you really did love me and that I wouldn't get hurt in the end. But you kept pursuing me, proving I was worth it and that you loved me. You make me feel beautiful and special, and I was actually everything you said about me. Because of the way you make me feel, I love you even more. I adore you, Finn McKenna," I confessed, tears filling my eyes.

"We're pretty sad, aren't we? We're two insecure people. But together, we're an amazing couple, and I know we'll have a wonderful future together, my lovely bride-to-be. I love you too, my sweet. Now, if we could only make love, my dreams would be complete," he said, then laughed. I giggled with him, then we toasted our upcoming wedding and finished our delicious tiramisu.

CHAPTER 46

$\mathcal{W}$e boarded the plane and headed for Aruba. I held Finn's hand and was as giddy as a child on Christmas morning. When Finn and I snuggled together, I questioned him about the tropical seascape painting he'd given me. Did the palm tree contain six coconuts or three? He gave me a strange look, and I said I was positive when I first received the painting, there were only three, but just before I left for this trip, the palm tree now had six. He said he couldn't remember, and I laughed it off, telling him I must have been wrong.

When we landed on the island, Mom waited on the tarmac. I missed her immensely and was ecstatic at seeing her. My brothers and I gave her a big kiss and a hug, and Finn stepped over to her. Mom took his hands, smiled, and said, "I'm so happy God brought you to my daughter. I know you'll take precious care of her, my amazing new son." She kissed him on the cheek and hugged him. There were tears in Finn's eyes as he embraced his new mother.

I was staying in a suite with my mom, which was connected to another room that housed Gracie and Si. After introducing Gracie to my mom, my precious little girl hugged her and wanted to be held by her. Mom picked her up and gave her a loud kiss. They were instantly family, like grandmother and granddaughter. My heart felt light as I watched them bond so quickly.

Our wedding day had arrived, and Mom helped me into my exquisite wedding dress. It was a white stretch crepe, fit-and-flare gown. It had a romantic sweetheart neckline with banded off-the-shoulder straps. The silky material draped down my body and hugged my curves. The back zipped up beneath fabric-covered buttons, which extended down the chapel-length train. I selected low-heeled silver sandals and a simple stringed jeweled headpiece for my hair. Topping off the ensemble, I added diamond stud earrings to my lobes which Finn had given me as a pre-wedding gift.

My bridesmaid and flower girl wore matching dresses in pale turquoise, which were both cool and lightweight for a summer beach wedding. Gracie was excited and said she felt like a princess in the matching tiara.

Jonas and Aaron entered the room. They were handsome in their white tuxedos and kissed me on the cheek for good luck.

We left the hotel and strolled onto the beach, where Finn had arranged the ceremony details. There was a beautiful floral archway up ahead that had been set on a large, raised wooden platform. A boardwalk was also created, allowing easier access for the wedding party and guests. Gardenias and roses were everywhere, and I could already smell their heavenly fragrance. Si handed me my bouquet, Jonas and Aaron gently took each of my arms in theirs, and we walked to the beach where my good friends and family waited. Peach rose petals covered the entire beach wedding area, and the strong tropical breeze caused them to swirl in gorgeous patterns across the sand.

I then spotted Finn up ahead under the floral archway at the altar, and I smiled with joy. He wore his lightweight, black James Bond tuxedo and looked elegant and handsome. Edison and Si were also up at the altar and waited patiently. I heard a violinist playing lovely music.

As I was about to start on my walk to my future husband, something soft brushed by my legs, and I thought I spied a flash of white. I looked down and around but saw nothing. Whatever it was wasn't malevolent, so I ignored it for now. Jonas and Finn gave me a questioning look, but I shrugged my shoulders and nodded I was ready.

As we proceeded down the raised aisle, Gracie danced as she moved forward ahead of us. She threw rose petals onto the ground and skipped up to stand next to Si. As I gazed at Finn again, his loving survey traversed my body in my wedding gown, and tears glistened in his bright green eyes.

The wedding was short but traditional, as we exchanged vows and rings. We also took the body and blood of Christ to emphasize that our Lord was to be a significant part of our marriage. We kissed and were pronounced husband and wife. Everyone jumped up as they yelled and clapped with their congratulatory responses.

I wrapped my arms around Finn, and he held me close and whispered in my ear, "It's about time. Now, let's go cuddle under a beach blanket." I laughed and turned a pale shade of pink. He chuckled at my embarrassment and gave me a frisky wink. He gently caressed my hair where a curled tendril laid against my cheek and said, "Have I ever told you your hair looks like warm fire in the sunlight, my love?" I smiled with delight at his compliment and kissed his cleft chin.

After the wedding ceremony, we posed for dozens of photos with our family and guests. Finn had hired some of the best photographers and videographers to record the wedding, and they would return the night of the reception. He thought of everything.

Finn and I returned to our rooms, changed into comfortable clothing, packed our bags, and met again in the lobby. When we were about to leave for our honeymoon, we hugged everyone goodbye. I picked up Gracie because she was sniffling. We told her we'd video-call her often and would see her soon. We held her close and then placed her in my mother's arms. Finn whispered something into Gracie's ear, and whatever he said lit her face with a gigantic smile.

On the drive to the airport, I asked Finn what he'd said to Gracie. He explained, "I told her Jonas and Aaron were going to take her for a pony ride on the beach. It would be funny to watch everyone bounce up and down like balloons in their saddles."

"Finn, that's cute. The pony ride would be perfect for her. Thanks for scheduling it."

"Actually, it was your mum's idea. I simply made the arrangements with your brothers and the hotel."

We arrived at the airport and boarded the plane. It wasn't long before we landed on another island that was slightly larger than Aruba. After we deplaned, we boarded a boat and set off at great speed across the turquoise water.

About ten minutes later, we came upon another beautiful island that didn't appear inhabited. We approached a jetty where two other power boats were docked, and three young men were waiting. They welcomed Finn back to the island and collected our luggage.

Finn ushered me to one of the all-terrain vehicles on the beach. He drove along the shore and around the curve toward one end of the island. As we came around the bend, Finn pointed up ahead, and I saw a sprawling, gorgeous house that overlooked the long, sandy, and incredible beach. The sand looked like golden sateen, and the waves that were gently splashing to the shore were the color of azure and sparkled under the sun's beaming rays. A couple of thatched-roof cabanas were placed in the sand, and large chaise lounges sat beneath them.

He parked the vehicle and led me up several steps to the house. Off to one side was a large and inviting infinity pool, plus a hot tub. The landscaping around the back of the house and the pool was designed so that it appeared to be occurring naturally. Several palm trees, tropical flowering plants, rocks, and sand were strategically placed to give the house and the yard privacy, yet they didn't block the view of the ocean from the house. There was one enormous flat rock at the edge of the pool. It was set vertically, so water flowed from the top of the rock and landed gently into the swimming pool below.

"Oh Finn, I don't know what to say, except this is stunning."

"Clinton left me this island in his Will; the man who was like a father to me. We had many wonderful times here, and I'll always cherish them. But now, I can share it with my lovely bride and create new, incredible memories. This island is private, and we'll be the only ones here after the staff departs for the mainland. They take care of the island and the property when I'm away and have kindly prepared the place for our arrival."

"We'll be alone for an entire week?"

"They'll come and restock everything for us if I call them, but yes, we'll be completely and utterly alone." Finn whispered some exciting things he had planned for me in the near future.

I replied to him, "I sincerely hope you'll put those words into action."

He chuckled, then gave me a sweet kiss. "Now, let me show you my lair, my pretty." Finn spoke in a devious tone as though he was a lascivious pervert. I laughed loudly and kissed him in return.

The house was as lovely as the outside landscaping. Finn guided me into the home through the spacious, sprawling back deck. The enormous kitchen was near the front of the house, and the living area was to the rear. The main floor was built in an open-concept plan and was beautifully decorated in light, tropical colors and comfortable furnishings.

Windows covered the beach side of the room, providing a spectacular ocean view. Finn led me to the left of the living space into a large main bedroom. It also had a massive glass door and several windows with a view of the beach, and the bed faced the windows so you could watch the gorgeous sunsets. There was an ensuite that was large and luxurious, and the two-person soaker tub looked inviting. The house had three more bedrooms and three full baths. The front of the home was immaculately landscaped with tropical flowering plants.

I placed my arms around him and enjoyed being close to the man I loved so much in this world. We heard a polite cough behind us, and a voice uttered, "Mr. McKenna, we've done everything as you requested. There's also champagne on ice in your room. If you or your bride need anything else, please call me."

"Thanks so much, Arturo. As usual, you and your family have done a splendid job." Finn gave the young man a handshake and a pat on the back, and Arturo quickly departed with his two brothers.

"Arturo and his family have been with us for several years. His father used to care for Clinton when they were both still alive; God rest their souls. Now his progeny takes care of my family and me. They have a house on this island and generally stay there, but since I'm with my bride, I rented them a delightful place on the mainland. This island is self-contained with its own power and fresh water. Now, let's change into something more comfortable and go for a long walk."

"You've got to be kidding, buster. We aren't going anywhere but to the honeymoon suite!"

He turned and gave me a shocked expression with a look of feigned innocence. "What are you talking about? We've so much to see, my love. What else would we possibly do on this delightful island?" He batted his eyes at me and I punched him lightly in the arm.

"You rat! You're messing with me!" I barked in an impatient yet teasing tone, then pointed to the other room. He roared with a huge belly laugh, picked me up in his arms, and carried me over the threshold.

"Your wish is my command, your highness." He put me back on my feet and stared deeply into my eyes. I bit my lip and quickly turned away.

"Finn, I'm going to use the bathroom and prepare for our next harrowing yet very important mission, my love."

"I agree with you, soldier; I think I'll do the same. But don't dawdle—we have much to accomplish," Finn said with a chuckle.

"Don't worry. It won't take me long to prepare." I kissed him deeply, grabbed my smaller travel bag, and entered the bathroom. I heard Finn laugh as I closed the door.

Preparing for what was to come in the romance department with Finn, I lightly bit my lip in nervousness, and yet, I couldn't wait to consummate our relationship. I pushed the jitters aside and prepared myself for being with Finn in the most intimate way.

As I returned to the bedroom, Finn had thoughtfully turned on some romantic music. He stood by the open balcony door and the warm breeze wafted into the room. I could smell the sweet ocean scents and hear the waves gently washing against the shore.

Finn's back was to me and he only wore a pair of silk pajama bottoms. I enjoyed the view of his strong bare back and shoulders as he sipped a glass of champagne. He turned to me and choked on his next swallow. He coughed, then put down the glass before he spilled it.

"Mara, that's some outfit. You realize it won't be on you for long."

He strode toward me and ogled me up and down. I wore a dark purple teddy with a matching pair of tiny, thong panties. Running my hands down his beautiful, hard-muscled chest, I wrapped my arms around him. All I wanted was to be as close to him as humanly possible.

Finn groaned, then picked me up and carried me to the bed. He gently laid me down, and I commented, "That move was very cliché, my love, but it was beautifully romantic." I ran my hands through his thick, silky hair and pulled his head down to mine. "I can't believe our wait is finally over." He kissed me deeply, then he was true to his word. My teddy and panties were now piled in a soft heap on the floor.

Very few words were spoken after that, but none were needed. It was amazing how patient Finn was and how much tenderness this man could impart. This was what falling in love should be, and all I knew, is the long wait in finding Finn was definitely worth it. I had thought my first time would be awkward, but my new husband was patient and thoughtful.

A while later, I woke up to Finn kissing the back of my neck. When I turned over, he kissed me once more.

"I'm sorry I woke you, my love, but I'm starving for food."

"Me too. I'll go take a hot shower, then meet you in the kitchen." Throwing off the sheet, I strolled toward the bathroom. I heard Finn inhale a deep breath as he watched me saunter away.

As I started my shower, I felt strong arms encircle my waist from behind as Finn joined me under the hot watery jets. Needless to say, it took us quite some time to finish our shower and everything that followed.

We had a leisurely lunch, and when we finished, Finn replied, "I want to show you the island, my love. What do you say?"

"I'd love to. But can I put on a few more clothes? I hate to scare away all the wildlife on the island," I joked with a beaming smile. He gazed at my body which was clad only in a tight tank top and a pair of tiny bikini panties.

"Well, if you insist. But I'm hoping your clothing this week will be minimal, my gorgeous bride."

"Only if you do the same." I wiggled my eyebrows in suggestion.

After we changed, he handed me a bottle of sunscreen, and we both covered ourselves liberally to prevent sunburn. We grabbed our sunglasses, strolled to the beach, and waded in the warm turquoise water. He guided me down to the right side of the beach and showed me the extensive area Clinton had constructed as a breakwater. The sea was much calmer here, and it was used for swimming, snorkeling, and personal watercraft.

As we continued following the beach line, we were now on the opposite side of the island; the wind picked up, and the surf was much stronger here. It was also a lot rockier at this northern point. The gigantic waves awed me as they crashed to shore against the giant boulders. Finn saw my amazement at the sight, so we sat at the top of a dune. We watched the monster waves sending water sprays high into the air. Sitting there for over an hour, we enjoyed God's fantastic show of nature.

Finn informed me it was time to return, as the sun would set soon. We spent a wonderful evening together, dining on cheese and tropical fruit, then gazed at the sun as it went down over the water's horizon. The solar lights kicked on around the pool, and Finn suggested we swim—in the nude, of course. After a few laps, we spent time in the hot tub.

After sitting in the frothing bubbles for several minutes, I commented, "I feel like my body weighs three hundred pounds. I'm suddenly exhausted but in a good way." Finn smiled, kissed my shoulder, and hugged me close.

"Let's go to bed, sweetheart. You're already falling asleep." He helped me out of the hot tub, we dried ourselves off, and he picked me up and carried me to the bedroom.

He gently laid me on the soft bed and pulled the sheet over me. I watched Finn as he turned out the lights and returned to bed. He climbed in and pulled me close, then stared into my eyes. I looked at him and we both smiled, and I laid my head on his chest and listened to his heartbeat.

This entire day had been perfect and I wouldn't have traded it for anything. Snuggling against Finn's warm body, I enjoyed the tropical evening breeze coming in through the large windows. I could smell the sweet-scented flowers and salty ocean. The sound of the gentle ocean waves caressing the sandy beach made me yawn with exhaustion.

"Goodnight, my gorgeous bride."

"Goodnight, my amazing husband."

We spent seven glorious days eating fabulous food, swimming, snorkeling, shopping on the main island, and simply learning more about one another. He got his way in the "minimal clothing" department—most of the time, anyway. However, I had to be sure I was always covered in sunscreen, and Finn insisted he was the one to lather it all over my skin.

As we spent this time alone with each other, it brought us even closer, and our bond grew stronger. I contemplated my previous life and how empty it had seemed and was thankful to God that He'd brought this remarkable man into my new life. Finn and I discussed this at length, and he said he felt the same way. We had a connection we couldn't explain, but it wasn't necessary. God, Finn, and I knew what we had; that was all that mattered.

We'd return to Aruba that afternoon and our wedding reception would occur in the evening. After attending Sunday Mass on the main island, we sat on the beach under the cabana and drank margaritas.

"Finn, we need to be ready when they come to take us to the airport."

I was about to get up, but Finn stopped me, grinned deviously, and countered, "We have a little time yet for a little more fun together before we have to leave. Now, where was I?"

"You're still a rat, my love. A wonderful, loving, and thoughtful rat, and I wouldn't trade you for anything." I giggled and playfully poked him in the chest. He did exactly what he said he would do and then a little bit more.

CHAPTER 47

$\mathcal{A}$rturo and his brothers returned to the island a few hours later, and they transported us to our flight back to the main island.

The plane landed at the Aruba airport and we drove to the hotel. I was eager to see everyone, especially Gracie and Mom. Finn was too, and I saw him looking for them as we walked into the hotel lobby. Gracie came running over, yelling our names, and Finn immediately picked her up and kissed her loudly. She talked a mile a minute about everything she and Nana had done while we were away. She also said Jonas and Aaron were so much fun and that the beach was the "funnest" ever. We smiled at her use of words. Mom took Gracie back into her arms since Finn and I had to go to our room to unpack and change.

We made it to our suite and began unpacking, and I told Finn I'd like a shower before I changed into my reception dress. He walked over to me, stood directly before me, and gave me a questioning eyebrow while he tapped his foot.

"Hmm? Feeling frisky, are you?" I flirtatiously wiggled my eyebrows at him and ran my hands over his chest.

Finn hunched over, lowered his eyebrows into a heavy scowl, clenched his lips and lower jaw, then made grunting noises. He looked exactly like a caveman and I laughed hysterically.

"My Wooman," he growled, then picked me up and threw me over his shoulder, which made me screech in delight. Then he ran sideways like an ape toward the bed. After tossing me lightly onto the mattress, he jumped around next to me while on his knees, beating at his chest. He continued to make that hilarious face, saying I was "his wooman," and I roared again with laughter. But our glee swiftly turned to romance.

A little while later, I shrieked, "Oh my gosh, Finn, I have to shower and get ready for the reception." I frowned at the clock beside the bed. Gazing at him again, I cupped his handsome face in my hands and said, "You know, I think your caveman look is very becoming. Would you keep it that way for the rest of the night?" I batted my eyelashes at him.

He made the caveman face again and crossed his eyes too. We both laughed joyously and he tickled me in the ribs. "I can do that, my love, if you put on your raccoon eyes and make that chipmunk face you do so well." I did my rodent imitation and gave him a quick kiss.

Finn walked with me to the shower and turned on the water jets. "Your bath awaits, my sweet." He kissed me again and walked from the room, still naked as a jaybird. I ogled his muscled body as he exited the bathroom, craning my neck to continue watching him as he went around the corner.

"You'll hurt your neck doing that, my love," he said from the other room and chuckled.

"Finn, you must have eyes in the back of your head. How do you do that?"

"I can always feel when your gaze is on me, my sweet."

After my shower, I carefully applied makeup, did my hair, and changed into my reception dress. It was a white, strapless, heart-shaped lace bodice cocktail dress with a chiffon skirt with an asymmetrical handkerchief cut that flowed around my legs. After his shower, Finn changed into a light-weight tuxedo shirt and comfortable yet classy khaki pants.

We entered the outdoor reception area, which was on the hotel veranda, and it was elegantly decorated. The food was placed inside the building, but the bars and several tables and chairs were outside. Finn hired a small group of classical musicians. Lovely music was playing, and it perfectly fit with our venue. The cake was made of chocolate, vanilla, and strawberry flavors. The frosting was buttercream, decorated with peach-colored rosettes and gardenias made from fondant.

The late afternoon sunset was a beautiful backdrop for the beginning of the reception. Finn and I drank in the view of the lovely beach and the wedding archway where we'd been married seven days ago.

Narrowing my eyes, I peered at the archway and surrounding area as hundreds of peach rose petals floated around in the breeze. I mentioned this to Finn, and we asked the wedding coordinator if there had been a wedding earlier today and if they used peach rose petals. He said no, but the strange thing was, those were the same petals we'd used on our wedding day. They never blew away in the seven days since our wedding, even with the strong ocean breezes, and they were still just as fresh and succulent. Finn and I looked at each other in wonder but smiled, looked up toward the heavens, and toasted God.

We ate our tasty meal, then cake, and it was time for us to dance. Finn pulled me into his arms and I folded myself into him. He held me close and whispered romantic things into my ear. Holding him tightly, we swayed to the delightful music. Finn also danced with Gracie as she stood on his feet. They glided across the floor and she giggled with glee. He also took Mom for a spin during a waltz, and it thrilled him that she asked him to call her "Mum."

I was elated that everyone was having a great time. Jonas and Poppy remained cozy and I also spied Si and Aaron boogying down. They held each other close during the slower songs and seemed to like one another. I wondered if becoming a priest was still on Aaron's mind, or after meeting Si, he'd decided against it. Only God knew for sure what was in their future.

I noticed Edison and his wife weren't at the reception and asked Finn about them. Apparently, Edison had an urgent call from the base yesterday, and they'd taken the first flight out this morning. Finn didn't know why, and Edison said he wouldn't bother a man and his new bride about work on their honeymoon. But if it became urgent, then he'd let Finn know.

A little while later, Mom said Gracie was falling asleep on her feet, and she'd take her up to bed. We hugged them both goodnight and they retired for the evening.

Finn and I were dancing again, but I felt his pocket vibrating. "Finn, is your phone ringing, or are you just happy to see me?" I asked, giggling.

He chuckled, then pulled his phone out of his pocket. Finn's smiling face turned into a worried frown, he grabbed my hand, and we moved to a quiet place to take the call. "It's Edison, sweetheart."

"Hello, Edison. What's the problem?.... I see....No, I understand. You need us sooner than you thought?" Finn rubbed his forehead. "Okay, we'll try to get a flight in the next few days. I'll let the team know....Edison, it's not your fault. You tried to keep us out of it, don't worry about it....Thanks, I will. I'll call you back tomorrow. Goodnight, my friend." Finn disconnected the call.

"Problems?"

"I'm afraid so. I wish it could have waited another week, but evil does what it wants when it wants. I'm so sorry, Mara; I didn't want our honeymoon cut short like this. Edison tried to handle it himself, but he needs the full team and the Gatekeepers for this one. The entire team has to return to the base and stop the next mess that's building."

"Finn, we're the Chosen Ones of God and here to do a job. We had seven wonderful days of bliss, but soon it's back to work. I'm with you, love, but we still have a couple of days to enjoy ourselves."

"You're right. I have to tell the team, but we can continue celebrating tonight with our friends and family. Then another full day tomorrow. Now dance with me, my love. I need you in my arms again." After we danced for a while, we then mingled with our guests. We eventually took a break and sat at one of the outside tables, where we kicked off our shoes and drank delicious cocktails.

A short time later, a young server approached me and said, "A man wants to speak with you and your brothers. He's on the beach by the wedding archway."

I peered at where the server was pointing, which was well-lit by a string of party lights. There was an image of a man, slightly stooped over with age, and I recognized the figure.

Finn and I walked over to Jonas and Aaron and gave them the message. They also remembered the gentleman who was waiting to speak with us. Finn looked at me quizzically, so I told him he was our spirit guide and we needed to talk with him privately. Finn smiled, kissed my hand, sat at the table, and ordered a club soda.

The three of us walked out to where the old man waited on the board-walk, and we asked one another if this was the person who had guided each of us at the beginning of our journey. We agreed it was the same man, but it was surprising that we each saw him differently. Jonas said the man he knew didn't have a beard, and I said he did. Aaron said the man was in his fifties, and Jonas and I countered he was easily in his late eighties. As we approached him, the old man turned and greeted us with a charming smile.

"Ahh, the Gatekeepers. You've done so well, and I must say, I'm proud of all of you. But then, I knew you'd do a wonderful job and that the Lord had chosen well."

He moved closer, then stopped directly in front of us. "I'm also thrilled by your accomplishments and love you very much."

The gentleman pointed to an area farther down the beach, but we only saw darkness. But then, three shadows moved closer, and we discovered who they were as they approached the lighted area of the boardwalk.

Spirit came running over to me, and I couldn't help but yell his name joyfully. "Spirit!" Crouching down, I wrapped my arms around his big beautiful neck and buried my face into his soft fur. "I missed you so much, my dear, wonderful friend. I'm delighted you're back and unharmed. You scared me to death; you know that?" Spirit licked the tears of happiness from my face and whined in response.

I looked over, and Jonas and Aaron greeted their long-time animal friends. My brothers were happy and relieved their companions were safe and sound.

The old man smiled widely and replied, "The good Lord above knew the three of you would've jumped into that portal to Hell without hesita-tion. You would have sacrificed yourselves to save your fellow brothers and sisters. God then sent these three wonderful creatures of His to take the fall for you. But the Lord sent them to Heaven for their sacrifice, and they never experienced the evils of Hell. They're now back, and if you need them, they'll always be here to assist you."

Looking to the heavens above, I said, "Thank you, Lord, for taking great care of them. We do love these precious animals dearly, and we're beyond thrilled to have them back."

The old man continued, "I'll be leaving soon, but I wanted to congratulate the three of you on your success. You've done a magnificent job and everyone upstairs is proud of you. Your sacrifices will give you many graces when you return to the Father. Mara, and Jonas, I wanted to let you know I've always been proud of you. I've loved you more than life itself, and if you ever thought otherwise, I've only myself to blame."

"I don't understand," I replied in confusion.

"I'm sorry. I completely forgot. Give me a moment and then you'll understand," he said.

His entire body shimmered briefly as we looked at him, and we understood. Dad now stood before us, our wonderful father, who had died way too early. But now he was back in his early thirties, with dark wavy hair, his twinkling blue-green eyes, and the dimple by his mouth that reminded me of Jonas and Aaron.

"Dad?" I cried loudly along with Jonas. We both stood in shock and couldn't think of anything else to say. I swayed, and Aaron grabbed my arm to hold me upright.

"Yes, sweet Mara, it's me," Dad said. "Aaron and Jonas, would you give me a few minutes to speak with Mara? But don't go far because I would also like to speak with you two as well," he added. Aaron and Jonas nodded, still obviously stunned, and stepped off the boardwalk and went over to play with the animals.

"Dad? Is it really you?" I exclaimed in awe, fell to my knees, and cried.

My father knelt beside me and took me into his arms. "Oh, Mara-Bear, please don't cry, my precious daughter." I was overjoyed to hear him calling me by the nickname he'd given me as a child. "I love you so much and never wanted you to think otherwise. When you were growing up, I made some horrendous mistakes, but they were mine and never yours." He helped me to my feet but held me close until my tears subsided.

I stared into his eyes and said, "Dad, I know you weren't proud of me —and I understand. But as a child, I needed to know you cared about me— yes, I know you loved me—in your own way, but I felt so alone. Mom did what she could when I was so sick, but I don't remember you ever comforting me or even being by my side when I felt I didn't want to go on living. You weren't there when I needed you, Dad, like you disengaged from me. All I ever wanted was your comfort and support." I was crying openly again and realized Dad was too. He held me again until we both were more composed.

He backed up a step, took my hands, and said, "Mara-Bear, I'm ashamed of how I made you feel. That was never my intention, and I'm sorry for everything. I knew how sick you were and how the exhaustion was overwhelming. It was because of the guilt I felt that I couldn't make you better, which made you think I wasn't proud of you or cared about your suffering. It killed me to see you so sick, and because of my stupid pride, I was afraid you'd witness me crying in despair at what you were going through. So, I hid away and tried to distance myself from both your pain and mine, and for that, I truly apologize." He hung his head in shame, and I saw his tears fall to the sand below.

"My dearest daughter, I was so proud of how resilient you were, and I never understood how you got through every painful day of your life. But you never gave up and always kept trying, no matter how difficult it became. All I can say is I'm sorry I never told you this, and that I wasn't there when you needed me most. I love you and was, and am, very proud of you." He explained all this as I wept in his arms again. "Now you need to stop crying because this is your honeymoon. God found you a perfect match in Finn, and I'm thankful to our dear Lord that I could witness your marriage ceremony. Yes, I was there and was ecstatic to see my precious daughter marry such a good man." He set me away from him after he kissed me on my forehead.

"Do you have any more questions for me, Mara-Bear?" I shook my head, kissed him on the cheek, and he returned the gesture. "I love you, my dear child." He looked deeply into my eyes, gave me a big smile, and wiped my tears away.

"I love you too, Dad, and thank you for explaining everything. It makes all the difference in the world to me."

"Thank you, sweetheart. Now, I need to speak with each of your brothers. I messed up with Jonas too, and I want to apologize to him, then get to know Aaron in the little time I have left."

"Dad, have you spoken with Mom yet? I mean, are you allowed?"

"Yes, I already did, but only for a few minutes. One special thing about your mother and me: we never left anything unsaid when we were together. When she saw me and got over her shock, we hugged each other. Then, she touched my cheek in understanding and told me to come and talk to our children. She was always such an insightful woman." Dad smiled joyfully, touched my cheek once more, then walked over to Jonas.

I watched the two of them speak for several minutes, then Dad took Jonas into his arms and hugged him fiercely. Jonas cried openly and hugged him in return. After a few moments, Jonas stepped back, and Dad kissed him on the forehead.

Then, I watched Dad walk over to Aaron, and they strolled together along the shoreline. Jonas returned to my side as we eyed the father and son who'd never met in their previous life. After several minutes, we heard their laughter, and they hugged each other.

Aaron and Dad returned to our side, looking happy and at ease with the world.

"Dad, thank you for being our guide and explaining everything from our past. I don't know why God permitted you to help us or allowed you to appear to us as your true self, but I hope you'll thank Him for everything," I said as I tried to stem my tears again.

"You're welcome, and I promise He knows how thankful you are. But be sure to tell Him yourself. God would like that," Dad replied.

"I love you, Dad, and I've missed you so much," Jonas admitted. "Will we see you again?"

"I'm sorry to say, I don't think so. Not on this earth, anyway. But we *will* meet again when you return to the Father. That, I can promise you."

"Can Finn meet you, Dad, before you go?" I asked him.

"I'm sorry, my precious daughter, but no. My instructions were only to speak to my three children and their mother. I don't know why, but that's God's wish. Please tell Finn I know he's a fine man, and I also know he's good for my precious daughter. Tell him too, that I'm proud to call him my son. Now, I must leave you and return to the loving home of our Father. You must undertake many more missions for the Lord, but stay faithful and true, and you'll be greatly rewarded. I love you, my beautiful children."

He started to walk away, but then I heard a squeak with every other stride as he crossed the boardwalk toward the beach.

"Dad, surely you're not still wearing that squeaky shoe?" I asked.

He turned to look at us and answered, "Why not? They're a perfectly good pair of shoes. Just because there's a small imperfection doesn't mean they aren't worthy of being worn."

After his comment, he smiled brightly and gave us a wink. We laughed as he turned away and walked down the boardwalk toward the sand below. He'd joined our spirit animals, and they all strolled down the beach. The animals ran and leaped in the sand, chasing the fresh rose petals left over from our wedding. The petals were gently lifted by the tropical breezes and spun in the air, and the animals found them especially entertaining to chase. We chuckled at their antics and waved goodbye until they, and our dad, vanished into the night.

We pondered what Dad had just said and realized what he'd meant. Our dad wasn't perfect and never was, and neither were we. But it didn't mean we weren't worthy of being loved by others or by God, Himself. We must always forgive, no matter what our or others' imperfections may be. "Thanks, Dad," I whispered, with a loving smile on my face.

To be continued...

WAIT. Don't go just yet. Please go to the next page and see other exciting books by Tamara Maudelle available at Amazon...

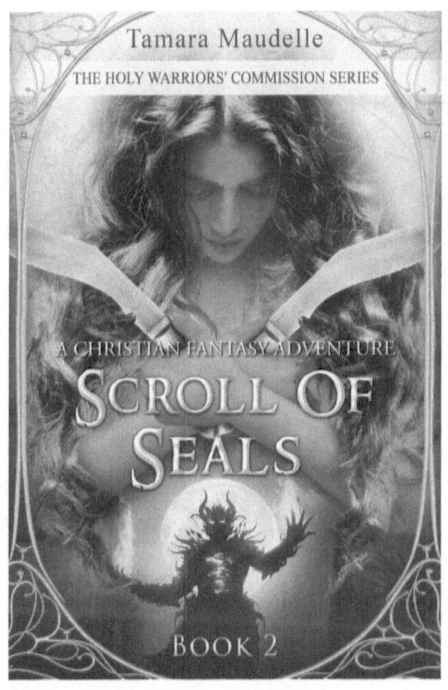

Mara and her team of God's chosen warriors must find a precious holy artifact hidden inside a one-thousand-year-old cavern while staying mere steps ahead of the demon Xerkamedes' foul-smelling servants, the myrmidons.

To gain the information they need, the team must interrogate and rely on the intel from one of the most heinous criminals they have ever encountered. Then they have to fight myrmidons and overcome personal and physical endeavors, which puts Mara and her team not only at odds with their enemies but also with each other.

Will they find the precious artifact in time, and should they believe the information given by a cold-blooded killer? Will this dangerous mission finally take the life of one of their own, and will they succeed in defeating Xerkamedes?

CHRISTIAN PARANORMAL ROMANCE

Hannah is on the run. She must not only escape from her childhood nightmares but also from someone who's supposed to love and protect her. The lakeside cottage she's inherited is the saving grace Hannah so desperately needs. Now, with a new home and identity, she's hoping for safety and a place to heal.

Storm Harbor Cottage provides her solace and peace, but how long will it last? After meeting the handsome veteran who is renovating her new home, she wonders if he will be another person who betrays her.

As danger closes in, who can Hannah rely on to keep her safe? And how can she explain the bizarre occurrences that keep happening? Learning to trust might be the only thing that saves her, but confiding in someone might also get her killed.

Will Hannah ever break free from her gruesome past,
or will it threaten her life once again?

JUST A NOTE...

Dear Reader,
If you liked my book, I'd be very appreciative
if you would leave a review on Amazon.
As an author, good book reviews raises our rankings on their website.
You can contact me at tamaramaudelle@outlook.com.
Thank you!

Tamara Maudelle